THE REMNANTS

PRAISE FOR
THE REMNANTS

"Peterson has built a bleak and visceral world as vividly imagined as *Dune*, then forced a group of optimists to survive it. Even amid a hopeless future coated in dust and self-made mutants, *The Remnants* is surprisingly funny and full of optimism about the incorruptibility of the human spirit. This book makes me wish I could travel into the future, not to the point at which this apocalyptic story takes place, but to when this book is already successful and I can play tabletop RPG version of it."
Soren Bowie, writer, American Dad!

"The level of invention here is off the charts. If you like your sci-fi sautéed in postapocalyptic motor oil and infused with the aroma of *Mad Max: Fury Road* bath salts, this is just for you. Pure fun."
Karl Mueller, writer/director of Rebirth (Netflix Studios) and Mr. Jones (Anchor Bay Films)

"*The Remnants* is a post-apocalyptic picaresque with more cool and invention than any dystopia in memory. Think *Smokey and the Bandit: Fury Road*. Peterson delivers massive heart and radioactive grit; the redhead rogue: Eldridge, friends to follow him into hell and lurid, lucid goons to fill it. A playful, sweet and brainy chase."
Brett Jackson, creative director

THIS IS A GENUINE CALIFORNIA COLDBLOOD BOOK

A California Coldblood Book | Rare Bird Books
californiacoldblood.com
rarebirdbooks.com
Copyright © 2019 by Robert J. Peterson

ISBN 978-1644280522

All rights reserved, including the right to reproduce this book or portions thereof in any form whatsoever, including but not limited to print, audio, and electronic.

Set in Minion
Cover art by Leonard Philbrick, Sergey Gudz, typesetting by Brett Jackson
Printed in the United States
Distributed by Publishers Group West

Publisher's Cataloging-in-Publication data

Names: Peterson, Robert Jason, author.
Title: The Remnants / Robert J. Peterson.
Series: The Deadblast Chronicles
Description: Los Angeles, CA: California Coldblood Books, An Imprint of Rare Bird Books, 2019.
Identifiers: ISBN 978-1644280522
Subjects: LCSH Dystopias—Fiction. | Adventure and adventurers--Fiction. | Humorous fiction. | Science fiction. | BISAC FICTION / Science Fiction / Apocalyptic & Post-Apocalyptic | FICTION / Action & Adventure.
Classification: LCC PZ7.P44531 R46 2019 | DDC 813.6—dc23

For Lauren.

"Lord, my body has been a good friend, but I won't need it when I reach the end."
—**Cat Stevens**, "Miles From Nowhere"

"Moats and boats and waterfalls,
Alley-ways and pay phone calls,
Lord, I've been everywhere with you."
—**Edward Sharpe and the Magnetic Zeroes**, "Home"

PROLOGUE
THE LAST WILL AND TESTAMENT OF BORIS HAGAN CHRONICLER OF DEDRICK

[BEGIN AUDIO TRANSCRIPT]
[AUDIO: A WATERFALL ROARS IN THE DISTANCE.]

THIS IS THE LAST will and testament.
I don't have much time, because they need me. Listen and take note of my words: this is the last will and testament. For me. For the world you knew, or thought you knew.

For my friends, especially one in particular.

This will, my last message, is for . . . whoever's listening. Whoever you are, out there in some gleaming future surrounded by silver glass, I'm talking to you. Right now, I'm holed up in hell: the world after Deadblast, the cataclysm that deleted most of the world. For the record, here's the sum total of everything we know about Deadblast:

Dick.

Precisely dick. Deadblast ran roughshod over the globe, laying waste to most of it and rearranging what was left. Cities and mountains got buried, while ancient secrets got heaved into the daylight for the first time in a life-age. In a blinding flash, all was wiped clean in an apocalypse that wasn't nuclear or natural. There were no mushroom clouds or hurricanes, no neutron bombs or earthquakes.

That was about five hundred years ago. We think. Hell, even that's a shot in the dark. Coulda been a thousand years ago, ten thousand. That's part of the reason why I'm making this recording. Y'see, after the horrors of Deadblast, there ain't many folks who go out of their way to set things down for posterity, but I'm one of 'em. Most folks don't see no reason to remember a world with so much suffering, but I don't see it that way. There's good in this place. I've borne witness to it. And I'm here to sing songs of the goodness and bravery of my friends.

But first, a little about me: the name's Boris Hagan.

Maybe you heard of me, maybe you hain't. I go by a lot of titles—Chronicler of Dedrick, survivor of the Xiang Tournament of '03, historian and expert on all things Deadblast—before and after. (Though to be fair, my knowledge of what came before Deadblast is built on a foundation of hearsay, rumortryst, and the occasional sparkling fragment of truth I pan from the stream of whispers that run to and from the remnants.)

I'm the world's only truth-prospector.

[AUDIO: BEDSPRINGS SQUEAK.]

Maybe in the future, you're reading my work. Heh. I might've set *down a thing or two back in my home remnant of Dedrick.* What The Fuck Just Happened?: Boris Hagan's Guide to Deadblast *is a favorite tome, as is* It Ain't Just For Porn (But Mostly It's For Porn): Boris Hagan's Guide to The Arpa (As Well As Porn) *is another. (Both were bestsellers in the southwestern basin—no big deal.)*

But maybe my grandest achievement was From Andros the Trenchant to Zzyzx the Zzyzxian: Boris Hagan's Underground and Unauthorized Guide to The Odds.

The Odds. The sonsabitchin' Odds. I ain't even mentioned them yet. Guess I should get down to it, because the Odds are the reason why I'm recording my last will and testament into a dictatryst instead of kickin' it with my friends back at Nix's rooftop bar. Here's the skinny on the Odds:

The Odds rule the remnants.

Simple as that. After Deadblast, we were left with a mostly barren world and a smattering of cities that we call remnants. Remnants come in all shapes and sizes. Some are just little outposts—huts and cabins and habitats in the deep deserts. Others are bigger, almost as big as them cities they had before Deadblast. Most of 'em are underground. The Odds are the ruling caste and class, a cadre of bookies who'll take wagers—or as we say in post-Deadblast parlance, "make odds"—on anything; and when I say "anything," I mean anything—from the day of our own death to the freakazoid happenings of our immune systems to the very minute and second the sun'll rise and set. If a dreg wants to make odds on an outcome, they'll take your hard-earned jenta. The Odds are the only game in town, the only game that ever was, the only game that ever will be. Either you make good with them or you make your way out of the world.

One of my friends actually made good with an Odd.

That's what started all this. It's why I'm sitting in a house perched on the edge of a waterfall, getting ready to dump my memory into this dictatryst so all of y'all listening from the shores of a better world can know we tried to make things right—or as right as we could.

—⚏—

But a moment ago, *I said this was the last will and testament for my friends, one in particular. Didja ever have one of those friends you couldn't quit, even though they were dumber'n dogshit?*

For me, that's Eldridge of Dedrick, my best friend.

Best friend.

We're a dying breed, best friends, because friends of any kind are a dying breed after Deadblast, but me and Eldridge—aka "the redhead"— we been tight since he was a boy and I was . . . well, a little less decrepit. My last will and testament is also his last will and testament, because even though I think he survived the tale you're about to read, I can't imagine he made it all the way to your era and became a Shore-Rider. (Not that I don't think he's worthy to become one of y'all; he's just . . . a little too much of a dipshit. In fact, his dipshittery is kind of what this story's all about.)

Over the last month or so, I seen me a bunch of the remnants, all of 'em alongside Eldridge, aka "El," aka the "Red Rook." (He's got himself quite a few nicknames.) He earned himself the title of "Red Rook" last year when he won the Xiang tournament of 2603. Here's a quick primer on Xiang: It's like a board game ya might've heard of: chess. Only it's played by real people, some of whom have bazookas, and everyone's basically trying to blow everyone's balls or ovaries or constituent sexual organs off.

The playspace for the '03 tournament was the Remnant-Protectorate of Dedrick. El won the tournament in a bit of cheat—he killed the fella who ran it, Jeb Goldmist, Dedrick's reigning Odd. (Earlier when I said he "made good" with an Odd, I might've been stretchin' the truth a little.)

I was trying to become an Odd before the '03 Xiang tourney. I stopped after Eldridge killed Jeb Goldmist. I'd always wanted to become an Odd because I was sick of it all—sick of being poor, sick of fightin' for my life every minute of every day, sick of feeling sick with worry for my friends. But when I finally laid oculars on Goldmist . . . when I finally saw what all that wealth could do to a person . . . I didn't want no part of it.

Eldridge killed Goldmist. As for why he killed Goldmist—well, that's a long story. Suffice it to say it involves intrigue, betrayal, and skullduggery. It also involves some old grudges—grudges that Goldmist stoked and exploited to turn Eldridge into his little pawn, so to speak. More on that later.

For now, know that I, Boris Hagan, Chronicler of Dedrick, am here today to set down my last will and testament. Before Deadblast, folks wrote up wills to tell folks how to divvy up their stash after they shuffled off. In those days, that usually meant divvying up their jenta, their homes, their worldly wares. I ain't got much in the way of worldly possessions, but what I do have is knowledge.

Knowledge about what happened.

Knowledge of how Eldridge wound up on the Chain of Tears.

Knowledge of how we put together a search party to go out lookin' for him.

Knowledge of how Eldridge and I wound up on the run from a grextet of bounty-mercs, including one by the name of Quillig, who'd had it out for the redhead since time immemorial.

Knowledge of how our friends Oksana, Stewart, Pell, and Crius got 'emselves in such dire straits.

Knowledge of how we trekked from remnant to remnant—from Dedrick to Penticton to Hemming; how we won the Mud Races, braved the slopes of Killermount, and met the toughest rabbit in the owsla of the fishfolk.

Knowledge of how we called down the wrath of god with the deadliest weapon known to humankind.

Knowledge of how the world's most beautiful woman transformed into the very first true-blue angel I ever seen.

Knowledge of how Eldridge, aka "Dipshit J. McStupidpants," finally faced up to his past.

Knowledge of how we blazed a path all the way up to Ikraam and Towertown.

And finally, knowledge of how we all braved the fires of the Fallen Tower, where Eldridge betrayed me.

Well, that ain't fair. Eldridge didn't betray me, exactly, but . . .

Wait. Lemme back up. If I'm gonna set down my last will and testament, I'm gonna do it using every trick in my saddlebag. Thank Crom the lady of Ikraam House is a chronicler like me. See, she's got herself a dictatryst, and I'm wearing it right now. Imagine an old footbomerico helmet outfitted with a bunch of glowing electrodes and a microphone. The electrodes're reading my thoughts, my memories, my feelings, my impressions as I speak into the mic. The dictatryst takes all that data and transfers it to an outputter that'll type out a full account of my sorry tale—with some side effects that can only be described as strange and unusual.

What you're about to read is part firsthand account, part rumortryst . . . and all a hundred percent righteous truth, even the parts I'm only speculating about. I don't know if anyone'll find this record, but maybe my story'll leave the shores of this world and float its way to a better one. If it does . . . if it did . . . if you're listening from the shores of that better world, it means two things:

One, that I'm dead.

And two, that somehow, the entire world as I knew it got swept off the board and changed.

Maybe for the better.

Hopefully for the better. By Crom, I hope and pray for the better.

This is the last of my great labors, this will and testament. I'm gonna tell you the whole tale, from the Chain of Tears, where Eldridge and I first made contact after we lost touch back in Dedrick, up to now, as I sit on a bed I thought was gonna be my coffin, wondering how I'm gonna help my friends.

[AUDIO: THE CLICK AND WHIRR OF A DICTATRYST DEVICE COMING ONLINE.]

If you're one of them high-toned Shore-Riders, this one's for you. Listen close, because I don't have much time.

My friends—including the dipshit—need me.

THE ULTIMATUM
&
THE DYNAMO

ELDRIDGE

THE ONLY THING THAT surprised Eldridge about winding up on the Chain of Tears was that it wasn't Quillig who caught him; it was an Odd.

To be sure, the plaid-faced bounty-merc *deposited* him on the dreaded Chain, which served as the endless, mobile shitcan for every deadbeat who defaulted on a wager made with the mighty Odds.

But Quillig didn't catch him.

Instead, one of the Odds themselves—specifically, one of the *stupidest*—had captured the redhead and turned him over to Quillig, who happily blasted Eldridge with a triplet of electro-crackling crimson mortarchains. Quillig inserted him into the Chain some thousand miles to the east of Eldridge's hometown of Dedrick. The bounty-merc's lipless mouth wheezed with cold laughter as he separated two of the Chain's permanent residents and positioned Eldridge between them.

That had been two months ago. Maybe.

No one marked the passage of time on the Chain. No one *could*. They only marked the passage of scenery. They marched single-file across a landscape that screamed toward both horizons with little more than the occasional hill or dead cactus to vary the view. Mortarchains dangled between each prisoner from their chest and back. The mortarchain implant tinged a prisoner's vision with glowing, electric red and simultaneously illuminated the night and darkened the day so no one could even tell when the sun, with all of its volcanic heat, rose and set. The chain also kept all the prisoners' internal temps tightly controlled. No one got hot, and no one got cold as they marched toward a horizon that would never arrive.

Until it did. Or so said the chainmail.

The chainmail messages had doubled in number and frequency over the previous week. They arrived as encrypted code; the prisoners' only secret from the swarm of hovertroids clouding the sky over the chain. No one knew who provided these tiny guardbots for the Chain. None of the Odds took credit for them. They simply *were*.

"I heard one tryst say they came from across the oceans," said Boris Hagan, speaking years before.

—⚡—

[AUDIO: THE CLICK OF A DICTATRYST DEVICE DEACTIVATING.]

Boris Hagan here again. I warned y'all that this dictatryst thing-amajig was gonna do some strange and unusual stuff, and that includes referrin' to yours truly in the third person. So don't get weirded out—it'll still be me thinking, talking, and reminiscing for the edification of all you Shore-Riders.

[AUDIO: THE CLICK AND WHIRR OF A DICTATRYST DEVICE COMING ONLINE.]

—⚡—

ELDRIDGE

EVERY PRISONER ON THE Chain knew the code and the encryption keys, which they immediately passed on to every new deadbeat who wound up on the Chain. People learned the code at different rates. It took a dunce like Eldridge a full ninety-two hours to learn the sturdy thirty-two-bit encryption that spontaneously changed every twenty-four to thirty-six hours. This led to periodic delays on the message system, but sooner or later, they all committed it to memory and learned the technique for delivering the messages:

To send a message forward: You walked forward and gripped the shoulder of the prisoner in front of you to get their attention. Once you had it, you tapped out the day's encryption key, followed by the message, which you delivered in a cunning combination of binary notation and what Boris Hagan would call "Borse code."

"Did you name that after yourself?" Eldridge asked him years before.

"You'd like to think that, wouldn't you?" Hagan said over beers in his under-Dedrick bungalow. "Maybe."

A similar procedure sent a message backward, except the prisoner delivering the chainmail would have to reach around and yank on the mortarchain spilling out of their back to get the attention of the prisoner to their rear.

That's how Eldridge first got word the end was near—someone yanked his chain.

The sharp tug pulled him forward a few sizzling steps as the nimbus of red energy swirled around his mortarchains and emitted a volley of sparks showering the sand around him. More sand stretched to the horizon on either side with only a lone mesa in the distance to his right, which Eldridge presumed was south. After he regained his footing, he looked up and saw the prisoner ahead—an ancient, white-haired woman who shuffled along silently day after day, her bones wrapped in a single layer of swaddling. She reached across her chest and took hold of her shoulder, where her birdfeet-thin fingers started to tap out a message. Eldridge activated his analytical centers and decrypted it:

We're almost there. Pass the word.

But before he passed the word backward, Eldridge wheezed, "Almost *where?*"

She reached around her back and jerked the chain with a force so surprising Eldridge stumbled into the sand, instantly drawing the attention of a few score hovertroids, each of which descended on him and unfurled hundreds of filaments of superstrong fiber that wisped down to him and pulled him upright, their internal servos clicking and whirring at him. As soon as he was back on his feet, one of the larger hovertroids—a chief lieutenant, apparently—zipped over and extended a fibrous snake-arm that coiled around his neck and squeezed just hard enough to make him wince.

"*Stay on your feet, macta,*" it barked in a computerized voice similar to what his friend Crius Kaleb used to sound like back when he only spoke through his electronic speechmouth. That was until Eldridge got together with another old friend, Pell Yannick of the Narsyans, an order of body-worshippers who lived in the mountains north of Dedrick and spent every waking hour either lifting weights or engaging in a dark copulative art known only as "powerfucking." Pell was a Narysan chieftain and, as such, had braved the order's greatest physical challenge, a device called the Typhoid Maiden. Weathering the Maiden's horrors had endowed Pell's blood with remarkable palliative effects. One drop of a Narsyan chieftain's blood could cure anyone of anything—and that included the brain parasite that had been slowly driving Kaleb insane over the years.

Pell and Eldridge had cured Crius Kaleb. But how long ago had that been?

The redhead couldn't remember.

Once again came the *jerk* on his chain. This time he stayed on his feet, but the old woman's message came again:

We're almost there. Pass it on, fuckhead.

"All right, all right," he mumbled as he reached around and got the attention of the prisoner immediately behind him. Eldridge had never looked at him directly, but he was fairly certain that the prisoner behind him was a young man; a boy, really. He passed on the message: *We're almost there. Pass the word.*

Unrest shook the Chain as the word passed along it. Eldridge sensed it in the form of a tremor that shivered through the dim and distant collective neural link they all shared. He also *heard* it in the form of murmurs, yelps, and the occasional wail.

What the hell's at the end of this thing?

Wheels rumbled in the distance and drew Eldridge's attention away from the mysterious destination that lay somewhere ahead. He craned his neck and looked backward, where he saw a dark shape approaching. The rest of the prisoners looked way, too, including the presumably young man behind him, who indeed had knobbly joints, a mop-head of hair, and a pimply face. Eldridge put his age at around twelve or thirteen. *Kid's young enough to be my son,* he thought—and stopped in his tracks long enough for the next Chainmate to give him a nudge forward. He frowned at his hands, his thumbs and forefingers kicking off sparks like flint as they made frantic little circles. The unmistakable sense that he was forgetting something overtook him. Only in this case, he hadn't forgotten something small, like the keys to his motorcycle. As happened more and more often in his advancing years, the redhead spoke to himself:

"What was it? Did I leave something in Dedrick?"

Even stranger, when he tried to remember what he forgot, his mind delivered up a dreamlike tableau: He was flying—*soaring*, really—over a chasm that dove into the earth and stretched from horizon to horizon like a massive maw that grinned at him, as if to tease, *What can't you remember?*

Jesus, the redhead thought to himself. *That's a good question. I can't remember when I cured Crius Kaleb. What* else *have I forgotten?*

He hustled the thoughts out of his head and narrowed his focus on the vehicle that approached from the horizon and spewed smoke from a pair of stacks flanking a wide cabin. Eldridge recognized it as an old-time big rig for an eighteen-wheeler. Boris Hagan told him these trucks used to haul all kinds of cargo between the remnants before Deadblast.

This one, however, only carried a cargo of two people—familiar to the Eldridge—who both got out of the big rig after it hissed and squeaked to a halt.

The first person had traded his standard red kevlar three-piece suit for an electric-blue vest and pants, which he held aloft with a set of black suspenders that jangled with hand grenades and other explosives. As always, a patch of threadbare plaid fabric covered his face from brow to chin and cheekbone to cheekbone. A rectangular black device he had plugged into his eye sockets gave him the ability to see through a single aperture.

Quillig, the bounty-merc.

He carried his standard weapon—a triple-spiked mortarchain rifle, which had seen some recent action. Three glowing red chains hung from the rifle's razor-sharp spires, their ends lancing into the back of the big rig's second passenger, who fell to the ground when Quillig yanked him out of the cabin. The second passenger's white beard had once been a sandy brown. His eyebrows met with a permanent, woeful arch in the middle of his forehead, while drool dripped from both corners of his mouth. He wore a corduroy vest and ripped denim pants. Gold-rimmed glasses clung to the end of his nose and threatened to fall with each of his staggering steps.

Eldridge found the strength to turn completely around and get a better look at his old friend.

"Boris," he whispered.

Boris Hagan was joining the Chain of Tears.

—⁂—

QUILLIG HAD TO GLOAT. The redhead couldn't even blame him.

"The Odds don't care for you and your friends, Eldridge," the bounty-merc said, dragging Hagan alongside the redhead as he marched with the rest of his Chainmates. Quillig continued: "You'll never guess where I found this one—Penticton."

"Penticton?" Eldridge asked. "Boris, what the hell were you doing there?"

But Quillig was already dragging him farther down the Chain and away from El, who scanned his databanks for anything Penticton-related. He reckoned the remnant lay roughly southwest of his current position, and he knew the chief Odd in Penticton was a woman named Lilya Hanna.

Eldridge watched Quillig climb back into his big rig and ride away, the occasional burst of bloody static electricity from the Chain casting his truck in sporadic silhouettes.

Boris had been trying to become an Odd, last Eldridge knew, and after the redhead disposed of Hagan's old boss, the Odd Jeb Goldmist, Hagan's plan had been to ramp up his own oddsmaking.

So what happened?

—⁂—

ELDRIDGE WOULDN'T FIND OUT for another week—or however long it took Boris Hagan to learn the chainmail code—because as soon as his white-haired friend learned it, a message came speeding up the Chain from the rear, specially marked for him. As they all marched through a crevice that spanned a mere fifteen feet, the kid behind him kicked him in the back of his calve.

"Red alert, stupid," the kid said. "Back up, would ya?"

Eldridge slowed his pace until the kid behind him could grip his shoulder. He could hear the kid shuffling through the sand and dirt of his tippy-toes as he tapped out the message on his shoulder.

The dreenqueen has taken Dedrick.
Pell in trouble.
Stew in trouble.
Crius in trouble.

And finally:
Oksana in trouble.

The redhead stumbled, and once again, he tried to turn around to see his old friend, but this time the hovertroids sliced through the sky, extended their filmy arms around his shoulders, and spun him around toward the front again.

"Always face forward, *macta*," one of them said. "*There is no behind.*"

Indeed there wasn't, because as soon as the hovertroid turned him back around, something swallowed the horizon. Incredibly, despite the featureless expanse of tundra, Eldridge had managed to miss the gigantic structure that now rose up before him. Heretofore, the gigantic structure had hidden behind a wall of mist, but as they finally crested a miles-long sloping hill, the mist cleared and revealed their doom.

"What the hell is that?" Eldridge asked.

The old woman answered: "The fuck you think? It's the dynamo."

—⁂—

ELDRIDGE HAD SEEN AN old-time centrifuge in Dr. Enki's office back in Dedrick, and the dynamo looked like a giant centrifuge covered with countless doodads and accoutrements of science. Hundreds of utility pipes ran around its circumference, all of them coiling around windows, turrets, and ramparts where human guards kept watch on the Chain-gang that slowly marched through a thirty-foot doorway that yawned at the bottom-center of the dynamo, which itself stood as high as Jeb Goldmist's tower but ten times as wide. As the Chain trudged on, Eldridge strained to see the edges of the dynamo, but both sides disappeared into the mist.

A shadow blocked the sky; the gigantic door was upon him. The double doors themselves—two slabs of solid steel—stood against the interior walls of the hallway, their hinges crusted with rust that flaked into piles of grime on the floor. Everywhere Eldridge looked, he saw strange ancient glyphs—black triangles arranged in three-pronged formations against a yellow background. He saw several signs warning about "spatiotemporal-kinetic radiation," but he didn't know what that meant.

The vaulted ceiling gave view into dozens of windows that looked down onto the Chain. Eldridge spotted at least a few score human guards. He also noticed the hovertroids hadn't followed them into the dynamo.

But where were the guards from?

They weren't dressed like Jeb Goldmist's magnars, who used to stomp around his hometown of Dedrick in black body armor that bristled with silver spikes. No, these guards wore the same dust-caked jackets, slacks, jeans, corduroy, leather, and canvas that every dreg from here to the coast wore—only all of these guards, men and women, were outfitted with sidearms and ear-mounted headsets that glowed green from within. (He guessed green based on their purple shade in his red-soaked mortarchain vision.) One of them took a personal interest in the redhead.

She stood a full five inches shorter than Eldridge but was able to shove him around with one arm, as her other arm held one of those weird green-glowing rifles. She had braided her hair into hundreds of blond cornrows—undoubtedly to keep any Chainmates from pulling it—and she had eyes that looked like tiny black targets floating on a sea of white. If she hadn't been roughing him up, the redhead might've thought she was cute—but then he remembered Boris's message:

Oksana in trouble.

Whatever that meant. But all of his other friends were in trouble, too. A burst of green light interrupted his thoughts.

"Move your feet, deadbeat," said Target-Eyes, the blonde guard, leveling her weapon at his face. Looking down the barrel of it felt like looking down an endless tunnel that led to a glowing green pool. She flipped the rifle around and rammed the butt into his stomach. He bent over, then *fell* over as the old woman, who had walked several paces ahead, pulled his chain to its limit and yanked him to the floor. The kid stumbled into his prone form, as did the Chainmate behind him (a middle-aged man).

And that's when Eldridge felt it.

The middle-aged woman stumbled to her knees and stopped her fall by holding onto the kid's shoulder with one hand while her other hand came to rest on the redhead's thigh—and the hallway turned *white*.

It was only for an instant, but the redhead's vision flashed an instant, blinding, information-less white when he touched both the kid and the middle-aged woman. Target-Eyes yanked him to his feet.

"*Move!*" she yelled.

He did, now scuttling at a half-jog down the shining steel hallway, passing by more and more observation windows until he arrived at the main event: the dynamo itself. The hallway spilled out into a spiral platform that made a slow, coiling descent around the inside of an open-atrium chamber roughly half a mile wide in diameter and filled with red-and-white lightning that licked and flashed from below. A guardrail was all that sat between him and a hundred-foot drop into the earth. The ceiling opened out onto the night sky above. Eldridge and his fellow Chainmates packed this spiral hallway, all of them rushing around it down and down toward what must have been the dynamo itself—and air caught in the redhead's chest when he finally saw the source of the dynamo's power.

It was *them*.

The lower they got towards the dynamo, the faster they ran, and the brighter their mortarchain links glowed. All of them started to merge together into a single bolt of light that eventually streaked directly into the dynamo's turbine, which whirled endlessly at the bottom-center of the room. For some reason, his memory called up the image of Qi Li, the previously unstoppable Xiang pawn he had dispatched in the last tournament. Li had moved like some of the doomed Chainmates below.

Had he once walked with the Chain, too?

That same message blipped across his brain again: *Oksana in trouble.*

And she wasn't the only one in trouble. Eldridge had already jogged around two levels of the spiral walkway. By his rough estimate, he had less than ten minutes before he (and Boris, who was about a hundred people behind him in line) would transmorph into a streak of light and sprint headlong to his doom. Ideas. He needed ideas. He had one, and he reached into his pocket and found two shell casings, which he threw down into the dynamo—but they splattered into an invisible barrier that hovered twenty feet above the dynamo turbine, their destructions marked by a pair of crackling blue ripples.

A force field.

"Shit," he muttered as everyone's pace quickened, including his own. They ran round and round the walkway, lower and lower, until Eldridge felt a familiar dimming of his vision around the edges. The blackness that crept in at the periphery of his world didn't come from the dynamo; it came from within.

Maybe Doc Enki had been wrong after all.

His vision flashed black for an instant, and when he came to, he had propped his feet onto the guardrail and pressed his back against the wall behind him, both of his hands full of his mortarchains, his mouth stretched wide in a howl that vanished into the churning roar below. The chains burned his hands and sprayed sparks everywhere. He sensed his fellow Chainmates were screaming, too, although his eyes were shut for fear of being blinded by the sparks. The chain in his right hand—the chain that linked him to the old woman, the chain that led *forward*—strained in his grip as he called on every last grise of his old Narsyan strength. If he had kept up his Narsyan training over the years, he might've been able to yank the mortarchains out of his body himself, but as it stood, he needed help.

A fucking lot of it.

"Last chance! Pull! Pull! Pull!"

And they joined him—kids and old women all. Everyone in a hundred-person range of Eldridge stopped, planted their feet against the guardrail and pulled on their mortarchains. Up ahead, Eldridge could actually see one of the dynamo's victims slowly emerge from the streak of white light as he was pulled free from behind. Smoke rose from his form, but he was moving, and best of all—or worst, depending on your point of view—the Chainmate ahead of him had been consumed. *The Chain now had an end.*

Everyone crashed to the floor on top of one another as an alarm sounded from somewhere inside the dynamo. Red bolts of lightning flashed across the half-mile divide of the turbine chamber as hundreds of circuits—human circuits—were shorted. Eldridge pushed the old woman off of him and struggled to his feet, his mortarchains still dangling from his back and chest. He gripped the one in his chest and pulled until he felt his sternum starting to come unglued from his ribcage, but he finally exhaled, gave up and turned to look back. Plainclothes guards were streaming into the turbine chamber, and even though his vision was still tinged a permanent red, he sensed the purplish (green?) flash of their weapons above. The walkway was too narrow and too crowded to accommodate all the guards, so they started blasting their way through the mass of Chainmates, their weapons blazing. Eldridge grabbed his chains and *ran*. He ran for the nearest bunch of prisoners, most of whom had collapsed to the ground, their eyes slits, their limbs shaking with exhaustion. The redhead often forgot his endurance level was triple or quadruple that of the average dreg.

He screamed, *"We need to touch! All of us! It's gonna hurt!"*

Before they could protest, he yanked his chains together and wrapped his arms around six other prisoners, including the old woman and the kid. Once again, his vision flashed white, and a red-hot vise closed around his chest. His heart stopped for a full four counts, then gurgled back to life. Stunned, he lurched back against the guardrail. When he opened his eyes, his vision had returned to normal—the turbine below shone with neutral white light, and the guards' weapons flashed with a deep green light. His chains fell away from his hands, their charge gone.

Some of Chainmates were gone, too. Three of the half-dozen people he had touched lay dead on the floor around his feet, including the old woman. The kid had made it, though, and Eldridge immediately took his shoulder.

"We need to help each other," he said. "Now!"

They propped their feet on each other's chests, grabbed hold of their mortarchains, and pulled as hard as they could. Even without their red-electric charge, the chains were still coiled around their nervous systems in some tangible way, and as he pulled, Eldridge feared he would pull the kid's spinal column out through his chest like a party-conjuror performing a crazy magic trick. Fortunately, the chains came free without causing any permanent damage, but pulling them out was like pulling a network of deeply rooted tree roots from the ground—a dozen tiny mouths opened in their flesh as the chains slid free, but finally they *pop-pop-popped* out. Eldridge looked up and saw more guards forcing their way farther down the spiral rampway, which he scanned for any sign of Boris Hagan.

Eldridge called out: *"Boris?!"*

A wave got his attention. Although the redhead's gambit had disabled the mortarchain's charge for the dozen prisoners around him, all of the prisoners *behind* them still glowed with the chain's red power. Two levels above him, amidst that red aura, Eldridge spotted the white beard and sparkling spectacles of Boris Hagan, and not twenty feet behind him a platoon of dynamo guards approached, green-glowing rifles at the ready. They shouldered their way past prisoners, blasting the occasional Chainmate who tried to block their path. In horror, Eldridge watched as Boris turned to face the guards who were about to pass him. The redhead started to scream again—but Boris let them pass unhindered.

All but one of them.

In a flash, Boris wrapped his mortarchain around the neck of the rearmost guard in the platoon and pulled him back against the wall. The rest of the guards reacted instantly and blasted them with emerald light, but Boris used the helpless guard as a human shield, giving everyone a full view of the effects of the green-glowing rifles.

They didn't do a damn thing if you weren't on the Chain.

It was simultaneously a security measure and the guards' greatest blunder, because as soon as enough of the Chainmates did the math— *if we free ourselves of the Chain, the guards' weapons can't hurt us—* mayhem took hold, sparked by the redhead's shouted orders:

"Push together! Touch each other! Touch as many people as you can! Push!"

And they pushed, all of them, Hagan included. Luminescent red sparks, green muzzleflashes, and white lightning filled the turbine chamber as hundreds upon hundreds of Chainmates charged backward and pressed into each other, shorting out thousands of circuits. Eldridge tried to run forward with the kid by his side, only to find the dead who hadn't survived the overload weighed both of them down. Eldridge winced and yanked his chain out of the old woman's chest.

"Sorry," he whispered—but there was no time. He helped the kid pull his chain out of the chest of a withered man who might've been same age as the redhead if the endless march on the Chain hadn't spent his soul. Chains dangling from their backs, Eldridge and the kid hugged the guardrail and started running back up the spiral pathway. They passed by more and more prisoners, and the redhead realized with horror that the survival rate for breaking a mortarchain bond was roughly 50 percent—prisoners were yanking chains out of dead people by the scores. He ignored the thought and continued his ascent up the pathway, the kid by his side.

They rounded a few levels until finally they met the platoon of guards, all of whom were occupied with prisoners who were punching and kicking and trying to wrap their own mortarchains around their necks. Their rifles flashed and flashed in the blinding brightness of the chamber as the noise of the dynamo started to decrease by a few minute decibels.

There's gotta be a better way to generate energy, Eldridge thought, then drove his boot heel into the side of one of the guards. He fell to the pathway, and the redhead kick-shoved him down into the dynamo turbine, where he disintegrated in a crackling flash of blue electricity. Two other guards wheeled on him, but a dozen other prisoners grabbed them from behind. The revolt was on.

That's when he spotted Boris making his way down to him, rifle in hand.

"El!"

"Boris!"

Eldridge harmlessly absorbed one of the guard's green blasts and rammed his shoulder into the guard's midsection. He churned his legs and drove him into the chamber's outer wall, where the guard fell to the floor. The redhead stuck his heel into the guard's throat and wrested the rifle from his arms. With a slam of the rifle's butt, he knocked the guard unconscious, then turned his attention to two more of the guards, whom he dispatched with a roundhouse swing of the rifle. He caught them both in the face, and they reeled backward into the waiting arms of more Chainmates, who pitched them into the force field below. More blue lightning joined the brewing thunderstorm as they perished.

Eldridge and Boris met and hugged instantly.

"Keep moving," Eldridge said. "Where's everyone else?"

"Long story," Boris said. "I'll fill you in later. Assuming, y'know, we don't die."

Both of them sprinted up and around the pathway, wielding their rifles by the barrel and smashing any errant guard in the face. More prisoners freed themselves from the Chain and joined their rearward rush out of the turbine chamber, but as soon as they reached the entrance to the huge vaulted hallway that led into the dynamo, a pair of dark eyes stopped them—the twin black barrels of an old-school shotgun. A certain blonde female guard had it leveled at the heads of both Eldridge and Boris.

Hagan said, "That's a thirty-aught-six, isn't it?"

"Shut it," Target-Eyes said. "I always told 'em we should have these instead of rayguns. Had to break the glass to get this one. Now, we're gonna *talk*."

Eldridge nudged Boris with his elbow. "Talk, she says."

Boris smiled. "Talk about what, I wonder?"

"Nice weather we're having."

"Feels like rain."

Target-Eyes: *"Shut up!"*

Eldridge: "Duck."

Hagan ducked, and Eldridge pivoted on one foot, spun around and whipped Target-Eyes across the face with the chain still implanted in his back. Thunder echoed against the vaulted ceiling as her shotgun discharged into the air. Boris bum-rushed her and tackled her to the ground as the rest of the freed prisoners streamed out of the turbine chamber and packed the hallway. Eldridge kicked the shotgun out of her arms, grabbed it off the floor, and followed the rest of his former Chainmates as they erupted out of the dynamo and into the freezing desert night.

—ɯ—

THEY RAN. ELDRIDGE AND Boris, side by side, both of them running alongside hundreds of escaped Chainmates. A black sky awaited them outside—black from the night and black from the layer of clouds that hung overhead, threatening to explode with snow or hail or freezing rain at any instant. And the cold. All of them had escaped the horrors of the dynamo and into the standard-issue horrors of the night: negative-fifty-degree temps stabbed their skin like a million needles.

Once outside the dynamo building, they were met with a thousand shocked screams from the rest of the Chainmates who had yet to escape. The revolt inside the building hadn't quite turned into the chain reaction Eldridge had hoped would free the *entire* Chain, but all the same, he saw sunrays of hope in the eyes of the remaining prisoners who lined up to the horizon. Part of him wanted to stop and tell them how to break the Chain's charge, but Boris Hagan must've sensed his intention, because he grabbed the redhead's elbow and steered him southward into an oncoming blast of frozen air.

"Can't save 'em all," Hagan said. "Now, *run*."

But the stabbing needles of the cold night had allies in the form of the thousands of hovertroids that monitored the Chain outside the building. Yellow lights flashed on the faces of a few hundred of them, all of which disengaged from their regular positions and flew off in pursuit of the dozens of escaped prisoners. They darted through the air and extended their filmy filament arms around the helpless necks of escapees. Once entwined, the hovertroids jerked the escaped prisoners into the air, where they hung. No one knew who handed down the law, but everyone knew the punishment for deserting the Chain was death.

Not that anyone had ever escaped the Chain before.

A trio of hovertroids swerved into the sky and leveled yellow beams of light at their eyes. They attacked with an array of strong-wire filaments, but Eldridge and Hagan took them down with their bare hands. Hagan reached into the last hovertroid to cut out its hydrocell; he and Eldridge both frowned at it.

"You sure that's a hydrocell?" Eldridge said. "It's so small."

"I recognize its workings," Boris said, already jumping to his feet and shivering his ass off. Sweat dried on both of their bodies in the unthinkably cold air. Eldridge called up some old Narsyan training from his databanks:

"Bor, when you run, don't pump your arms. Tuck your hands under your arms and hug yourself. It'll slow you down, but it'll help keep your core warm. But first, let's get these chains out of our backs."

They took turns extracting the chains from each other, both of them muttering shits and motherfuckers at the pain. Eldridge grabbed the empty shotgun, and they both ran like a pair of armless silhouettes over a massive dune that spilled out onto a rocky expanse that stretched on for a good five to ten miles. Eldridge and Boris had left behind most of their fellow escapees—except the kid, who slogged his way through the brittle, frozen sand and rock a few yards behind them.

"That kid's following us," Hagan said.

"I know," Eldridge said. "We can't leave him."

"We might have to."

The kid's voice came floating up from behind. "You assholes better not be talking about leaving me! I'm just a kid!"

Boris rolled his eyes. "Then hurry it up!"

The kid came clambering over the dune. Shadows composed his form; the only light was the glow of the Chain, now a mere threadline of crimson on the horizon. Hovertroids continued their endless scan of the area, their golden eyes dancing in the distance, but besides that, only inky arctic desert night awaited them to the south. Huffing and puffing, the kid stopped before them. He stood about five feet and wore rags that hung off his frame. His black hair partially covered his ears and green eyes. His olive complexion came from the same extraction as Yasim, an Odd of Dedrick and one of Eldridge's old friends. Even in the dark, Eldridge saw light glint off some of the kid's ribs.

"Thanks for waiting," the kid said.

"We don't need an extra mouth, kid," Boris said.

"Name's Faz, short for Faizel. *Faz*. Think you can remember that?"

"Kid—"

"What's your name?" Faz asked him.

Hagan glared, then sighed. "Boris. My buddy's Eldridge."

Faz turned. "Hi, Eldridge. Guess what?"

Eldridge gave Boris a look, then said, "What?"

"You two fucksticks need me more'n I need you."

The redhead cocked an eyebrow. "How'd you figure?"

"Because I know how to get to the nearest outpost."

"Great!" Eldridge said. "Lead the way."

The kid smirked and stepped in between them. The night flashed green. The kid froze. He teetered on his feet for a moment before the seam appeared. Running from the top of his head to the center of his groin, the seam came loose as the kid split precisely in half; his brains, guts, entrails and viscera tumbling out of his sundered halves as they collapsed to the rocky ground. Eldridge and Boris spun around and saw Target-Eyes, her eyes lamplights in the night. She sat astride a triangular hover-skiff built for one person. It looked like a wheel-less motorbike outfitted with ten-foot triangular panels that flanked the driver and jutted forward like a pair of giant blades. Target-Eyes sat between the blades, her arm raised, her hand packing some kind of hand-cannon—the kind that could slice a kid in half, apparently.

"Get your fucking asses back to the Chain," she growled.

"How about no?" Eldridge asked.

"How about I fire this thing and drop you like I did *little-shit* there?" she yelled, brandishing the cannon.

Boris held up his hands. "We're all freezing out here. Why don't you come with us? You don't owe them anything."

"Fuck off. If I put in my years, they'll bring me across the oceans. Where it's warm. And green."

Boris made a face. "What?"

But then the redhead spoke: "Freeze." He leveled the shotgun at Target-Eyes.

She laughed. "It's empty."

"You sure?"

Her lower eyelids crept upward. "I spent both rounds back in the dynamo."

"Is that a question?"

"No, I shot 'em both," she said.

Eldridge glanced at Hagan.

"Boris, how much more of a diversion do you need?"

"Oh!" Boris chucked the 'troid's hydrocell at Target-Eyes's head. It exploded—her head, that is—as the hydrocell flew harmlessly into the sand. Her body slumped off the skiff, which floated to the ground. Both Eldridge and Boris shook the noise out of their ears. They looked at the shotgun. Smoke spumed out of one of its barrels. Eldridge lowered the shotgun and turned.

"Well, thank Crom I had a round left, dude! *That* was your plan? Throw a hydrocell at her face and hope for the best?!"

"At least I *had* a plan! Did you even *know* you had a round in there?"

"Maybe."

"Enough," Hagan said, turning to the remains of the kid. They walked over and knelt, both of them convulsing with shivers. The two halves of the kid lay in sopping, blood-saturated patches of red sand.

Eldridge touched one of the kid's cheeks. It was already crusting over with gray frost. Hagan looked up.

"Come on," he said. "We better hope this kid had a map on him."

They each took a half of his body and searched the remains of his clothes. No map. They stood.

"What now?" Boris asked.

Eldridge looked at Target-Eyes's motoskiff. "Well, at least we've got transpo. And the kid was heading due south."

―⁂―

THE RUMORTRYSTS HELD THERE was only one cure for a dreen: the blood of a Narsyan chieftain.

―⁂―

[AUDIO: THE CLICK OF A DICTATRYST DEVICE DEACTIVATING.]

Whoa, whoa, whoa! Hold up there, friends and neighbors—my apologies!

Boris Hagan here, reporting to you from Ikraam House, mere moments before my final departure. Listen, this dictatryst gizmoid's one impressive piece of tech, but it keeps leaving out important pieces of the puzzle. I mean, ya can't spring a word like "dreen" on an unsuspecting Shore-Rider and not expect some confusion.

Here's the scoop on dreens: They're people. Used be, anyway. But they're folks who . . . well, who went off the rails for one reason or another, and in the process, short-circuited their endocrine systems. Some dreens are ragers—strength-junkies whose muscles'll never be big enough. Or hypofidgets, mirror-phobes who'll never be pretty enough. Or murungis, depressives who'll never be sad enough. Others can't get high—or stay high—enough.

Enough is never enough for a would-be dreen, and as soon as their endocrine systems go haywire, the rest of their bodies follow. Some dreens are monstrous, others just sorrowful, but regardless, like the dictatryst was saying: once you go dreen, there's only a few ways back. We used to think the only way was with the blood of a Narsyan chieftain.

But there's one other way, and it ain't pretty.

Let's back up a bit and try again, but for this next part, we're shiftin'

the scene about twenty miles north of the Chain of Tears, where we find bounty-merc Quillig trying his level best to keep not being a dreen.
[AUDIO: THE CLICK AND WHIRR OF A DICTATRYST DEVICE COMING ONLINE.]

—⚞—

QUILLIG

THE RUMORTRYSTS HELD THERE was only one cure for a dreen: the blood of a Narsyan chieftain.
That assumption was wrong.
There was one other cure, although strictly speaking, it wasn't so much a cure as it was an ongoing stopgap against a relapse into dreendom.
Bounty-merc Quillig had stumbled down the road to becoming a dreen some years ago. Everyone thought he had been a rager who slipped, but in reality he had been a tary-fairy who had happily subjected himself to hundreds of microsurgeries, endocrine cocktails and DNA splicings—all in an effort to mold his face and his form into something that didn't make him weep when he looked in the mirror. The lie about being a wannabe rager had emerged from the need for a bounty-merc—*any* bounty-merc—to craft an appropriately fearsome personal narrative.
After he dumped Boris Hagan at the Chain of Tears, Quillig rode his truck north to a remote outpost called Basil. Unlike remnants, which were almost exclusively subterranean (like Dedrick), outposts usually made their home aboveground. Little more than a smattering of well-insulated shacks in the middle of a frozen gray tundra, Basil was home to a few dregs and one of the "deep-desert sawbones" Boris Hagan often spoke of in hushed tones. These dark physicians supposedly helped merge the psychoskags of Dedrick with their technology, and they also offered dreen-reversal services—for the right price.
The sawbones' shack sat on the perimeter of Basil, encircled by a line of gray dust Quillig knew was dried brain matter. Quillig carefully stepped over the circle of brain dust. The kooky old physician had built the shack out of plywood, cyclone fencing, and the blue plastic remains of an ancient shitter. A hydrocell-powered climate-condi-

tioner chugged away and pumped hot air through a window into the shack, which was dark except for one white-hot light that the sawbones kept trained on Quillig's face at all times. An ancient medical chair awaited the bounty-merc inside, with a pair of raised leather hoops for his feet, although the bounty-merc had no idea why he'd need to raise his feet for what the sawbones had to do.

As for the sawbones himself, he regarded Quillig from above. Pustles and bubucles covered the sawbones's face; bumps and knobs the size of hailstones or play-marbles, all of them rock-hard to the touch, their inner-abscess having long since petrified. White stubble lined his face and sprouted tributaries of facial hair into regions where it didn't belong—up his nose, onto his eyelids—its boundaries having expanded across the patches of scar tissue that carved up his head. Coils of flesh bloomed on the sides of his head like misplaced outie navels, marking where his ears had once been. He had shit-brown eyes and wore a black raincoat when he worked.

Quillig often wondered how he had been cured. After all, as a dreen, there was no way he could have come to the sawbones voluntarily. Someone must have *caught* Quillig and brought him in. But who cared that much about him to want to see him cured? It was a mystery.

Not even two hours after Eldridge and Boris had escaped from the Chain, Quillig was sitting in the sawbone's home and *howling*. The sawbones was completing his latest anti-dreen treatment, a full endocrine scrub. This required the bounty-merc to strip naked and remove both the plaid fabric that covered his face and the black cartridge that gave him sight. Quillig sat topless, his eye sockets empty, his chest an anatomical diagram of the human muscular system— every muscle exposed in perfect relief, every vein visible, and all of it coated in the same purple-red scar tissue that covered the rest of his body.

But Quillig thought about none of it because his whole world had turned to fire. The endocrine scrub turned his blood to acid just as it transformed every muscle fiber to flame and every bone to embers. While the machine did its work, his body was locked in a frozen arc of torment, his lipless mouth stretched wide, his lungs hoarse from screaming.

He never remembered when it stopped. At some point he would

black out from the pain, and the next thing he knew, the sawbones would be stitching the patch of plaid fabric back over his face. A rectangular opening had been cut into the fabric. The bounty-merc's empty eye sockets stared through the opening. Black bionic implants sat in the inner-bottom corners of his sockets, which were coated with livid red and purple scar tissue. The sawbones slid his sight-cartridge into his sockets and plugged it into the bionic implants. Quillig stirred. The bounty-merc flexed an array of muscles on his face to activate the cartridge.

His sight-aperture narrowed around the sawbones.

"Was the procedure successful?" Quillig asked, his chest heaving.

The sawbones grunted his usual affirmation and started to remove a series of intravenous tubes from the bounty-merc's arms and legs. Quillig rubbed the needle pricks on his inner elbows.

"How long till I'll need another scrub?"

The sawbones crossed over to a rusty steel table that held equipment and dumped the used needles. He grunted, then held up three kinky-haired talons.

"Three months," Quillig said. "That's grea—"

Knock.

The blue plastic door shook with the pound of a strange fist. A shadow blocked the starlight outside. The sawbones regarded Quillig and cocked his head at the door, his look saying, *What the fuck is this?*

Quillig shrugged. "I don't—"

Knock.

The whole shack shook. The sawbones turned and opened the door, and Quillig felt his ears pop as the warm air from the climate-conditioner rushed out and the frozen desert air rushed in.

But no starlight followed the cold.

An image out of an old horror show filled the doorway. Quillig figured it was a man or a creature of some kind, but from his viewpoint, it simply looked like the door was filled with black. And then someone spoke.

"May I come in, please?"

Given the nature of the scene, the voice sounded about three octaves higher than Quillig expected. It sounded like a *child's* voice. The sawbones turned to Quillig again and looked a question at him.

The bounty-merc said, "Yes, come in."

Again, that childlike voice: "Thank you, sir."

The blackness that blocked the door crouched and inserted its knee and foot into the door. Both looked like they had been carved out of steaming, newly poured concrete—reminding Quillig of the freshly paved streets he had seen in wealthier remnants like Port Stafford. The creature lowered its head and slid into the shack, taking care not to touch anything or knock anything over. It waited a few beats to let the sawbones scuttle to the rear corner, where he cowered and peered at the creature from behind a rolling gurney. The creature slid its other leg into the shack. Once inside, the creature used one of its fingertips—which was the size of Quillig's head—to slowly close the door. That was when Quillig felt the sudden need to switch the climate-device from *heat* to *cool*, because the creature's presence choked the room with the hot stench of pavement. The creature sat on the dirt floor and crossed its legs, hunching to avoid hitting the plywood ceiling. It left tracks and traces of tar wherever it moved and on whatever it touched.

Finally, it raised its head and revealed no face.

Its head was a raised cylinder of concrete, and its "face" was simply the flat top of that cylinder. That same childlike voice emitted from it.

"You are bounty-mercenary Quillig?"

Quillig felt a sudden urge to put his feet in the leather stirrups. He fought it and answered, "Yeah."

"Were you aware there has been a security breach at the Chain of Tears?"

Quillig sat forward. *"What?"* He started to ask how many escaped, but he stopped and simply spat, "Who?"

"The Red Rook."

Quillig's gorge rose at the sound of the words. Ever since his triumph over Jeb Goldmist's Xiang tournament, the rumortrysts had started referring to the little cocksucker as the *Red Rook*. The bounty-merc jumped up and crossed to the wall, where his shirt and vest hung. He whipped them off a hook and pulled them on. As he buttoned his Kevlar vest, he asked, "How many others?"

The creature said, "It doesn't matter to you."

"And why not?"

"Because *he* wants the Red Rook recaptured. Personally. By you."

Quillig's fingers paused on the last of his vest buttons. His hands floated down to his sides. He took a step forward and tilted his head toward the creature.

"'He'? As in *him* 'he'?"

"Quite right."

Quillig's weight shifted from one foot to the other. Absent-mindedly, he patted his chest with both hands. "You're going to have to say it out loud."

"Very well. The man across the oceans."

Quillig shook his head. "How is that even possible?"

The creature chirped, "He has a gift for you."

The bounty-merc had heard a lot of death threats in his time, and a lot of them began with such pronouncements—"I've got a gift for you"; "Special delivery"; "I'm about to shoot you in the face with a gun." But the concrete creature simply put forth its three-fingered fist and uncurled its digits, which cracked and crumbled as they shed chunks and particles of pavement.

In its palm sat a castle surrounded by a world of glass.

A cracked glass sphere housed the tiny castle, which had apparently once been painted bright colors—pink and powder blue—but the years had sapped the paint of its brilliance just as it had it sanded away the hand-carved detail that had been lavished on it once upon a time, leaving behind the smooth, melted remains of its former self. The castle and its cracked glass home both sat on a small, ornate pedestal. Petals of gilding peeled from it.

The sight of the castle unhinged the bounty-merc's knees. He lurched back into the chair and stared at the castle.

The creature spoke: "Take your gift."

Quillig hesitated a moment, and then used his fingertips to slowly lift the castle out of its hand. He cradled the glass sphere as if supporting the head of a newborn baby.

"When—when exactly did this breach happen?"

"Approximately two hours ago."

Quillig's sight-aperture opened and closed with barely audible *whirrs*. "Two hours? How did he find out so fast?"

"He found out instantly."

"How?"

Concrete bubbled around the creature's shoulders. Within a few heartbeats it had doubled in size, its limbs fattening and filling the corners of the shack. Its knee blocked the climate-conditioner—and with it, all incoming breathable air. The sawbones yelped and fell to the floor behind the gurney. The reek of black concrete throttled the room. Quillig recoiled into the chair as the creature's circular flat face filled his worldview and spoke with that same childlike voice.

"This is a one-way transfer of information, bounty-merc. The man across the oceans knows you brought the redhead to the Chain, and he expects you to capture him now that he's escaped. Do you know where Port Stafford is?"

"*Yes,*" he said, his lungs full of tar. "*On the western coast.*"

"Correct. You will bring him to Port Stafford. *Alive.* For delivery to the man across the oceans."

That said, the creature shrank. Rolls of concrete undulated back into its body. Its knee unblocked the climate-conditioner, and breathable air flowed back into the shack. Silent, the creature opened the door. Quillig sighed at the inrush of freezing air. The creature started to (once again, very carefully) extract itself from the sawbone's home.

But as its head was about to vanish through the door, Quillig felt a crackle of courage in his chest. He stood shoulders squared and brow knit, although he still held the castle as if it could shatter at the slightest touch.

"How much bounty for the redhead?"

The creature paused. Slowly, it raised its flat face, but this time, a glowing, red-hot crevice slashed across the diameter of the cylinder. Molten lead poured out of its mouth as its voice—still childlike but a thousand decibels louder—thundered:

"*No bounty. You bring him in. Alive. We let you live. You have thirty-six hours.*"

The words blew Quillig back into the chair. The creature slammed the door, dragging the blue plastic through the pool of steaming, congealing molten lead on the ground. Toxic white smoke billowed from the melting plastic as it curled upward and admitted a never-ending draft of freezing air. Quillig's aperture narrowed. He sat in silence for a moment before the sawbones shuffled out from behind the gurney.

"You owe me for the door."

―⚬―

ELDRIDGE AND BORIS HAGAN

Fortunately for Eldridge and Boris, Target-Eyes's skiff had a surprisingly powerful heating system. Even though it was an open-air vehicle, the heater generated an invisible dome of warmth around the seating area. *Un*fortunately for the two escapees, the skiff only seated one, which meant the other had to sit with his head tucked between his knees and crammed into the space behind the driver. They also scavenged clothes from Target-Eyes's corpse, taking care to clean as much blood and brain matter off the former guard's duds as possible. Because Hagan was already wearing one of his zillion standard-issue sweaters, he grabbed her pants while Eldridge pulled on her coat and a strangely familiar T-shirt. It read: *Play at the Prometerium.* Eldridge stared at the words.

Hagan asked, "What's the Prometerium?"

"Just a place out on the coast," he said, thinking of a simple game he had played that caused him a lot of trouble.

Hours later, the skiff sliced through the desert night, its halogen headlamp casting a single cone of light into the ink. Their ears and noses and fingers were all stained with the unmistakable red of the nearly frostbitten, but they had made it out of the cold just in time to save all their bits and pieces.

Eldridge took first shift driving, but he insisted Hagan stay up with him.

"Yo, Boris! How long's it been since I killed Jeb Goldmist?"

Curled up behind him, Hagan said, "You don't remember?"

"No."

"About three months ago. Can you remember how you got on the Chain?"

"Yeah. That mactabrain Walter Torsten snatched me up in Hemming."

"And do you remember why you were up in Hemming?"

Eldridge thought. "Something to do with Goldmist's jenta?"

"Damn. The rumortrysts were right about the Chain. It *does* scramble your brain."

The skiff listed leftward as it swooped over a rise in the terrain. Up ahead, Eldridge saw a break in the graphite-black clouds that loomed overhead. Pinpricks of starlight twinkled in the distant sky. Once again, the redhead found himself soaring over that same grinning chasm in his mind.

What am I forgetting?

A thought jostled loose in his mind, rolled around, and fell out his mouth in the form of a dreamily asked question: "Did Nadia ever tell you why she left me?"

Hagan's expression held fast. Only a slight contraction between his brows reflected that the redhead had just referred to the mother of his child by name for the first time in years.

Nadia. Nadia Tola.

"I remember her," Hagan said, steely.

"Did she . . . ever tell you why she left me?"

Hagan's expression tightened. "Which time?"

"What?"

"She left you more than once. She left you to raise Zora by yourself, and then she left you . . . well, later."

The redhead frowned. He slipped a hand into his pocket, lost in thought.

"Zora," he mumbled.

"Yeah," Boris said. "Your kid? Your daughter?"

"My daughter."

"In Junktown," Hagan said.

Eldridge's eyes went foggy. "It's warm there." Eldridge stared into space for another moment before he gave his head a shake and said, "Sorry about that. Lost in thought." His expression brightened. "Wait. Was Goldmist's jenta . . . booby-trapped?"

"Right," Hagan said, mentally noting the redhead's strange episode. "So after all that bullshit, you still couldn't pay off . . . whoever you need to pay off."

"It's not important."

"You sure about that?"

Eldridge thought. "The guy's called 'the man across the oceans.' That's all I know. Some kind of big shot on the eastern continent."

"How'd you get in hock to the likes of him?"

"Long story."

"Looks like we got a long ride ahead of us."

"Some other time. Now, tell me what happened after I found out about the booby trap."

"You don't remember?"

The chasm grinned at him. "I feel like I've forgotten a lot of stuff."

"Well, you needed jenta. And you went to Hemming."

After a moment, Eldridge nodded and said, "Yeah. Right. I remember now. I wanted to play the hyperlotto."

—✵—

[AUDIO: THE CLICK OF A DICTATRYST DEVICE DEACTIVATING.]

With some folks, gambling's a sickness, an addiction. We used to think El had him a sickness when it came to making odds, but we were wrong. Turns out, he's just the most durnfool unlucky dipshit I ever known.

See, some years back, El got himself deep in debt to this highfalutin' potentate called the man across the oceans. Damn if any of us know who he is—he rules the eastern continent, or so sing the rumortrysts. Eldridge had been planning to pay off his debt by winning what's called a "deathday wager." You place a bet predictin' the exact day you'll die. Eldridge thought he had it licked, but when he missed his deathday, he was forced to enter Jeb Goldmist's Xiang Tournament.

But even triumphing over Jeb Goldmist didn't change his luck. Goldmist being dead may have freed up his jenta stores, but the evil bastard was a cunning one. He'd smart-glommed a temporal-snare onto his jenta. Any time Eldridge tried to spend his winnings, the jenta smart-characters vanished into the past.

So Eldridge was still in hock to—and on the run from—the man across the oceans.

But as we saw earlier, he wasn't the only one.

[AUDIO: THE CLICK AND WHIRR OF A DICTATRYST DEVICE COMING ONLINE.]

—✵—

QUILLIG

THE MAN ACROSS THE *oceans*.

Did he have a name? Hadn't Quillig heard it somewhere before? After all, he had taunted the redhead with his identity when he caught him in Dedrick for Jeb Goldmist, although he knew as much as the redhead knew about the famed odd—his gender (man) and his location (across the oceans). That was all *anyone* knew about him, even those who *lived* on the other side of the oceans.

"You know who you owe," Quillig had told the redhead as he dragged him down Sinister Street to Goldmist's tower. Little did the bounty-merc know at the time that he was setting Goldmist up for a titanic smackdown in his own backyard, but that wasn't his concern. After he shot Eldridge in the head, the bounty-merc left town.

Good thing.

Now, three months later, as he drove his big rig across the endless desert south of the Chain of Tears, Quillig looked at the tiny castle in the glass sphere. He had wrapped it in a burlap blanket and tucked it into a cup holder that sat between the truck's two front seats. The bounty-merc thought back to his previous encounters with Eldridge: how the mouthy little shit had thwarted him in the remnant of Le Ponce and sullied his name six years ago in Glaucio. Eldridge had stood atop the bar in a saloon, brandishing a bottle of ancient whiskey he bought with the jenta he won off a half-witted Odd, Walter Torsten, who insisted Quillig capture Eldridge in retribution though he didn't owe Torsten any jenta.

"You can't put a bounty on someone who doesn't owe you anything," Quillig said six years back, his plaid patch new and freshly sewn onto his face.

Sitting behind a desk made of solid diamond, Torsten snorted a drag of trox-laced gelatin through a two-foot straw from a sippy cup. He fidgeted with his cybernetic arm, one of four major limbs he'd replaced from his love of cutting, which did not exclude his own body; he constantly tried to cajole his subordinates into doing the same.

"Bad news!" he'd say while backslapping a leggy trixie-waitress on his floor. "We have to amputate at the neck!"

No one laughed, and neither did Quillig laugh at the idea of capturing the redhead without obeying proper Chain protocol. That wasn't good enough for Torsten, though.

"He cheated."

"He cheated," Quillig said. "How exactly do you cheat at sportsbook?"

Eldridge had won the bottle of whiskey off of Torsten by predicting which footbomerico team would get blown to bits by a pre-game IED during that week's play.

And all those years ago, Torsten took another snort of his spiked gelatin and glared at Quillig with bloodshot eyes whose vasculature squirmed like two plates full of angry red snakes.

"He cheated by *winning*. Just bring him the fuck *innnnngggg!*"

Torsten's words degenerated into guttural howl as the gelatitrox hit his brain and fried his nervous system. Quillig took that as his cue to leave.

And in his ears, he heard a series of *pops,* like buttons being torn from a shirt.

Red Rook, my ass.

Now, years later, Quillig aimed the headlamps of his big rig at a dark mesa that rose on the horizon. He had to admit: He shot Eldridge in the fucking head, and the little shit just kept on coming. And now he had thirty-six hours to deliver him to Port Stafford, which was a thousand leagues away on the western coast, and he realized he needed a little something extra to bring in this bounty—*help.*

It was time to visit a sectan confine and round up a grextet.

FROM A DISTANCE, THE mesa looked abandoned, but up close it swarmed with activity. As he approached in his big rig, Quillig adjusted a setting on his sightbox, giving him a better view of the infrared visual spectrum. A network of vertical tracks ran up the side of the mesa that would otherwise be invisible to passersby. Not that there *were* any passersby in that deep part of the desert.

Quillig parked his rig next to an eclectic dozen other vehicles—motorbikes, hovertrikes, shit-shakers, and rusty old wrecks. After stowing the tiny castle in a vest pocket, he wrapped himself in a Mylar coat and climbed out, instantly shivering in the double-digit negative-temp cold. Needles of frozen hail-rain started to fall across the desert. The eastern horizon remained pitch dark, sunrise still hours away.

But even though it was the middle of the night, Quillig knew the sectan confine would be buzzing.

The bounty-merc jogged around to the back of his rig where he maintained a tiny habitat used during long stretches in the deep desert. He pulled out a T-shaped device resembling an old children's toy—a "pogo stick," he had heard it called. But this wasn't a toy. Quillig ran over to the side of the mesa, chose one of the vertical tracks, and affixed the bottom of the pogo-device to it. Servos and machinery groaned from within the mesa, and the track chugga-chugged to life. Quillig propped his toes on the pogo-device's footholds and rode up to the top of the mesa, the *ratta-tat-tat* of freezing rain-hail sounding on his Mylar wrap as he rose into the frozen churn of the desert night. Without realizing it, he hunched over to protect the castle in his pocket. Once he crested the top of the mesa, Quillig deactivated the infrared display on his sightbox, thereby rendering the track invisible, but that didn't matter—the sectan confine of Pestus wasn't hidden from view.

One of hundreds of such confines, Pestus and its ilk served the near thousand bounty-mercs who operated around the eastern continent at any one time. Their locations and appearances were as varied as the bounty-mercs who used them. Some confines hid in the center of mountains, accessible only through secret caves, while others huddled at the bottom of the ocean, located as far offshore as the bounty-mercs dared venture for fear of angering the undersea marauders who ruled the waters.

The location of some confines—one in particular—was a secret to most, even Quillig. The rumortrysts held that it lay in a remnant to the east, but the plaid-faced bounty-merc had never found it.

No matter: Pestus made its home inside of an ancient stone

battlement that supposedly once housed mortar-cannons and other weaponry from a conflict that happened soon after Deadblast. No one remembered, but in the intervening years, the bounty-mercs had claimed it and gutted the insides. As Quillig strode in the front door, he saw the result:

A big-ass map.

Everyone watched the map, and everyone contributed to it. Dozens of bounty-mercs ran to and fro, writing notes on the map, which stood ten feet tall and spanned forty feet of the confine's interior circumference. To be sure, the confine included some tech—a few computer monitors here and there spilled out information about live bounties—but the map was low-tech. *No*-tech. Bounty-mercs would post notes around the map and then run lengths of string from the notes to specific locations they would mark with brightly colored thumbtacks. They did this until they covered the map with information about live bounties. Once every two weeks, one of the attending bounty-mercs would clear the map, no matter what. Underneath, the map was peppered with enough tiny holes to make it look like corkboard.

The inside of the confine was all gray stone—walls, floor and ceiling—except for a polished wood bar that stood opposite the great map. A barkeep wearing an eye patch manned the bar and served basic food and drink—but no booze.

No one fucked around in the confines.

Dozens of wooden tables sat strewn around the room in a constant state of squeaking shuffle as bounty-mercs scooted them from one place to another to make room for meetings, confabs and strategy sessions. Despite Pestus' remote location, Quillig counted at least twenty fellow bounty-mercs who came and went within the first five minutes of his arrival. Styli scribbled and jenta smartcharacters scurried from hand to hand—the tables danced with red wealth.

And Quillig was about to bring the room to a standstill, he knew.

The plaid-faced bounty-merc pulled up a chair, stood on it and called out:

"The Chain of Tears has been breached!"

Boom. Silence. Hands froze mid-deal and dozens of faces swiveled his way. His lipless mouth curled in a sneer, even though the thought of the concrete creature's ultimatum made his heart feel like it was made out of lead.

He continued: "There are hundreds of new bounties on the grid. You're welcome to 'em, but I'm here *for one motherfucking bounty.*"

A female bounty-merc wearing a chainmail cocktail dress snorted. "The redhead," she said.

"Fuckin' A right it's the redhead. He's got his little shithead sidekick with him, too—Hagan. But Boris Hagan's not my concern. I just want Eldridge, and I want to split the bounty with a grextet. Who wants in?"

The same female bounty-merc asked: "Who's paying the bounty?"

Quillig was ready with the lie: "The man across the oceans."

It landed like a punch line. The room was silent for a beat, and then hands started slapping tables and knees as guffaws broke like a wave across the room. Bounty-mercs young and old, fat and thin—they all bent over with glee, and after they laughed their asses off, their asses laughed their asses off. Even the barkeep laughed—he had listened to enough stories over the years to be in on the joke—and when Quillig glanced over at the bar, his mind's eye showed him an image of the redhead dancing in that saloon in Glaucio years ago. He heard *pops* over the laughter, like someone was squeezing a fistful of bubble-wrap next to his ear.

The bounty-merc in the chainmail cocktail dress stepped forward, shaking her head and touching her chest, which rose and fell with her chuckles. She emerged from behind a few other bounty-mercs and revealed that her cocktail dress was only part of a larger ensemble of bulky black boots with three-inch treads, missile launchers strapped to her back, microfabric tights, and a device that cupped the sides of her neck and blinked with digital readouts. Most female bounty-mercs braided their hair, but this one left hers hanging in flowing waves of umber.

The woman said, "You expect us to believe that the man across the oceans is interested in a single dreg who owes him some jenta? *Legions* of dregs owe him jenta. His debtors are everywhere. Some of 'em owe him and don't even *know* they owe him. What's the redhead to him?"

Quillig said, "I don't know. But he gave me this."

He held up the tiny castle.

The only sound in the room was a slight hiss as the air drained out of everyone's chests. Slack jaws and slapped foreheads prevailed. The plaid-faced bounty-merc chuckled.

"Not so fucking funny now, is it?"

—⚊⚊—

BOUNTY-MERCS CROWDED AROUND THE map where Quillig stood and held aloft the tiny castle. They waved their hands, their weapons and their good bounty-mercing names in an effort to get on the plaid-faced man's grextet, which would consist of himself and two other specially chosen bounty-mercs.

He dismissed the first wave—which included an identical twin set of knife experts and an armpit-smelling grotesque who was covered head to toe in some kind of organic scales like willowy lengths of tree bark.

For the next bunch of hopefuls, he pulled up a table and started taking notes in his own coded shorthand. The female bounty-merc in the chainmail cocktail dress straddled a chair and grinned at him.

"You want Lady R with you on your little journey," she said.

Lady R looked like she was weeping mercury, but she had simply pierced the outer corners of her eyes and affixed silver studs in both holes. Small, flowery black tattoos surrounded the piercings and curled around her eyebrows. When she puckered her mouth, her lips made a perfect red heart—the result of some carefully applied permanent makeup. Like most bounty-mercs, dozens of scars covered her face. In her case, the densest collection of scar tissue made a cup under her left eye. Quillig indicated the injury.

"Tell me what happened there," he said.

"Some other time. For now, let's—" At that moment another bounty-merc—a suckling babe with spiked hair and an overbite full of sharpened black teeth—groped her hair.

"Nice locks, chickie," he said, but when he brought his hand away from her head, his arm terminated at a flat cross-section of flesh. He frowned at where his hand had once been like it was a jigsaw puzzle, then stammered, "Where—hand—go?"

The female bounty-merc jumped to her feet, rounded on the impulsive over-biter, and took a deep breath. When she opened her mouth, her voice rang: "I sent it to the Lost Realm of Mohana where the Loog Giants rule from the peaks of the Agots and the little Ottos scurry in their shadows. Be not afeard—your hand now floats in a pool of scale-honey hewn from the hides of night-dragons."

The over-biter gave her an incredulous one-eye squint, then slammed his handless wrist down on a table and used his remaining hand to draw a splatter-iron hand-cannon. Lights flared on the woman's neck-mounted device, and the missile launchers strapped to her back slammed forward, flanking her head, and fired a pair of jenta-stylus-sized missiles, which implanted themselves in the over-biter's eye sockets. He stumbled backward, screaming and clawing at his eyes. The two missiles beeped, then detonated in a pair of cube-shaped explosions that left behind cubic cavities in the over-biter's dead head. His corpse collapsed to the ground.

In the back, the barkeep flipped a DAYS WITHOUT INCIDENT sign back to zero.

Quillig's sight-aperture expanded. "You're in."

She nodded. "I know."

"What's the R stand for?"

"It stands for the end of it all, sibbie-merc. I am she: Lady Ragnarok."

—ᴡ—

QUILLIG REJECTED A HUNDRED more hopefuls before he met the jellywoman.

The jellywoman had been skulking in the back of the confine, sitting and staring at a smartpad-sized device that lay on her table and displayed a never-ending rush of data. A plate of liquefied food sat in a bowl next to the device. The food had been solid when the confine's barkeep served it to her, but the gel-woman used a handheld emulsifier—a tiny propeller—to turn the synth-beef and rubbery vegetables into soup. Using an eyedropper, she dripped samples of the soup into the middle of the pad. Every drop exploded against the pad with a rainbow starburst of data that dispersed and settled into modules of nutritional and (most important) *toxin*-related information. Once she was satisfied that the soup was free of toxins, she fed a three-foot straw into the glop and attached the other end of the straw into the gel that encased her body.

That's how the jellywoman got her handle, of course: her coating.

She looked like she had been encased in a moving ice sculpture of herself. Some time ago, she had paid a deep-desert sawbones to create an impenetrable layer of gel armor for her body, and some time ago she had allowed herself to be lowered into a vat of the molten glop wearing nose plugs and with nothing but a mouth-mounted O2 canister to keep her alive. Once she was fully submerged in the gel, the sawbones used a pair of extendo-tongs to remove the O2 canister, and she had to endure a full three minutes unable to breathe while the glop lowered in temperature enough to be able to accept the injection of CO_2-scrubbing nanotroids the sawbones had invented. Once they were active in the glop, the sawbones nodded at the jellywoman, who then inhaled the gel into her lungs, where it hardened into the same semi-flexible state as the rest. Nanotroids attached themselves to the alveoli inside her lungs and scrubbing the CO_2-saturated blood that arrived. Growing calm, she sat in the gel for an hour to let it cool into a block. When it was solid, the sawbones cut her out with a laser-scalpel.

Never did her personal ecosystem come into contact with the outside world. Because the protective gel wasn't perfectly transparent, the jellywoman wore socket-mounted oculars that could un-distort her view and allow her to see normally. To an average dreg, the oculars would appear to be opaque black, but the jellywoman could see through them normally. The gel was impervious to viral or bacterial invasion, but more important for Quillig's needs, it could also withstand the impact of a point-blank shot.

"RPGs bounce right off it," the jellywoman said, speaking through a speechmouth that had been wedged into the gel while it was still congealing.

In response to the jellywoman's claim, Quillig's head cocked and his sight-aperture narrowed.

The jellywoman said, "Ah. You have certain requirements. I do, too, but for now, I want to satisfy yours. A demonstration—a *demo*—is in order." She stood, a moving plastic blob-woman, and said, "Shall we step outside?"

A dozen hopeful bounty-mercs volunteered to test the jellywoman's armor, but Quillig insisted on doing it himself, lest he find himself the victim of a clever confidence game. They stepped out into the freezing night. Atop the mesa, the light from inside the confine cast long shadows all around, the menagerie of silhouettes a who's-who of freakery. Colossi lumbered alongside bamboo-skinny figures that crouched and scurried alongside mesomorphic strongdudes who flexed and preened in the darkness. The jellywoman gave herself a good buffer zone between herself and the other mercs, while Quillig accepted and inspected a grenade-launcher from Lady R, who assured him that it was "fully functional and very killy."

The jellywoman stood alone and spread her arms. "I'm ready for—"

Thoonk! Quillig had already fired. A column of firesmoke billow-streaked across the mesa and slammed into the jellywoman's chest, where it exploded in a sideways mushroom-cloud that dissipated in an instant and left the jellywoman standing in the same pose. Meanwhile, the grenade Quillig had launched tracked a parabolic trajectory up and away from its target. A hapless bounty-merc wearing desert camo-fatigues was just coming up the side of the mesa on a personal pogo-transport. When he saw the grenade, his forearms made an X over his face. The explosion sent him flying into the darkness. The other bounty-mercs immediately headed back into the confine, grumbling about how that kind of body armor "wasn't nothin' special."

The jellywoman crossed to Quillig and Lady R.

"Hello," the jellywoman said. "You have certain requirements. I believe I have met those requirements. I also have requirements. Requirement the first—"

"Okay, okay, you're in," Quillig said. "Can we go inside?"

"Yeah, jellywoman," Lady R said. "I'm freezing my ovaries off."

"Requirement the first," she said, louder and harder. "You mustn't ever call me jellywoman. You mustn't. My name is Kieron. That is the name you shall use."

Quillig said, "You got it, Kieron. And I've got a crazy idea—let's go catch some bounty."

—⚜—

ELDRIDGE AND BORIS HAGAN

They continued riding due south. Boris had taken over driving after a couple of hours. Thankfully, he kept the prescription on his spectacles up to date, so when a dust mote of light appeared on the horizon to the southwest, he was able to spot it. He woke up Eldridge to get a second opinion.

"I think that's Penticton," Boris said.

"Yep, that totally nondescript speck of light looks Penticton-ish to me, too."

They headed toward it. Eldridge checked the skiff's fuel-meter. Like most post-Deadblast vehicles, it was hydrocell-powered, so they could ride it for as long as they wanted, but the redhead didn't like their chances of staying alive outside with no real shelter. He also saw that the skiff had a cooling system, but would it be as effective as its heater? He didn't want to wait for the sun to explode over the eastern horizon to find out.

In the meantime, it was still story time.

"You're telling me that Torsten tried to clean out the Old Mine?" Eldridge asked. "Is he fucking insane?"

"Nope, just stupid. Well, *and* insane. But you knew that, didn't you?"

"Hey, it's not my fault he was such a sore loser back in Glaucio!"

"Yeah, but you didn't have to be such an asshole about it, El."

"Whatever. So after I went up to Hemming to play Torsten's hyperlotto, he snatched me, turned me over to Quillig, then set up shop in Dedrick?"

"That's about the size of it. And he decided he wanted reopen the Ancient Sea and the Old Mine for some reason."

"Bad idea."

"The dreenqueen thought so, too. We got out before the main wave of dreens hit, but they got to Crius before we could warn him. He's the new dreenking."

Crius Kaleb. An Odd and a lifelong friend of the redhead's. Crius had been mind-crazy for most of his life until Eldridge cured him, and now he was the dreenqueen's parasitic mate. Calling him a "king" didn't connote the truth of his new station.

But if Kaleb was the *new* dreenking, there was also the matter of the *old* dreenking to consider. Eldridge had met the old one: Milos Tola. The redhead had never told anyone that he had seen his former son-in-law attached to the side of the horrific mountain of mutated flesh that was the dreenqueen.

The thought of Milos caused Eldridge to see that grinning chasm in his mind again. He ignored it and concentrated on his current predicament. If Milos was no longer the dreenking, where had he gone? There was no time to ask or answer that question.

"Shit. Shit, shit, *shit*. Any idea where the dreenqueen's holed up?"

"Nope," Hagan said. "But under-Dedrick is the new dreen stronghold. The Old Mine's practically abandoned now."

Eldridge fumed for a minute. "Boris, where the hell were the Narsyans during all this?"

"They're gone."

"What do you mean they're *gone?*"

"They lost a lot of people during the attack on Dedrick. Pell got booted from the throne, and then they all bolted for better odds."

"They don't *have* a thro—Pell got booted? They made him do the Circle Walk?"

"No, I don't think they drummed him out. But they've got a new leader. Yamuna?"

The name sparked something on the redhead's memory-horizon—something that lay in the vicinity of the grinning chasm he had sensed earlier—but he couldn't see it. Not yet.

"So where's Pell?"

Hagan took a breath. "El—"

"Wait, before you answer that—*where's Oksana?*"

—⚏—

QUILLIG AND THE GREXTET

"Can I see it? Please?"

Quillig and Lady R hunched over a rocky rise, both of them holding sophisticated binocular devices that bristled with add-on modules, antennae, and other sensing apparatus. Quillig's, naturally, was retrofitted with a female in-port that allowed him to plug his sight-cartridge directly into it.

Lady R had spoken, glancing away from her binoculars to needle Quillig. Kieron stood silently by, her bodygel glistening in the moonlight as she stood over her fellow grextans and kept watch on the dark desert, which swirled with eddies of sand and the occasional tumbleweed. Quillig's big rig sat parked behind them. Both Kieron's and Lady R's transpos were secured to the back of the rig. Because she didn't have to worry about the elements, Kieron drove a minimalist powerbike that looked like an impressionist stick-drawing of a bicycle but had the hydrocell-powered ability to hit 250-mph land speed. Lady R's transport was a personal hover-litter; it looked like a metallic, electronic throne encased in a dome.

Quillig ignored her question, which had been the tenth time Lady R had asked to see the tiny castle since they left the sectan confine.

"Seriously," Lady R said, her eyes hidden behind her binoculars. "Give us a look. It won't kill ya."

"Do you two have *any idea* how we're going to track our quarry?" Quillig asked.

"The usual," Lady R said. "Heat-trails. Biosig waves in the electromag."

Kieron looked over at Lady R, then echoed, "Indeed. Biowig saves in the electrozag."

Quillig stared at Kieron. Lady R pounced: "Electro-*zag?* You ever tracked quarry before?!" She cackled. "It's *biosig* waves in the *electromag!*"

Kieron's head drooped, prompting Quillig to play peacemaker. "Lady R, shut the fuck up." She did. He continued, "You can just say 'biosignature' and 'electromagnetic spectrum.' But that's not the point. The usual means of tracking aren't even necessary in this case."

"Why?" Kieron asked.

"Because they escaped from the Chain," Quillig said. "Now, the bad news is that the people running the Chain were so confident that this would never happen that they didn't implant the prisoners with tracking chips. The good news is that anyone who's had a mortarchain up his ass is *marked.* Look."

Quillig removed the sight-cartridge converter from his binoculars and handed them to Lady R. She peered through them. The view showed two hot-pulsing threads of cherry red—one for the redhead, one for his shithead sidekick.

"Fucking *boss,*" Lady R said. "I can see the two little dingleberries a coupla clicks ahead. What're those red trails?" she asked, handing the binoculars to Kieron.

Quillig remained silent. Kieron spoke up.

"Microwaves," said the jellywoman.

"Microwaves is right," Quillig said. "They're leaving a nice, bright trail."

"How long will it last?" Lady R asked.

"Not much longer, but it's a start," Quillig said. Kieron's head perked up.

"I may have a means to improve the trail's longevity," she said, turning one of her hands palm-up and flicking open a small chamber set into her forearm. With an audible *whirr*, a black tube, roughly the size of a pencil, rose from the jellywoman's forearm. She leveled the device in the direction of their quarry.

"What's that do?" Lady R asked.

"Nearly nothing," Kieron said. "But almost everything." She cocked her wrist and—

White.

The world was white. Instant and sudden was its advent, this world of white, white, white, white. Somewhere in the distance, Kieron heard screaming.

Lady R: *"Ohmygod my eyes my eyes my EYESSSSS!"*

Quillig: *"Turn that fucking thing OFF!"*

Kieron uncocked her wrist and returned the world to its former, far-less-completely-white state. The desert landscape faded back into view, with it, the sight of Quillig and Lady R both pressing their hands against their eyes (or in Quillig's case, across his visor). Slowly, they lowered their hands. Quillig's breaths came slow and steady, his chest rising and falling in tune with what he was muttering:

"One . . . two . . . three . . . four . . . must . . . not . . . kill—*what in the everloving fuck was that?!*"

ELDRIDGE AND BORIS HAGAN

"WAIT, BEFORE YOU ANSWER that—*where's Oksana?*"

Hagan hesitated a full ten seconds before he answered.

"She went dreen."

One of the skiff's wings clipped an outcropping of rock and sent the vehicle fishtailing off to the southeast. Eldridge righted their course.

"How?" he asked.

"She was trying to help. After the psychoskags left—"

"They left too?"

"Yeah. With Feruccio. Anyway, after they left, we didn't have any way to fight back against the dreens. It was Doc Enki's serum—Feruccio's serum. She got hooked."

"And? What happened? Is she down in under-Dedrick?"

"Worse. Once she went dreen, she rounded up a contingent of dreens and headed north for Towertown—*whooaaaa!*" Hagan wheeled, his feet thrown from under him by a sudden change in direction; Eldridge had spun the skiff northward, maxing out the accelerator at the same time.

"El! El! Stop, stop! We can't go to Towertown yet! We have to go to Penticton!"

"But Oksana's in Towertown."

"El, I know. But *Pell's* in Penticton."

"He is? How'd that happen?!"

"Turn this thing around, and I'll explain!"

"Forget it! We're headed to Tower—"

A white flash filled the horizon behind them in a blinding instant. Eldridge's and Boris's forearms slammed across their eyes—a reflexive instinct every resident of the post-Deadblast world had honed since childhood. It meant one thing:

The sun was rising.

And that meant the desert was about to instantly transform from a freezer to a pressure cooker.

"Shit, Boris! It's morning! How'd it come so soon?"

"Wait," Boris said. "El, sunup's not for another half hour, at least. Look."

The blinding flash was fading. More important, the *temperature* was holding steady around fifty below, meaning that morning had indeed not broken. Boris pointed at the horizon, where something was taking shape.

"This is a shot in the dark, El, but does that look like what I think it looks like?"

Eldridge squinted into the distance. Three silhouettes emerged from the flash like a trio of dark figures rising from a pool of milk. The redhead's squint turned into a wide-eyed gape.

"Shit. It's Quillig. And he's rounded up a grextet. Looks like they're a couple hours behind us. We gotta move. Penticton it is."

QUILLIG AND THE GREXTET

KIERON STOOD, SHOCKED.

"I . . . I wasn't expecting that to be so bright. Where I come from—"

But Quillig was already raging: "Wasn't *expecting?!* You just blasted a fucking *klieg light* at those shitbirds! Might as well've sent a moto-express to tell 'em we're coming!"

"I . . . I beg your forgiveness, fellow bounty-merc—"

Lady R shoved her full in the chest. "You fucking *cunt!* I need this jenta!"

"I'm so sorry, I—"

"Shut it, jellywoman," Quillig snapped. "In the fucked-up hypothetical world where that blinding light *wasn't* a colossal fuck-up on your part, what was it *supposed* to be?"

Kieron held up a pair of pleading palms. "Why, a spectramp, of course."

Quillig looked at the ground. "And what, if I may ask, is a fucking spectramp?"

"You don't know?" Kieron's voice had jumped a full octave. "Oh. Of course you don't. You don't have them—"

"Just tell us *what. It. Is.*"

"Spectramp is a portmanteau for *spectral amplifier.* You said our quarry's trails would fade soon. The spectramp simply enhances their microwave trails so they would sustain longer."

The plaid-faced bounty-merc reattached the converter to his binoculars and plugged his sight-cartridge back into it. His view showed nothing but a pure black field. Quillig heaved a frustrated sigh.

"I got nothing."

"Nothing?" Kieron whispered.

"Zippidee-doo-da. Ragnarok, can you confirm?"

The armored bounty-merc was already nodding as she peered through her binoculars. "Their microwave signatures are gone. Wiped clean."

"That doesn't make sense," Kieron said, pacing. "When I was a young scout, our amplifiers always *enhanced*—"

"*When I was a young scouty-poo,*" Lady R sang. "Jellywoman was a scouty-poo, Quillie! You hear that?"

"Ladies, be silent for thinking time," he said, wondering, *Where could the redhead be going?*

In his mind, Quillig sprinted down a hallway. It was an imaginary conceit he had developed as a child. When faced with a problem, his mind generated a random hallway filled with possible solutions. Some of these were nightmare hallways—snaking (and snake-ridden) passages that slashed through maggoty old mineways that coiled into the earth and offered nothing but dark doorways to doom. Other hallways offered more hope in the form of bright wallpaper lined with bouncy woodland creatures; somehow those creeped out Quillig more than the nightmare hallways. In the case of his current pursuit of the redhead and his crotchety old friend, Quillig's brain generated a short hallway that dead-ended mere yards ahead of one of his internal avatars:

A man with dark brown skin, blond hair, and green eyes.

His true self.

Quillig tried not to think of how he looked before his dark days as a dreen, but sometimes his brain forced him to, and on that particular day, his old self looked at a few doorways before he opened one. Inside was the obvious answer:

"Penticton," Quillig said. "That's where I snatched his shithead friend. Hagan."

"Penticton?" Lady R asked. "What's in Penticton?"

"The old bastard was trying to win someone's freedom. Someone... one of the redhead's old friends. A Narsyan. That must be where they're headed. It's close by, too. Now listen *up*. This quarry we're tracking is different than your usual bounty. Rare is the debtor who gets to die.

To die means escaping their debt. This one's no different. We take him alive, but that's the part where fate's gonna laugh at us. *Because I've already killed him. Twice.* This little macta's got more respawns than a neckbeard, but more important: He's got *friends*." Quillig had intended to sneer the word "friends," but a note of envy crept into his faltering tone. He continued: "All over the fucking place. And they're powerful. Eldridge couldn't get himself jerked off without someone pointing the way to his dick, but know this: *He will always have help.* He'll get help from strange quarters and at the very last motherfucking moment you expect it. 'Oh, I'm about to shoot him in the head. *That'll* kill him.' But it won't. 'Oh, I'm about to *throw him out a fucking window.* That'll *definitely* kill him.' But it won't. Because he'll always have help. And it'll always come. Be ready. Saddle up, bounty-mercs." Quillig prodded Kieron. "You too, dumbass."

Lady Ragnarok muttered, "Pathetic excuse for a bounty-merc."

Kieron said something in response. The wind carried it away.

"What was that, little B-M?"

Kieron raised her voice: "I wasn't *born* a bounty-merc."

ELDRIDGE AND BORIS HAGAN

The remnant of Penticton was easy to miss. A dreg driving at a normal speed would blow right by it, unaware that they were passing one of the largest remnants in the eastern desert. A single standpipe about thirty feet in diameter marked the entrance to Penticton. It rose out of the earth in the middle of an anonymous, endless stretch of desert. The elements had scoured away the standpipe's original color and smoothed away any of the text that it originally bore until all that remained was a burnished cylinder that gleamed in the deathly sunlight that bathed the desert. A road ramp led up to the front of the standpipe, and when Eldridge and Boris Hagan arrived in their school bus, a full-on traffic jam was backed up for a mile leading up to the standpipe.

Eldridge and Hagan had found a small outpost between the interchange and Penticton where they traded two barrels of gasoline for special glass that replaced all of the windows on the bus. The opacity of the glass would change depending on the outside temp. The hotter the temp, the darker the glass. The two men sat inside, enjoying the bus's air-conditioning and marveling at the eclectic jumble of vehicles that streamed into Penticton—behemoth-y four-wheeled internal combustors that chugged along and belched black smoke; lithe three-wheelers that bore a single, insulated passenger above a rear-mounted cockpit; scores of motorbikes that drew Eldridge's lustful gaze; hundreds of pre-Deadblast antiques retrofitted with hydrocells; shit-shakers of every variety.

One thing united them: almost every vehicle that streamed into Penticton that day had a companion. All of them hauled some kind of *secondary* vehicle whose make and purpose Eldridge didn't immediately recognize. None of these secondary vehicles had wheels. Instead, they all bore some kind of propulsion system on their rear ends in the form of giant fans, arrays of propeller-motors, or bulky rockets that dangled from support struts mounted to the vehicle's chassis. Hagan must have noticed the redhead's puzzled expression, because he bumped his elbow.

"Those are boats."

"Oh. Is Penticton underwater?"

"Nope. But part of it is under *mud*. That's what everyone is here for. The Mud Races."

"Got it. So how'd Pell get waylaid *here?*"

"Long story. Pell, Stew, and I all struck out to save you and Oksana, but . . ."

"What?"

"Well, our plan didn't exactly *go* to plan."

Eldridge chuckled.

"What's so funny?" Hagan asked.

"Nothing." He weighed his words. "Well, it's just . . . Pell . . . came *with* you guys?"

"That he did."

Eldridge shook his head, smiling. "Wow. That's pretty cool. So Oksie's in Towertown with a bunch of dreens?"

"Yeah, her and Stewart."

"Shit."

Stewart Kaleb. Son of Crius Kaleb and best friend to both Eldridge and Boris Hagan. Like Quillig the bounty-merc, Stewart had once been a dreen, but Eldridge had used the blood of a Narsyan chieftain to bring him back more or less intact. The redhead winced when he heard that Stewart was in trouble, too—*again*.

"Did he go dreen again?"

"No, he went fire warden."

"The hell's a *fire warden?*"

"Heat-freaks that live in Towertown. They look like they've got lava for blood, and they live for extreme temps. They can travel safely outside, day or night. They're the caretakers for this place called the Fallen Tower. Ever hear of a 'skyscraper'?"

"Yeah. Old-timey pre-Deadblast building. Really tall. Saw some pics of 'em in the Old Mine."

"Right. Well, this one fell over and landed along a river of lava. And that's where Towertown remnant came from—an Odd called the Creep moved in and started making odds on how far you could get into the tower. It turned into the local religion. The fire wardens guard the tower and monitor everything that happens inside. Well, everything except that central chamber where Oksana's hiding. Oksana and Stewart."

"Wait, what? Why is Stew hiding in there? *How* is Stewart hiding in there?"

"Stew volunteered to make a deep run into the tower, but he never came back. When he didn't come back, we couldn't pay off the Creep."

"You needed to pay off the Creep?"

"Yeah. No one gets into the Fallen Tower without making odds with the Creep. We made odds that Stewart could make it to the central chamber. They said he didn't. I think they were lying—"

"An Odd, lying? That's crazy talk. You feeling all right, Bor?"

"Har har."

"So *any*way, that's how Pell wound up waylaid here in Penticton. We needed jenta to pay off the Creep, so we came down here to win some. I know the Odd here, so I liked my chances."

"You *know* Lilya Hanna? How?"

"Can you ask me some other time when we're not running for our lives?"

"We're stuck in a line of cars and boats inching our way into a subterranean remnant, slowly suffocating on carbon monoxide in a tunnel that's tighter'n Pell Yannick's *everything*. If Quillig and his crew stage an assault right now, it'd be way out of character. Trust me. We go back a-ways."

"That's for damn certain. Seems like we're sittin' swans to me."

"Nah," Eldridge said, checking their six. "Well, maybe. But if I'm remembering right, I don't think ol' plaid-face knows this remnant too well. If he's gonna try and bag us here, he'll hang back, gather some intel. Quillig's more of the 'wait for the perfect shot' kinda bounty-merc."

"So you're not worried? At all?"

"Didn't say that," Eldridge said. "But I'll worry when Quillig throws down, not before then. Trust me, we've got a few minutes for you to dish on how you know the master of all sportsbook in the eastern desert."

Hagan fidgeted and waved away the question. "It's not important. What matters is that as soon as we got into a room with her to make odds, she snatched Pell and threw me out."

"I don't get it—she grabbed Pell but let you go? Why?"

"The only thing I can think of is . . . well, maybe she used to be a Narsyan."

The redhead rolled his eyes. "Well, who the hell *wasn't*? What did she do with him?"

"Nothing good. You'll see. I tried to win him back with some odds, but . . . well, it didn't work out."

"What kind of odds did you make?"

Now it was Hagan's turn to sulk.

"I don't want to talk about it."

THE PINKEYES,
PELL,
&
PENTICTON REMNANT

QUILLIG AND THE GREXTET

THE REDHEAD WAS RIGHT. Quillig was indeed the "wait for the perfect shot" kind of bounty-merc. Trailing the two targets by a few clicks—and a couple hours—the plaid-faced man slowed their forward progress to allow for the worldwide nuclear detonation that was the sunrise. In a giddy instant, the world flipped from a frigid midnight to a kiln-like two hundred, the sun a single shriek of white fire overhead. In response, everyone polarized their oculars—Quillig lowered his visor's opacity by 99.99 percent, while Lady R donned a pair of wraparound shades, the word "SLUT" glittering along the side in genuine pre-Deadblast rhinestones.

Meanwhile, Kieron was still fucking around with her oculars, moaning. "Laurentius be damned, this *light!*"

Quillig shook his head, injecting himself with a vial of super-coolant. "You okay there, jellywoman?"

"Yes, yes, yes, my liege," she muttered, pressing her plastic-coated fingertips to the side of her head. "I'm just not used to these days."

Lady R frowned at Quillig, who shrugged. Kieron grunted.

"One moment," she said. Her brow creased, a shadow shifting slightly within her coating. Suddenly, her fingertips lanced into her plastic, prompting as faint *yip* from Lady R.

"The shit's going on in there, jellylady?"

"*Kieron*, if you please," she wheezed as her fingertips pressed against the sides of her head—her real, organic head—and slowly turned forward, like she was rotating a cylinder set into her skull.

Which she was.

Click. The jellywoman's oculars turned black, and she sighed in relief. "Thank the Citadel. I still can't abide how bright—"

"Show's over," Quillig cut her off. "Jellywoman, can those doodads mounted over your eyes see our quarry up ahead?"

Kieron jogged forward, her every movement attended by a plastic *squeak* and dropped to a knee. Placing her first two fingers to her temple, she peered ahead and the Penticton standpipe.

"I see them," she said." They've vanished into the main entrance."

"C'mon, Quillie," Lady Ragnarok said. "They're sitting fucks. Let's pinch 'em now."

For a hot moment, Quillig considered it. *There'd be a body count, but that's never stopped me before. And I could be done with this. But the man across the oceans said he wanted the dipshit alive, and it'd be just like the redhead to croak the one time I gotta keep him breathing.*

"No," the plaid-faced man finally said. "There's a back door. It'll take a couple hours to reach. Let's go."

—⋙—

ELDRIDGE AND BORIS HAGAN

While Quillig and his grextet were making their way to the back door, Penticton, remnant of many rooms, welcomed Eldridge and Boris Hagan by way of a giant tunnel that started at the standpipe and sank into the earth. Boris Hagan had heard about how Penticton's reigning Odd, Lilya Hanna, had used her wealth to dominate the trade of metals across the eastern remnants, but he had no idea of the scope of it until his first, ill-fated trip to the remnant. As he steered the hover-skiff deeper down the forty-five-degree access ramp that led into Penticton proper, the redhead wouldn't stop asking him about that first trip.

"Okay, so you came here to win jenta to pay off the Creep. Hanna grabbed Pell. You tried to win *him* back, but you lost. So what happened after that?"

"El, believe me—it'll be better if you just see it for yourself."

Hagan tapped the brakes to avoid rear-ending a pontoon boat being hauled in front of him. Meanwhile, a trio of motorbikes coasted down the ramp immediately behind them. Eldridge glanced aft. The cylindrical tunnel gave barely eight feet of clearance overhead. Light slanted down from above and glinted off the hundreds of details laid into the walls—reliefs of men and women fighting against unusual, serpentine monsters; runes and other languages unfamiliar to Hagan (despite all his years researching the Arpa); various ancient signage for all kinds of forgotten establishments—KINK'S, SLEEMY'S, TUCK IT & FUCK IT.

"Choch-kees," Hagan enunciated.

"Is that what those are?" Eldridge asked, indicating the signs, which included old metal plates that they used to put on cars. "Is there one from Missouri?"

"Probably—whoops." The ramp flattened out suddenly, and Hagan found himself hovering along a new path he remembered from his first trip. The cylindrical tunnel widened by a few feet as the path curved around another standpipe that rose out of the steel floor. A few windows looked out and gave view to interiors lit with oil lamps and electric bars of fluorescence. One dreg sat reading a book, while another simply watched the caravan drive past.

Then, a deluge of lights, smells, and sounds.

The tunnel rounded another corner and circle-wiped in an outward explosion that yanked ten levels of open atrium into view. Deep within the earth sat Penticton and its hundreds of interconnected levels, but the remnant centered on its primary atrium, an open cylinder that spanned 1,200 meters in diameter. Wrought-iron balconies encircled the outer edge of the cylinder, all of them churning with thousands of dregs that ran to and fro. Some of the lower floors included circular mezzanines that extended out into the atrium. Each mezz was built from a different-color glass—level four was yellow, level three was blue, level two was red. Varying staircases connected mezz to mezz to mezz. From above, those mezzanines would resemble old-timey science diagrams, an oddity that gave the primary atrium its nickname, the Venn Room.

The uppermost mezz (purple glass) stood apart from the others and floated parallel to the fifth floor, its weight suspended by micromags that dotted its circumference. This mezz held aloft the home office of the remnant's resident Odd, Lilya Hanna.

"There she is," Hagan said, pointing up.

In the Venn Room, the citizens of Penticton could always look up to the fifth-floor mezz and see the glowing pink skull and eyes of their resident and ruling Odd as she paced back and forth, never sleeping and always watching her datareads.

Ah, the datareads—the pulsebeat of Penticton.

Dozens of the flatpanel datareads hovered over Hanna's head, all of them borne aloft by micromags and all of them rotating in endless concentric circles around each other as they spilled forth info and results on the thousands of games happening in the lower atria. That was Hanna's specialty: games. She had turned Penticton into one of the eastern continent's primary destinations for games, professional and otherwise.

As Hagan and Eldridge followed the main traffic circle that coiled around the atrium, dregs of all shapes, sizes, and psychoses scurried around the mezzes, each of which held restaurants, smoke bars, inns, and homes. Thousands more dregs packed into the balconies overhead, disappearing into and reappearing out of the tens of thousands of doors and passages that led into the deeper reaches of the remnant. Some of them ran up, some down, and all of them bore styli in hand as they looked up at the datareads that rotated around Hanna.

"What is she wearing?" Eldridge asked.

Hagan knew that Hanna wore a succession of brightly colored, ornate gowns that originated from some unimaginably ancient pre-Deadblast era. The gowns themselves hugged her surgically altered waistline, which had been shrunk to the width of a baby's fist. Meanwhile, a zeppelin-like wireframe (covered with fabric) hung off her waist and amplified the size of her backside. The whole apparatus bounced as she paced around her mezz, her pink eyes glowing high above, her hands buried in a muff.

"I think it's called a . . . tussle?" Hagan said, feigning ignorance when he knew exactly what it was called—and what was hidden underneath.

Meanwhile, Eldridge had noticed the mud. All around them, conduits and pipelines from above dumped water onto the street, which was lined with hundreds of small grooves, all of them filled with fast-running flows of brown muck.

"What's with all the mud?" Eldridge asked. "Is it for the races?"

"Nope. It goes deeper than the races."

Up ahead, a pair of dregs directed them away from the traffic circle and toward another cylindrical tunnel that dove into the earth. A dreg wearing a handlebar mustache and a lot of spikes waved them to a halt.

"Here for the races?"

"No, just visiting," Hagan said. "We're here to see Lord Macta."

Eldridge started. "What?"

The corners of the dreg's mustache rose as his lips curled away from green teeth. A smile. He said, "Then you need to take *that* passage."

He pointed at another cylindrical tunnel that sprouted off from the Venn Room and led deeper into the earth. A blank green plaque was bolted into the wall over it. Hagan steered them off the main path and around the traffic circle toward the green tunnel, and along the way, they passed by half a dozen other tunnels—some of which led down, while others led up.

But that wasn't all. Some of the tunnels were *moving*.

Huge gears flanked the entrances to some of the tunnels and cranked to life as they passed. Some of the tunnels slanted downward, while other lifted upward.

"We're not going to get lost, are we?"

"Relax," Hagan said. "The one we're taking doesn't move."

Hagan steered into the tunnel, a circle of black stones that gleamed with the perpetual sweat of moisture that beaded and condensed on every surface in Penticton. When the secondary path met the tunnel, the grooves curved away from the center of the road and spilled into gutters that ran down the sides. Mud flowed freely into both gutters. Hagan slowed the skiff's progression downward.

The green tunnel was lined with windows that looked in on habitats, bars and other rooms. In the next room, a dozen dregs were packed into the balcony, cheering on a video feed of a balimpsest game. One of the players onscreen climbed the hundred-foot cage surrounding the court, leaped off the cyclone fencing, and threw the orange ball through the hoop. As the dregs exploded with whoops and cheers, Hagan felt an analogous roar from somewhere far below.

"Feel that?" Hagan said. "That's where we're headed."

Eldridge nodded as the bus dipped and started another slow descent down a tunnel that, like every tunnel in Penticton, was flanked by a pair of mud gutters that collected all the stray dirt, shit, and piss from around the remnant and delivered it down, down, down. They rode past ten more of these levels—some large, some small—before the green tunnel finally deposited them on the remnant's lowermost level: the Green Room.

Although "room" wasn't an accurate description for it. The lowermost chamber in Penticton Remnant was only half the height as its uppermost atrium, but it was twice as wide, covering nearly a square mile of floor space. By that depth, the steel walls had given way entirely to black stone, which composed all of the walls and floors. Similar to the uppermost atrium, mezzes stuck out from the walls, but all of these were wrought-iron platforms, buttressed with iron struts.

Dozens of tunnels from above emptied out onto one of its twenty primary streets, all of which were interconnected by a network of alleyways and mud canals. The mud gutters from above all fed into the canals, which teemed with hordes of mudworthy seacraft, including single-person boats, pontoons, rocket-gondolas, and pedal-powered rafts that kicked up sheet after sheet of mud in their wake. Foot messengers wearing broad-soled shoes sprinted along the canals, swift enough to skip along the churning mud's surface tension.

But none of these features earned the Green Room its nickname. No, that sprang from its central purpose, or *purposes,* as they all sprang out of a network of round floor holes—vines, stalks and shoots of plant life. Hagan recognized some of the vegetation, though the names eluded him.

Penticton's plant life made it one of the jewels of the eastern continent. Aboveground farms established by foolhardy Odds and dregs always fell prey to the elements. Only those with the vision and the know-how to grow food underground actually made it happen with consistency. The days of open cannibalism were hidden in the mists of the earliest days after Deadblast, but if a remnant like Penticton were to fall (or be overtaken by dreens), then those days might come screaming back.

Other vehicles rumbled around on the streets, cutting between the smattering of buildings. Nothing stood higher than a few stories tall, because Hanna had declared the Green Room as the site of the remnant's balimpsest cage.

A hundred feet tall, the cage dominated the center of the atrium and provided a home for an energetic colony of ivy and kudzu that crept up the sides. Scores of ivy-covered bleachers surrounded it, all of them equipped with micromags that carried its spectators higher or lower depending on the action in the game. Like all post-Deadblast sports, balimpsest echoed an earlier, less dangerous game, although no one could remember what it was called. Roughly, the game challenged two teams of seven to climb up and down a hundred feet of cyclone fencing and throw a ball through a hoop. Fourteen players scrambled around the fencing as Hagan and Eldridge drove past to the tune of thousands of screaming dregs, who all cheered in concert with tens of thousands of other dregs all throughout the remnant's hundreds of subterranean chambers. Their voices reverberated through the walls and floors.

Boris Hagan steered the skiff around the cage and rode over a wooden bridge that arched over one of the canals. A messenger vaulted off the hood of the bus and leapt into the canal, his feet an elliptical blur of speed that carried him down the mudway. A few other vehicles sat parked around a twenty-foot iron gate that stood in the middle of a patch of stone surrounded by canals. The gate itself led nowhere; it merely rose out of the stone ground without an accompanying fence and framed an attraction housed in Penticton's lowermost chamber.

"We're here," Hagan said.

He parked the bus, and they got out. The redhead shook out his legs as they walked through the gate. A few dozen other dregs jabbed their fingers at the sight before them—a mountain of naked flesh. The flesh mountain oozed around a stone platform that bore a wooden sign that read LORD MACTA, KING OF ALL SORROW. Somewhere amidst the linking piles of corpulence, a pair of eyes and a mouth floated on a sea of fat. Moans floated up from the spittle-encrusted mouth, the sound only interrupted when a spats-wearing barker-dreg slopped a ladleful of lard into the maw. Patches of livid, chafed red skin marked where the mountain's folds rubbed together, every swipe of flesh against flesh scraping away yellow flakes of cheesy smegma that had dried there. The mountain bucked upward a moment and gave the crowd a view of the hole that had been cut in the platform underneath it and through which the sad creature's waste dribbled.

Hagan looked over at the redhead, whose expression held no surprises for the old man. Eldridge's chest collapsed inward as his mouth hung open and expelled an ongoing sigh that vanished into the jeers and taunts from the crowd of dregs.

"What. The fuck. *Is*. This, Hages?"

"Keep looking," Hagan said.

The redhead kept looking. Hagan tracked his eyes and watched them until they lighted on the flesh mountain's right leg, which looked less like a leg and more like a swollen scrotum capped with a twitching blue foot, but when the redhead looked at the creature's leg, he saw the final thing Hagan had seen before Quillig blasted him with mortar-chains and dragged him out of Penticton.

A purple scar.

The scar coiled around the flesh-mountain's leg and flashed across its quivering belly and chest like a lightning bolt. The redhead placed his hands on his hips and bent over. He took a deep breath, then stood up straight.

"I'm so sorry. *Pell.*"

Pelagius "Pell" Yannick, unspoken high chieftain of the Order of the Narsyan, swallowed another mawful of lard and groaned, a Narsyan no more.

—⚇—

ELDRIDGE SLAMMED BORIS AGAINST the side of the hover-skiff, his sunburnt face somehow redder than normal.

"What the fuck *happened,* Boris? I get snatched, and all my friends wind up at the mercy of the Odds? What the hell kind of rescue operation *is* this?"

"El, go calm, go calm."

The redhead backed up a step and squinted, trying to ignore the moans coming from Lord Macta. Finally, he looked over at Pell again. "How is that even possible? Who could gain that much weight in three months?"

"It's been less than that, and he didn't *gain* weight. Hanna *did* something to him."

Eldridge shook his head. "This is bullshit. Odds aren't supposed to . . . Only when you default . . . *Where's my fucking gun?*"

Hagan blocked the door to the bus and the weaponry that waited inside, but Eldridge buried his shoulder under his arm and bull-shoved him to the ground. The white-haired man fell on his hip and cried out. The redhead paused with one foot inside the bus and looked down, his face elongating with sympathy.

"Bor, I'm sorry, I didn't mean—"

Hagan rammed his boot into the redhead's groin, scoring a double-nut shot. Eldridge spun, backed into the bus, then slid to the ground, cupping his wounded plumbing. Hagan sidled up next to him.

"That play won't work, El."

Grimacing, Eldridge said, "We'll load him on the bus and cart him back up to Burbage—oh."

"Right. Burbage is empty. And besides: We're not getting him out of here."

"Why *not?* I took out Jeb Goldmist. I can get a fat fuck out of a measly remnant."

"Do you even know what 'measly' means?"

"What's that gotta do with it?"

"Never mind. Here—go ahead and try. Get your cute little gun and try to spring him."

"You're not going to stop me?"

Hagan shook his head. Eldridge took a few tentative breaths, then stood, his legs shaking. He climbed into the bus and grabbed the thirty-aught shotgun. He loaded it, then packed some extra shells into his pockets. Stepping off the bus, he cocked an eyebrow at Hagan. "You just going to sit there?"

Hagan waved. "Good luck."

Eldridge shook his head, then turned his attention to Lord Macta and his jeering audience. The balimpsest game continued to clatter and roar behind him. One of the teams must've been mounting a comeback, because the crowd's roar grew louder and louder as the cyclone fencing shook—all while Eldridge marched toward the fat blob that had once been Pell Yannick. As he made his way through the crowd of onlookers, he raised his shotgun and trained it on the spats-wearing barker who was feeding Pell from a seemingly bottomless bucket of lard.

"Buddy, I need you to stand back, so I can—"

The barker's ladle paused. He said, "Pleeeeeease?"

Eldridge faltered. "What?"

A small voice from below. "Mister? Pleeeeeease?"

Pink. Pink surrounded him. The redhead looked down and directly into the glowing pink eyes of a young dreg, barely more than an infant, who wore mitten-toed pajamas emblazoned with the logo of one of Penticton's balimpsest teams. She tapped the logo, a prickly, italicized rendering of a virus that slashed through a splatter-of-plasma drop shadow under a bold font that shouted, THE CONTAGION. Her glowing pink eyes sparkled. She asked, "Do you like Contagion-ball?"

More pink. More eyes. As the volume of the balimpsest game doubled to a red-noise racket, the crowd gathered around him and peppered him with questions.

"What's the third letter of your favorite color?"

"How many brain cells do you have?"

"What's the biggest prime number you know?"

"Whoomp!" the cage-crowd intoned behind him as a player executed a high-flying, acrobatic slam-dunk—quite a feat, as a balimpsest ball weighed thirty pounds. The crowd of onlookers ignored Pell and focused every one of their pink eyes on Eldridge. But had they been pink a moment before? Hands clapped him on the back, all camaraderie, but somehow his shotgun had disappeared. Eldridge slapped his thighs like he had lost his keys, then noticed the little Contagion fan on the ground, playing with his gun.

"Honey, don't," Eldridge said. "Dangerous!"

A bemonocled dreg wearing a bloodred vest over a white-hairy chest wrapped an arm around him and said, "I like you, old bean. I think I want to hug you and kill you."

"What?" Eldridge said as two more toddler-dregs locked their arms and legs around his calves. Two more latched onto his thighs, all of them squealing, "I love Uncle Dingleberry!" Their weight pulled Eldridge to his knees. Someone placed another toddler on his shoulders, and the little shit squeezed his legs around his neck. He heard the gruff voice of the bemonocled dreg above him.

"Everyone hug Uncle D!"

Eldridge looked up just in time to see the young Contagion fan hook her toe around his shotgun's trigger. The report stung his ears. The blast ripped a strip of scalp off her head. She giggled, her eyes still glowing pink. The image of Constable Tola's face floated up before the redhead. He sensed the incursion of the yawning void in his memory, but he shook it away for now. Eldridge looked up and saw the spats-wearing barker grinning down at him with the same pink glow in his eyes.

That's when he saw the tendril.

A smoky tendril of crackling pink energy drifted down from above. The tendril delta-split into hundreds of filaments that lanced into the ground all around him. Two more pinkeyes took hold of his hands and shook them like a pair of whips, his shoulders cracking with the force of their greetings.

"Hey hello hi. Hey hello hi," they repeated in unison.

Eldridge screamed. *"All right, Hages! You made your point!"*

Nothing. No response. His limbs covered with hanging toddler-dregs, Eldridge dragged himself in a small circle until he faced Hagan, who was reclining against the hover-skiff.

The old man smirked. "You're still thinking about it!"

"About what?"

"About saving Pell. Soon's they let you up, you're going to jump up and free him. She's got her pinkeyes on you. She can't read every mind in the remnant, but when she's got her pinkeyes on you, she can yours. Stop thinking about doing it, and they'll let go."

He was right. That was *exactly* what the redhead had in mind. And the instant he decided not to do it, the tendril retracted into the ceiling above, the dangling toddlers dropped from his limbs, and the crowd shifted its attention back to poor Pell.

The little Contagion fan started screaming, too.

The child's mother scooped her into her arms and sprinted away. She leapt over a canal and ran over to one of the tunnels that led upward. That's when Eldridge noticed the network of ropes and pulleys that ran along some of the tunnels. Child in arm, the mother propped her feet on either side of the mud gutter and grabbed onto a perpetually moving rope set into the wall. The rope carried her up into the tunnel. Eldridge stood and straightened his clothes. He walked back over to the hover-skiff and propped his hands on his hips. Hagan stood, too.

"Satisfied?" No answer. Eldridge stared at the ground. Hagan touched his shoulder. "El?"

His head snapped up. "I don't deserve this. Any of this. You should've just let me go. Let me stay on the Chain."

"If it's any consolation, we had more on our minds than just you. The dreenqueen's got Dedrick. And I think I left my oven on."

The redhead's jawline shifted with the grinding of his teeth; a familiar sign he was about to dig in his heels, Hagan knew. El opened his mouth, closed it again.

"What is it?" Hagan asked, already tired of the exchange.

"Nadia wouldn't have done this."

Hagan rolled his eyes. "Well, yeah—no *shit* she wouldn't have. She wouldn't have done most things, including piss on your face if your teeth were on fire, show any common decency whatsoever, or—oh, I dunno—*not do what she did to you.*"

"C'mon. It's not nice to stick a lance into someone's grave."

"It's not nice to *dance* on someone's grave," Hagan corrected. "And just because she's gone don't mean I gotta be nice to someone who never did right by you, not even once."

"That's not true," El said. "She saved my life."

Hagan scoffed. "You mean the night you *met?* There's another word, one folks had *before* Deadblast, for what she did to you."

"*Fuck* you."

Hagan leaned forward, palms up in pleading. "Are we really fighting about *Nadia* when we've got *all* our friends to save?"

"You never gave her a chance. I remember the night you met. You were shitty to her even then."

Hagan winced at the acute onset of memory. The night he met the redhead's wife/not-wife, he also *discovered* two things:

One: The Arpa.

Two: The reason why Nadia left Eldridge for good: *Zora.*

The night Boris met Nadia, he had long since turned his under-Dedrick apartment into a shrine to the world that was. He'd bring folks back there to show off his collection of pre-Deadblast books (dusty paperbacks and threadbare hardcovers), or he'd show them his wall of dustcovers (the shiny coverings they used to wrap around new books), or he'd show them his wall of sports posters (the 49ers, Arsenal, the All-Blacks).

No one gave a shit. Until Eldridge.

Like always, bright-eyed joy beamed from the redhead's face when he visited Hagan's apartment, and as he had on any of his countless previous visits, Eldridge spent half an hour in delighted silence as he examined every one of the old man's artifacts, asking questions, making comments and cracking jokes.

Nadia stood in the corner, silent.

She leaned against the wall, arms crossed. Every few minutes, Hagan looked over and invited her to join in the festivities, but she would only shake her head, her brown eyes simultaneously warm and cold, and smile a smile that was all teeth and no joy. (At least to Boris's eyes.)

"I'm fine right here," she said. "I'm just waiting for Billy-Bill to finish up."

Boris often forgot Eldridge even *had* a first name: William. Nadia was the only one who ever called him Bill (or Billy, for that matter).

The night Boris Hagan met Nadia was special for another reason: It was the first time Eldridge had seen Nadia in years. Soon after she gave birth to Zora, she had vanished, leaving the redhead to raise the future Dedrick constable by himself in Junktown. She had offered no explanation for her disappearance—an oversight that rankled Boris—and then she simply reappeared in Dedrick one day.

Her presence disabled all of the redhead's defenses. That night in Hagan's apartment, she eventually came out of the corner and padded across the room to the redhead, who was kneeling to get a closer look at Hagan's shelf of hardcovers. When he stood up, she wrapped her arms her around him.

Thinking back to that night, the old man had to concede: for reasons he couldn't fathom, Nadia made Eldridge happy. Eldridge was constantly jumping at strange noises and walking into doorjambs, but when Nadia snuck up behind him, he didn't so much as flinch. He simply accepted her embrace and held her hands against his stomach, his head a few inches lower than hers. (That woman was *tall*, Hagan reflected.) Her black hair rested on his shoulders, her complexion similar to Yasim's—several shades darker than the redhead's pale-stark skin.

Their embrace emboldened Hagan to show off the altar of his shrine: his computer. It sat on a glass desk and hummed along. A black wire fed into the back of the computer—a wire that Hagan had discovered earlier that day. Deep in the basement of his under-Dedrick apartment building, he had spotted the finger-thick black wire in the dirt. When he pulled it out, he found that it *ended* in the dirt. The wire was still buried, and it still led somewhere. Curiously enough, the wire was capped with a male out-port—a metallic ring encircling a single steel needle—that happened to fit a female in-port on the back of his computer. It had been a stupendous hassle to run the wire all the way up to his apartment without anyone noticing, but he did, and he had plugged it in a few minutes before Eldridge and Nadia arrived, but he hadn't tried to *use* it yet, whatever "using" it would entail.

For a long time after that first night online, Hagan wished he'd never found that black wire.

"You guys wanna see something?" Hagan asked.

"Sure," Eldridge said, then whispered to Nadia: "We can talk in a minute, okay?"

"Take your time, love," she said, her utterance of the word "love" phony to Boris's ears.

Hagan booted up his computer, which cycled through a few screens before it landed on a simple prompt:

>

Eldridge: "What's it do?"

"I don't know," Hagan said, then explained how he had discovered and plugged in the black wire that fed into the back of the device. "I'm curious to see if it leads anywhere."

"How would you find out?" Nadia asked.

Hagan shrugged, then touched his chin. "Well, let's try this . . ."

He typed HELLO and hit enter. The cursor jumped down a line, then spilled out new data:

COMMAND "HELLO" UNKNOWN

TYPE SEARCH: [ENTRY] AND PRESS ENTER

He glanced at a poster on his wall—OAKLAND RAIDERS—and, intuiting the input syntax, typed SEARCH: OAKLAND RAIDERS.

The computer churned for a moment, then returned:

OAKLAND RAIDERS. NFL HLKVN;LKNJ.>>>>-FOOTBALL TEAM THAT COMPETED IN THE NATIONAL FOOTB&&6^LEAGUE IN THE 20TH, 21ST AND 22ND CENTURIE.........404.

Eldridge leaned closer. "What the hell? Where is this coming from? The wire?"

"I guess so," Hagan said.

"Isn't this dangerous?" Nadia asked.

The old man looked at her. "How so?"

"What if one of the Odds finds out about this? They'll take it away, won't they?"

"Oh, no one would care. They never do..." He trailed off, mumbling. A book caught his eye: *The Complete Works of William Shakespeare*. He searched for the playwright's name and waited.

The computer returned two things. A single word—PLAYWRIGHT—and a pixilated black-and-white image of a longhaired man wearing a ruffled white collar.

Hagan grunted. "Hoping for more on that one." He thought, then said, "Wait a minute." The old man entered SEARCH: DEADBLAST.

Air whistled through Nadia's nose as she inhaled sharply. Eldridge shrugged out of her embrace and leaned in close to the computer. It churned. And churned. A few additional cursors appeared, then vanished. Finally, more than a minute later, it returned:

NULL.

The redhead straightened. "Damn. Worth a shot, I guess."

More whistling. The two men looked to the lady and saw that she was finally exhaling. Tendons settled back into her neck as a grimace faded from her face, leaving behind only a ghost of dread that darkened her brow. Eldridge took her hands.

"What's wrong?"

She shook her head, once. "Nothing. Well..."

"What is it?"

"Can you search for 'terrormonger'?"

Eldridge hung his head. Terrormongers shared some figurative DNA with dreens, except that their dead-eyed mania sprang from actual agency, unlike dreens, which chugged along on pure instinct. They mostly skulked around the marshes of the north, where the climate was one step more temperate than the deserts. Junktown lay on the boundary of the desert and the northern marshes. The redhead had taken their daughter, Zora, to Junktown to raise her, but he had parted ways with her about a year earlier.

After a terrormonger attack.

The attack had left Zora with blackened, charred eyelids. Eldridge never spoke much about the incident, and he had never told his daughter the truth about what happened, even going so far as to invent a new narrative. After all, the attack had blanked most of her memory, so Eldridge filled in the gaps with whatever suited him.

But Hagan didn't know that at the time. He just typed in the search entry. Moments later, he was bent over his bathroom sink, fighting back his gorge. For whatever reason, the Arpa returned the definition of napalm, along with an image of a young man in the final moments of his life; *final*, because his skin was bubbling off his body. A bright orange paste clung to his skin and danced with flames.

From the bathroom, Hagan heard Nadia whisper something unintelligible.

"No, no," Eldridge said in response. "That's not what happened."

Hagan emerged from the bathroom. Nadia stared at the wall, her arms limp by her sides. She swayed back and forth, repeating the same sentence.

"Is that what happened? Is that what happened? Is that what happened?"

The redhead kept repeating "no" over and over in response until she fell silent. Hagan remained still. Nadia looked at the redhead, who returned her eye contact, his gaze steady. She slowly shook her head.

"I can't believe you left her alone. In this . . . *world.*"

"Nadia—"

"Don't follow me."

She left. The redhead never saw her again.

Years later in the remnant of Penticton, Hagan looked his friend dead in the eyes. "I didn't like Nadia because she wasn't nice to you. Simple as that."

El tilted his head, cooling down. "I know she could be a pain in the ass, but she was really cool, too. We had some good times."

"I believe you."

"And she was right," Eldridge said, but as he said it, his eyes went foggy. "About what I did."

The redhead was doing that "thousand-yard stare" thing again, like he had back on the hover-skiff, when Boris had brought up Zora.

"What did you do?" Boris asked.

His eyes still foggy, Eldridge said, "I left her alone."

"Left *who* alone?"

Eldridge didn't answer. In fact, he was only marginally present in the remnant with Boris, whose concern was growing.

Hagan stared at him. "You all right, El?"

Eldridge gave his head a shake. "Yeah, yeah. Of course." He forced a chuckle, then glanced back at the crowd of people. He pointed at his forehead. "Man. Good thing I had the doc raze the scar off my head, huh?"

Boris's brow furrowed at the jump in topic. "What? Your scar? What's that got to do with Nadia?"

The redhead's breath caught in his throat. "Oh. Well, I guess I was thinking of Nadia, and then I was thinking about how every third asshole in my life was a Narsyan, *then* I remembered Hanna used to be a Narsyan—or might've been—and I thought how weird it'd be if she knew *I* used to be one, and . . ." his speaking paused, but his lips kept trying to form words he couldn't find or didn't know. Finally, he added: "I guess that was a pretty big jump, wasn't it?"

It was, but Boris sensed his friend needed compassion more than honesty in that moment. "Nah, I got it, old buddy. Now, what say we go request an audience with her Oddness?"

"You going to tell me how you got in hock to her?"

Clouds gathered over Hagan's head. "Later."

—⚏—

QUILLIG AND THE GREXTET

While Boris Hagan met with Lilya Hanna, Quillig and his grextet rode the rest of the way to Penticton. They bypassed the traffic jam leading into the standpipe and rode out into the blank expanse of desert.

As the standpipe shrank behind them, Kieron spoke up.

"Is there always so much traffic leading into Penticton?"

"It's for the Mud Races, dipshit!" Lady R yelled from her hoverthrone.

Not many knew it, but the giant standpipe was only one of several ways into the remnant of many rooms. Quillig himself knew of three other ways into Penticton, all of them located within a ten-mile radius of the main standpipe. Not even Quillig knew how large the remnant's footprint was. The rumortrysts held that its interconnected rooms linked on for miles and miles, each one smaller than the next, all of them protected by their remote location, as well a veritable mountain of dirt overhead.

Quillig, Lady R, and Kieron didn't have to range quite that far to find a door down into Penticton. Fortunately, the plaid-faced bounty-merc knew of a vertical shaft that led down into one of the remnant's more remote upper chambers. Most passing dregs would drive right by it, its location lost in the sunspots of light that covered the desert during the day, but Quillig remembered its exact location. Quillig parked his big rig in a seemingly random patch of desert and hopped off, taking his boltgun with him. Lady R and Kieron parked their vehicles nearby, securing them in place with various tech.

Quillig scanned the horizon and estimated they had another couple of hours before sunrise. The standpipe was an inch-high feature on the southwestern horizon, the traffic jam a glittering line that led away from it. Quillig walked around, his aperture trained on the ground.

"May we help?" Kieron asked.

"Shut up," Quillig said as his boot rapped on something metallic. He crouched and used both hands to shovel sand away from a round wheel attached to a round steel hatch set in the earth. The elements had burnished the steel to a shine and kept the finger-thick hinges free of rust. Quillig crouched, laid his boltgun next to the hatch, and rapped his gloved knuckles on it three times. Then four times. Then two times. Then once.

Then he grabbed his boltgun and crept back on his knees, training his weapon at the hatch.

"Back up, you two."

They did. Moments later, the muffled rattle of metal sounded from underground. The steel wheel jerked counterclockwise with a shriek, then slowly rotated until the hatch hissed open a single inch. Cold air gushed from the dark opening and washed over the three bounty-mercs.

Quillig fired a red bolt over the hatch.

"Don't you fucking move. I can end you before you slam it shut."

The hatch remained motionless. A voice growled: "You the plaid?"

"That's me. Conrade still down there?"

"Connie still here. How you know Connie?"

"We got history. You gonna let us in?"

"I gotta check. I gotta close this up. You okay with dat?"

The concrete crreature said I had thirty-six hours to deliver the redhead to Port Stafford. At least six have passed since then. Barely more than a day till I'm dead. The voice in the hatch spoke again:

"You hear me, mate? I gotta close this up."

"Move it. I'm in a fucking hurry."

Quillig nodded. The hatch sealed shut. Lady R kneeled next to him.

"You sure that was a good idea?"

He ignored her. Ten minutes later, the hatch opened again. The same voice growled from within.

"Connie say it all right."

A swollen creature rose from the earth as the hatch opened. Presumably this creature had started life as a man, but some combination of allergic ailments, failed meds, and early-dreen endocrine experimentation had caused the man's flesh to take on triple the amount of moisture it needed. Standing still, his physique might be mistaken for that of an overly muscled rager, but whenever he moved, his "muscles" swayed back and forth like bags of gelatin. His face peeked out from between his overstuffed brow and chin, while his attire consisted of a few score straps of red and black fabric that cut trenches around his body. The creature aimed an old-time revolver at Quillig.

It growled, "Connie say you come with me."

"Then we'll come with you. What about our ride?"

The creature leaned to the side like a statue tipping over. "I send some men. Come on. Connie's waiting."

The creature vanished into the hatch. Lady R touched Quillig's shoulder.

"Who the hell is this Connie?" she asked.

"The man with the map."

Quillig stood and secured both his boltgun and his mortarchain rifle to his waist-belt and suspenders. That done, all three bounty-mercs climbed down into the hatch, which they sealed shut behind them. They climbed down a metal ladder bolted to the side of a concrete tube that descended into darkness. A few flickering light bulbs dangled from the walls and lit the way with sporadic bursts of piss-light. The going was slow, given that the swollen creature's waterlogged joints weren't designed to handle ladders. Finally, the ladder terminated into another cylindrical passage that ran horizontally, only the walls of this passage were brick, not concrete. More light bulbs dangled from a wire that hung from the wall. The passage extended in both directions. The creature led them to the left and through an interlocking labyrinth of cylindrical tunnels, each one built from a different color brick—some red, some blue, some green. Quillig noticed that gutters lined the pathway and ran with a trickle of water and dirt. The mud always flowed in Penticton, even as high in its subterranean altitude as they were. Eventually, they reached a tunnel that slanted forty-five degrees downward and was lined with super-slick foot slides on either side of a channel of mud that ran down its center. They all propped their feet on the foot slides and rode down, although Kieron's ultra-tacky plastic coating forced her to waddle down, foot to foot. The tunnel emptied into a circular, brick-walled room. Two wooden doors led off from the room, while a window looked out onto another down-tunnel that itself was lined with windows. Quillig looked and could dimly see down through another few levels of Penticton before the view vanished in darkness.

Back to the room: A desk sat to the right, surrounded by a few leather easy chairs. Various framed images hung from the walls—one painting depicted a starry night, while other photographs tracked the progress of a single father and his daughter. The single father in the photographs had lost his face to a flesh-eating bacteria some years ago, and a few of the photos reflected that version of the father—the version who had a black hole where his face should have been. But some years later, the father had acquired a prosthetic face-piece that he affixed in that black hole. Not only was the face-piece a remarkable replica of his old visage, but it also plugged into his nerve endings and gave him control over his expressions. *Some* control. He had also replaced his eyes with glittering black oculars that sat in his old sockets.

That man, the father from the photographs, sat behind the desk, which was cluttered with discarded smartpaper, bowls of jewelry, jars full of styli, photos of various dregs, as well as a bottleflask of bourbon and an accompanying tin tumbler. The father wore a black vest over a white, sleeveless T-shirt. Tattoos coiled around his forearms—hundreds of triangular glyphs; characters from an ancient tongue. He held a stylus in one hand and a pad of smartpaper in the other. He scribbled notes and sipped bourbon.

Quillig stepped forward.

"Conrade."

The father, Conrade, didn't answer but continued scribbling. Silence rolled by, along with more of Quillig's precious time. Conrade glanced up, then scribbled some more. He finally nodded a dismissal at the swollen creature, who opened a door and left. Conrade reached an apparent stopping point and dropped the stylus. He twined his fingers and looked up.

"There's a matter of balance here, Quill," Conrade said. His lower lip, having been spared by the flesh-eating bacteria, moved normally, but his prosthetic face-piece always moved one step behind his organic parts. It looked like the center of his face was moving in slow motion compared to the rest. "See, I know the score, but you know *me*. Right? There's a debt. *My* debt to you. I know it, you know it. But now you come knocking on my back door. And the rumortrysts say the funniest things."

"Such as?"

"Well, such as you're tracking the Red Rook. Eldridge." He smirked. *"Again."*

Quillig heard a series of *pops*, like the seams of a burlap sack giving way.

"So what if I'm tracking him again?"

Conrade's lower lip smiled, followed by his upper. "Usually if someone's in your debt, you come barging in acting like a hard-on. Not now, though. Now you're all back-dooring it with these two *iacios*. Seems desperate. Kinda makes me feel like I don't need to pay that debt of mine. Nothing personal. It's just a matter of balaaa . . ."

Before he could finish saying "balance," Quillig was crossing the room. From a pocket, he produced the tiny castle—the totem from the man across the oceans—and set it on the desk without a sound.

Light flashed off the glass sphere that enclosed the castle. Conrade's face tilted down as his lips stopped smiling one by one. He sat back in his chair and took a sip of bourbon.

"Well, I'll be hornswoggled. He's a player in this?"

Quillig placed both hands on the desk and leaned over the castle.

"Yeah. He's a player in this. So you're *goddamn fucking right I'm desperate*."

ELDRIDGE AND BORIS HAGAN

"Great. More shenanigans," Eldridge said.

The redhead and Boris Hagan sat inside the hover-skiff on one of the many mid-range levels of Penticton. The level spanned about two hundred feet and held only two levels of floorspace. The second-floor balcony wound around half of the level's cylindrical circumference. Boris sat munching on a chunk of dehydrated something-or-other that resembled a petrified turd. In response to the redhead, he shook his head.

"It's not shenanigans. She's an Odd. There's no other way."

"Won't she just throw us back on the Chain? Don't you *owe* her?"

"She won't. Trust me."

Eldridge drained a canteen of water and glowered at the floor.

"What?"

"Nothing. I just hoped I wouldn't have to . . ." He trailed off.

"Associate with an Odd?"

Eldridge looked up and nodded.

"You wanna take on the pinkeyes all by yourself?"

Eldridge shook his head.

"Me neither."

Hagan jumped to his feet and called for one of the attendants. While they waited, Eldridge fidgeted with his fingers, his mouth hanging open. Hagan looked over.

"Something wrong?"

Eldridge nodded. "Hages, when I was on the Chain . . . my memory . . ."

He trailed off. Hagan said, "I know. It scrambles your memory. It should all come back. Why? Are you missing something?"

"My—" The redhead cut off his words at the arrival of an attendant. A preteen-looking dreg ambled up, his skin shrink-wrapped around his skeletal system, his hands bone-boiled and reinforced with strong-wires. Hagan knew that even though the kid looked weak, he could crush a diamond-sphere with those bony hands. The kid wore a bright orange baseball cap emblazoned with a white letter T. Hagan stood.

The kid scowled at them. "What'll ya have?"

"We want to see the Odd," Hagan said.

"Miss Hanna? She's busy."

"Can you deliver a message to her?"

The dreg smirked and snorted.

"Tell her that Boris Hagan, newly liberated from the Chain of Tears, wants to know the name of the sixty-first president of the United States."

The dreg frowned, then dashed over to an upward-progressing tunnel, where he (and his bright orange ball cap) rode a rope into the darkness. Eldridge stood and walked over.

"What the hell are the United States?"

"Nothing. Some old country."

A ghost-smirk passed across the redhead's face. "Boris, what kind of odds did you make with Hanna?"

"I *said* I don't want to talk about—"

Zam! A tendril of pink shot like a spear through the floor nearby. The stone ground coughed up dozens of glowing pink filaments, all of which found hosts in the vehicles surrounding the hover-skiff. A platoon of pinkeyes crowded before the bus. One of them, a bald hunchback with a fringe of prickly white hair that framed his face, stood forward.

"The good Miss Lilya Hanna will see you now."

He motioned for them to leave the hover-skiff. They did. The pinkeyes congealed around the two men and led them over to an up-tunnel, where they queued up and each grabbed a rope. Two of them pushed Eldridge and Hagan toward the tunnel, where they both took hold of ropes, too. They straddled the mud gutter, which flowed between their legs as their shoes silently slid along some kid of low-friction alloy lain alongside all the gutters. More windows looked out on the tunnel, some blocked with curtains, others open and giving view into dark hallways that twisted up and down. A stairwell led sideways. A door led into the ceiling. Hagan looked up. This particular up-tunnel carried them past floor after floor. At each floor, various dregs started to take hold of the rope, but backed off when they saw the pinkeyes.

"I'll wait," they all said.

Finally, the mud gutters ended, and the tunnel emptied out into the Venn Room. Hagan instantly felt the pink gaze of Hanna burning into him from her floating purple mezz. Above, two glass circles detached from Hanna's mezz and floated down before them. The hunchbacked pinkeye gestured.

"She'll see you now."

Eldridge and Hagan stepped onto the micromag-equipped glass circles, which lifted them into the air through the chattering atrium. Dregs on all sides on all axes paused and watched them rise up to the purple mezz, where Lilya Hanna awaited.

As they rose, Hagan said, "I'll do the talking."

A pair of holes awaited the glass circles. Hagan and Eldridge rose through the purple glass and came to a stop. Lilya Hanna stood before them.

Each Odd had their own history, although no one knew the truth about any one of them. The redhead's run-in with Jeb Goldmist had revealed that particular Odd's penchant for disguise, subterfuge, and misinformation, but despite all they learned about Goldmist, Hagan and Eldridge still had no idea how or why he was older than Deadblast. (Neither had they any idea why Shanta Feruccio was endowed with similar longevity.)

But in the case of Lilya Hanna, Odd of Penticton, the rumortrysts held that she had risen to prominence in the eastern remnants through charm and cunning. Unlike Jeb Goldmist and his magnars, she maintained no formal standing army, instead relying on the "loyalty" of the citizens of Penticton to protect her—along with a shitload of high-end tech she had liberated from rival remnants over the years.

Indeed, the trysts also whispered that after she took the Circle Walk, she had worked as a bounty-merc once upon a time, scouring the northern territories for bounties as her body slowly melted away from the inside.

That same deep-desert sawbones had installed glass windows all across her frame. One sat in the middle of her chest and displayed the mechanical workings of her artificial heart. Two more windows ran the length of her forearms and showed off every twitch of her robotic ulna and radius bones. Another window encased her nonexistent brain—nonexistent because she actually kept it separate from her body as a security measure. She housed the mucky old gray matter that remained of her organic self somewhere deep in Penticton, its remote presence manifested in the glowing neon-pink gas that swirled inside her glass cranium and tinged the irises of her eyes, as well. The end result was that Hanna's body glistened like the well-polished brass innards of an ancient grandfather clock.

Hanna stood alone on her mezz, which was otherwise empty. Hagan tried to place the origin of her floor-length dress, which combined modesty with exhibition. The word "Victorian" occurred to him. Navy blue fabric covered the Odd's neck, but her arms remained exposed, while a cleavage-window revealed her mechanical heart. It looked like a bronze fist that kept opening and closing.

Hagan's eyes dropped down a moment, and he saw a five-story drop below his feet, all of it tinged purple. He felt a rush of vertigo, so he focused on the Odd.

"Well?" he asked.

"Glxt," Hanna said.

"I beg your pardon?" Eldridge asked.

"El, shut up and let me concentrate," Hagan said. *"Revolvo?"*

"Glllxtyyyyyyyy." When she spoke, her body smeared laterally like she was shifting back and forth at great speed, which she was. Hagan peered into an unseen distance and soft-focused his mind on her form. He had picked up this trick from a goofball named Zak Chamberlain who used to make Odds back in Dedrick.

"Some of these mechanorgs outpace our computations, Hages," Chamberlain had said years ago. "You haveta Zen *out* to take it *in*."

Hagan had never asked him what it meant to "Zen out," but as he'd worked with Chamberlain back in the day to decipher the rapid-fire rants of a mechanorg bounty-merc they had braced, he discovered that the Zenning-out of oneself involved a sort of astral projection. You had to look at your inside from the outside. If you could pull it off, then you could hit the brakes on everything else—and that included a hyperactive mechanorg's speedspeech.

Case in point: Odd Lilya Hanna.

The Zenning commenced. Hagan closed his eyes and deactivated the world. Parts of Penticton fell away. First smells faded, then sights. Finally sounds faded, and Hagan was left alone on the purple mezz with Hanna and a slow-motion Eldridge. Hagan knew that from the redhead's perspective, both he and Hanna were now conversing in unintelligible consonant-clots, but he'd worry about El's confusion later.

"*Revolvo?*" Hagan repeated.

"Calvin Garfield," she said, her voice an amalgam of tones that reminded Hagan of an organ being tuned. "And you're looking good, Hagan. Show me those buns."

Hagan rolled his eyes and thumbed his glasses. "I'm not showing you my *buns,* Hanna, I need—"

Hanna's pink eyes flared. She jerked forward, her tussle bouncing in tune with her body, which lurched side to side as her mechanical legs carried her closer. As she lurched, her body's windows danced with the whirl of servos and the pump of brass pistons. Hundreds of tiny muscles twitched at the corners of Hanna's mouth. Brass teeth glinted into view.

"Ooooh. 'Hanna,' he says. Tough guy. Why won't you call me Lilly?"

Hagan dropped back a step and felt the heel of his boot slip off the mezz. He dimly wondered what Eldridge thought of his sudden ability to move at super-speed, but he ignored the thought and found his footing before he fell to his death.

"I'm not going to call you—"

Her tussle bounced again. "And! *And.* And why aren't you on the Chain?"

"I escaped. And I want something."

"To show me your buns?"

"*No.* I escaped from the Chain with my friend here. We want Lord Macta."

At the sound of Pell's pejorative nickname, all of Hanna's internal mechanisms sprang into life—pistons pumped, servos spun, and steam leaked from her joints. She crouched and bared her brass teeth.

"Why do you even want *that?*"

"Hanna, why do *you?*"

The Odd's back bucked as her gears misfired. Her brain essence cycled through shapes—at first it was a long, pink wisp, but then it broke apart into crackling clumps that flashed with tiny lightning bolts.

"Ask me again. Later."

"Is it because he's a Narsyan?"

Radiant pink exploded and flooded the Venn Room. Hanna's mind essence had filled her glass cranium with solid, luminescent pink that emitted a bloom of white-bright flares that danced around the surface area of her head like hyperactive spotlights.

She opened her mouth fast enough to lock it in place. Her voice screeched from some kind of internal speaker: *"Your face used to be a Narsyan!"*

Panic-shrapnel strafed Hagan's body, and for a delirious moment, he thought that Hanna had spotted the scar on Eldridge's forehead that marked him as a former order member, but then he remembered that Dr. Enki had removed it.

Maybe the redhead's thought-jump earlier from Nadia to his scar hadn't been so strange.

Hagan smiled a fake-as-hell, panicked smile. "Sorry I struck a nerve—or whatever fiber-optic analog for nerves you have. And by the way—it was Tutweiler."

Hanna's forearm pistons slowed as the shock of pink light retracted back into her head. She used a fist to slam shut her mouth. "It was not. Tutweiler. But! *But the Chain, Hagan.* How did you escape from the Chain? And the sixty-first president wasn't Tutweiler, just like the fifth chapter of the old legend wasn't called *Vengeance of the Evil Alliance.*"

"All right!" Hagan said. "You were right about that one. But it was Jacob Tutweiler. Former senator from Calitah. I've been studying."

"I *bet* you've been studying. And working out." One of her eyelids snapped down and up with an audible scrape of metal. "But why are we even talking, Hagan? I can have a B-M here in minutes to take you *and*. And. And your friend away. Away to the Chain. Why are we talking?"

"Because I escaped from the Chain of Tears."

"That's a reason?" Her posture snapped straight. "More than you deserve. Someone doesn't know his pre-Deadblast trivia very well."

She emitted a sound like bicycle spokes flicking a playing card ad infinitum. Laughter. In the corner of his eye, Hagan saw the redhead holding up a palm, his mouth puckered around an oncoming *W*, no doubt the beginning of a *What the hell?* He refocused on Hanna.

"Be that as it may. But what if I had a better proposition?" Hagan said.

Hanna's gearworks settled into place with a series of muffled *clicks*. "I'm listening."

Hagan took a breath and concentrated on steadying his voice. "You tell me."

Her brain essence shrank to a prick of pink. *"Revolvo?"*

"I escaped from the Chain of Tears. We both did, my colleague and I." Hagan indicated Eldridge, then continued: "No doubt such an industrious pair could prove useful to you—and our price is modest. We want Lord Macta."

Gears ground, and Hanna lurched closer, her brain essence flattening into a shimmering ribbon.

"All right. We make Odds. But no trivia. I want you to deliver something. And I want you to enter the Mud Races. And. And I want you to *win* the Mud Races. But first, show me those buns."

QUILLIG AND THE GREXTET

QUILLIG AND HIS GREXTET were still playing catch-up.

A deal was struck: Conrade would dispatch some of his operatives into the deepest reaches of Penticton to gather intel regarding the redhead's whereabouts and intentions. In addition, he would provide them with a map of Penticton's ever-shifting tunnels and hallways. After all, he was the man with the map.

But Quillig still wasn't satisfied.

"We're gonna need some kind of transpo," Quillig said.

"First, I'll get you a map," Conrade said. "Follow me."

He led them out of his office and into a network of brick and stone hallways that composed the upper levels of the remnant. A human's heart was located in the middle of its chest, but the heart of Penticton was located in those upper hallways, which hid in the earth a few scant meters below the surface level.

"Sometimes you can hear dreens screeching overhead," Conrade said as he led the three bounty-mercs down a long brick hallway lined with windows that looked in on various utility chambers where dregs carried buckets full of dirt and dumped them into hoppers that agitated the dirt until it separated into fine clumps that scooted down a rolling trough that led into other chambers where dregs holding hoses misted the dirt with water that was collected in *still more* chambers that enclosed gigantic moisture-farms. The farms centered around ten-foot-wide circular filters that sat before other tunnels—tunnels that Quillig knew led far away into the earth where unknown stores of water hid. Like most of the remnants that rose from the dust of Deadblast, the remnant of Penticton had survived because it hid from the elements and discovered a steady source of water; or in Penticton's case, *sources* of water. Most of the sources were springs, although some rumortrysts held that Lilya Hanna's moles had discovered an entire subterranean lake. In any case, as they walked past dozens of such rooms—all of them dedicated to processing water and earth—Quillig knew that there were hundreds of such chambers scattered through the layers of earth that hovered above Penticton's primary atria, which lay far below.

As they marched down the hallway, dozens of dregs streamed around them, all of them carrying buckets or troughs full of water and dirt. As they passed, running pairs of dregs reopened dozens of utility chambers. Some of these chambers had simply been locked, while others had been boarded over with signs that warned Do Not Trespass. As more and more dregs worked to process more dirt and water, the omnipresent gutters that lined every pathway in Penticton flowed with more and more mud. Quillig's boots squish-crunched through gritty puddles of it that overflowed onto a footbridge they crossed. The footbridge arced across a vast vertical passageway that slashed across the main pathway and extended hundreds of feet above and below. A cool, green-scented breeze wafted up from below. On the far side of the bridge, the pathway continued into another enclosed passage. A steel guardrail ran along the sides of the bridge.

As they crossed the bridge, Kieron came prancing up and tapped his elbow.

"Sir, sir," the jellywoman said. "I have a notion. You said that the redhead had returned to Penticton to retrieve an old friend, correct?"

"Shut the fuck up," Quillig said.

"But sir—"

Her boothells clacking on the brick path, Lady R flounced over and yanked the jellywoman away from him.

"The boss said shut the fuck up, jellywoman."

Kieron reared up. "It's *Kieron,* you painted pretender."

They paused on the footbridge as Kieron and Lady R screamed at each other.

"We shoulda *left* you out in the desert, *jellywoman.*"

"And you're an embittered *harridan* who can't recognize a simple *truth!*"

Conrade examined the tattoos on his arms. "This gonna be a problem, Quill?"

"Nope," Quillig said as he grabbed his two fellow bounty-mercs and pushed them down the path away from Conrade. Lady R shook out of his grip.

"Watch it, bub!" she said.

"I'd shitcan both of you, but I can't," Quillig said. "I need the help."

"But you won't *accept* my help, sir," Kieron said. *"They're in the Mud Races."*

Recognition flashed in Lady R's eyes, which slanted in different directions as her heart-shaped lips smacked around silent words.

"Sh-*shit,*" she stammered. "Yes. They are. *Obviously.*"

Kieron's weight shifted from foot to foot. "You concur?" she squeaked.

Lady R's posture stiffened. *"You* concur with *me."* To Quillig: "Boss, you said the Red Rook—"

"Please don't call him that," Quillig said.

Lady R stared at him. Quillig waited for her eyes to roll, but they didn't.

"Boss," she continued. "You said the red . . . *head* was coming back here to get one of his old buddies, right?"

Quillig looked back at the footbridge, where Conrade was leaning against the guardrail, his arms crossed. Quillig looked back. "I did say that. So what?"

Kieron broke in: "The reigning Odd here is Miss Lilya Hanna, is it not?"

"Wow, you read that in a storybook or something?" Lady R said.

"It is *Hanna,* is it *not?*" Kieron repeated.

"Yeah," Quillig said. "Hanna makes the big odds around here."

"If she is holding their comrade captive, and their goal is to win his freedom by making odds, it stands to reason that she would assign them an incredibly difficult feat—a well-nigh impossible task—to accomplish."

"And what would be *more* impossible than winning the Mud Races on your first try?" Lady R asked.

"Indeed," Kieron said. "We saw hundreds of conveyances making their way into this remnant for these races."

Conrade's voice rang out. "Hey, Quillig!"

They turned. Someone had joined Conrade on the footbridge, a young dreg. Quillig would have thought him a dreen, except that this newcomer was standing still and not shrieking. The bounty-merc figured the newcomer's age at around eleven or twelve years. He stood before Conrade with his bone-boiled hands clutched before him, and in those strongwire-reinforced hands, the young dreg held a bright orange baseball cap that bore a single white capital T.

Conrade addressed Quillig: "The kid says he saw your principles meet with Hanna. Says she put 'em in the Mud Races."

Quillig looked at the other two bounty-mercs. Lady R was smiling, but he ignored her and nodded at Kieron. Her eyes darkened, and she glared at the jellywoman. They turned and walked back onto the footbridge.

"You're sure about this?" Quillig asked the kid.

"It true. All true. They went down to the Green Room and got a boat."

Quillig asked Conrade, "Any idea what kind of boat they got?"

"Nope, but I can ask around."

Quillig turned to the kid. "When do the races start?"
"In a few minutes."
"What?" Quillig screamed, wheeling on Conrade. "Gimme the map. *Now.*"
"Dial it down, plaid," Conrade said. "It's coming, but if the race is getting underway, I'm gonna have to get ya a different map. Follow me."

—⚡—

ELDRIDGE AND BORIS HAGAN

"Tell me one way that thing isn't a bomb."

Eldridge reached forward and tapped an ornate box that Boris Hagan cradled under his arm. They both straddled a mud grate and slid down one of Penticton's many tunnels as a river of mud rushed between their feet. Hagan led the way. Light grew ahead, and the tunnel emptied out onto the mid-level floor where their school bus awaited. They both hopped off the twin slides. The redhead had to pinwheel his arms to stay upright, while Hagan planted the landing. He turned to Eldridge.

"It's not a bomb."

He held it up. Cubical in shape, the package had no apparent keyholes or opening mechanisms, and neither had it any seams or weak points that Eldridge could see. Its base color was a shimmering electric blue. Overlaid on that base was an iterating series of golden designs that ran along the edges of the box and swelled with self-replicating detail at its vertices, the work of some ancient arithmartisan. It was called a thmart box.

And it was ticking. Loudly.

"It might be a bomb," Hagan said. "Let's get back down to the Green Room."

After Hagan had stopped conversing with Hanna at super-speed—which from Eldridge's perspective lasted only about ten seconds—he explained her proposition: Win the Mud Races, and deliver the thmart box to Odd Walter Torsten in Hemming. When Hagan explained the proposition to Eldridge, the redhead's eyes darkened. He nibbled his lower lip.

"What's the matter?"

"I'm not exactly besties with Torsten."

"You're not exactly besties with the Odds in general. It's our best shot."

Eldridge couldn't disagree. Now they had to secure some kind of mudworthy vehicle capable of winning the Mud Races, which were set to green-flag later that afternoon.

As they climbed into the school bus, Eldridge asked, "Who's in the Green Room?"

"A guy who wants to help us. He just doesn't know it yet."

They rode the rest of the way down to the Green Room enveloped in a cacophony of roaring engines, chattering dregs, and boasting potential Mud-Racers. Cars, vans, trucks, skiffs, and motorbikes crowded into every down-tunnel and jockeyed for position. One dreg speed-pedaled a bicycle outfitted with suction-cup wheels along the ceiling of a tunnel. Others had abandoned their rides on the upper levels, choosing instead to jump from the roof of one vehicle to another as they made their way down. Meanwhile, Hagan negotiated with the traffic jam and screamed *macta* at every third asshole.

Finally, they spilled out into the Green Room, where thousands of dregs flowed away from the balipmsest game and thousands more battled for parking spaces in anticipation of the Mud Races. Directly opposite the entrance tunnel, Eldridge saw a quartet of dregs pulling a banner skyborne that read, X9TH ANNUAL RACES OF MUD. A giant portcullis blocked a black-dark passage leading into the earth. All of the mud canals—and by association, all of Penticton's mud—dumped into a single channel that ran under the portcullis and disappeared into the tunnel. Scores of vehicles massed around the tunnel entrance, all of them disgorging dregs by the thousands. Datareads leapt skyward and floated around the tunnel entrance, each one displaying readouts of some of that year's favored competitors in the races. Hagan pointed.

"Here's who we'll be up against."

A 3D readout electromorphed its way out of the dataread and hovered in the air over the mud-river. Green letters spelled out a name: TUCKER BEELZEBUB. A 3D bust of Mr. Dyanmo appeared next to his name and rotated in space next to his smiling face. Although to be fair, Tucker wasn't so much smiling as he was trying to crush his own blinding white teeth together. His jaw muscles protruded a full inch away from temples lined with blond sideburns as thick as shag carpeting. His forehead bore a tattoo that read TRUE LIFE. His conveyance looked like a giant, triangular brick, a quarter-mile-long barge that had been carved out and lined with hydrocell-powered boosters. The end result was a twenty-thousand-pound hovercraft that could skim along the mud-river at more than a hundred knots.

Tucker's dossier faded away, and another name scrolled out: MOONDOG. His appearance stood in contrast to Tucker—hairless and unsmiling, although at a distance he would *appear* to be grinning ear to ear because he had removed the skin of his cheeks. He wore a necktie over a bare chest. Moondog was known for playing as a mean flightless Xiang knight back in '87, and he had used his winnings to build his dream ride: an insane-looking quadruped contraption that looked like a suprafeline built out of chrome gizmos, steel struts, and miscellaneous metallic crap. No really knew how the damn thing worked—or even how it held together—but it did, and its organic functionality gave it incredible mobility across the mud river.

The rules of the Mud Races stipulated that all competitors' vehicles had to interact with the river's surface in some way. This disqualified simple flightcraft but allowed for hovercraft like Tucker's and weird creations like Moondog's.

Hagan guided the school bus up an impromptu ramp. A concession dude jogged by, holding up a fistful of steaming femur-slurps (human bones packed with a protein-rich, savory slurry), while small-time Odds made odds on who would crash first, who would be destroyed mid-race—everything *but* the outcome of the race. None of them would dare risk such an indiscretion in the shadow of Lilya Hanna.

One of these small-timers stomped up to Eldridge and Hagan, his eyes alight, his body coated in latex, his head glittering with inch-wide steel spikes. When he spoke, his mandible unfolded like a pair of labia. He jabbed a talon'ed finger at the redhead's T-shirt, which was visible under his open coat.

"Gentleshits! Someone's made odds at the Prometerium! Care to make odds with the Prometerium of the east?"

"Nope," Eldridge said. "Hages? Which way are we going?"

Hagan looked at the redhead's shirt again. "Wait. What's the Prometerium, anyway?"

"It's nothing. A place out west."

The Odd said, "It's a lot more than just a *place!* It's *the* place. A superplace. Care to make odds, gentleshits?"

He blocked their path through the crowd. The redhead's posture stiffened.

"I said *no.*"

Hagan must have sensed the increase in tension, because he grabbed the redhead's elbow and tried to guide him around the trouble—but the Odd persisted.

"No no no, gentleshits. Waity-wait, get your styli. Make some odds on who'll go bye-bye."

Eldridge gave him a hard look. "No thanks."

"But hey-dee-hoo. Gentleshits. I'm not talkin' about *destruction.* Lots of 'em'll get ka-boomed. But no—who'll go *no-trace* on us?"

"No trace?" Eldridge asked, directing his question to Hagan.

"It means, who'll vanish entirely from the race course."

The Odd glee-wheezed. "That it do!"

Vanish entirely. The redhead touched his Prometerium shirt as Hagan's words turned into corrosive ink that corrupted his thoughts and once again cracked open the grinning chasm in his mind. Unintelligible voices whispered from below, asking questions he couldn't answer.

Asking questions he could *no longer* answer.

A voice whispered, *It was warm in Junktown. But what did it look like?*

The redhead's face clenched. He got in the Odd's face.

"Pound sand, Odd."

Hagan gave Eldridge a *what the hell* look as they continued to weave their way through the crowd toward one of the far walls. But the Odd wasn't giving up.

"Waity-wait, my shits!"

And then he laid a hand on the redhead.

The small-time Odd's paw, three-fingered and capped with steel talons, dropped on Eldridge's shoulder and squeezed. The redhead spun on a heel and rammed his palm-slammed the Odd's sternum.

The Odd flew back thirty feet, leaving a wake of fallen dregs between him and the redhead.

Overhead, a few minute tendrils of pink grew out of the ceiling, all while smatterings of Penticton's citizenry started to glare at Eldridge with faintly pink eyes, although they themselves hadn't transformed into full-on pinkeyes . . . yet.

But Eldridge didn't notice the tendrils or the eyes. He was too busy glaring at the Odd, his chest heaving. Hagan stepped in front of him.

"*Eldridge*," he said, using the damn Voice again. "Don't show off."

The redhead glared past Hagan, his eyes still locked on the Odd.

"Wasn't. Showing. Off."

"Hey. C'mon. Look at me."

The redhead's breathing slowed. He looked at his white-haired friend.

"Look up. Look around."

The pink tendrils had doubled in length. They swayed overhead like the branches of ancient trees Eldridge had seen in a book. Willows. He noticed the burgeoning glow of pink eyes all around him, too. Eldridge frowned, but then he got it.

"Hanna's a Narsyan."

"*Used* to be," Hagan said. "Don't let her find out. Don't show off."

The redhead nodded. "Let's go."

The pink faded, and as the hapless Odd struggled to his feet, Boris Hagan led Eldridge through another crowd and toward an area of the Green Room that glistened with green light from somewhere below. Eldridge flashed on his adventure in Dedrick's abandoned quarry during the last Xiang tournament. A gaggle of bottlenecking dregs, their eyes locked on the datareadout overhead, blocked their way. They pushed their way past, and the floor dropped out from underneath. Eldridge kicked backward onto the slippery black stone floor before he saw that the ground hadn't disappeared—it had turned to *glass*.

A glass-encased chamber lay underfoot, all of it packed with thousands upon thousands of gently waving fronds, stalks, and plant life. As Eldridge walked across the glass, his feet felt warm. Below in the glass chamber, hot lamps stood at regular intervals and shone light on the plants.

Hagan tapped his shoulder. "This way."

The humidity of the glass chamber presented a new sensory challenge. Irrigation spigots like old-style fire-sprinklers protruded from the black stone walls and misted the room with a constant haze of moisture. Fans churned from floor-grates while shadows danced overhead as dregs walked across the glass ceiling. The redhead's clothes stuck to his skin. Hagan removed his glasses and tried in vain to wipe mist off the lenses.

And the *smell*. Never had Eldridge encountered it. To be sure, he had smelled trees and seen patches of grass and plants before in various parts of the eastern continent, but his nostrils had never before contended with the thick, sweet, organic superodor that engulfed him in the bowels of Penticton.

Hagan called out: "General?"

Plants rustled. A man emerged. Naked but for a loincloth, the man sported a bodyful of black hair that had been slicked to his flesh with moisture. The same black hair covered his head and face, its darkness only interrupted by flashes of gray that streaked back from temples and dusted his jaw. Underneath the hair, his skin hung off of a still-formidable muscular system. Inlaid copper tubes danced in his forearms like organ pipes, evidence of hydro-powered cybernetic enhancements. Vasculature lined his biceps, calves, and neck. A blue light glimmered from within his chest, another sign of cyber-enhancement.

Around his neck, a pendant dangled at the end of a silver chain. The pendant depicted two silver triangles. One pointed up, the other down. Their points overlapped and created a diamond shape, into which had been laid a red gemstone. Behind the triangles sat a horizontal gold bar.

Eldridge recognized pendant as the icon of Rene Rosaire's Church of the Ancients—or did it have another name?

Dazzleglow.

El teetered. A voice from the past had unmoored him: *Dazzleglow. You know the Church had another name.*

"The Shattered Heart," Eldridge whispered, staring at the old man's pendant.

That isssss correct, the voice hissed. *The Shattered Heart, for that is where I was reborn into the dreenking. The first dreenking, that is.*

The voice cackled. *Because I'm no longer the dreenking, am I? I've been deposed.*

Suddenly it was months ago, hours after Jeb Goldmist had canceled his own Xiang Tournament. Eldridge was standing in the Old Mine, talking with Milos Tola; Tola, who had disappeared near Rosaire's church years ago only to turn up in the Old Mine as the parasitic mate for the dreenqueen of Dedrick.

Tola. Milos Tola. Why do I know that name?

Once again, that same dark chasm grinned at Eldridge.

The redhead opened his mouth to ask the general about Milos, but Hagan was already smiling and extending his hand.

"General Mebus!"

The redhead's flashback had taken less than an instant—so little time that Boris hadn't even noticed. But how was that possible? Hadn't the redhead whispered to himself mere moments before? Wouldn't his old friend have heard him?

Unless you only thought *you whispered those words,* Milos said in the bouncy cadence of a youthful taunt.

—⚹—

QUILLIG AND THE GREXTET

Not long after Eldridge and Boris Hagan had met with General Mebus, Quillig and his grextet rode down a tunnel, finally catching up with their prey. A moving walkway carried them deeper into the earth. Windows on either side of the tunnel afforded them a view of a two-hundred-foot chamber that had been excavated to show off some of the remnant's many rooms. Dozens of cylindrical pods protruded from the interior walls of the chamber. The walkway spilled out onto another brick hallway.

"This way," Conrade said.

The man with the map led them down the hallway. He had dispatched the kid with the orange ballcap to collect more intel about the Mud Races. The hallway ended at a steel door. Conrade paused before it.

"Fucking rumortrysts. Never know which one to believe. Some of them have it so Penticton used to be a command center for one of the big, pre-DB nation-states. Others say it was a stronghold for extraterrestrials."

"What's an extra-blozestrial?" Lady R asked.

Quillig's dark aperture swung around. She clammed up. He turned back to Conrade. "Can we hurry it the fuck *up?*"

"Easy now, plaid. Come on in and don't touch anything."

He pounded on the steel door. A beat later, it opened inward. The swollen creature stood at the door and let them pass into a room that spanned 250 yards and rose a hundred feet. Mounted to the walls ahead was a matrix of monitors whose surface area was larger than the floor space of your average dreg's habitat. Dozens of other workstations sat around the room, all of them equipped with computers, some of them equipped with switches, dials and hundreds of unmarked buttons.

But the monitors lay dormant and dark, the workstations empty. The action waited in the middle of the room, where Conrade's lackeys congregated around the maps—but unlike a sectan confine's paper maps, 3D-rendered electromorph maps hovered in a nimbus of yellow light. Penticton's many rooms hung in the air like a gigantic, three-dimensional, dynamic family tree decorated with hundreds of interconnected, cone-shaped pods. Two of the pods stood out as the largest—one was the Venn Room, which hung at near the top-center of the remnant, while the other was the Green Room, which resided near the bottommost boundary.

Conrade conferred with one of his lieutenants. There was a bang at the door. The kid with the orange ballcap ran in.

"Be with you in a moment, Quill."

The plaid-faced man nodded. Lady R wandered through the room. Kieron stepped up next to Quillig. Plastic squeaked as she crossed her arms. Quillig stared at the map.

"Nice *mensando* back there, jellywoman."

"Thank you, sir." She hesitated. "And if you please, my name is Kieron."

Quillig took a moment to respond.

"Have you heard of the man across the oceans?"

Kieron pivoted to face Quillig. "Only via what you would call 'rumortrysts,' sir."

Inside Quillig's throat, two pieces of parchment rubbed together. A chuckle.

"Conrade's right. You never know which rumortryst to believe. But they agree on one thing: Him."

"The man across the oceans."

Quillig nodded. "They say he lives in a sea of green and never gets sick. They say his people don't know sorrow or want. Until he punishes them. They say he can destroy men with a thought. They say other things, too."

"Such as?"

Quillig shook his head. "Some other time. But the point is: *That's who holds me in thrall.* The buck-stopper. The tryst-weaver. The mightiest of the mighty. So I'll call you 'jellywoman' if I damn well please."

Kieron absorbed that statement, then nodded an acknowledgement.

Lady R wandered over. "Did you see the rest of the map?"

"You mean this?" The plaid-faced man indicated the dancing network of golden pods that hung in the air before them: the many rooms or Penticton Remnant. Lady R's hair bounced as she shook her head. Quillig's breath caught in his chest. She spoke.

"Nope. It's even bigger."

She led them throughout the room, which appeared to be empty.

"What're you talking about, Ragnarok?" Quillig asked.

"Wait a minute. Let your eyes adjust."

He did, and after a moment, the rest of Penticton shimmered into existence. The map of Penticton glowed brightest near its center, where the concentration of pods was highest, but the rooms of Penticton *filled* the space. Thousands of rooms extended into every corner, each one connected by a glistening filament of tunnel.

Conrade called, "Quill! Don't move. You're in the perfect place." He mumbled something to the swollen creature, who stood over a keyboard/monitor interface. He typed out a command, and the room turned green; *green* because another map, a *blue* map, had joined the yellow one.

But unlike the map of Penticton, which depicted a clearly man-made network of rooms and connecting tunnels, the blue map was a single, coiling tube that ran underneath Penticton, passed through the Green Room, and then continued past the sprawling remnant's boundaries where it terminated into the far wall of the map room.

Quillig asked, "What am I looking at?"

"It's the tunnel for the Mud Races."

Only Conrade hadn't spoken up. Lady R had.

Conrade walked over. "She's right. Here, look." He led them over to the edge of the Penticton map. One of the remnant's outermost rooms hung in the earth directly over the racecourse. Conrade tapped it. A pair of luminescent red crosshairs blinked to life around the room and spun in alternating directions. He continued, "You wanna catch these bounties, your best shot's gonna be right here."

The kid in the orange ballcap walked over. "He's got the general's waterboat."

"Come again?" Quillig asked.

"Old General Mebus," Conrade said. "Bastard's been working on a boat for years. Kept saying he'd win the Mud Races if he ever gave it a go."

Quillig shook his head. Even in this faraway remnant, the redhead had friends.

Kieron spoke up. "Sir? An interrogatory?"

"A *what?*" Lady R said, a sour face among her auburn locks.

"It means a *question*," Quillig said. "And an extra*terrestrial* is someone from another planet."

"Oh."

Her temple-tattoos opened like flowery archways as her eyes widened. The sight sent a libido shockwave through Quillig; something he hadn't felt in years—not since before he turned dreen, but that was before he migrated across the oceans to this continent. Or rather, before someone *brought* him across the oceans.

Quillig looked away and addressed Kieron.

"Go on."

"Thank you, sir. I wonder why we don't simply try to apprehend them at the *end* of the course. In Hemming. If we left now, we would have ample time to stage an ambush."

The jellywoman was right, of course. Attempting to apprehend the redhead in the middle of the Mud Races would require—

bare minimum—some amount of spelunking and digging though hard-packed earth or solid rock to gain access to the race tunnel. Any sensible bounty-merc would disregard such a scenario in favor of an easier acquisition point. But Quillig couldn't answer her honestly, of course, as both Kieron and Lady R were expecting huge bounties for their services; bounties that would most likely have to come out of his own pocket. If he told them that the only "bounty" to be paid was "his own life" and that he was racing against an impossible clock ticking down to his demise, they might not be so keen to help.

Quillig nodded and stalled. "It's a fair question."

Lady R spoke up. "It's simple, dummy. The answer is the Odds."

Kieron looked back and forth between them.

"I don't understand."

Lady R held up a hand. "Mind if I field this one, Quillie?" The plaid-faced man nodded. She continued, "It's like this: the Odds like their jenta. They make jenta all the time, but some events are like big, fat Odd jenta-making *holidays* that keep them in the black for the rest of the year. The Mud Races are like that—a jenta-making holiday for Lilya Hanna and that crazy fuck Torsten over in Hemming. Quillie, what'd they used to call that holiday? The one in December?"

"Krissmess?"

"Right. Krissmess. So when we're talking about these things, we'll call 'em Oddsmesses. The Mud Races is an Oddsmess for Hanna and Torsten. Fucking with an Oddsmess would be like diving into a woodchipper: *painful* and *dumb*. Torsten's goons'd overpower us in two shakes of a lamb's twat."

Behind the plaid fabric, what remained of Quillig's lips curled in a frown. Why was Lady Ragnarok making this argument? Sure, messing with the Mud Races was a bad idea, but so was chasing their quarry through hundreds of miles of subterranean tunnels. If Quillig hadn't been operating under such a dire deadline, they would've already booked it for Hemming and set up shop outside. As soon as the redhead left the remnant, *bam!* They'd snatch him.

What was Lady Ragnarok up to?

You've got less than twenty-four hours, Quillig. If that.

A massive *bah-whooming* horn sounded from somewhere deep below them.

"What was that?" Quillig asked.

"The Mud Races," Conrade said. "They just started."

Quillig's shoulders tensed. He indicated the room on the map Conrade had highlighted moments before. "This room is our best bet. But we're gonna have to haul some ass." He called over his shoulder, "Turn on the tracker!"

The swollen creature tapped a few more buttons, and a few hundred glowing white dots flared to life all along the blue tunnel—each of the racers, all of them flying along. Fast. Kieron leaned over.

"Which one is Eldridge?"

Conrade turned to the kid. "Well?"

"It's this one," the kid said, activating another spinning pair of red crosshairs around the last-place dot.

"He got started late. He's way in the back."

The plaid-faced man heard it in his ears: *Pop-pop-pop-pop.*

"That won't last," Quillig said. "Let's get moving. Conrade!"

"Yes?"

"You promised us transpo."

"Right this way. I've got something that's perfect for your little *ménage à trois.*"

—⚞—

ELDRIDGE AND BORIS HAGAN

GENERAL MEBUS SHOOK BORIS Hagan's hand.

"Borishagan, you bastard!" When he said Hagan's name, he ran both names together into one clot of sound. Mebus continued: "What're you doing back in this remnant? I thought Hanna, that old whore, Chained you."

"She did, but I got out. With some help." Hagan indicated the redhead. "General, this is my friend, Eldridge."

Eldridge offered his hand, but the general's eyes narrowed behind his mass of hair. "You were the rook. The *Red Rook.* Weren't you?"

"Excuse me?"

The general pointed at him. "The Xiang tourney. In Dedrick a few months back. You were black's rook on the kingside, weren't'cha?"

Eldridge looked at Hagan, who nodded to say, *It's all right. Go ahead.*

"Yeah, that was me."

The general's head split open and blasted them with laughter-shells. Hagan winced. Eldridge covered his ears. Mebus grabbed the redhead's hand in a death grip. Only the redhead's Narsyan strength kept his bones from breaking.

"You're lookin' at the original Black King! That's right. Indeedy. Nix, that old fuck, signed me up. Little did I know! Then he gives me the boot after things got underway. I'd made some development moves, then whoopdeedoo! *Adios, Generale!* Hah! Well, I guess I should thank you, seeing as how the White Queen laid waste to half the board! Heh! Ho."

"That's hilarious," Eldridge said. "Can we stop shaking hands now?"

Mebus dropped his hand. "And you got my boy off the *Chain?* That's quite a resume you got there, Mr. Eldridge. Well done!"

More laughter-shells. Eldridge thought about making a break for it. Hagan grabbed his elbow and yelled over the laughs:

"General! We need to win the Mud Races!"

Silence. The general's fingertips leapt to his chin-beard and started stroking as thought overtook him. He turned and wandered back into the plants, muttering to himself.

"Hmmm. Races. *Mud* Races. Races . . . of mud. Hmmm." He pinched a plate-sized leaf and spoke to it. "What to do about that?" He vanished behind a wall of green.

Eldridge whispered, "Is he okay?"

"He's been in charge of this conservatory since I was a kid. And he was a field marshal in one of the first post-Deadblast wars. If you think *I'm* an old fart, I think *he's* an old fart."

The general reappeared, pushing a stalk out of his way and chuckling.

"Borishagan, you bastard!"

"Yes, General?"

"Heh. Larry told me something crazy."

"Did he now?"

Eldridge asked, "Who's Larry?"

"Never mind," Boris said, waving at the redhead to say *hush*. "What did Larry say, General?"

Mebus spoke between sobs of laughter. "That . . . you needed . . . to . . . *win*. The Mud Races!"

Laughter-shells. Eldridge and Hagan *both* covered their ears. It took the general a good five minutes to get his mirth under control. When he did, Hagan spoke.

"You want to hear something even *more* crazy?"

"Hah. Maybe. I dunno if my gut can take it!"

Hagan laughed, too. "I know, right? Well, here it is: I need your waterboat to win the races! We'd like to trade for it."

The following onslaught of mirth drove Eldridge and Hagan running out of the conservatory, up the spiral staircase and back out into the Green Room, where they saw puzzled dregs looking around for the source of the mysterious mad laughter that rose from the floor.

But when the general had laughed himself out, Eldridge and Hagan looked down into the conservatory. Mebus was holding up his middle finger—which meant something quite different in the days after Deadblast.

"We're in," Hagan said.

—⚒—

THE CANALS WERE CLOSED and the shunts were open. The Mud Races were about to get underway.

Huge aluminum slides clanged down from the ceiling as the mud of Penticton converged down on the Green Room and just as all the competitors converged on the dark tunnel—still guarded by a portcullis—that led into the main racecourse, which extended through the three hundred miles of earth between Penticton and the remnant of Hemming. Mud flowed in from all quarters of the remnant. Hagan knew that the wild increase in mud production was necessary because the racecourse itself wasn't fully submerged yet. A few miles ahead in the tunnel was a giant, retractable dam manned by a pair of dregs who would release it at the arrival of the first competitors. The race's leaders would ride an onrushing wave of mud as they blitzed from Penticton to Hemming.

Boris Hagan stood behind the wheel of General Mebus's waterboat.

Eldridge stood over to the side of the waterboat and held onto the guardrail, his pallor a slight green from the neck up. The boat danced and bucked on the wake of the other mudcraft. Ten-foot waves of mud rolled from one side of the river to the other and slapped together in the middle. Mud gushed over the guardrail of the general's waterboat, which was equipped with an automatic bailing and draining mechanism—a mechanism that hadn't originally been intended for mud races, because the waterboat hadn't originally been a boat. It had been an *invention*.

Back in the conservatory, the general led them through the endless thicket of green to his habitat: little more than a room with a lidless toilet bolted to the wall. Hagan and Eldridge sat on green protrusions from the wall—chairs buried under plant life—while the general flopped into a hammock covered with coils of ivy. As he swung in the air, he snapped his fingers and summoned his assistant.

Eldridge screamed. Hagan stayed cool.

The thing emerged from the carpet of grass and vines at his feet. It looked like a thousand vines had coiled together and flash-evolved into a slithering, wheezing tube of sentient plant life. A mouth, webbed with mucus, opened on the top of its "head," while a single, staring oculus regarded them with a bloodshot, feline eye.

And it rammed the redhead's leg. Eldridge nearly fell off his grass-chair.

"Bor. What the fuck *is* this?"

But Hagan was already kneeling before the general's assistant.

"Good girl, good girl," Hagan said as he petted the thing's head. "How many of these are there, General?"

"Just the one," Mebus said. "But she's a beauty, isn't she?"

The general's assistant laid its head in Hagan's hand and smacked its lips. Eldridge relaxed a little and knelt down next to him. He offered his hand, and the assistant closed its maw around his fingertips. A smooch. Eldridge petted its head. The general sat up.

"Delilah, can you get me the plans for my waterboat?"

The plant-thing, Delilah, slithered back under the carpet of plants. Hagan hooked his thumb at where she had been.

"The result of experimentation?" Hagan asked.

"Negative," Mebus said. "Pure evolution. She just came rising up out of the grass one day. The little darling's *herbi,* so I didn't have to worry about her biting my balls off. She keeps all the floor holes and grates clean. Eats just about anything organic."

"Then she pretty much has to stay here, right?" Eldridge asked.

Hagan smiled at the redhead. The general did, too.

"That's an affirmative," Mebus said. "Not much plant life topside. And not many other remnants with our kinda agriculture."

The floor rustled and disgorged Delilah, who bore a tube of rolled-up smartpaper in her maw. The general petted her, dismissed her, and laid out the plans on an ivy-covered makeshift table he kept at the side of his office.

The plans did not depict a boat.

Instead, they depicted an elaborate irrigation system. Hexagonal in shape, the general had designed his irrigation system to be arranged in a grid of modules that would affix to the ceiling of an enormous, enclosed farm. But because his life in Penticton had never afforded him the chance to build such a space, he had only built the one prototype, which he had never used for irrigation.

"Follow me," he said.

The general led them out of his office and through the conservatory, leaving the glass ceiling behind. They delved into a dark, green maze that hid under Penticton, and only the general knew the way. Intermittent shafts of light cut through the darkness from above as they passed by the Green Room's many floor holes. Greenery and darkness closed in around them as the general led them farther and farther away from the glass ceiling and into the deepest reaches of the conservatory.

The sensation brought memories bubbling to the top of Boris Hagan's mind; memories of the time he spent in hiding during the last Xiang tournament in Dedrick, the one that led to the fall of Jeb Goldmist. Like Penticton, Dedrick had a network of tunnels that hid underneath its lowest floor, but in Dedrick's case, those tunnels held fire instead of foliage. All of Dedrick's trash eventually fell into those tunnels, where it was incinerated according to a specific schedule—a schedule that Hagan had to follow with detail-oriented mania if he didn't want to perish in a column of flame.

But the darkness also did something else for Hagan: it let him *rest.* As soon as they passed out of the light and into pure pitch, his shoulders fell, and his knees started to shake. His chest and back both ached from the mortarchains implants. Heretofore, Hagan had been tapping deep stores of willpower to keep himself upright, and as he walked through the dark jungle of the Penticton conservatory, he simultaneously had to contend with his failing body and his uncooperative memorybanks, which constantly pinged his terror centers with the nightmare of his time spent under under-Dedrick.

Finally, General Mebus spoke.

"Stop," he said. "Delilah?"

Something slid between Hagan's legs, forcing them apart as it passed. Delilah was apparently the living key to this door, because they heard a series of fiddling clicks and clacks before a rectangle of light bloomed and admitted them to another chamber where the waterboat awaited.

The chamber's architecture was at odds with the rest of Penticton. Where Penticton's walls were mostly built from steel or black stone, this vaulted room had three crumbling brick walls and a reinforced wood ceiling. That same wood covered the fourth wall. All told, the room covered about a thousand square feet of floorspace, roughly the same size of a Dedrick city block. Circular openings in the wall led nowhere, having been blocked up by earth or concrete ages ago.

"How'd you find this room?" Eldridge asked.

The general chuckled. "Me and Delilah found it a while back. Not sure what it used to be, but it made a great staging area for *this* beaut."

He gestured at the waterboat, which sat in the center of the room. Their entrance to the chamber had activated a set of lights that stood on steel legs. Hagan recognized the vestiges of the general's irrigation system in the craft. It looked like a hexagonal metal catwalk. The general had mounted a sitting and steering area near the front of the hexagon, while a simple wooden deck stretched to the aft of the boat, where the primary propulsion lay.

And in the case of the general's waterboat, propulsion was the same thing as irrigation.

The general waved them over underneath the boat, where they could see foot-wide scoops that yawned from its hull.

"Y'see, when I converted this little shit into a boat, I cranked up the power of the moisture scrubbers." He indicated the yawning orifices above. "But here's where it gets good. The scrubbers can scrub more than just water from the air. They can also scrub water from *anything*."

"Including mud?" Hagan asked.

"That's right. Hah! When you activate this little baby, you'll skate along that river on a surface of nice, clean water. And no one out there'll be able to keep up. Of course, if someone *hits* you, the boat'll fly to pieces, so you'll just have to stay out in front!"

The general left them with those words. They hired a few dregs to help transport the boat through a series of tunnels that led up to the Green Room. Mebus cautioned them against bragging about the functionality of their boat.

"Because I just ain't sure it's *legal,* is all, fellas. No one'll be able to *see* the water underneath if they don't look too close, and everyone'll be hauling so much ass, no one'll even care to look. Still—'loose lips' and all that, right? Heh!"

"Loose lips?" Eldridge asked.

"Some old saying," Hagan said. "General, what can we trade you for the boat?"

"Nothing."

"Nothing?" Hagan asked. "General, we'd pay the jenta if we had it."

Mebus shook his head. "You've got the one and only Red Rook by your side. I'd . . . Well, I'd just be so tickled if you two old fucks could cross the finish line down in Hemming in my little boat."

The general would entertain no more discussion on the matter. They hired some dregs to bring the boat up to the Green Room, where they lowered the boat onto a plywood ramp. They released the waterboat, and it splashed into the river, where it bobbed in place. Hagan and Eldridge climbed into the boat, where the redhead's face immediately took on a greenish hue as mud slopped over and sprayed out the sides by the craft's bailing mechanism. Hagan secured the package in a steel strongbox mounted next to the steering wheel alongside the boat's throttle. Farther up the river, Tucker Beelzebub's barge-brick growled in the water while Moondog's suprafeline crouched knee-deep in mud, its green eyes glowing. Hagan regarded them with a slack jaw—but drooping eyelids.

"I wish I had time to practice driving this thing," he said. "Like, a *year*."

The Mud Race's other competitors included various pontoon boats, jon boats, as well as the occasional fan-powered hovercraft.

"Those are called airboats," Hagan said. "They used to ride those on swamps, which was a region where water and—"

"I know what a swamp is, Hages," Eldridge said, managing a smile right before he upchucked over the side of the boat. As Eldridge puked, a horn sounded from behind while cheers rose from the crowd of spectators that surrounded the river on an array of floating bleachers. They all turned, and from the far canals of the Green Room came puttering a single-person hover-platform that bore a man who screamed into a megaphone.

"Green flag imminent! Green flag imminent!" yelled the Odd; specifically, it was the spike-headed, labia-mouthed Odd whom Eldridge had attacked earlier. *"Green flag immi—"* his barking (as well as the crowd's cheers) trailed off when he spotted the redhead in the boat, and for a moment, his eyes flared pink.

Everyone's eyes flared pink. The room fell silent. Lilya Hanna had arrived.

She descended from above on a floating circle of purple glass, her eyes a blaze of pink light that sprayed the room with glowing tendrils. In her cranium, her essence had assumed the shape of an ancient character—like an L turned upside-down.

A gamma, Hagan recalled.

The reigning Odd of Penticton hovered over the entrance to the portcullis, the burbling of mud the only sound. Two tendrils snaked forth from her eyes and yanked the portcullis groaning and shrieking up out of the mud, which dripped from its pointed ends as it rose into the ceiling. Once the portcullis was up, Hanna curtsied. When she spoke, her words came out at a normal pace:

"First one to Hemming wins."

The instant she said "wins," an enormous something *thudded* from behind as a final, massive dam was released and a tsunami of mud came rolling up the river. In concert, a massive *bah-whooming* horn sounded, prompting everyone in the room to simultaneously cheer and cover their ears. The sudden onrush of mud surged into the canals like an excess of electricity dumping into a power-grid. Mud flooded over canal-banks everywhere as the black stone floor of the Green

Room disappeared under brown and the tidal wave of mud rushed forth. Hanna zipped upward through a tunnel in the ceiling, her pink tendrils spiraling into the sky with her. The crowd snapped out of it and once again erupted into applause, hoots, howls, and jeers.

Done vomiting, the redhead looked up and pointed at the tunnel. "Hit it!"

Hagan rammed the throttle. Nothing happened.

"What the hell?"

But even though nothing happened with the general's waterboat, plenty was happening all around them. Tucker Beelzebub's barge-brick rumbled into the tunnel while dozens of smaller mudcraft sped past it. Tucker, himself a two-time Mud Race champion, stood at the helm of the barge-brick, chewing on a cigar and smiling. Everyone knew it took him a while to build up speed, but once he got going, not even a nuclear shockwave could stop him.

Not that there were any nukes left to begin with. According to the rumortrysts, the horrific weapons of old had simply up and vanished one day, unused.

Hagan shook his head out of the past. The Mud Races had already left them behind. Spectators gawked and jabbed fingers at them as they floated in a listing circle down the river toward the tunnel, their forward momentum a side effect of the other boats' departing wake.

Eldridge ran to the front of the waterboat.

"What the fuck is the problem?!"

"I don't know!" Hagan yelled back as he slammed the throttle forward and back. As they spun in the water, Lord Macta came floating back into view. They had to look through the balimpsest cage to see him, but there he was, alone on his display platform. They couldn't hear his moans over the taunts of the crowd overhead, but they could see his mouth stretch into a yawn of sorrow. The redhead's face fell.

That's when they saw General Mebus jerking off.

Not that he was *actually* jerking off. The general stood on the riverbank, ankle-deep in mud, his theocrazzic pendant sparkling, his fingers curled into a circle that he pumped over his loincloth-clad crotch. The redhead's temper flared.

"What's *your* malfunction, asshole?!"

"Crank it, Boris, crank it!" the general yelled.

"What?"

"The throttle! Crank it! Like so!" He made the jerking-off gesture again.

The gray-haired old man spun, grabbed the throttle and pulled. It snapped up. He pushed. It snapped down.

And the waterboat took flight.

The boat's water-scrubbers flared to life with a deep *hum* while simultaneously spraying mud in every direction. Unfortunately, they hadn't been facing the tunnel when the scrubbers activated. Instead, the boat blasted skyward over the general's head. They both grabbed a guardrail and hung vertically in the air as the boat sailed into one of the many flooding canals. Hagan pulled back on the throttle to get the speed under control while the redhead struggled to his feet. Hagan steered the boat through the network of canals and back to the main river. He waved at the general as they passed. Eldridge waved, too, although his eyes rolled.

They disappeared into the tunnel, and once again, Boris Hagan's memory challenged him with the image of the flaming garbage tunnels that lay under Dedrick. He ignored the memories and opened the throttle. They blasted into the empty tunnel and rode in silence for a few minutes before Eldridge spoke.

"Hages?"

"What?"

"Back when we met with Hanna and you were moving at superspeed . . . did you show her your ass?"

—⚏—

[AUDIO: THE CLICK OF A DICTATRYST DEVICE DEACTIVATING.]

I gotta take this thing off, because it's givin' me one humdinger of a headache!

Hoo boy. Breathe in, breathe out, Boris. You got this, old man.

Hey there, all you Shore-Riders, I'll be back in a minute. I just need to check on everyone else.

[AUDIO: BED SPRINGS SQUEAK. FOOTSTEPS.]

Okay. Phew. Everyone present, accounted for, and still sound asleep. Wow. So, everything you just read or heard took me about five seconds to enter into the dictatryst. No bullshit! I'd heard these gizmoids were fast, but I had no idea. Reminds me of an old story—

Hush up, Boris, because time's a wastin'. What's the hour? Oh, no. I've got so much left to do, such a long road ahead of me before my labors are complete.

But I've got to get all this down, lest I croak too soon, like I almost did during the Mud Races. Yes, you heard that right, you Shore-Riders—your humble Chronicler almost bit the big one midway between Penticton and Hemming. Your humble Chronicler almost abandoned his best friend in his time of greatest need.

Well, until now, that is. He needs me more than ever, but he's so far away, and I don't even know if he still wants to see me; if he still thinks of me as his best friend.

Boris Hagan, that's some durnfool crazy talk. Like hell he doesn't. He has since the first day you hopped off that wheat caravan dead of noon. Felt like you was jumpin' onto the surface of the sun. You hustled your old bones down the ramp into under-Dedrick, and lo and behold, who was the first bugger I met inside? Some snot-nosed lil' ginger on his brand-spankin'-new motorbike, who offered me water and asked if I knew anything about something called "comix."

I ain't never forgotten the first time we met, and I'll be damned if our last meeting is gonna be the last time—or the last way—I see your stupid face.

[AUDIO: THE CLICK AND WHIRR OF A DICTATRYST DEVICE COMING ONLINE.]

Let's get this story down for the Shore-Riders. Then I'm coming to save your ass.

THE MUD RACES
&
HEMMING REMNANT

ELDRIDGE AND BORIS HAGAN

The general had delivered. The old field marshal's waterboat rocketed along the mud river's surface at more than a hundred knots. Once Hagan mastered the boat's controls, Eldridge found some rope stowed in the back and used it to provide them with makeshift seatbelts.

Darkness fell. Hagan flicked on the boat's headlamps. The black stone of Penticton soon faded into a cylindrical natural stone tunnel that glimmered in the passing light. Every half-mile, they passed a set of temporary utility lights that had been bolted to the rock walls. The miscellaneous roar of dozens of engines reverberated from the tunnel ahead. Eldridge tapped the throttle and hooked his thumb back toward the Green Room and General Mebus.

"Ya think he could've mentioned that *before* the race started?!"

They rode headlong into a bank of chilly mist. The temperature dropped twenty degrees in an instant. Hagan buttoned his corduroy vest and leaned over.

"Go easy on the general. He did some time as a monk or a priest or something up in the deep desert with René Rosaire. Drove him buggo."

"The Church of the Shattered Heart?" Eldridge asked.

"I thought it was called the Church of the Ancients?"

"Me too," Eldridge said. "Someone told me otherwise."

"Got it," Hagan said, giving him a look. "Isn't that where Milos—well, where your son-in-law died?"

Milos. Milos Tola. His former son-in-law and the one-time dreenking. Eldridge had last seen Milos in the Old Mine, an ancient roadside attraction that also served as a backdoor into his home remnant of Dedrick. (Well, Dedrick was *kind of* the redhead's home.) At the time, Milos was the parasitic mate for the dreenqueen of Dedrick, who had been holed up in the Old Mine for untold decades, but in the months since Eldridge deposed Jeb Goldmist, the dreenqueen had acquired a new king—Crius Kaleb, one of the redhead's oldest friends.

The thought made the redhead's heart hurt; that he had fought so hard to bring Crius back from the brink only for him to succumb to the allure of dreendom months later.

But something else unsettled Eldridge. He could remember Milos well, calling up his face from across all eras of his life—human, dreen, or otherwise. He further remembered the first time he met Milos; it was high atop a mesa where he lived with . . .

Once again, that same dark chasm grinned at him, taunting him.

"El?"

The redhead started. "What?"

"Did you hear my question?"

"Uh," he trailed off, his eyes fogging up again. "What was it?"

The waterboat carried them past the race's rearmost competitors and into a tunnel that opened onto a vast cavern that held a natural stone bridge where the mud river crossed. Hagan steered the waterboat around two airboats and a hovercraft that lost control and flew off the bridge.

Hagan said, "Isn't the Rosaire's church where Milos died?"

"Boris, Milos is alive. Well, he isn't dead."

"What?"

The cave ended, and the mud river narrowed into a small canal barely wide enough for the widest boat. They passed a dozen more competitors. Eldridge wondered how Tucker's barge-brick had handled the passage, but he refocused on Milos Tola.

"He was the dreenking. Before the queen replaced him."

Hagan gaped at him for an instant, then turned his attention back to the race.

"Why didn't you ever tell us?"

"I . . . I felt *bad* for him. Embarrassed. How he wound up that way."

Hagan nodded. "I get it."

"Boris, you don't think that old guy, Mebus, might know anything about Milos, do you?"

They entered a stretch of rapids. More cold mist gushed by as the river churned into a shitty, light brown, like a toilet flushing for eternity. By the opening solid wood floodgates and two giant wheels flanking the river, a pair of dregs held up large smartboards that displayed their place on the leaderboard.

It read 227/335. They rode on.

Eldridge repeated his question: "Do you think he might?"

"I doubt it, El. He left the church a long time ago."

"So why's he still wearing the pendant?"

"I don't know. He could be wearing it for *any* reason. Maybe he still feels a connection to the faith. Maybe it reminds him of where he grew up. I don't know. Why are *you* wearing that shirt?"

He pointed at the redhead's T-shirt for the Prometerium. Eldridge zipped his leather jacket.

"It's just some swag."

"Some swag? You made odds there, didn't you?"

"So I made some odds there this one time. Shut up."

"'*Some* odds'? We wouldn't happen to be talking about the odds that got you hip-deep in shit, would we?" They rode in silence past a two more jon boats and a large pontoon boat. When no answer was forthcoming, Hagan continued, "El, everyone makes odds. That's why I wanted to become one. But come on—you know you took it too far."

Eldridge chuckled. "Wanna hear something funny? I don't actually have a gambling problem."

"You don't?"

The redhead shook his head, then his finger. At the steering wheel. His jaw dropped open.

"*Look out!*"

The boat scraped the outer wall of the cave. Their speed halved instantly. Eldridge slammed into the boat's dashboard. The three competitors they had just passed zoomed ahead. The waterboat threatened to spin out of control, but Hagan wrested it back on course and maxed out the throttle.

"Damage report!"

The redhead pulled himself to his feet and crawled over to the side of the boat, where he saw a fissure in the network of steel struts. The damage was centralized around one of the vertices in the boat's hexagonal shape; a mist of water sprayed out of one broken pipe and soaked a bundle of wires that had survived the close scrape without fraying. Eldridge frowned and called up some knowledge that he had picked up over the years.

"Hey, Hages! Metal conducts electricity, right?"

"Like a motherfucker it does—why?"

They passed underneath a giant stone arch that stood at the entranceway to another gigantic chamber, except in this case, the cave extended for a few miles, and the mud river curled through it like an enormous playslide for a child. Scores of boats churned through the glop ahead. There was still no sign of Beelzebub or Moondog, but Hagan quickly gained on the three boats who had passed them moments before. Eldridge ran over and pointed at the damage.

"Because this contraption runs on electricity, and Mebus ran wires every which way. If one of 'em snaps, we're screwed."

Hagan's lips pursed in consternation. He looked over his shoulder at the damage, the back at the redhead. He jerked his chin to the rear of the boat.

"There's a repair kit in back."

"I don't know how to fix one of these things," Eldridge said.

"You do now! Or we're dead. Get crackin', grasshopper."

"What's a grasshopper?"

Boris Hagan wrenched the wheel. The bus fishtailed around a corner and passed by those three pesky boats. The white-haired old man glanced over his shoulder and grinned at Eldridge, who was holding onto a guardrail and flopping on the wooden deck.

"*You* are, old buddy," Hagan said with a grin.

The river dove through the giant cave, and they rode the muddy wave deeper and deeper into the earth.

—⚡—

QUILLIG AND THE GREXTET

"GET THE HELL OUT *of the way!*"

Quillig's gloved fist coiled around the accelerator and revved the engine while a triplet of gape-eyed dregs huddled on the black stone floor and watched a double-sidecar motorbike (courtesy of Conrade) roar across a twenty-foot chamber that lay a several miles west of the Venn Room and some three hundred yards below it.

The room was little more than a makeshift habitat for the three dregs, who all wore tattered denim and canvas. They had been boiling water over a small fire when Quillig's motorbike came crashing down a tunnel and sprayed their home with mud.

The room had actually been clean before the grextet arrived.

As Quillig steered the bike across the room, he ran over a few ancient cans of vegetables, which spat their green and orange treasures onto the muddy floor. The dregs cried out and started to shovel the mud-veggie glop onto their tin plates and into their open mouths. On the far side of the room, Quillig paused at the tunnel, which was moving up and down.

"Which way, jellywoman?"

Kieron referred to a scroll of smartpaper, which displayed a monochromatic (and far less detailed) version of Conrade's map. The jellywoman had immediately volunteered to handle "navigation control" (as she called it) when Conrade presented them with the map, which worked like this:

Penticton had end-points. *Terminas.* Places where the rooms actually ended. Over the years, Conrade and his comrades had traveled to each of those far reaches and carefully hidden transponders that could, if activated remotely, broadcast a signal at a frequency that lurked in the spectrum well below the dangerous bands banned by the Cell Phone Edict of Deadblast. They had compiled telemetry from those transponders to construct their dynamic map of Penticton, which managed to stay current up to the last hour, or whenever the transponders last pinged the map room.

A bright red dotted line marked the route to the ambush point. To get there, they had to keep going *down.* The jellywoman used her fingertips to zoom in closer on their position, then nodded.

"Down, sir."

Quillig nodded. They waited an awkward minute for the tunnel to pivot downward. The three dregs' expressions shifting as the whites of their eyes turned to slits and their fists slowly closed. Before they could make a move, Kieron and Lady R both spun around. Lady R's neckmount produced a pair of missiles, while Kieron stared them down with her wrist-cannons. The dregs backed off.

Lady R chuckled and pressed a button on her neckmount, which produced a stylus-sized device. The lady pointed it at the remainder of food on the ground.

"I should Chain you cunts on principle. But failing that . . ."

Kieron stared. "My lady, what are you—"

Her wrist flexed, and the stylus sprayed fire across the floor, incinerating the food and setting the three dregs alight, and as they howled, the Lady wagged her finger at them and cackled.

"Dammit, Ragnarok!" Quillig yelled. "Don't torch anyone till we're ready to leave!"

She flicked her hair out of her eyes and laid a hand on his thigh.

"But they're *real* now, boss. They weren't really real before. They were lost in the night. Now they're—"

A column of water doused the dregs, who fell to the ground, their skin bubbling. Lady R glared across the sidecar, where water dripped from one of Kieron's hand-cannons. She pointed at Kieron.

"You. *Later.*"

Deep inside her plastic shell, Kieron's chin rose. She said nothing, but merely waited for the motorbike to rumble into the tunnel as it pivoted downward and they left the three charred, moaning dregs behind them in the remains of their home. They rode down and emerged into another chamber, this one empty and much smaller, but it had *two* tunnels on the far side.

"Which way?" Quillig asked.

They paused while Kieron consulted the map. As they rode closer and closer to the edge of Penticton, the rooms got smaller. This forced Kieron to zoom in closer and closer on the map—which turned to water in her hands.

Everything turned to water. Black water.

Water.

Water.

Down below, where the Admiral awaits.

In the Oceans.

Kieron, still coated in plastic, floated away from Quillig's motorbike and descended deep, the black stone walls of Penticton giving way to vast, linking columns of lightsteel. The columns stood like giant legs in the oceans, grouped in threes, extending to the surfaces far above and below. Every few hundred fathoms, a set of hinges allowed the legs to bend with the surrounding current.

The jellywoman activated a pair of lights mounted to the sides of her head.

The triple columns of lightsteel each encased a glass tunnel that, like Penticton, linked one chamber to the next. As she sank deeper into the water, Kieron encountered one of these chambers—a thousand-gallon steel tank—which acted as a way station for those diving into the abyss. Kieron opened the hatch, and a surge of water from inside pushed her upward. When the surge subsided, she swam into the tank and pulled the hatch shut above her.

Darkness. Pressure.

All around her, density grew as pumps packed the tank with more and more water. Twenty of these chambers lay between the ocean's surface and the floor below, and anyone who dared to travel so deep had no choice but to pause within every chamber and slowly acclimate themselves to the crushing pressures of the abyss.

These glass tunnels were known to the natives as *abnatrips*. The way stations were called *premingers*. Some of the abnatrips were equipped with premingers filled with air instead of water, but not many extraterrestrials dove into the abyss.

Extraterrestrial. Quillig said it meant one thing, but to Kieron it meant something very different.

The jellywoman waited until the light came. When the preminger had brought her to the appropriate pressure, a tiny, superbright light flashed overhead, and the hatch below automatically popped open. She swam through it and dove even deeper, and the deeper she got, the *closer* she got.

To her home.

And the admiral.

Admiral Govannon, with his cruel eyes and face of a thousand scars, an atlas of suffering he had inflicted on himself over his life, cutting himself over and over, the dense tissue having healed into a lattice of sickly powder blue. Like all of Kieron's people, his chest was outfitted with a bulky, brass contraption that sprouted a pair of tubes that fed into a mouthpiece. From a reservoir housed within the contraption, a black, O2-rich respiro-paste was pumped into the mouthpiece and from there to the lungs.

It was still the best way to breathe under the crushing pressure of so many thousands of fathoms.

But not for Admiral Govannon. No, instead of breathing through his mouth, the fearsome admiral breathed through his *eyes*, retrofitting his apparatus to feed in under his ocular nerves, which in turn made his icy green eyes bulge dangerously. All of Kieron's people had mostly solid black eyes—their pupils perpetually expanded to take in all light—but because of his leaky retrofitted apparatus, the admiral's pupils churned like grainy pools of black ink. The modification served the admiral's sense of theatricality; his mouth free, he was able to vomit forth his lungs' contents like a squid.

That was Kieron's last memory of the admiral—his mouth a geyser of black hatred, his hands carving out a profane farewell in their native undersea sign language.

"They'll never forgive you, general, for abandoning them in their darkest hour. Never, never, never, never, never. They'll never forgive you—I'll never forgive you, coward, for sullying this, my moment of triumph! Come back! Come back to me, Kieron! Come back!"

"Hey, jellywoman!"

The water faded. The abnatrip faded. The preminger faded.

The admiral faded.

She was sitting in the sidecar once again, staring at the map. She twisted her torso and looked at Quillig, who had just yelled at her.

"Pardons begged, sir. One moment."

Kieron focused on the map. If her eyes hadn't been replaced by oculars amidst her plastic coating, she would have squinted in concentration. A moment later, she pointed at the leftmost tunnel. Quillig revved the bike.

"Status on the race?"

The jellywoman gave the smart-scroll a shake, and the map of Penticton was replaced by the map of the racecourse. Hundreds of black dots sped along the coiling gray line that demarcated the mud tunnel, but there was something else. Midway along the racecourse, the thin gray line mushroomed into a short, wide, rectangle—some kind of holding cavern. A few of the black dots had already spilled into the cavern, where they scurried about.

"We're still ahead of the leaders," Kieron said. "There's some kind of bottleneck about a mile back."

"What?" Lady R sniped. "No '*sir*'?"

"S-Sir," Kieron added, stammering under the glare of the lady.

"You shut up," Quillig said to Lady R. Then to Kieron: "And you don't have to call me 'sir.' Let's hustle."

They rode into the leftmost tunnel, not noticing that the moment they left, someone entered the room behind them—one of the charred dregs they had left for dead. The remains of his denim overalls hung from his clavicles, which jutted from his chest. His ribs looked like a pair of ladders that crawled up his trunk. Webs of bloodveins crawled through the whites of his bulging eyes. The flesh on his left arm bubbled, then detached and slapped onto the floor.

From his pocket, he produced a thimble-sized pinch-syringe—a tiny packet of drugs capped with a needle. He jabbed the needle into his eye and squeezed, and his eye popped and burped white glop onto his cheek. That was the *downside* of the injection. The *upside* was that he started *thrumming*. Every muscle fiber on his body twitched a hundred times a second. He jittered across the floor like he was standing on an earthquake. The dreg was unaware that he had just passed an unseen and unknown endocrinological threshold that he had been inching toward for the last few years.

No longer a dreg, the newmade dreen took off down the tunnel in pursuit.

ELDRIDGE AND BORIS HAGAN

THEY PASSED ANOTHER PAIR of dregs who hunched on outcroppings of rock and held up smartboards that told them their new place: 12/335. Hagan smiled.

"Check the package!"

As they swooped around a curve in the tunnel, Eldridge popped open the strongbox and peeked in.

"We're good—*aaaaaaaaaaahhhhh!*"

They fell. The river rounded a corner and appeared to end, but instead of ending, it made an eighty-degree turn *down*. The waterboat hung in the air for a delirious moment. Hagan propped his feet on the dashbord, while Eldridge hung in the air vertically.

And the package fell out of the strongbox.

"Shit!" Hagan screamed. "Grab it! Grab it!"

Eldridge recalled the words of Marko Marinus, Narsyan.

"There are times in life we call 'one-chance moments.' You might be scaling the sides of the Oasis Mountains, and one of your fellow initiates falls. In that moment, you have only one chance at perfection. Typically, you might practice for hours, days, weeks to prepare for such a moment, but sometimes you only have those few fleeting instants to prepare. Understand this: That is enough time. If you are in balance and your mind is true, you can divine the one thing you must do to prevail."

They were falling vertically. When the thmart box fell out of the strongbox, it floated in space for a moment, and then started to fall downward. In those fleeting instants, Eldridge figured out what he had to do: he let go.

The redhead released the rope and sailed past Hagan, a mist of mud all around him. The cave faded into darkness far below. From Hagan's perspective, Eldridge was floating above the deck of the waterboat, but they were all falling faster and faster, and in the precise instant before the package's momentum would carry it beyond his reach, Eldridge plucked it out of the air and placed it back in the strongbox.

"Hages, hand me my rope, would ya?"

His feet still propped on the dashboard, Hagan leaned over and tossed the rope up to him. Eldridge grabbed it just as the boat finally slammed back onto the river's surface. Mud spewed through the boat's open grates as the hull sank underneath the river's surface for an instant before it bobbed back up, caught more air, and then finally settled on its way, all while still plummeting along the eighty-degree slope, which fell into a black hole. The redhead crashed to the deck, sliding back and forth on the layer of mud that covered everything. He pulled himself up to his feet just as the river finally flattened out and entered into a long, straight stretch. Another leaderboard flashed by and confirmed that they had climbed into tenth place.

"Hages!" Eldridge yelled. "Let me take over for a while."

"Not now! If I let loose of this wheel, we'll crash right into the wall."

He wasn't wrong. After their earlier mishap, Hagan had barely blinked, despite the onrush of mud. He stood in a constant, spraddle-legged crouch over the wheel, his forearms and knees trembling from the effort.

And that's when the waterboat gave way.

It split along the same fissure that had opened earlier—struts of metal catwalk sprang away from each other and opened a seam along the boat that began at one hexagonal vertex and split diagonally. The vertex lay at the front-left of the hexagon, and when the boat broke, it looked like a hexagonal head opening its mouth. The boat listed to the right. Hagan steered to back to the left, leaning into the turn. As he leaned, his knees started to quaver.

"Okay, *now* I need help!"

Eldridge dropped his rope and ran around to Hagan's left to pull on the wheel. The hexagon's mouth opened wider, and they started to spin in circles from the two sources of momentum—the front was moving forward, while the sundered rear was pushing them to port. Three racers passed them by as they continued to spin in place.

"Stop the fucking engines!" Eldridge yelled.

Hagan did. The spinning slowed. More racers passed. Eldridge ran to the split and dropped to his knees.

"Damn, shit, damn. Pell. Pell."

He held his head in hands. Hagan stepped over.

"El, it's okay. We'll find another way to save him."

Eldridge jumped up. *"How?"*

"What?"

"How will we save Pell? Stew?" He paused. "Oksie?"

"We'll get help."

"Help? *From who?* Who do I got left to ask? The dreenqueen? Milos isn't her king anymore. The Narsyans? They're fucking *gone,* and they wouldn't give a shit about Pell or Stew or Oksie anyway."

"You don't know that."

"Whoever their new leader is—" He broke off his own speech. His hand jumped to his cheek. He nodded, hard. "Yamuna. I remember her now. We were in the order. Back in the day."

More racers roared past and sprayed them with mud. They were spinning as fast as a second hand moves around a clock. Hagan folded his arms.

"This Yamuna. Do you think she'd help?"

The redhead made a dubious grunt. "When we took down Goldmist, we were only fighting him and the magnars, not a whole remnant. I don't know how Hanna controls her people or what that pinkeye shit is, but we'd have to kill a whole lot of innocents to save Pell, even *if* the Narsyans pitched in. Besides, she gave him the boot, Yamuna did. Do you really think she'd step up for him now?"

Hagan thought, then shook his head. "Nope."

"Okay, then let's cut off this boat's butt."

They got to work. Eldridge leaped across the churning mud river and ran to the back of the boat to grab the repair kit and propane torches. Eldridge handed one to Hagan, and they dropped to their knees and started cutting. As they worked, Hagan's hands shook.

"Watch it, old-timer," Eldridge said, smiling. "You're gonna melt my face off."

"Sorry," Hagan said, pausing for breath between syllables.

It took them ten minutes and cost them another twenty spots on the leaderboard, but finally, the back half of the boat fell into the river, and the hexagon was now an awkwardly slanting trapezoid. Eldridge stowed the repair kit inside the strongbox on top of the package. Hagan jumped up, but his knees buckled, and one of his ankles rolled. Eldridge touched his arm.

"Whoa there, buddy! Perfect time for me to take over."

"Not a chance, El. This thing's gonna be a bitch to handle, and I already know how she rides."

"You're about to fall over. Come on, let me—"

A ten-foot wave of mud drenched them. They didn't even see it coming, but one of the racers was piloting a pontoon boat equipped with a dozen internal-combustion outboard engines. They had passed him a few miles back.

The wave had knocked Hagan to his knees. Eldridge helped him to his feet.

"Break time, Hages."

Hagan nodded and fell back onto his rear, dislodging droplets of mud that rained from his hair. He clutched his chest.

"I'm sorry, El. The . . . the mortarchains. It . . . it—"

The redhead smiled. "Sorry, Bor! Can't talk now. I'm too busy trying to win this race."

Hagan grinned and closed his eyes. Eldridge took the wheel—and frowned. He felt a sudden urge to steer the boat into a wall. Boris Hagan grinned and gaped at him from the deck, mouthing the words *the mortarchains, the mortarchains* in endless, silent succession. That same dark chasm cracked across the redhead's mind and spewed forth unintelligible whispers. Without realizing it, he had allowed the boat to list to starboard. Reality shimmered back into focus, and he jerked the wheel back to port, but even when he aimed the boat straight ahead, it continued to drift.

Boris Hagan stirred and pointed aft.

"You'll have to knock some of them out. The scrubbers."

"On it."

The redhead disabled some of the boat's portside scrubbers with a propane torch. That done, he got behind the wheel and slowly eased forward on the throttle. The boat rotated counterclockwise before it started moving forward in a (nearly) straight line. A few more competitors passed them. The redhead eased forward on the throttle more and more.

It worked. The boat zoomed ahead, but only at half its previous top speed.

They both wrapped ropes around themselves, Eldridge standing behind the wheel, Hagan still seated. The old man thumbed his glasses into place and smiled.

"Good enough for government."

"Huh?" Eldridge asked.

"Nothing."

—⚍—

QUILLIG AND THE GREXTET

T*HEY'RE LIKE THE RINGS of a tree,* thought the bounty-merc. The three of them ran down a tunnel barely wide enough to admit their passage. The westernmost room of Penticton waited somewhere in the pitch darkness ahead. The narrow width of the tunnels had forced them to park their motorbike about twenty rooms back, and the three of them—Quillig, Kieron, and Lady R—had made the remainder of the journey at a hard run, blitzing up and down tunnels crusted with decades-old mud, the rooms having long since been abandoned. Kieron and Lady R both lit the way with their tech—Kieron with her wrist-mounted lighttorch, the Lady with her neckmount.

But back to the rings of trees.

The thought surprised him in the hallway of his mind. Quillig's usual mode of processing crucial decision points—the mental image of his avatar-self walking down a hallway full of doors—didn't always work according to his internal discipline. Sometimes those decision doors held *other* secrets hidden inside, and in this case, as he was considering the best way to take the redhead captive from the Mud Races course, one of his internal doors swung open and gave him view of a much, much younger version of himself—age six.

Or was I five?

Quillig the bounty-merc sat behind a desk in a classroom, surrounded by other children who all sat at small desks. Floor-to-ceiling picture windows composed the walls. Outside, the world was white because the sun filled the sky like it always did after Deadblast. But no heat entered the room. Instead of cooking in their seats, the children sat in a cool breeze that was pumped in through grates in the ceiling.

Their teacher stood at the front of the classroom in front of a dancing array of 3D electromorph props, one of which was the cross-section of a tree.

"If we look at the rings of a tree, we can learn a great deal about the past," their teacher said. He wore a white T-shirt, slacks, and a black jacket whose sleeves were capped with electromorph-sensitive gloves.

He indicated the rings. "This is three years ago. This is ten years ago. This—" he pointed in between those two rings, "—is when most of you were born."

Quillig raised his hand.

"Yes?" the teacher said.

"Which one of those rings is Deadblast?"

Desk legs screeched as Quillig became the epicenter of a circle of bare floor that suddenly appeared in the room. Quillig looked around at his receding classmates, his blue irises swimming in white and water—tears. His teacher hulked into view and laid his black hands on his desk.

"Lay your hands on your desk, please."

"What'd I say? What'd I say?"

One of his classmates spoke up. "He's new. He didn't know."

Glowing red slime filled the teacher's mouth and dribbled from the corners of his mouth in two bloody lines that dropped to the floor and pooled in expanding puddles.

"There are no first chances. No second chances."

The glowing fluid spread to his eyes, which flashed a bright red. He emanated heat and stench like a new street Quillig had ridden his bike across. The street had been gray one week, black the next. And the *smell*. The new pavement reeked a hot stench that made Quillig sneeze.

He sneezed in his teacher's face that day. The teacher reared back, slinging red fluid everywhere. That same instant, one of his classmates, a little girl with her hair in ringlets, leaned over, her eyes huge, her eyebrows steepled, her mouth drawn in terror.

"It's a *myth!*" she hissed before instantly snapping back into her seat, but alas, Quillig didn't hear her warning.

The teacher wiped Quillig's spit out of his eyes and flat-palmed his desk with both hands. His face filled Quillig's world.

"Lay your hands on your desk, please."

Quillig did, and the desk turned white. His palms felt cold at first, but as the moments ticked by, Quillig realized that his palms were on fire. He tried to lift them, but his flesh had melted to the surface. He opened his mouth to scream.

The teacher said, "Don't scream."

He didn't scream.

"Repeat after me," his teacher said. "Deadblast is a myth."

"Deadblast is a myth!"

"What's a myth?"

"Deadblast!"

"And why does the sun shine so hot?"

"Because *he* makes it shine hot!"

"When and why does he do this?"

"To *punish* us!"

"And why does he block the sun with clouds?"

His teacher pointed outside, where as if on cue, clouds rolled in and shrouded the land in cooling shadows.

"So we can go outside and enjoy the green!"

"And why does he warm the air at night?"

"So we can go outside and enjoy the green!"

Air rushed back into the room. Shoulders sloped forward as spines relaxed. A few of his classmates even ventured smiles. The glowing red fluid evaporated, and the teacher's face returned to normal.

"You may remove your hands from the desk now."

Quillig lifted a pair of shaking hands from his desk. He stared at the tops of his hands, not daring to turn them over. The teacher grabbed his hands and wrenched them upright. Lancets of pain shot up his forearms—but his palms were undamaged. The teacher released his hands and returned to the front of the room.

"In this classroom, we talk about *facts*. Not myths. If it's myths you want, you may discuss them with one of your three epochs, but remember, class: Take care not to disturb their nubis-periods. Because if you do, what might happen?"

The little girl with ringlets spoke. "We might run out of *us*."

"Very good, Yamuna. Now, let's turn our attention back to the lesson."

Quillig the child looked at the rings on the tree and peered into the past.

And then he was an adult again, his face covered in plaid, his body covered in Kevlar.

Kieron and Lady R flanked him as they sprinted through the last of Penticton's outermost rooms. As they progressed through the remnant's rooms and hallways, the walls and floors melted from stone to steel to brick to stucco. Some of the rooms were little more than pockets of air shored up with crumbling plywood. But still the tunnels led farther and farther on. The plaid-faced bounty-merc imagined Penticton as a giant tree, with concentric rings progressing outward, each ring made from a different material or alloy.

Finally, they scrambled down another connecting tunnel and emerged into a room with no doors. Quillig turned to Kieron, whose head jerked back and forth from within its plastic coating.

She gave a nod of confirmation.

"We're here, sir."

Quillig surveyed the room amidst the slanting flashes of his grextet's light-torches. A jumble of multicolored bricks (blacks, yellows, and blood-reds) covered the walls. Black dirt leaked through every crack in the mortar, while the ceiling hung a scant twelve inches over their heads. The floor was dark brown hardwood, the planks having long since faded into a rough matte finish.

"Gimme an X-poly, jellywoman," Quillig said, whereupon Kieron stepped forward, only to be met by the plaid-faced bounty-merc's outstretched palm. "You *do* know what an X-poly is, yes? They have 'em where . . . well, wherever it is you come from?"

"They do indeed, sir," she said, squatting on her haunches (her plastic coating made it impossible to kneel). She tapped a few buttons on her wrist. A black stylus popped out. She took it in hand and drew on the floor. Instead of ink, the stylus produced a luminescent black smartline that hovered a few centimeters above the floor. The jellywoman drew a rectangle, and then small circles at its corners. That done, she tapped the center of the rectangle with the stylus tip, which left behind a single dot that flash-expanded until it filled the shape.

The end result: they could see straight through to the mud tunnel.

Tiny smartcharacters danced along the edges of the X-poly, one of the older smart protocols. Stylus users could draw different polygons to achieve different results. A circle would produce a mirror, a small triangle would produce a basic command line (as long as it was accompanied by the drawing of a rectangle with the letters "qwerty"), while a rectangle with a dot would produce a low-level X-ray scan of the current view. The display wasn't as powerful as, say, Dr. Enki's symbioleech back in Dedrick, but for the three bounty-mercs, they didn't need detailed information—they just needed to know which way to *dig*.

"Make it happen," Quillig said.

Lady R dropped to her knees as her neckmount produced a pair of hotcutters. They sprayed forth a sparking laser that sliced out the section of floor around Kieron's X-poly. The floorboards dropped an inch onto something solid. Lady R removed the wood and revealed solid rock. Quillig cursed under his breath. Kieron stood and faced Quillig.

"Sir, I suggest we abort the plan as it stands. Let's withdraw and simply capture the principle once he leaves Hemming. We know he has to return to Penticton to retrieve his fallen comrade. There will be ample opportunities to capture him—"

Quillig's senses diverged. All sound vanished from the room, like an unseen hand had hit the *mute* button on existence. In the next instant, a white explosion flared from the center of the jellywoman's chest. She flew against the opposite wall and left an elliptical divot in the bricks, which silently rained down around her as she fell to her chest. Quillig turned around.

Just in time to see the mortarchains coming his way.

They emitted from Lady R's neckmount, which had produced three long spikes, two of which flanked her face, while the third rose above her head. Quillig's every muscle flared backward as the chains lifted him off the ground. His body hung in repose for a quiet moment, his arms spread and his legs bent behind him.

Sound roared back into his ears as he fell to his knees, hard. Pain shot up his legs and lightning licked around his body, casting the room in a flashing, flickering blood-red as the Lady extinguished her primary light-torch. She detached the three spires from her neckmount and assembled them into a single mortarchain module that she fastened to her wrist. The electro-crackling crimson mortarchains drew taut as Lady R reeled them in and dragged Quillig across the room on his knees. Quillig took hold of the chains and tried to pull them out of his chest, but his greatest effort only caused them to tighten their grip on his nervous system. He tried to reach for his own weapons, strapped to his waist, but the Lady held the mortarchain module above her head and took control of his arms like an ancient marionette.

"You ... fucking ..."

"There is no bounty, sweetie. You can admit it now."

Quillig's aperture narrowed. "There ... are *endless* stores of jenta to—"

"Let's be calm and candid. Drop the charade ... and drop the castle while you're at it."

He hesitated. She gave the chains a twitch, and he pulled the tiny castle from his pocket. He held it up in his quaking hand. She snatched it, stowed it in her dress, and kissed the air twice, taunting him with smooches.

"You're good, Quillie. He lives *across the oceans,* and you managed to piss him off. If I had to guess at the story, I'd say he blamed you for the escape on the Chain, and he wanted the Red Rook back. You catch Eldridge again, and he lets you live. Am I close?"

Quillig grunted. "You're close."

"Goody."

"But . . . *why?* Why capture *me?*"

She graced him with a white smile and shook her head. "Silly. There's a bounty on *you.* And since I don't want to get killed catching the Red Rook for jenta that doesn't exist, I'm bringing you out to Kirabo to claim my bounty, and then you're off to the Chain."

"Kirabo?! I've never even *been* there!"

A high-pitched *hiss* stuck a needle in Quillig's eardrum.

"Well, you're about to see it for the first and last time. Time. Time. Time. Time . . ."

Her arms dropped, and the mortarchain module clattered to the ground. The Lady's expression fell as her eyes rolled back to whites and a halo of light appeared around her head. Smoke rose from behind her. She fell to her knees and revealed Kieron, who stood behind her, wrist-cannon smoking, light-torch gleaming. Lady R collapsed to her back, her legs curled underneath. Kieron bent over and fiddled with the mortarchain module until they disengaged from Quillig and slurped back inside.

Quillig fell forward and caught himself with his palms, his breaths coming hard, fast, and ragged—like a tracheotomy patient hyperventilating. Kieron sat before him.

"Are you injured, sir? Try to control your breathing."

"She's . . . She's right. There's no bounty. And I'm dead in twenty-four hours if I can't get him to . . . Port Stafford."

"Then we shall bring him to Port Stafford in less than a day, sir."

Quillig looked up and narrowed his aperture on her.

"I treated you like shit. Why are you helping me?"

Kieron considered the question.

"I always had a difficult time making friends, even back home. When I . . . *emigrated* and became a bounty-merc, that task became even more difficult. A moment ago, when I regained consciousness, I thought about letting her take you away, but . . . you showed me a measure of respect earlier. For my *mensando*."

"But . . . the bounty. The man across the oceans isn't gonna pay me."

"Oh, I intend to be paid. I trust that you have your own jenta?"

Quillig's aperture narrowed around Kieron's face. He wondered if the jellywoman was smirking underneath all that plastic shit.

"Yeah."

"Then we shall work out a bounty between ourselves. May we agree that you are now in my debt, Mr. Quillig?"

Quillig's aperture expanded, then narrowed, then expanded again.

"We may."

"Then let's get to digging."

—⚟—

THE JELLYWOMAN ACTIVATED A wrist-mounted hotcutter and started to melt through the rock. Quillig adjusted some settings on her boltgun so that it could deliver periodic explosive bursts into the rock. It took them about half an hour, but finally, they broke through a thin layer of sandstone and revealed the mud river rushing by underneath. Quillig retrieved the tiny castle from Lady R's body, then lowered himself through the hole. Kieron struggled to insert her uncooperative limbs into the opening. Finally, her plastic coating took prehensile hold of the rock opening, and she began her descent.

But then she heard a voice.

"Ki . . . Kieron?"

She looked into Lady R's eyes. While they had worked, she had rolled onto her side, her legs splayed out behind her. Her eyes betrayed the glassed-over gape that the jellywoman well remembered from the scores of deep-sea drowning victims she had seen back in the day. She paused as Lady R took her last breaths.

"I'm sorry. Kieron. Sorry I was . . . so mean."

"I've never much trusted deathbed apologies, my lady."

Kieron started to climb down. Lady R rasped.

"Wait."

She stopped. "Yes?"

"Are there . . . *really* people on other planets?"

Deep within her plastic covering, Kieron's eyes brightened. "My lady, it may surprise you to know that *I* am from another world."

Lady R smiled.

"Wow."

Quillig's voice echoed from below. "Get a move on, jellywoman!"

Kieron started to climb down, but Lady R's voice stopped her one last time.

"Pssst," she said, her eyes twinkling.

"My lady, I need to be on my way."

"Wanna know a secret?"

She shrugged. "Certainly."

"*Let's go!*" Quillig called.

Lady R whispered, "There's a sectan confine in Hemming that hardly anyone knows about, not even Quillie." As life drained from her eyes, she said, "Look for the scars."

Kieron waited until Lady Ragnarok fell silent. Then she climbed down and left her buried in the deepest reaches of Penticton remnant.

—⚡—

ELDRIDGE AND BORIS HAGAN

THE RIVER HAD BECOME a lake.

The Mud Races were an effort undertaken with grudging cooperation among the chief lieutenants of both Lilya Hanna of Penticton and Walter Torsten of Hemming, and every few years, they concocted new obstacles for the racecourse itself, lest it become too easy to navigate. The undertaking of this presented formidable engineering challenges as it required them to dig deep into the earth and carve out a diabolical new curve or add a stomach-turning new drop. The year that Eldridge and Boris Hagan entered the races—and wound up rewriting its rules—the committee of designers added in a new twist: a *mystery*.

After they'd jettisoned the shattered rear end of the waterboat, Eldridge and Hagan rode along for another half hour. They inched their way back up the leaderboard, climbing back up into tenth place. That's when they reached the demolition derby.

The tunnel opened out onto a massive subterranean lake of mud that stretched for miles to the left and right, while a few hundred yards directly ahead, dozens of tunnels presented themselves for the racers to choose from.

Mayhem greeted them when they arrived. A pontoon boat and an airboat beset them and started carving circles around them in an effort to capsize Eldridge and Hagan with their wake. Still another jon boat outfitted with a kestrel drive zipped over and attacked them openly, its pilot chucking powerful firecrackers their way. Eldridge waited for an opening between the two circling boats and sped between them, the waterboat still nimble despite its reduced speed. The attacking boats apparently decided they weren't attractive enough prey and headed off to wreak other havoc. Eldridge surveyed the tunnels.

"Which one do we take?" he asked.

No answer came. Boris Hagan, still lashed to the deck, lay bent in two, his forehead hovering above his knees, his torso bobbing in tune with the boat's movements. Eldridge hadn't even notice the old man fall unconscious.

"Bor?!" he yelled, then thought, *Shit. On my own.*

He surveyed the cavern and saw some good news. By default, they had overtaken the leaders, because the great Tucker Beelzebub and Moondog didn't know which way to go, either. Their problem was compounded by the sheer size of their conveyances. On one end of the cavern, Tucker's barge-brick sat idling in place, while a half dozen of his crewmates rode around the cavern on single-person watercraft ("jetskis," Eldridge recalled) in search of the way out.

Meanwhile, Moondog's mechanical suprafeline was slightly better equipped to deal with the mystery. Eldridge looked to the opposite end of the cavern and saw the giant robotic cat scamper into one opening after another, only to return to the gigantic cavern, unsure of the proper course. More engines roared from behind, and Eldridge turned to see a dozen more competitors emerge into the cavern. He steered away from the entrance tunnel and started to survey the exit caves. *There's got to be a way to figure out which one's which.*

"Boris, old buddy, it sure would be nice to have your help right about now."

But Hagan continued to slumber. Panic dusted him like flakes of ash raining from above. Was there something wrong with Hagan? Had his heart given out somewhere along the course?

Fuck it. Eldridge parked the waterboat in one of the far corners of the cavern, and as wave after wave of mud made the mudcraft dance in place, he knelt over Hagan and lifted his head.

"Hages?! You all right?" No answer. Eldridge thought back to lessons he had received from Dr. Enki. He tucked his first two fingers underneath Hagan's chin and felt around for a heartbeat. At first he felt nothing, which sparked more panic, but then he felt a light throb against his fingers—and sighed. He lifted Hagan's head and yelled into his face. "Hages! You gotta wake up! You gotta—"

Fire surged up through the waterboat's grate floor like a hundred rectangular polyhedra of yellow light. The explosion blew Eldridge onto his back and sent him sliding aft along the now red-hot metal flooring. Hagan's ropes were instantly incinerated. A sphere of fire heaved the boat into the air, where it hung for a moment before it slapped back onto the river surface. Eldridge slid off the rear of the boat and grabbed onto the grating, his entire lower half submerged in mud. Hagan fell forward and came sliding toward the redhead on his chest. His flesh burning from the metal's sudden heat, Eldridge pulled himself onto the deck, landed on his side, and caught Hagan in his arms before he pitched headlong into the mud.

Wheezing, the redhead sat there for a moment, holding his friend and surveying the scene. Scores of competitors rode in circles around the cavern. Any one of them might have chucked an explosive their way, although the jon boat with the kestrel drive seemed the likeliest candidate. He spied it tearing back and forth across the cavern, the thrust from its drive a ribbon of white light streaking behind it.

"Son of a *macta*," Eldridge hissed as his boots sank under the mud. His legs jerked and kicked mud everywhere as the onrush of mud consumed the boat, which was sinking. He took hold of Hagan and climbed up to the front, which was still above the mud's surface. Chunks of the waterboat fell away and disappeared under the churning mud. Meanwhile, scores more competitors spilled into the cavern, all of them wondering which way to go.

"Gamma."

Another voice. Hagan's. Eldridge cradled him in his arms.

"Bor?!"

"Gamma," he said, his eyelids fluttering, his skin gray.

"What?"

"Hanna. Her brain was a gamma. That's the way out."

"A gamma? What? What the hell's a gamma?"

A wisp-smile passed across his face. "A letter. A . . . gamma. Looks. Like. An L. Upside. Down." Hagan made an L with his thumb and forefinger and held the upside-down figure against his chest for an instant before he fell unconscious again. The waterboat continued to sink. The engines were dead.

And the words of Marko Marinus, Narsyan, offered the redhead his only guidance.

"There exists no individual challenge that is impossible to overcome. But when seen as a single challenge, discrete challenges may well appear to be insurmountable. When you encounter such a scenario, take care to mind-divide the larger challenge into smaller ones."

Eldridge surveyed the scene. He and Hagan sat on the sinking waterboat, which was parked at one of the far ends of the cavern. Tucker Beelzebub's barge-brick sat on the opposite side of the cavern. Scores of other boats circled around in between. Moondog's suprafeline galloped in and out of caves, still baffled. The redhead scanned the caves. Most of them were too far away to properly examine, but one of them yawned a few yards ahead, and sure enough, carved into the rock over each cave was a single character. The cave nearest them was marked with a little table (Π). He couldn't see any of the other caves, much less the elusive gamma. But he was pretty sure no one *else* had figured it out. If someone did, it stood to reason that the other competitors would all follow that boat down the winning tunnel in one mass.

The waterboat continued to sink. He needed options. But Marko reminded him what he needed to do first.

Mind-divide the larger challenge into smaller ones.

They had to ditch the waterboat, but he couldn't leave Boris on the sinking ship. A quick scan of the surrounding walls revealed a small stone shelf. Eldridge removed Hagan's belt and lashed his friend's wrist to the deck. Hagan still slid to his back, but he remained above the mud-surface—for now. Eldridge jumped up to the controls and tried the throttle. Underneath, the shattered scrubbers screamed with effort. The remains of the waterboat crept toward the wall until the scrubbers finally sputtered into silence at the cavern's boundary. The waterboat bumped into the wall. Eldridge sprang at Hagan, unbound his wrist, and swept him into his arms. As the front of the waterboat went under, he ran off the prow of the boat, Hagan in his arms, and leapt onto the stone shelf, where he and his friend collapsed to the ground in a mass of muddy denim, corduroy, leather, and flesh. Eldridge propped up the unconscious Hagan against the wall and turned to see the boat's dashboard about to disappear. He jumped onto his chest and grabbed the boat's grating. His bicep locked in place and instantly turned to fire as he held the boat above the mud's surface long enough to pop open the strong box and retrieve the thmart box, which he slung onto the stone shelf. He released the boat. It slipped under the mud with a *slorp*.

We're gonna need a new boat. And a bigger one wouldn't hurt.

He stood, boatless, on a shelf in a cavern filled with mud set deep in the earth and watched the movement of the other competitors. Could he *swim* out to another boat and commandeer it? No way. The redhead trusted his Narsyan training, but they had never trained them to swim a mile through mud. Maybe he could jump onto one of the smaller boats if they passed close enough.

But maybe he didn't need a smaller boat. Maybe he didn't need a boat at all.

One of Tucker's crewmen was approaching on his jetski, no doubt scanning the exit caves for any sign of clues. Eldridge knew they didn't have much time before the other racers figured out Hanna's subtle riddle. He also didn't count on the jetskier to ride close enough to the cavern's boundary for him to make the jump.

Smaller challenges.

So he started climbing, his days high up in the Oasis Mountains riding back into his mind on gleaming mounts—*horses,* Hagan called them. He turned around and made a forty-inch flat-footed jump that lifted him high enough to grab hold of a swell in the rockface. Luckily, the dried mud on his hands had dried into a helpful crust.

As he climbed the wall of the gigantic mud cave, Eldridge looked back and figured that Marko had another reason for filching the chalk.

"Here, El. You can use it," Marko would say.

The image of a youthful, smiling Marko vanished. In its place stared Marko in the final moments of his life as he died among the remains of the Narsyan conventuary in his best friend's arms.

Eldridge slipped but found his grip. He kept climbing.

Engines roared around the cavern as he climbed. He craned his neck and checked over his shoulder. *Could they not see the fucking letters?* Eldridge thought. But maybe they could and simply hadn't cracked the code—the very simple, one-letter code that Hanna herself had provided. He continued his ascent, searching the rockside for another shelf or at least a convenient arrangement of rockswells where he could pause and get himself turned around.

He found none. But it turned out he didn't *need* one.

The stupid bastard stopped by the stone shelf (and directly underneath him) to peer at Boris Hagan. Eldridge peeked between his legs at the crewman, who wore plaid flannel and denim, along with a black domed helmet and a sidearm strapped to his belt. Eldridge let loose of the rockside and fell. He crashed onto the crewman's shoulders and drove him and the jetski under the mud's surface for an instant. The crewman revved the engines and blasted the jetski out of the mud and into the air. A column of mud-sludge sprayed skyward from the rear of the jetski as Eldridge rode it, hand hands curling around the crewman's neck. The crewman drew his sidearm, but the redhead's grabbed his wrist and held the barrel away from his face as they rode in a swerving circle around the far end of the cavern. A few gunshots fired harmlessly into the air. Eldridge dug his fingertips into the tendons of the crewman's wrist. The gun dropped into the mud. Eldridge returned his grip to the crewman's neck and squeezed while the crewman threw increasingly weaker and weaker punches until his arms fell limp. Eldridge sat on the seat behind him and shoved him into the mud. Panting, the redhead took control of the jetski and glanced over at where the crewman had fallen. He floated facedown in the mud. Eldridge looked away.

He rode over to the stone shelf where Hagan still lay alongside the package. He parked the jetski, set it to idle, and jumped onto the stone shelf, where he started to wrestle Hagan into his arms.

"El?"

The redhead stopped. Hagan's eyes were open.

"Hages? Can you move?"

"Where'sss . . . the boat?"

"Um, it kind of sank. I got us a new one!"

Hagan's head lolled over. "A jetski?"

"Yeah! Cool, huh?"

But Hagan shook his head. "Gas."

"Huh? C'mon, Hages, let's go."

"It's not hydrocell. We won't have enough gas to make it."

"We'll figure that out later. Let's go!"

Eldridge looped an arm under his friend's shoulder and hefted him to his feet. They staggered over to the jetski. On shaking legs, Hagan lowered himself on. Eldridge grabbed the thmart box, jumped behind the control, revved the engine, and took off into the cavern, which was still jammed with scores and scores of other boats large and small. He tucked the package between his legs. Tucker's barge was still idling on the far side of the cavern, while Moondog's suprafeline galloped past it, checking the other caves. The redhead slalomed around the other competitors, his eyes checking the special characters carved above the exit caves. Hagan moaned.

"Gamma."

"You got that right, old buddy."

And there it was. Not a hundred meters away was an exit cave that bore an upside-down L over it; the ancient character gamma: Γ. The redhead didn't want to attract too much attention, so he watched the competitors for a moment, trying to determine if anyone was watching them. Various packs of boats rode around the cavern, grouped in twos and threes, checking the caves. But none appeared to be checking the gamma cave. Eldridge eased back on the jetski's throttle, and as he rode into the cave, he disengaged the engines and let the jetski coast into the darkness. When they had proceeded far enough, he reactivated the engines and sped down the cave.

That's when the alarm sounded.

When he had ridden a certain distance into the gamma cave, an array of lights on the ceiling flared to life, blinding him momentarily and revealing two sets of micromag-equipped bleachers that floated over the racecourse, all of them packed with dregs who cheered when they saw Eldridge and Hagan. Another dreg held up the leaderboard, which read: 1/335.

The redhead smiled and revved the engines just as an alarm sounded in the cavern behind and alerted the other racers to the solution. Eldridge looked over his shoulder and saw a dozen boats converge on the gamma cave and crash together into a mass of outboard engines, metal, and wood and lodged in the cave entrance—until the barge-brick arrived.

Tucker Beelzebub's barge-brick smashed through the wreckage and thundered up the river toward them.

"Holy *Cromshit*," Eldridge muttered as he wheeled the jetski around and took off down the tunnel.

QUILLIG AND THE GREXTET

"THEY'RE MOVING, SIR."

KIERON unfurled the smartscroll and indicated the mass of black dots headed their way. After burrowing down from Penticton's westernmost room, they had climbed down onto a stone shelf that stood about twenty meters above and ten meters removed from the racecourse. Various stalagmites, stalactites, and other rock formations provided cover as they crouched and consulted the map by the glow of Kieron's light-torch and a single, exposed, dangling light bulb. For the last half hour, all of the racers had been bottlenecked, but in the last few moments, they had apparently triumphed over whatever had blocked their path.

Quillig examined the racers and found his eyes drawn toward the activity of the two leaders. The black dot in the lead danced around the racecourse like a gnat, darting from one side of the tunnel to the other; while the competitor in second place appeared to be piloting something much larger and heavier. It had a higher top speed than the one in the lead, but it took much longer for it to accelerate, decelerate, and change course. The plaid-faced man tapped the leading black dot.

"You wanna make odds that's the redhead?"

"I don't make odds, sir."

Quillig suppressed a sigh. "You don't have to call me 'sir.' But if you *did* make odds?"

"I'd wager that is he."

"All right. Let's get expo."

Their hands moved in a blur, a flurry of action. Kieron extinguished her light-torch and primed her weapons and mortarchain. Quillig double-fisted his boltgun and mortarchain rifle.

An engine echoed. They sprang to their feet and looked down the tunnel.

Kieron reduced the gain on her speechmouth and said, "The young lad said that the redhead would be piloting a hexagonal mudcraft, not unlike a section of catwalk."

"I know. Shut up. Listen, I lost my binocular-module a while back. Do you have some long-range specs in all that goop?"

"Yes, sir—I mean, yes," Kieron said, tapping out a series of commands on the side of her head. The oculars wedged deep in her gel became opaque red. "Currently scanning the oncoming tunnel in infrared."

"When you spot him, we'll climb down into position."

"Understood."

The tunnel started to rumble as the approaching engines roared louder and louder. Kieron kept her oculars trained on the darkness. Quillig shifted from one foot to the other.

"Well? Do you see him?"

"I see nothing yet—wait. I see the leaders. The first is . . . a small mudcraft. Like an aquatic motorcycle. Two-seater. Not the redhead. Immediately behind is a much larger mudcraft."

"The redhead's not in the lead? Do you see anyone else?"

The third-place competitor hasn't come into my view yet, sir. Here come the leaders now."

Sure enough, the aquatic equivalent of a motorcycle came tearing out of the darkness, bearing two men—one with white hair, the other with darker hair. Quillig looked past the aquabike and peered into the darkness, which had started to growl in anticipation of the second-place competitor.

An internal door opened. His mind said: *Red.*

Quillig dropped his weapons as the message arrived from within. He leapt onto some rocks and opened his aperture to take in all the cave's light, and when he saw the two men on the aquabike, he screamed, *"Fuuuuuuuuck!"* loud enough to cause the man driving the aquabike—the one in front, the one whose hair wasn't so much *darker* as it was *redder*, the one who had earned the suck-my-macta nickname *the Red Rook*, the one who had eluded him *again*—to glancce over his shoulder at the source of the noise.

But Eldridge saw nothing and simply rode away.

Standing in full view on the rocky promontory, Quillig balled his fists and wailed. He continued to wail even when the second-place competitor—a gigantic barge—exploded into the tunnel and knocked him onto his back. He lay on the ground screaming at the sky buried high above, his mental doors iterating and permutating, slamming open and shut, each one holding back a different flood; some doors held fire, others held water, others snow, others earth. He remembered the satisfaction he got when he delivered Eldridge to Jeb Goldmist, and he remembered the embarrassment he felt when he heard that the redhead had destroyed the mighty Odd days later.

Another door opened. And his stitches popped off.

They were the stitches that held the patch of plaid fabric to his face. Quillig was standing in the remnant of Glaucio, six years ago, watching the drunk redhead carouse on a bartop in a saloon so ancient that it supposedly predated Deadblast. Deep-dark finished wood composed the bar. A yellowing mirror hung behind the bar, its glass having warped over the years so that it reflected a wobbly, pulsating version of the redhead as he took shots from a bottle of priceless whiskey; whiskey he had bought with jenta won from Glaucio's then-reigning Odd, Walter Torsten. Torsten had paid Quillig to capture and bring in the redhead, even though the redhead hadn't broken any rules. He had made his odds with Torsten, they balanced, and the redhead prevailed.

All the same, Torsten snorted his trox and demanded the redhead's red head.

But when Quillig approached him that night in Glaucio years ago, he had balked at using his mortarchain rifle, instead simply yelling at the redhead to get down off the bar and come with him. In response, the redhead had dropped to his knees and patted him on the shoulder.

"Let's see what'cha really look like under there, pal!"

It didn't happen all at once. Drunk, the redhead had to fumble his fingers in between the stitches to get a grip, and when he pulled, the stitches popped out one by one. Quillig used both hands to grab the redhead's forearm, but the son of a macta was just too fucking *strong*. The whole process took ten seconds, which gave the rest of the dregs at the bar plenty of time to turn and watch Quillig's fleshless, post-dreen face come into view. When Eldridge was done, he dropped the fabric on the bartop and stared at Quillig, his drunk smile slowly fading. Everyone else in the bar was starting to turn away—when Quillig started to scream.

Only he didn't scream so much as *squeal*. The sound rose from his gorge and gurgled in the back of his throat before it escaped his mouth as a keening bleat; the same helpless *waaah* that an infant might make when vexed. He stood in that bar and bawled tears he couldn't shed, so very sure he was that his face—fleshless, exposed, dark red muscle tissue with a black cartridge where his eyes should have been—would horrify the crowd of onlookers.

But no one gave a shit, all of them having witnessed far greater horrors in the post-Deadblast world.

They did, however, find him *hilarious*.

The laughs came quick, like a clown had just de-pants'ed himself for all to see. Fingers jabbed and jeers flew his way, all while the redhead watched his humiliation from his knees atop the bar.

Quillig snatched up his plaid fabric and left Glaucio that night, and from that day forward, the rumortrysts became one of his archnemeses. They said the redhead defeated him in single combat on that bar. They said the redhead kept that original patch of plaid as a trophy. They said Quillig lived in terror that the redhead would return and kill him for all to see.

They said. They said.

The roar of engines returned to his ears. He was still lying on the stone shelf high above the mud river. Kieron stood over him. He sat up, head hung, then climbed to his feet and turned to Kieron.

"Sir?"

"You—"

Vision blanked, sound tripled. The rock floor rushed up and slammed into his ear as *arms* closed around him; arms capped with scrabbling, scraping, clawing talons that attacked his neck. And the sound. Screeches emitted from seemingly a dozen different voices, all at different registers, including those just above and below human hearing. Heat. Steaming body heat pressed against him, bathed in putrid stenches from a hundred different sources and different glands. Sweat. Insulin. Serotonin.

And dopamine. Lots and lots of *dopamine*.

When the dreen struck, it fell from above and knocked Quillig's weapons to the ground. In his peripheral vision, Kieron reared back and tried to get a bead on the creature with his wrist-cannons, but they rolled over so that Quillig blocked her shot. The plaid-faced man felt his boltgun underneath him. He tucked his knees against his chest and pressed his feet into the dreen's stomach, and as he pushed him away, he recognized the creature as one of the poor dregs that Lady R had burned to death earlier.

Ragnarok, you macta.

Holding the dreen at leg's length, he reached underneath himself, yanked the boltgun free, and wedged the barrel under its chin—just as its head exploded. Boats sped down the river below. The creature fell back, and Kieron leaned over.

"Let me help you up—"

"*No! It's not dead y—*"

No, it wasn't dead. Shoot a dreen in the head, and it'd keep coming. Shoot a dreen in the heart, and it'd keep coming. Shoot them both, and you had a dead dreen.

Headless, the creature bounded to its feet and whipped back and forth. Countless hypothecaries and rumortrysts speculated on how a headless dreen processed sensory input. Was it some kind of sonar? An enhanced sense of touch? A sixth form of perception unknown to normal dregs? Quillig remembered very little from his time as a dreen—just intermittent flashes—but he knew that it only took a headless dreen a few moments to reorient itself before it struck again.

Quillig yelled, "Shoot it in the—" But his words vanished into the clamor of a giant robotic cat that sprinted down the river. Kieron wavered above him. Quillig jumped to his feet, but it was too late. The dreen lurched forward, grabbed him around the neck, and drove him back over the rock shelf. They fell, skidding and sliding together all the way down to the mud river, which by that time was packed with racing boats.

Waves of mud slapped against the shore as Quillig and the dreen rolled down a rocky embankment, dislodging an avalanche of small stones as they fell. They came to rest by the riverside just as an airboat motored past and showered them with mud. Quillig wrestled the dreen to a standstill—both of them on their knees, facing each other, hands around each others' necks. Quillig faced upriver, and he spotted an oncoming jon boat with an array of outboard motors. Arms screaming from the effort, he held the dreen in place until the boat was close enough, and then he shoved the creature into the mud, hoping to hell the thing would get tangled in the motor's propeller.

Unfortunately, the dreen had a pretty good grip.

A wave of mud enveloped him and carried him downriver. The dreen fell out of his grasp and floated away to who-knew-where. Quillig swallowed a mouthful of mud and choked. He flailed his arms, thinking back to the swimming lessons he received as a child, but the lazy days he had spent paddling around clean blue swimming pools hadn't prepared him to swim through thousands of gallons of gritty, shit-tasting sludge. There was enough water in the mix to keep him afloat, but his flailing limbs barely did anything to carry him toward the surface. All the same, he managed to get his head above-mud for a brief moment when he gulped a few breaths—right before the pontoon of a passing boat struck his head and turned the world into starless night.

THE JELLYWOMAN WATCHED QUILLIG and the dreen roll down the embankment into the river. Quillig and the Lady had warned of the risks inherent in disturbing a major event like this, but then again, they had both been lying at the time. So she cast aside her doubt and lightly pinched the webbing between her thumb and forefinger. In response, her foot-rockets ignited and carried her over the rock shelf that had provided their cover. Looking back, some of the competitors in the

Mud Races of '04 would say that as they neared the finish line, they saw a woman encased in plastic hovering over the racecourse.

But Kieron could do more than hover. She could *fly*.

She wasn't *good* at it, by any means, but she could scoot along just fine, using an ongoing, hydrocell-powered surge from her wrist-cannons as stabilizers. The jellywoman soared through the cave tunnel, scanning the river for Quillig and the dreen, which could apparently survive decapitation. What had Quillig been trying to tell her? That it was still alive? How exactly did one kill a dreen? Kieron figured that both the brain and the heart had to be neutralized. She shook her head.

How can I know so little when others know so much?

Simple: she wasn't *from* here. She wasn't from Penticton, she wasn't from Hemming, and she wasn't from anywhere in between. There weren't any dreens where she was from. There wasn't a Chain of Tears.

There weren't spectramps that turned the world white.

Kieron had been fretting over the mishap since it happened. She'd used the device to track enemy scouts and incursions into friendly waters for more than a decade. When she'd activated the device *back home*, the device emitted nothing more than a faint blip of light. More to the point, the device also *worked* back home, dramatically enhancing a target's trail instead of extinguishing it as it did here.

Because you were underwater, she thought more than a year later as she flew over a river of mud, searching for Quillig. *Here, above water, the device's function is completely different.*

She spotted Quillig. The river coiled around a column of stone, and right before the turn, Quillig's head bobbed above the surface just in time for a passing boat to smash it. The plaid-faced man vanished under the brown waves. Kieron adjusted her trajectory downward, dodged around an airboat, and plunged into the mud. When she was submerged, her senses came alive, even in mud. Deep within her plastic coating, her oculars—two flat disks that sat wedged in her eye sockets—retracted and exposed her natural eyes, which glittered like a pair of black gemstones, their surfaces nothing but solid pupil, naturally selected to absorb all possible light. Months ago, when Kieron had cut the deal with the deep-desert sawbones to encase her in plastic, she had been forced to wear two-inch-thick sunshades over her eyes. The sunshades would appear to be opaque to a surface-dwelling dreg, but they weren't, having been specially crafted by Kieron's people to make it possible for them to move about among extraterrestrials.

But now that the jellywoman rocketted through a river of mud, her superpupils gave her the ability to see *everything*. The details of the riverbottom stretched out before her and revealed the details of man-made engineering—multicolored bricks and tiles lined the river floor and depicted various landscapes and images from times past. Men and women stood on pixilated cliffsides and pointed at sunsets that were apparently safe to look at. (Kieron at least knew that much; that for anyone not encased in plastic, the days and nights were equally treacherous.) Every few hundred meters, the word SEWER passed underneath her.

She looked up and saw she had lost ground on Quillig, who was still somersaulting through the river, unconscious and helpless before the river's current.

Despite the setback, Kieron smiled, though not at the situation. She smiled at the *sight*. None of her kindred choose to visit the surface realm encased in plastic as she had. No, most of them ascended through the network of abnatrips to the ocean's surface wearing nothing more than their O-paste tanks, which they kept strapped to their chests. Once they reached land, they removed the tanks and retched the O2-rich respiro-paste out of their lungs and went about their business. Some of them visited the surface as a part of a coming-of-age tradition that allowed her people to visit the surface to see if they wanted to stay. Few did. Still others actually had business on the surface, high up in the mountains to the west, where an ancient order, the Narsyans, had tasked Kieron's people to engineer the most powerful hallucinogenic substance ever devised.

They gave the credulous extraterrestrials harmless dried seaweed in exchange for periodic deliveries of the Narsyans' food, which was the deadliest poison ever seen among Kieron's people. Somehow the Narsyans were able to eat it, but for Kieron's scientists, it was the deadliest biological agent they'd ever seen.

Which was exactly why Kieron had demanded they acquire every last drop of it. They weren't a warring people, Kieron's clan, but all the same, they had been engaged in an undersea war with a rival faction— led by Admiral Govannon—for the last generation. Kieron herself called upon all willing souls to defend their waters. She herself had led the resistance against Admiral Govannon's navy, the Ivory Armada. But no matter how brutal the warfare, she steadfastly refused to make use of the deadly bioagent.

"To use this weapon runs counter to every ethic we hold dear," she told her people's high assembly. "Let the extraterrestrials use it if they choose. We won't. I won't."

And she didn't. Not even when the tides of war turned against her. Not even when Admiral Govannon's Ivory Armada breached the Downtide Frontier. Not even when New Chattanooga fell.

Not even when her people begged her to use it did she relent.

"If I did, the cost would be too much, from so many," she thundered at the assembly. "If I did, we would cease to be *us*."

But later, Kieron abandoned the cause. So she wound up among the extraterrestrials.

As she watched Quillig, imperfections wove through her plastic coating and distorted the world. Her oculars corrected for it, but while they were retracted, the world shimmered before him. Just like she was underwater.

Quillig was close. Boat-wake churned through the water overhead like faraway mountain ranges surging in and out of existence, all of them capped with snow. Kieron barrel-rolled deeper to avoid any passing propellers and juiced her foot-rockets for more speed. She zoomed through the mud, dodging the occasional chunk of debris—a stray chunk of shattered hull, a guardrail, entire engines that hemorrhaged billowing black clouds of oil—an image that stirred old memories inside the jellywoman. Memories of a battlefield. Memories of a war still raging far, far away.

The jellywoman hadn't been keeping track of the time. She had no idea if Quillig would still be alive when she found him.

She also still hadn't seen the dreen.

No matter: she accelerated and zoomed through the water toward her quarry, which grew larger and larger in her shimmering view. Overhead, two boats collided. A blinding hemisphere of orange light flash-expanded into the mud and drove Quillig deeper. Kieron course-corrected around the explosion, then juked left and right around the remains of what appeared to be a giant, steel spinal-column.

Quillig, his plaid-fabric dangling from his face, came rushing into view and into her arms.

Speed was the need. Kieron pumped her foot-rockets and carried the plaid-faced man to the river's surface. The jellywoman exploded through the surface, raining a trail of mud behind them. The sludge beaded away from Kieron's plastic suit in a few brief moments, but Quillig hung heavy in her arms, his clothes soaked through with the shit. Kieron squinted into the dim light of the cave and reactivated her oculars. The extraterrestrial world returned to normal. She sighed—just in time to get her picture taken.

Lights flashed from everywhere. Despite her protective oculars, Kieron blinked and reduced speed. When her eyes adjusted, she realized that the tunnel had spilled into a gigantic *mouth.*

She flew into a room hundreds of feet high and wider than she could see. High above, a ceiling constructed of some kind of plaster or stucco arched over the scene—the roof of the gigantic mouth, but in color, it was a tertiary rainbow of beiges and dark browns. Underneath, hundreds of city blocks stretched into the distance, the entire city broken up by the rises and falls of hillocks and mountains.

All of that lay beyond. Immediately before Kieron hovered hundreds of bleachers, all of them packed with cheering dregs. A banner lined with black and white flowers arranged in an alternating pattern hung over the river. It read FINISH LINE! WELCOME TO HEMMING! The flashing lights were the work of dregs packing smartscopes that could capture images for printout or hardline delivery. With Quillig in her arms, Kieron descended to the riverside, where thousands more dregs congregated and cheered.

The jellywoman laid Quillig on the sandstone riverside under the shadow of bleachers. The patch of plaid fabric had been partway torn off. It lay folded over, exposing one-quarter of his ruined face. Kieron sat down and immediately set about reviving him. Dregs gathered around the unusual sight—a woman encased in plastic, and another covered in mud, both of them having just emerged from the racecourse. Threads of panic settled over Kieron as she unwound a tube from her wrist and fed it into Quillig's windpipe. She activated the pump buried within her plastic. The tube turned brown as she sucked mud out of her fellow bounty-merc's lungs.

"What happened there, mister?" one mustachioed dreg asked. Kieron looked up into the eyes of a dreg clad in denim and leather. He wore a denim shirt with ruffled sleevecuffs and leather pants. On his head sat a white, rimmed leather hat big enough to hold ten gallons of water. A leather belt hung from his waist on a diagonal slant, bearing a holstered revolver-pistol. Dozens more dregs, mostly children, crowded around the scene, waving their fingers and chattering.

"Wow!"

"Who's that?"

One of them poked Kieron's plastic coating. "Is this your race suit?" Mr. Ten Gallon held them back.

"Hold on now, young'uns! We got a man down!" He addressed Kieron. "Anything I can do ya for, ma'am?"

"No, thank you," Kieron said, inaudible because the gain on her speechmouth was still so low. She accidentally increased it too much and barked, *"No, thank you, sir!"*

Eyes bulged all around her. The kids scuttled backward, whimpering. Ten Gallon chuckled.

"Mighty good trick you got there. Them littlefolk don't know better'n to crowd around a dying man. How's he doin'?"

Kieron's pumps drained the last of the mud from Quillig's lungs. That done, she tapped a few buttons on her wrist and produced a small triangular module that she set on top of Quillig's heart, while simultaneously, she adjusted the pump so it started feeding air *into* his lungs instead. The heart module beeped and delivered a charge into Quillig's chest. Nothing.

"Oh, dear," Kieron said, still too loud.

Ten Gallon said, "I seen me some drowning cases in the races before. Ain't a pretty way to die, suffocatin' on mud."

The heart module beeped a second time, and Quillig lurched upright, projectile-puking one last chestful of sludge. He sat, chest heaving, mud dribbling down his chin, his plaid mask askew, his sight-aperture *whirring* open and shut while his whole system rebooted. He looked over at Kieron, who patted him on the back.

"Sir! We've arrived in Hemming!"

Ten Gallon extended his hand. Quillig's arm floated up and offered a handshake as firm as an earthworm. Ten Gallon tipped his hat and smiled.

"Name's Mack. Yer cohort, the lady here in her fine attire, did you right just now. Brought you back from the beyond, lickity-split. And you fellas is just in time. They's announcin' the winners."

Still panting, Quillig shifted his weight around and watched. Mania swept the crowd, both at the sight of the winning racers, but moreso at the sight of the remnant's reigning Odd, Walter Torsten, who was making his way through the crowd on a wave of backslaps and attaboys. Joyful voices heralded his arrival:

"It's him! It's him!"

"Ohmigod, Walter, please touch me! *Pleeeease!*"

"Walter! Marry me!"

"No, marry *me!*"

He emerged from the crowd—the torso and head of a man, the arms and legs of a robot. His human half wore a tuxedo, his cybernetic half nothing. At the riverside, he whirled around to face the crowd and spread his arms. More cheers. A trixie jumped out of the crowd and shoved a thousand-count bouquet of black and white flowers in his arms. The flowers seemed to give him the ability to fly, because as soon as his face disappeared behind them, he floated up to the deck of Tucker Beelzebub's barge-brick, which floated at the end of the Mud River. An arch of micromag-equipped bleachers formed a winner's circle.

But Tucker Beelzebub wasn't standing on his boat.

Eldridge was.

He stood on the deck of the barge-brick alongside his white-haired friend and waved at the crowd with a bloody hand. The head of Moondog's suprafeline sat on the deck beside him. Mack slapped his knee and hooted.

"Them boys done rewrote the rule book, boostin' a boat in the middle of the race. What do y'all think about—"

Behind Mack, the river expelled a mud monster. It began as a bubble of mud that popped and spat forth a humanoid creature that rained sheets of mud as it flew through the air toward them, strangely silent.

The mud monster spun in the air, head over heels, and landed on its back before them, where they all saw that it *had* no head. Kieron didn't even hear the shot. Mack simply slid his smoking gun back into its holster and marveled at the sight on the ground. The rest of the crowd continued to cheer on the winners.

"Whee-oo! Lucky I got me a heart-shot just then! They usually roust alla them thangs from the course before the race. Musta missed one. Heck, I remember me the Mud Races of '67. Now *that* was a helluva year..."

While Mack talked, Quillig had plucked his revolver out of its holster. Still sitting, he shot Mack in the heart. No one even heard the shot over the cheering of the crowd. Mack crumpled to his knees, wheezing and clutching at his chest as tears streamed from his eyes. Quillig fired another round into the center of his forehead. Mack's head rocked back, and then he fell onto his chest, dead.

"Sir!" Kieron exclaimed.

Quillig spun and rammed the pistol into Kieron's speechmouth, crushing it, and with the revolver lodged deep in the jellywoman's plastic covering, he pulled the trigger. Speechmouth-shrapnel burst from Kieron's face as she fell backward, trailing a plume of black smoke.

The bounty-merc stood, gun in hand. He touched his face and found it exposed. He fumbled with the plaid fabric for a moment, trying to secure it in place, but he gave up and simply held it in place with his hand as he disappeared into the cheering crowd.

—⚜—

ELDRIDGE AND BORIS HAGAN

Back in the day, Eldridge had worked as a moto-express carrier, delivering hard copies of messages from one remnant to another. Such work demanded extensive aboveground travel, which any inhabitant of the post-Deadblast world knew held countless dangers—dreen attacks, hordes of outlaws, freaky deep-desert psychos, and of course the ongoing challenge of dealing with the elements. Eldridge had once moto-expressed a letter from a comely young woman in the remnant of Bainsbridge to a wiry, bug-eyed dude in the remnant of Doughty some twenty leagues to the south. As he rode his old hydro-cell-powered motorbike down the wide wooden ramp that led out of Doughty (which stood on stilts), a gigantic truck—easily twice the size of Quillig's big rig and trailing an ancient flatbed that still bore a tatted old banner that read OVERSIZE LOAD— screamed down the ramp in pursuit with the bug-eyed guy at the wheel. Looking back, the narrative had been obvious to Boris Hagan, who seemed to know everything.

"You delivered her 'Dear Jack' letter to him, El," Hagan had said.

Regardless of why the letter upset him so, the spurned lover from Doughty remnant chased Eldridge into the desert for hundreds of miles, his wide-load truck always inches behind him, the heat of its huge internal-combuster engines radiating a sphere of swelter that made Eldridge sweat despite his bike's cooling mechanism.

That's what the final stages of the Mud Races *physically* felt like for the redhead as he sped through the tunnel, his purloined jetski kicking up a pair of brown waves in its wake, all while Tucker Beelzebub's barge-brick dominated his mental rearview, the prow of the twenty-foot-tall brick slicing through the mud's surface a few treacherous inches behind. Somewhere behind Tucker, Eldridge could hear the clanking charge of Moondog's suprafeline as it galloped along in third place and looked for a way to bound into the lead. That's what it *felt* like.

Psychologically, however, the race presented far different challenges. When the spurned lover from Doughty had chased him into the desert, youth and hydrogen kept the redhead cocky as he rode in circles around the wide-load truck. The redhead had already retrofitted his bike with a hydrocell, so he could ride on until the heat-death of the universe. The spurned lover's truck ran on plain old gasoline, and Eldridge knew he just had to outlast him. Not so in the Mud Races, as the jetski's fuel gauge was already tipping toward E.

He also didn't have an ailing friend along for the ride back then. Boris Hagan's head rested against his back, where Eldridge could feel a triplet of aching sores from where Quillig had implanted his mortar-chains. He felt analogous sores on his chest, and if the redhead with all of his Narsyan strength, training, and fortitude could feel that pain, he blanched when he considered how Hagan must be feeling.

Crunch! The thoughts vanished for a moment as the barge-brick slammed into the rear of the jetski and broke off a chunk. His hand leapt between his legs to secure the thmart box in place. The jetski threatened to fishtail out from behind him, but the redhead maintained his grip and steered around a turn in the river that opened into a straightaway. A flickering light bulb hung from the ceiling and cast an intermittent, sickly yellow glow. The redhead gained some leadway on Tucker as he accelerated down the straightaway and passed under the light bulb.

Red on the right.

But it wasn't red. It was *blue*. Something blue flashed in the redhead's peripheral vision. He had spotted it high up a rocky embankment to the right of the river. Something blue . . . and something that *glistened*, both of them near a column of light that shone down through the stone ceiling. The sensory input struck receptors in the redhead's memory, but the connections weren't quite strong enough to close any circuits. Electricity hummed in his head, but the exigencies of the race silenced it.

Although he was quite sure he heard someone yell the word *fuck*.

Boris Hagan's grip loosened. Soon after they had solved the mystery of Lilya Hanna's riddle-chamber, Eldridge had instructed him to wrap his arms around his waist and clasp his palms together.

"Don't twine your fingers, Bor. You'll just get sweaty and lose your grip. Press your palms together and hold on as tight as you can."

His white-haired old friend did, and for the first few miles after they used the ancient character *gamma* to take the lead in the race, Hagan had held on just fine. His head snapped up periodically as he kept nodding off in spite of the circumstances and surroundings.

They passed another leaderboard that again confirmed their first-place status, but this one also offered other news: they were almost there. As before, a pair of dregs held up smartboards that displayed their place in the race, but a third dreg held up a smartboard that said 2 MILES TO FINISH. Incredible. How far was it from Penticton to Hemming again? Whatever. They zoomed between the dregs and another few bleacher-sets of cheering dregs and raced on. Eldridge checked his fuel gauge and dared a glance over his shoulder. The barge-brick grumbled louder as it increased speed and crept up behind them, while the suprafeline had taken advantage of the widening tunnel and climbed up the side of the tunnel until it galloped along the ceiling, its head a few yards above the barge-brick's main deck. Upside down, Moondog's master creation glared at Eldridge with spectral green eyes and gnashing steel fangs that chomped in tune with the rest of its workings.

The redhead chuckled, both at the theatricality of Moondog's conveyance and at the idea that had knocked on his mind's door and asked to come in.

Knock, knock.
Eldridge answers the door. It's the idea.
"Hi," Eldridge says.
"May I come it?" the idea asks with a wink.
"Sure," Eldridge said. He admits the idea, who immediately flops down on an easy chair in his mind's habitat. Eldridge says, "I don't remember inviting you."
"That's because you're a dumbshit. You know it's the only way."
"I can't do it."
"Remember what Marko Marinus said. 'There exists no challenge.'"
Yep, the idea is his old friend Marko, returned in his mind as Eldridge would have liked to remember him. Instead of looking like a grotesque anatomical diagram of muscle and sinew, good ol' Marko simply looks like he works out a lot.
"I work out a lot," Marko says.
"Me too."
"So why don't you do it? All you'll need to do is carry him."
Eldridge nods. "A fireman's carry."
Marko smiles. "A fireman's carry. And remember . . ."
They speak as one: "Maintain the rage."

The redhead returned to the race in time to see that they were a mere mile and a half away from Hemming and the finish line. The jetski lurched and brought his eyes down to the fuel gauge, the needle of which was bouncing on the E. Their speed dropped by a quarter.

Maintain the rage.

He wrenched the handlebars to port and flipped a U-turn around the barge-brick. If he had been a little more conscious, Boris Hagan might've said he "flipped a bitch." The jetski zipped down the narrow strip of mud-river that ran alongside the barge. Tucker must've seen the maneuver, because the barge smashed into the side of the tunnel just as the jetski passed by. Eldridge flipped *another* U-turn and twisted the accelerator. With its final combustible fumes, the jetski blasted forward and eased up behind the barge-brick.

But Eldridge wasn't concerned about the barge. Not yet. He was too busy chuckling at the aforementioned theatricality of Moondog's suprafeline. In an effort to intimidate his opponents, Moondog had sought to recreate every detail of the fearsome mountain creature as a metallic monstrosity. It had eyes, it had fangs, it had claws.

And it had a tail.

It reminded Eldridge of a diagram of the human spinal column that Dr. Enki had shown him once. Hundreds of steel segments composed the tail, which lashed back and forth, always in concert with the overall feline's movements. The tail hung *so* low that it cut gashes in the deck of the barge-brick before it flicked out over the river a few yards above the surface—and right above the jetski's current position.

Had he been alone, he wouldn't have needed the fireman's carry, of course, but the ancient water-warriors of yore demanded the redhead's allegiance as he used his belt to lash the handlebars in place and gave the accelerator a hard twist and jammed it at full speed. A flick of his fingertips was enough to unclasp Hagan's grip. In one smooth motion, he hopped up onto the seat. Next, he grabbed the package, reared back, and heaved it up onto the barge-brick, hoping the Crom it would remain on the deck. In another smooth motion, he grabbed Hagan's wrist and looped his body over his shoulders.

His stomach sank. The old man felt *light*.

He dismissed the thought and concentrated on the suprafeline's tail, suddenly faced with another of Marko's "one-chance moments." It lashed back and forth three more times. The jetski lurched, and Eldridge almost pitched into the mud with Hagan over his shoulders, but he kept his footing and just fucking *went* for it. Pushing off with his left foot, he bounded onto the front of the jetski and focused all power-force into the heels of his feet as he jumped into the sky, his vertical leap blunted both by the weight of his friend and the dip that the jetski took when he jumped off. His trailing foot actually splashed into mud along the way.

But he had enough height. The tail flashed through the air. Eldridge hung onto Hagan with one hand and reached out for the tail with his other. He caught the very tip of the tail, which was capped with spikes that dug into his palm. No time for pain; he only needed *momentum*. The tail whipped forward and carried them directly over the barge-brick. Eldridge released his grip. They fell. He hadn't planned for how he would land. Blood flowed from his shredded palm. Hagan was prime. He wrapped his arms around his old friend and flexed his leg muscles—he couldn't afford a sprained ankle or a broken bone now. His feet hit the deck first, his knees buckling an instant afterward. He rolled forward and deposited Hagan on the deck, who rolled onto his back, unhurt, but then Eldridge rolled directly over him. Hagan's eyes flashed wide as he expelled a gust of air. The redhead tried to complete his roll by finishing on his feet, and he did—but only for a moment. His overall forward momentum threw him into an arm-pin-wheeling forward fall. He staggered across the deck and slammed into the waiting arms of two of Tucker's men, both of them clad in leather overalls and sleeveless denim tank tops. Eldridge scanned the deck and saw no sign of the package. *Shit.* Tucker himself manned the helm, a large round wheel that had been specially mounted into the top deck. His henchmen caught Eldridge by his arms and held him upright while his hand continued to spill blood on the deck. Tucker glanced over his shoulder.

"What the *fuck* is—"

Crack! Moondog's suprafeline tail-slashed the deck and decapitated one of Tucker's henchmen. They roared past the one-mile-to-go marker. Eldridge shook free of the other henchman and elbowed him in the face. He went down. Hagan lay on the deck, his only defense. Hatches flipped open all over the deck, and a dozen more henchmen streamed out, all garbed in hectic ensembles of leather and denim. Eldridge ignored them and bum-rushed the helm. Tucker spun around, a cigar clenched between his incisors, and met the redhead with a roundhouse kick that Eldridge stooped under.

He wasn't going for Tucker. He was going for the *wheel.*

Hard to starboard. Eldridge spun the wheel, dropped to his chest, and sent all twenty thousand tons of the barge-brick smashing into the side of the tunnel at a hundred knots. Moondog's suprafeline charged ahead, still clinging to the ceiling. Inertia carried a half dozen of Tucker's men off the prow of the boat. Eldridge grabbed hold of the steering column and flipped around so he was facing aft. Hagan came sliding forward. The redhead propped his feet on a hatch and propelled himself across the mud-slick deck, where he caught Hagan in a swirling splatter of sludge-mist. The barge-brick continued to grind against the side of the tunnel, the friction shaking the deck like an earthquake. The redhead got to his knees and dragged Hagan across the deck to a hatch, where he gave his old friend's cheek a slap.

"Hages! Can you hear me?"

"Don't fucking slap me."

Eldridge grinned. "Hang on to this." He wrapped Hagan's fingers around the hatch's handle. "Got it?"

"I got it. Slap me again, and I fuck you up, boy."

"Understood. Just hold on."

He jumped to his feet and stumbled as the barge hit a rocky outcropping and listed to port. A pair of competing boats got crunched as the barge-brick made its passage across the river, which ran in a straight line toward a burgeoning spot of light far ahead. Moondog's suprafeline continued its gallop toward the finish line. Eldridge spun around—and saw the package.

But Tucker Beelzebub was holding it, flanked by what remained of his men.

"Shit-kickin' sumbitch. Wanna comman-*deer* my boat, do ye?"

Even over the noise of the barge-brick's engines, the roar of the river and the clanging footsteps of the suprafeline, Eldridge could hear something else.

Ticking.

Boris Hagan must've heard it, too, because when the redhead looked over at him, the old man's eyes had snapped wide and alert despite his fatigue. Hagan gave him a curt nod and slipped into the hatch. Backed by his men, Tucker advanced on him, the ticking package in his hands, his golden sideburns flaring around his ears as he bit his cigar in two and swallowed half of it. Eldridge pointed at the package.

"Don't you *hear* that?"

Tucker hesitated. One of his men nodded.

"That thing's tickin', boss."

The thmart box seemed to turn red-hot in Tucker's hands. He dropped it.

"The hell's *in* that thang?!" he screamed at the redhead.

Eldridge shrugged, spun around and rammed the throttle. The barge-brick surged forward and sent Tucker and his men stumbling around the deck. The package continued to tick louder and louder as it slid around the deck, its presence repelling all humans like a reverse-polarized magnet. Henchmen went pitching into the water to avoid it, and Tucker danced a crazy jig back and forth as the redhead upped the speed and swerved right and left. Finally, Boris Hagan sprang out of his hiding place on a sudden burst of energy and grabbed the thmart box. Tucker wheeled around to attack him, but Hagan leapt to his feet and used both hands to swing the package in a giant upward arc that cracked Tucker under the chin. He reeled backward and fell to the deck. Hagan searched the thmart box for seams or openings, but he didn't have to—it popped open in his hands.

"El-*dridge!*"

Hagan ran to the front of the boat, his knees wobbling but his eyes alive, and thrust the newly opened package into the redhead's hands. And Eldridge smiled and looked ahead.

"What're you acting so surprised for, Hages?"

The package had bloomed like a steel blue flower, revealing a few bricks of boompaste and some kind of liquid-analog timing device. A vial full of green fluid was draining into a reservoir one drop at a time. The origin of the ticking was a shunt that clicked back and forth, admitting a drop of the green fluid with each click—and there wasn't much green fluid left to drain.

Mere meters ahead, the suprafeline galloped, and not far ahead, they could see the remnant of Hemming as it slowly crept into view. Eldridge reached into the package, grabbed the bomb, and rammed the throttle to full. The front of the barge-brick actually rose a few feet out of the mud as it gained speed and crept up behind the suprafeline. Eldridge hugged the side of the tunnel to avoid the always-lashing tail of the suprafeline.

And then a voice sounded from behind.

"*Yew sumbitches!*"

They looked back and saw Tucker standing in the middle of his ruined deck, his broken nose gushing blood, his men strewn about him, his fists clutching a hand-cannon he had liberated from one of his henchmen.

Shaking with fury, he screamed: *"I'm a-gonna—"*

The tail knocked him to pieces. Swinging around, it caught him diagonally across his torso and sent his limbs flying in every cardinal direction. His head remained suspended in midair for one moment after his body exploded, his eyes rolled to whites. Tucker's severed head bounced off the deck and pitched into the mud.

Eldridge looked at the bomb. One drop of green remained.

Hagan nodded. "Time's a-wastin.'"

"Take the helm."

Steady as a Narsyan balance, Hagan grabbed the wheel and maintained speed while Eldridge ran to the middle of the deck and chucked the package up at the center of the suprafeline's back with his bloody hand. As he wheeled around to scream something at Boris, the package blew.

A diagonal streak of white flashed across the cave's diameter. A bulge of yellow at its midpoint marked the origin of the explosion. The suprafeline split in twain, raining fire and spewing sparks across the deck. Its tail snapped off and slammed into the mud, while its rear section continued to gallop through the air as it bounced off a wall and splashed down. The front section caused the most damage; the head landed on the rearmost portion of the barge's deck and crushed several of Tucker's men, while the torso broke free and scraped down the stern on its way into the river.

When the smoke cleared, Eldridge lay on the deck on his stomach with his hands over his head. He looked up, saw Hagan at the wheel, and smiled. Hagan waved him over. As he walked to the front of Tucker Beelzebub's barge-brick, the tunnel opened up into the remnant of Hemming and its mountainous interiors. They passed under a banner festooned with black and white flowers. It read FINISH LINE! WELCOME TO HEMMING!

The river ended. The barge stopped. The crowd went apeshit.

They had won the Mud Races.

But they had lost the thmart box.

Eldridge waved to the crowd with his bloody hand. Someone in the crowd was so excited, they fired off a gun. Eldridge wrapped an arm around his friend, whose weight collapsed against him the second they touched. Hagan's ankles rolled, and only the redhead's grip kept him from crumpling to the deck.

"Let's find you a bed, old buddy."

Two more shots rang out from the crowd.

"We can't," Hagan said. "If Hanna finds out we lost the package, we're dead. We . . . we have to keep running. It's okay. I'm on my . . . second . . . thing."

"Second *wind?*"

"Whatever."

"If she wanted us to kill Torsten, then we'll just have to kill him," Eldridge said.

Another voice piped up. "Guess who's your best friend in the whole entire fucking wide, wide world of sports?!"

"Speak of the bevel," Hagan said.

A bouquet of black and white flowers hovered onto the deck of the barge-brick and settled down next to them. The crowd cheered even louder at the sight of the bouquet. A face popped through the flowers, grinning with two teeth, but it wasn't that he was *missing* most of his teeth; no, he had *replaced* his normal teeth with a pair of shiny white tooth-blades that spanned the arcs of his mandibles. He dropped the flowers on the deck and revealed a mechanorg lifeform. Only his torso remained intact. A pair of spindly prosthetic legs supported his torso, their knee joints bending in the wrong direction, which gave him an avian gait. Robotic arms rotated from ball joints set into his shoulders. A sleeveless and legless tuxedo hung off his torso. A strip of black hair was slicked to his steel skull. A T-shaped patch of flesh that included his eyes, nose, and mouth was all that remained of his original face. It was more than enough for the redhead to recognize him.

The mechanorg ambled up before them.

"Long time no *fuck*, Eldridge."

"Hey there, Walter."

Walter Torsten, Odd of Hemming, closed his tooth-blades with a *click*. His eyes crossed for an instant, then fixated on the redhead.

"Hey. Hey. Hey."

The cheers of the crowd audio-smeared into white chaos.

Eldridge grimaced. "What?"

"Hey. Hey-hey—why don't you guys come up to the *mountain?!*"

Torsten's voice would quantum-leap from normal to *shout* in the space of one word. *"It's really nice up there! Maybe your cocksucking old friendy-pal there could get some rest and suck some . . . cock."* His robotic arms swung in gesticulating circles as he screamed, and then he came to a sudden stop. His arms fell limp by his sides. His accent shifted— his vowels elongated, and he started dropping his Rs. "You gentlemen could also perhaps have a *spot of tea!*" Balled metallic fists and the click of tooth-blades accompanied each of his shouted syllables. Then he got quiet again. "With your . . . hee-heh . . . *permission!* Why don't we head up there and trox together like it's old times? Maybe you can play the lotto again."

"I drank all the whiskey, Walter," Eldridge said.

Torsten's lips closed over his tooth-blades. Solemnity overtook him. He raised a palm to the sky and spoke like a supriest, which he had once been. "Then . . . my Eldridge . . . it pains me to say that the only course of action that remains—correction, the only course of action that could *possibly* remain . . . is to chop off your nuts. And your dingaling."

Eldridge's eyes increased in diameter by a few freaked-out millimeters.

Torsten waved a hand, spread his tooth-blades and emitted a guffaw that ended in a shriek of audio feedback.

"I'm just fuckin' with ya. *Or am I?!* No! No yelling, little Waltie. Ha! More like *all* yelling! *Yeahhhh!* Let's go to the mountain. For the chopping. *No chopping!*" His torso rotated on a pivot set into his spinal column. Now his legs bent like normal. "Follow me, and don't forget your dingaling!"

―⁂―

KIERON

THE JELLYWOMAN'S SPEECHMOUTH SAVED her life.

The device was jacked directly into the speech centers of her brain, as the plastic coating in her lungs prevented the use of air currents. She simply had to *think* words, and she would speak them. But the speechmouth, one of the few connections between her internal systems and the outside world, wasn't actually connected to her *mouth*—it was two inches away. Quillig's gunshot had destroyed the device and knocked her unconscious, but Kieron remained unharmed.

She regained consciousness quick enough to see Walter Torsten float up to the deck of the barge-brick and escort Eldridge and Boris Hagan away. Kieron half expected her former partner to attack the redhead immediately.

But Quillig didn't attack. And neither would the jellywoman.

Kieron found herself alone by the riverside as soon as Torsten left with the two winners. Hemming and all of its thousands of dregs followed him everywhere, throwing hands and hats and babies into the air. When the crowd was far enough away, Kieron stood up, her face still spewing smoke and sparks from the cavity that had once held her speechmouth.

She needed a plan.

She started by digging out the remains of her speechmouth, taking care to sever the wires that linked it to her brain. That done, she plunged into the remnant, which was largely deserted anywhere Torsten wasn't. A few stray dregs wandered the streets, scurrying up and down staircases into the myriad storefronts that remained open.

The jellywoman stopped into a building that looked like a giant, three-dimensional E. Something about it had caught her attention, but she didn't know what. One wall rose from a grassy swell in the earth, and three floors protruded from that wall. Stone staircases linked the floors of the building. Between city blocks they shared with other structures, jagged brick walls acted as partitions. Moss grew on everything, including the building's sign, which read GENERAL STORE AND ART SUPPLIES.

That's what had caught her eye—the sign. Specifically, the word ART. Someone had scrawled two tiny additional letters, an S and a C, in front of it, so it read SCART.

Look for the scars.

The E-building held three stories of general store. Kieron stepped inside and found hardwood floors, various pots and pans hanging from the stone walls, and shelves packed with plates and silverware lining the walls. A dreg wearing a burlap apron and nothing else leaned against the far wall, a jenta-catch clutched in his fist. He didn't move at Kieron's entrance.

The jellywoman walked over and used her index finger to scribble on her palm. The dreg grunted and hooked his thumb at the stairs. Kieron climbed to the second floor, and the world opened up. Stacks of paper, cups of pencils, and racks of brushing implements filled table after table. Artificially rendered images hung from the walls. Kieron stepped closer to one and peered at the waves of pigmented paste that covered them. One of these images depicted a fantastic landscape—the sun set behind a pair of blue lakes that looked up from a rolling, green valley. Snow-capped mountains stood on the distant horizon. Another image depicted a man and a woman locked in embrace, while still another simply depicted a bowl of fruit.

There were even images hung from the *open* wall. Someone had bolted a strip of wood into the stone ceiling. The wood ran the length of the open wall, and from it were hung three wires that each bore an image. Kieron stepped over. The three images swung in the gentle breeze that blew through Hemming. Beyond the three images, rolling hills and hundreds of city blocks stretched out. In the distance, an unusual blue object glowed over a mountainpeak. The jellywoman turned her attention to the three images.

The one on the left depicted a band of ancient adventurers around a heat-blossom ("fire," as the extraterrestrials called it). The one on the right depicted a map of an unfamiliar land—"North America."

But the center image depicted nothing. It was completely white, its blank surface only interrupted by an occasional ribbed ridge, like someone had stuck wet paper to the image and fashioned it into a series of unusual, alien spinal columns. The jellywoman lingered and examined the strange ridges until she discovered that two disparate regions in her mind shared a border with each other. She crossed to a table that held spiral-bound pads of rough-edged parchment paper. She tried to use her stylus to write on it, but the parchment wouldn't hold the smartcharacters. The red letters spilled out of her stylus and faded away.

A voice said, "That won't work. It's the old kind."

Another dreg, this one presumably the proprietor of the store's second floor, stepped over. He wore the same burlap apron, but his was smeared with streaks of color—the same pigmented paste that composed the images on the walls. Kieron looked over and cocked her head in a question.

"That's not smartpaper," the dreg said.

The proprietor ambled over, favoring a leg. As he approached, Kieron saw that the limp was only *one* of his injuries. A bionic sight-cartridge, not unlike Quillig's, sat in one of his sockets. All told, he only had seven total fingers—four on his right and three on his left. Both thumbs survived, lucky for him. Light glinted off a patch of synth-flesh that had been stitched over one of his cheeks. Scar tissue flared around the side of his neck like a system of ancient rivers.

"Here, try this."

The proprietor handed him a stylus-sized cylinder of brittle black stone that had been sharpened at one end. Kieron stowed her standard stylus and tried writing with the stone one. She found that it left a trail of dark gray on the unusual paper's surface. The point of the cylinder flaked away as she wrote.

The jellywoman wrote a question.
What kind of paper is this?

The dreg slid his fingers across the surface of the paper. His fingertips smeared some of Kieron's question.

"It's like the old kind. Made from trees. Pulpaper. It'll cost ya if you want it."

Kieron ran her fingers across the surface of the pulpaper. Her plastic was equipped to deliver a wide array of sensory inputs to her brain, but for a moment, she wished she could touch the paper with her bare fingers. She nodded and wrote:
I'll want a pad of standard smartpaper, as well.

"Very good, ma'am."

The proprietor sifted through a mess of paper stacks and smart-receipts crammed into cubbies, fished out his stylus, and set it to smartpaper to record the transaction. Still holding the pad and pencil, Kieron regarded the strange white painting and had a thought. She looked over at the proprietor—his neck, specifically—and crossed the room, writing a new question. When she reached the roll-top, the proprietor handed her a rectango-stack of perfect white smartpaper. Kieron stowed the smartpaper and laid the pad of pulpaper on the roll-top.

Her question read: *Are those scars?*

The proprietor's stylus froze. He laid it down and looked at Kieron, a smile slanting across his craggy face.

"That's right," he said. "They're casts of scars. I made it myself."

Kieron wanted to smile, but her plastic prevented her. She wrote.

It's quite remarkable. Are they all your scars?

Silence greeted her question. The jellywoman scribbled more words onto the pad.

I hope I haven't offend

The black stone broke before she could finish. The proprietor shook his head.

"Do you know about the scar?"

Kieron started to shake her head, then stopped when she realized that the proprietor hadn't asked her about just *any* scar; he had asked her about *the Scar*, with a capital S. The jellywoman took up the remains of the black stone stylus and wrote another question.

What is the Scar?

Papers spilled off his roll-top as the proprietor tore off the piece of paper, crumpled it up, and dropped it into a small ceramic bowl. From his pockets he produced a stainless-steel heat-bloomer and set the paper aflame. Kieron held up her palms, silently asking *What's the big deal*, but the proprietor ignored her and walked to the edge of the floor and looked out. The crowd that had gathered to watch the end of the Mud Races had followed Walter Torsten clear across town, leaving the streets around the E-building deserted. He turned toward Kieron.

"You are a bounty-merc, yes?"

Kieron's posture tightened in surprise before she realized that it wasn't a great secret. She nodded. The proprietor waved her over to the three images.

"What are your confines? Lisken? Tannermort? Pestus?"

Kieron nodded at the name Pestus.

The proprietor smiled. "Well, now you have a new one to visit. Scar."

He knocked on the image of the scars. He knocked three times, then two, then five, then six, then one, then seven. The image swung on a hinge—and revealed a room inside. Purely on reflex, Kieron leaned around the side of the image and checked behind it. She saw nothing but the proprietor smiling at her through an empty frame. She leaned back around, and once again, she saw a room inside.

Kieron pointed and shook her head.

"It's new tech," the proprietor said. "Smuggled from across the oceans, smuggled right out from under *him*."

Him. Even the jellywoman knew enough about the man across the oceans to blanch at the invocation of his presence—but she couldn't stop looking into the room. Like the sectan confine of Pestus, it included a map that hung on the far wall, but unlike the quaint paper-and-string jumble of papers she had seen before, this map was a smart-monitor that blinked with lights and glimmered with a rainbow of information. Bounty-mercs in a variety of gear and of all shapes and sizes ran to and fro, hunching over tables, sharing drinks and intel.

Voices wafted out of the opening. A few beads of sweat popped out of the proprietor's brow.

"In or out, friend. You've just stumbled onto the biggest secret in all of bounty-mercdom. Only a select few of us know about the Scar."

A tingling wall of energy wiped through her as she stepped over the image-frame into the room. The "door" swung shut behind her and *clicked*. Her plastic-coated feet landed on a stone tile floor. Golden light shone from up-shaded troughs. Scar confine was made up of half a dozen smaller rooms, about three hundred square feet each, and each of them linked by doorways.

The primary room included the entryway into Hemming, as well as the smart-monitor that displayed a map of the surrounding region. A semicircle of stone stood against one wall—a tiny bar manned by a serving dreg. Bounty-mercs streamed in and out of the different rooms. Kieron crossed the primary room, stepping around a pair of identical twin bounty-mercs—each missing an arm, generating a glowing red plasmodic limb when they stood close enough together. A draft from one of the secondary rooms gusted across her ankles. The jellywoman dodged around a trio of mercs stepped inside.

And through another tingling wall of energy.

She paused and tried to sense her surroundings. There was no way for her to *smell* the air, but she could tell that the temperature had dropped by twenty or thirty degrees. A thin horizontal window, like a giant, narrowed eye, stood against the far wall. She crossed to it and looked out on a snow-covered mountainside dotted with juts of crags. Something didn't compute. She looked for a door and found a great wooden slab set in the wall. It opened with some effort, as she had to push it in a swinging arc through a bank of snow. She stepped outside and found herself surrounded by an endless mountain range.

A voice from within: "Close the door, numb-nuts! You're letting all the cold in!"

Kieron stepped back inside and pulled the door shut. She jogged across the room, back through the tingling wall, and ran into one of the other secondary rooms, which also stood behind a tingling wall. Inside that room, the temperature *rose* by thirty degrees. Bounty-mercs entered the room and removed their overcoats, which lay in a pile by the doorway, while a trixie-dreg clad in nothing but her trixie-overalls served cold drinks. Kieron saw another window, this one screened over. When she looked outside, she thought night had fallen, but the darkness was a result of the canopy of trees hanging over the swampland that stood outside.

Hard fingers tapped her shoulder. Kieron turned and looked into the single eye of an eyepatch-wearing bounty-merc who lit a cigarillo and stuck it into a porthole he had carved into his chest. As he chest-sucked on the smokestick, he jerked his chin at the swamp.

"Less'n you got business in the northern marshes, I'd suggest you stick to the main room, feller."

Kieron crossed back through the tingling wall into the primary room. She paced about as casually as she could and peered inside the remaining four doorways. She couldn't sense any of the environmental changes through the tingling walls of energy, but she guessed that each of the doors led to a distant region based on the attire of the bounty-mercs inside. One room was apparently on the surface of the sun, because the mercs inside wore nothing but underwear and towels, which they used to dry off their glistening skin. Still another room had a broad picture window that looked out on a sight that made her stop pacing.

It looked green, but Kieron knew that a few leagues away from the coast, the water would turn blue again. The shoreline arched away from the window and receded into the distance. The land didn't end in a beach; instead it terminated in a bluff that rose from the water in a great wall of stone and earth. Yellow foam broke against the wall, driven by those endless green waves. Portholes looked out from the side of the wall. The barge paused next to a few of them and popped open some of its own portholes. Each porthole disgorged a stream of dregs going ashore, all of whom had to make a tiny, precarious leap from the barge and into the waiting hole in the wall. The great vessel then continued up the coast toward a gigantic crane that hung over the water like a massive, upside-down L. Kieron knew that the crane would unload cargo from the barge in the form of huge steel boxes—the kinds of boxes they used to affix to the rear of vehicles like Quillig's big rig.

If Kieron could use her lungs, she would have sighed. She knew *some* things.

She also had to stave off a sudden impulse to use a hotcutter to remove her plastic coating and dive into the waves. She knew she couldn't; after all, she had lost her O2-chestpack, and she didn't know how to get the plastic gunk out of her lungs—although the deep-desert sawbones had warned her that if she took enough damage, her plastic coating might simply *fall* off. Kieron hadn't the slightest notion of how much damage that might entail, but in any event, she pondered the idea of abandoning her new life and returning to her old one.

But she couldn't. She could never go back. Not as long as the war raged.

Quotidian matters in the form of hunger pangs distracted her from her plight. She crossed to the food bar and wrote out an order for something high in protein and calories. The dreg served up a bowl of synth-meat and synth-vegetables, and the jellywoman used her handmounted emulsifier to liquefy it. Once she had tested it for toxins, she fed one of her bodystraws into it and slurped it directly into her system. As he absorbed the nutrients, she relaxed, listened to the chatter, and considered her next step.

She didn't have to consider for very long.

"Got a big new bogey on the board, assholes!"

A bounty-merc wearing three layers of corduroy and a vest fashioned from cyclone fencing jabbed his finger at the giant smart-monitor on the wall, which blinked with hundreds of faces—bounties—that lay scattered across the land. Each face included basic biographical data (height, weight, gambling addictions, amount of bounty), but whenever the board changed significantly, the map of the western continent would disappear, and in its place would materialize a large picture of the new information with all relevant details.

In this case, a picture of an old man faded into view on a chaotic wave of pixels. He sat on a rooftop restaurant under a brick ceiling and smiled at someone out of frame. His skin was dark brown, hair sandy black, the horrors that would whiten it still in his future.

The old man had actually been on the board for some time, but one of the Odds had just increased the price on the dreg's head by a factor of ten.

The Odd? Lilya Hanna.

The new bogey? Boris Hagan.

Kieron left a trail of protein-gruel on the floor as she strode out of the sectan confine of Scar with her food-tube still dangling from her wrist.

—༞—

ELDRIDGE AND BORIS HAGAN

From Uzziel to Goldmist, the Odds had ruled over the detritus that remained after the Deadblast cataclysm through a variety of means. Odd Lilya Hanna had her pinkeyes. Odd Deanna DuBois of the Tri-Remnants used a neural stimulant to induce orgasm in her populace every twelve hours, rendering them drowsy and subservient enough to wager their jenta on her odds, which related to the rising of the sun. Most dregs had learned to avoid the Tri-Remnants for fear of being driven insane like its population, which had wagered that the sun would rise from the *west* for 2,737 consecutive days.

Odd Trick Maxwell had, by contrast, hoarded all of the food in the remote remnant of Kendra, and he only rationed it out to his emaciated citizenry when they made odds with him. Like Jeb Goldmist of Dedrick, Maxwell had raised a standing army to quarantine his remnant and keep his citizens hungry while they frittered away their jenta on his odds, which centered around the struggles of one unconscious man's immune system. Maxwell's stronghold displayed a constant video-stream of the man's internal systems and lymph nodes. Even as their stomachs grumbled, the citizens of Kendra came to be obsessed with the man's day-to-day battles with various bacteria and viruses. Some of his individual white blood cells even had their own fan clubs.

Walter Torsten of Hemming had a different way of maintaining order—he was simply *stupendous*. Or so everyone thought.

Arm in arm with Eldridge and Hagan, the Odd levitated off the barge-brick and carried them into the air before the bleachers full of cheering fans.

"Congratulate the winners of the Thirty-Fourth Annual Mud Races! *They're kind of awwwwesoooooome!*"

Whites. Whites of eyes. Hands clapping so hard the palms turned red. *Ran* red. One guy shook his fists and screamed, apparently on one breath, for the entire two minutes that Torsten presented them to the crowd. Dregs young and old hugged each other. Finally, the Odd carried them down to street level, where thousands more faithful beset them. Torsten then led them on a march through the streets of Hemming, which thronged with dregs young and old, all of whom had raging megahuge boners for Walter Torsten.

Hemming looked like it had once been a city in the mountains, but over time, a cocoon had grown over the city. A beige-and-brown stucco-stone ceiling covered everything. The streets had once adhered to a grid, but as Eldridge bore Hagan on his shoulder and followed Torsten, he saw that nature—in the form of *elevation*—had slowly been reclaiming the remnant over the ages.

Dregs by the thousands lined the uneven stone-paved streets. As Torsten led them up one of Hemming's discrete city blocks, one building collapsed under the weight of so many bodies, all of which cheered as the cloud of rubble buried them. One dreg jumped off of a nearby building and smashed into the ground before them. He struggled to his feet and lurched to the side, one of his feet dangling on a shattered ankle. He eventually found his balance on one foot and smiled at his reigning Odd through agony. The dreg wore a T-shirt that read, HUG WALTER TORSTEN.

"*Aaaaa! Walter Torsten! You are the absolutely most greatest thing in the history of great great things! Eeeeeee!*" He pressed his palms into his temples and screamed. Torsten grinned at the crowd and made a downward gesture to the dreg.

"Take a knee, my friend."

More cheering. Someone yelled, "Holy dogshit!" Men's and women's underwear flew out of the crowd. By the time the dreg with the shattered ankle had fallen to a knee, Torsten was covered in undergarments. He extended his robotic fingers, which were capped with razor-sharp talons, at the loyal dreg. He showed the crowd his teeth-blades and held his index finger over his puckered lips.

"Shhh!"

The crowd fell quiet as the background noise of the remnant itself rose in relative volume—circulation fans hummed, distant dregs chattered, and (of all things) *birds chirped.*

Torsten's knees bent. He continued shushing the crowd as he extended his razor-talons into the dreg's neck. Backed-up blood swelled in a neck-vein for an instant before his jugular popped and sprayed a parabola of blood that pooled around Torsten's feet. The dreg felt his neck and looked at his red hands.

He raised his red fists. *"Yeahhhhh!"*

The crowd went wild and cheered as the dreg melted to the ground and faded away, bathed in his own blood. Torsten held up his hands.

"You're! Welcome!"

Using his talons, Torsten slashed all of the undergarments in half and stepped over the dreg, who died happy as fuck. He led Eldridge and Hagan over a rope footbridge, one of hundreds in the remnant. The footbridges linked the city blocks, and if one were so inclined, the remnant could be traversed without ever descending to the street level.

Buoyed by the cheering crowd, they marched over the swinging footbridge and stepped out onto another city block. A brass pole descended to the block's bottom level, which stood on a small hill a few feet above street level. Torsten hopped onto the pole and slid to the ground. Eldridge set Hagan on his feet. His eyelids twitched.

"Oh, look," Hagan said. "A fireman's pole."

A few dregs pounded them on the back, offering encouragement and congratulations. Eldridge shouted over the noise.

"You think you can make it?"

Hagan nodded. Eldridge looked at him for a moment longer before Torsten's voice sounded from below.

"The mountain awaits! *Let's go!*"

The redhead hopped onto the pole and slid down. Hundreds of dregs packed every floor. A wave of cheers followed him all the way down to the bottom, where he landed on a grassy hill that bloomed with flowers. Eldridge looked up through the cross-section of round holes cut through the floors. Boris Hagan almost crashed into him. The old man's knees buckled as he hit the ground. The redhead caught him before he fell over.

Wrapping an arm around Hagan's shoulder, Eldridge followed Walter Torsten as he robo-sauntered out of the block building and down the small hill. They stepped onto another street, which gave a better view of the remnant as a whole, which included the mountain.

At the far corner of town, one mountain stood hundreds of feet higher than the rest, its peak capped with a decidedly *man*-made object: a luminescent, glowing hyperobject, or more precisely, the *three-dimensional shadow* of a four-dimensional object that rotated in and out of a virtual space generated over the mountain's apex. Torsten pivot-whipped to face them, his teeth-blades glistening. The crowd gathered closer, a weather system of *shushes* passing through them. Quiet reigned.

"What's the atomic weight of lead?!"

"Um," Eldridge said.

"My balls!" More speaker-feedback squealed from his smiling mouth, accompanied by raucous laughter from the dreg-gallery. Another dreg jumped out and "demanded" a high-five or he would "cut his own face off." Torsten obliged and cackled.

"You should cut off your face anyway! Did wonders for me!"

"You got it!" the dreg yelled back.

That set off a high-stakes round of high-fiving in which Torsten saved many lives by gracing them with a high-five from his spindly, talon-tipped hands.

Finally, he waved to the crowd. "No more for now, folks! I gotta get *these* two good 'n' *killed!* Or is it *laid?*"

One comely female dreg screamed, "Time to amputate at the neck!"

The crowd roared. Smiling, Torsten gave her an approving nod, then made little guns with his hands and rat-a-tat-tatted her with praise. She mimed a dance of death and fell to the ground, shouting, "Medic!"

Torsten turned to the winners and pointed up at the hyperobject. "Look familiar, El? El? Eldridge?"

The redhead was frozen. The sight of the dying woman had sparked a deep dive into his memorybanks, where he searched for something from which he had heretofore shrank:

The grinning chasm.

But where *was* it? Which of his memories would trigger it? He remembered deposing Jeb Goldmist. He remembered the temporal-snare that Goldmist had smart-glommed onto his jenta stores. The redhead also remembered venturing up to Hemming to play the hyperlotto in yet another effort to pay off the man across the oceans— and that in turn finally brought him soaring over the grinning chasm that split his mind in twain.

Distantly, Boris Hagan's voice came to him: "Eldridge? You okay?"

"Yeah, I'm fine." Eldridge said. "And where the hell is my bike?"

"Oh, we impounded that sexy motherfucker," the Odd said. "You got good taste in motorbikery, redhead. Gives me *hardwood* every time I look at that hydro-packin' whore. All matte finish with the paint job, all chrome accents on the engine. It was filthy when we took it in, but you should see 'er now. Shinier'n *shit*. But don't you want to play the lotto again? You did so well last time. If ya don't mind me saying so—" he thundered his next words: "*—you kinda rocked the shit out of it!*"

Torsten led them up another stone staircase that coiled up six stories like a pencil stuck through six paper plates. A single load-bearing member shot up through the center.

As Eldridge climbed the stairs, his temples started to throb, but he didn't have a headache. When he accessed his memorybanks, he had only intended to call up the information related to his time in Hemming, and he found it—along with something else.

He had come to Hemming to win the hyperlotto. Winning the hyperlotto wouldn't give him enough jenta to pay back the man across the oceans, but if he won the hyperlotto *twice in a row,* he'd have enough. Of course, the odds of winning the hyperlotto *once* in a row were one in a hundred million, and the odds of winning it *twice* in a row were approximately one in however many elemental particles existed in the visible universe. That said, the redhead had found a way to win the lotto once, which was what brought him to Torsten's attention.

But that's not what was making his head hurt.

Eldridge and Hagan mounted the stairs to the sixth floor, where Torsten stood before a rocket-zipline that led up to his mountain fortress.

"Climb on, gents!"

Still supporting Hagan, Eldridge took a step forward and stumbled. They both fell to the stone floor. Torsten turned, already speaker-feed-backing at their clumsiness.

"Whoa! Get a room, fellas!"

Robotic claws closed around their collars and yanked them upright. The fall had jolted Hagan into alertness.

"You all right, El?"

The redhead's brow knit. He grimaced. "Yeah."

Hagan kept a watch on him. Torsten thwacked their shoulders.

"You boys ready to get *dead-y?!*"

"I don't know what that means," Hagan said.

The Odd stepped onto the rocket-gondola. "Let's rock."

Eldridge helped Hagan onto the gondola, his face still twisted around something inside. The gondola swayed under their weight. They both grabbed onto the guardrail. Hagan continued to watch the redhead's face.

"What's wrong?"

"Stop looking at me," Eldridge snapped, teeth clenched.

Torsten activated the gondola, and they rocketed over Hemming. As they gained speed, the redhead closed his eyes. The image of the gog-eyed mother shaking her baby appeared before him. The image vanished. The image of Constable Tola's ruined face appeared before him. Her face reassembled itself. She smiled at him, and then she vanished.

She vanished into the grinning chasm.

The noise of the rocket-gondola faded, leaving Eldridge with the sensation that he was flying over the chasm itself, and try as he might, he couldn't see into it.

But now he knew what was *inside* it.

His eyes snapped open to a view of darkness. The world reeled underneath him. Somewhere above, he felt Boris Hagan's arms wrap around him before he fell off the gondola. The old man's voice sounded miles away.

"El? *El?* What's the matter? What's wrong?"

Where had they all gone? He had them before. He knew that. He could remember a time when he could remember *them*. When was it? Before the Mud Races? No. Before they arrived in Penticton? No.

Before the Chain?

Yes. Before the Chain.

He could remember her before the Chain.

He could remember Zora Tola. His daughter.

But now he couldn't. Except for a few fleeting glimpses and feelings, she was gone. He could sense that he had once *had* a daughter. He knew she was brave, knew she was special, but when he tried to remember specific moments with her, he drew cold. He could remember almost everything *around* her—her husband, her mother, the fact that he himself had been the one to raise her in Junktown.

He also had some sense of her death. He knew that Jeb Goldmist had murdered her, which meant the Odds had taken his daughter from him.

Twice.

His vision returned just in time for Torsten's mountain to scream into view. The 4D hyperobject spun overhead, its surface a glimmering dance of blue-and-white fractal-soup. Up close, they could now see the elaborate system of windows carved into the mountainside. Dregs looked out from these windows, the largest of which were the three stone-lined vertical windows. The middle window stood fifty feet high and admitted the gondola line, which shook as they rocketed into the mountain.

Inside, a vast stone chamber opened before them. Ancient stonemasons had carved one quarter of a cylinder out of the mountain and laid it with stone. A flat wall rose before them, while the arch of the cylinder curved behind them, roughly following the slope of the mountainside. The gondola-line ended at a holding station where a half dozen of Torsten's volunteer brigade waited to receive them. Unlike

Jeb Goldmist's well-trained magnars, Walter Torsten had no standing army. Instead, an ongoing parade of loyal fans offered their services to the mighty Odd, whose appeal remained a mystery to the two winners of the Mud Races.

Volunteers beset them, offering hands and help. Three different vols asked to take their coats, while a few others held up glasses of water and sliced fruit. Torsten flicked a glistening yellow cube into his mouth. His lips puckered.

"You boys ever tasted pined-apples?"

Hagan shook his head. Eldridge stared at the floor. Torsten stabbed a pair of pined-apple cubes with his talons and offered them.

"Try it."

One of the vols said, "We swear to *fuck* they're not poisoned."

Hagan popped it into his mouth and chewed. His eyelids rose.

"El, you've gotta try this."

The redhead turned a hot gaze on Torsten. "What're we *doing* here?"

The Odd sipped a glass of water being held out by one of his vols. He smacked his lips and clicked his teeth-blades.

"Why, I want to pay you your winnings, El. You won the hyperlotto fairsies and squarsies. Don't you want the jenta? Don't you *need* the jenta?"

Hagan broke in, "What the hell's happening in Dedrick?"

Torsten's robotic shoulders rose. "How should I know? I left that piddlyshit remnant in my rearview months ago."

"It's a goddamn *dreen festival* down there, Torsten. And it's your fault! What kind of stupid, dumb-shit bastard tries to challenge the dreen—"

"Shut up, Hages."

Hagan shut up, his face drawn in shock, his eyes bright with betrayal. Eldridge, not Torsten, had told him to shut up. The white-haired old man glared at the redhead.

"What?"

Eldridge ignored him and addressed the Odd. "Enough bullshit, Walter. You're just going to put me back on the Chain. Like you wanted to in Glaucio. Like you did when I won the lotto. Like you're going to now that I won the Mud Races. Let's get on with it."

Hagan whispered, *"El?"*

The Odd's blade-smile faded. His eyes darkened, and he stepped closer, his every movement setting off a burst of backpedaling from his vols, who drew away from him. He approached the redhead and filled his worldview with the T-shape of flesh that composed his face. His breath smelled like motor-oil. Their eye contact was a laser that connected them. Torsten spoke first.

"You know explosives aren't allowed on the racecourse."

The redhead's eyes flickered. "Everyone breaks that rule."

The Odd stuck a talon in his face. "So you admit that it *is* a rule!"

"It's a rule," Eldridge said, his tone neutral.

"But holy *shitballs,* Eldridge! Moondog's dead, his ride all blown to hell. Tucker Beelzebub's dead, and you ride over the finish line on *his* boat, not yours. How the hell does that happen, less'n some foolio like you decides they can't win fairsies and squaresies?"

"What're you getting at?"

Torsten snapped at the redhead's nose with his teeth-blades. Eldridge staggered back a step. Torsten advanced.

"The rumortrysts say I'm the dumbest-shit Odd there is. Dumber'n Lestro Hepcat. Dumber'n The Great Ahmed. Even dumber'n Jeb Goldmist, who wasn't as smart as everyone thought. The rumortrysts may be right. But dumb as I am, I've got my vols, and they're not dumb. Nope. They can listen and report. And they can travel to other remnants." Torsten's tone turned high-pitched and pedantic. "And it's like this: They can find stuff out for me. Stuff my wittle brain can't figure out all on its own. Stuff like names. Names like Pell Yannick. Names like Lord Macta. Names like Lilya Hanna. Other stuff, too. Don't think I didn't notice her making a shitload of jenta when you won the Mud Races. And don't think I didn't know about—" his voice quintupled in volume, his face stretching, his robotic fists balling up, "*—the thmart box.*"

Eldridge and Hagan tried to stay cool, but both of them fidgeted, their eyes meeting for one telltale instant. Torsten offered up both of his hands for a high-five, which they accepted on reflex.

"*Yeah!*" Torsten said. "Way to try and bump off *another* Odd, dudes! So ya know what? I don't think I'm going to send anyone to the Chain. I think I'm going to keep the two of you right here in cozy ol' Hemming. I got me some hot little acid baths and these *boss* implements that go up your urethra and sprout thousands of sharp barbs. El, I don't know if I ever told you, but I kept a *second* bottle of that whiskey. I think I want to shred your dingaling and pour a *whoooole* bottle of booze over what's left. Whaddaya think?"

Torsten's vols rediscovered their nerve and crowded closer. Eldridge didn't move. Hagan searched for escape routes but found none. Ten-foot-tall steel doors stood at regular intervals along the back wall, all of them guarded by vols, while behind them, the zipline out of the mountain was the only escape—and Torsten himself stood next to the rocket-gondola. The Odd clicked his teeth, and as he turned to leave, he tossed an order over his shoulder.

"Lock them in the deepest, darkest, scariest, most ass-smelling dungeon we've got, vols. I'll have my fun with those two fucks later."

Twang.

Something hummed in their ears. The twang seemingly sounded from all around them, but Eldridge quickly realized that the zipline *itself* was vibrating like the string on an old guitar: *twannnnnggggg.* The redhead turned toward the great opening in the mountain and saw a black shape silhouetted by the shimmering blue of the hyperobject outside. The shape took form: a man holding onto the zipline with his hands and wearing a makeshift jetpack that spurted intermittent bursts of sparks and flame. Once he penetrated the mountain, the man released the zipline and cut loose the jetpack, which fell to the stone-tile floor and smashed to flaming pieces. They all turned to look.

A patch of plaid fabric covered his face. He had staple-gunned one corner of the patch back into place, the wounds crusted with black blood. Somewhere along the line, he had lost his blue Kevlar vest and was down to a pair of blue Kevlar pants and a white button-down missing its sleeves. Wisps of smoke rose from his gloves, the palms of which had been burned away by the zipline. Two straps crisscrossed his chest and held a pair of weapons to his back, a boltgun and a mortarchain rifle.

Quillig drew the boltgun and yelled at Eldridge and Boris.

"Get down!"

Hagan hit the ground, but Eldridge remained standing as Quillig blasted a red bolt of energy straight into Walter Torsten's chest. The

Odd leaned into the shot, apparently drawing on some deep-seated (and ill-advised) tactic for withstanding a point-blank boltgun blast. Black bloomed in the middle of his chest like a drop of ink splattering onto a blank page. Sparks spewed from his bionic limbs, which short-circuited and erupted into spasms. The blast left a smoking black crater in his chest lined with the cauterized cross-sections of his internal organs. With his last dying reflex, Torsten lunged in Quillig's direction, his teeth-blades opening wide, but he was too far away. Torsten's mouth chomped into the neck of a nearby vol, who shrieked as the Odd's corpse pulled him to the ground, where he bled.

The room turned white.

Forearms covered faces in response to the blinding burst. Everyone staggered around, blinking the light out of their eyes, including Eldridge. When his vision cleared, his gaze rose skyward. Hanging from the ceiling were several arrays of lightbulbs, their filaments still glowing orange from the flash they had just delivered. All across the remnant, sirens started to wail—and the vols started to wail with them. A voice joined the noise of the siren:

"Walter. Torsten. Is dead. Walter. Torsten. Is dead."

Powerful speakers scattered across the remnant delivered the message to the citizenry. The wails from the vols started to rise up from every corner of Hemming. Outside, blue light spilled over the mountainside as the hyperobject doubled in size. Quillig drew his mortarchain rifle and marched toward Eldridge and Hagan. Shrieking vols tried to block his path, only to find themselves flying backward through the air on a succession of red bolt-blasts. The sea of vols parted and revealed Quillig, who was training his mortarchain rifle on the redhead.

Hagan grabbed the redhead's arm.

"El! Let's—"

Eldridge shook away from Hagan's grasp. Quillig fired. Three crimson-crackling chains lightning-snaked across the room.

And Eldridge *caught* them.

In a blur of motion, he snatched them out of the air—two in his right hand, one in his left—and held their hook-ends inches away from his chest, his arms locked in ninety-degree angles before him, his whole body quaking with the effort. Hagan backed away, step by careful step, and looked at Quillig, whose sight-aperture slowly grew larger as he watched the scene unfold. Still the voice proclaimed outside:

"Walter. Torsten. Is dead. Walter. Torsten. Is dead."

As the wail of Hemming grew louder outside, Eldridge maintained the tableau for a few moments longer, and then in a flash, he swung around and slung the mortarchains into the floor, where they implanted with a trio of rapid-fire *bangs* and kicked up shards of stone. Red lightning licked around their lengths. Quillig tried to recall the chains, but they wouldn't budge. Vols crowded around them but kept their distance as long as the plaid-faced man was armed. Eldridge approached the bounty-merc, who pulled another weapon, but the redhead smacked it to the ground. He stopped, their faces inches apart. The vols closed in. Two of them took hold of Hagan's arms. He didn't even struggle.

"You want me to knock the other one out of your hand, or are you gonna let it go so we can talk?"

The mortarchain rifle clattered to the ground.

"Eldridge?" Hagan asked. "What are you doing?"

The redhead ignored his friend and addressed Quillig. "I'll go with you. But no mortarchains. Because you're not taking me to the Chain, are you?"

"No, I'm not."

"Because he's finally coming to collect."

"Who?" Quillig asked.

"You know who."

"Yeah," Quillig said with a nod. "It's him."

The redhead nodded. "Lead the way."

Quillig grabbed his boltgun and left the mortarchain rifle. They started walking.

Hagan yelled, "El?! What's happening?"

Tell him, said a voice in El's head. *He should know.*

No, he shouldn't, Eldridge replied. *Because then he'll try to help me.*

"Fuck off, old man," Eldridge said as Quillig led him away. "Nothing's happening. Go on home now."

"What?"

The only answer that came was the wail of Hemming.

"Walter. Torsten. Is dead. Walter. Torsten. Is dead."

[AUDIO: THE CLICK OF A DICTATRYST DEVICE DEACTIVATING.]

I know now why he did it. Why he didn't tell me.

And I get it.

Well, I don't entirely get it. I don't think he was justified. Hell, in point of fact, I think the motherfucker was dead-ass wrong to hide his pain from his one true-and-only best friend.

But at the very least, I can dig why he did it.

I don't know if any of y'all Shore-Riders got depressives among ya. You probably don't. Hell, I bet by your time, you done cracked that code.

"Take two of these, and your depression'll go away in an hour."

"Recite this incantation, and you won't work so hard to be alone."

"Read this book, and you won't spend your life trying to push your friends away."

Eldridge has always had that diseased gene that darkened the hallways of his mind. I could tell even when he was little. I'd find him sitting alone in some back alleyway of Dedrick. I'd stop and ask, "What's wrong, pal?"

"Nothing," he'd insist. I'd press him on it, but he'd just change the subject or run back to Burbage, even though I knew that was his least favorite place in all the world. That's how hard he worked to push me away sometimes, even then. Oh, he got better over the years—better and worse. He'd have good stretches, where he was present and accounted for in the lives of his loved ones. He'd show up for the big stuff, like meeting Milos Tola. Or going to their wedding.

Actually, shit—he missed that, too. All he did was moto-express up a growler of Claude's homebrew for the reception. So he had his bad stretches, his blind spots. I know the redhead felt ashamed for what happened to Zora, but he had no right to fade out of her life the way he did. That girl needed a dad growing up. Best she got was a guest star.

So when he finally remembered that Quillig's mortarchains had wiped out his memories of his daughter, Zora Tola, I understand why he didn't tell me. I understand why he swore at me.

He was trying to protect me by trying to get me to go away. He figured if he was mean enough to me, I'd take my old bones and shuffle off elsewheres.

Once a dipshit, always a dipshit.

I mounted a rescue for the redhead, but not before I ran into some trouble myself. We're gonna cover that next, and soon as we're done, I'm gonna set off on another *rescue, because that durnfool redhead done tried to push me away again.*

[AUDIO: SOME KIND OF VEHICLE HUMS IN THE DISTANCE.]

What the hell was that? Did you hear that?

Shit, Boris, you're losin' it. They can't hear nothing from where they are—they're Shore-Riders! But damn if that didn't sound like something approaching the house from a faraway distant place. I better check.

[AUDIO: BEDSPRINGS SQUEAK.]

[AUDIO: FOOTSTEPS RECEDING.]

[AUDIO: A WATERFALL ROARS IN THE DISTANCE.]

[AUDIO: FOOTSTEPS APPROACHING.]

Nothing. All clear. I better get back to it. There's still so much to tell, so much to do.

[AUDIO: THE CLICK AND WHIRR OF A DICTATRYST DEVICE COMING ONLINE.]

Hang in there, Eldridge. I'm comin' for ya.

KILLERMOUNT
&
THE RESCUE

BORIS HAGAN

"Walter. Torsten. Is dead. Walter. Torsten. Is dead."

So continued the litany as Boris Hagan watched Quillig lead Eldridge down the length of the great hall. They disappeared through a door in the far wall. As soon as the latch *clicked* shut, the vols yanked Hagan into the air and bore him on their palmtops toward another door.

"Hey! I didn't kill your dumbass Odd!"

"Shut up!" one vol yelled. "You *brought* his death to the mountain!"

Another yelled, "You took our Odd away!"

Still another, "And don't worry about your friends, the deathbringers. They'll never make it out of the remnant."

The vols then rejoined the wail that rang out across the remnant. Hagan fought to free himself, but hands had closed around his elbows and ankles to hold him in place atop the rolling wave of palms. As he bodysurfed toward one of the great doors, Torsten's body erupted out of the mass of vols, also borne on a table of palmtops. The Odd's corpse undulated alongside Hagan, who had an instant idea.

"I know how to bring him back!"

The crowd halted. Hands sprang loose, and Hagan toppled to the floor at their feet. Dried mud raining from his clothes, he lurched upright, then fell to his knees again. He remained on his knees, trying to wheeze his way out of oxygen debt. They drew back. One of the vols, a chief lieutenant who wore a rumpled old suit with a bare chest, stepped forward and helped him to his feet.

"How? We want him back, balls 'n' all."

Hagan smiled. "Oh, I'm skilled in these things. I'll bring him back, *starting* with the balls!"

A female Odd called out, "Maybe a little bigger this time! Don't tell him I said that when he's back."

Laughter greeted the vol's request while smiles proliferated and eyes popped wide across the group. Hagan's proposition was taking shape in their minds even as the wail continued:

"Walter. Torsten. Is dead. Walter. Torsten. Is dead."

Meanwhile, Hagan backstepped his way closer to the mortarchain rifle, its glowing red links still implanted in the stone floor. He didn't exactly know what he was going to do, and he couldn't stop thinking of the look on the poor redhead's face when he snatched those mortarchains out of the air.

What the hell happened between the end of the races and here?

He stepped over the still-crackling chains and continued his spiel:

"Doc Enki and I revived a lot of folks deader than Torsten is right now, no problem. All you need . . . um . . . all you need . . ."

The vols crept forward, fingers twining in anticipation.

"All you need . . . are some mortarchains!"

"*Yeah!*" exploded the cheer from the vols. They instantly dropped to their knees and teamed up to extract the chains from the stone floor. Six for each took hold of the three chains and pulled. Vols sprinkled to the floor one by one as the mortarchains' charge rendered them unconscious, but after a few minutes' struggle, the chains came free in an upward heave of stone tiles. The rifle slurped the chains back into itself. The chief lieutenant vol, Mr. Balls 'n' All, scooped up the rifle and presented it to Hagan.

"O great healer," he said. "Here is your instrument. Play your song of healing."

Hagan accepted the rifle, smiling in spite of the grief-weight in his chest.

"I thank you, O mighty vols, and I promise to revive your master. Please, present him to me now. I must ascend to great *heights* to bring him back from morpheus!"

All this time, Hagan had been backing away from the vols toward the fifty-foot window in the mountain. Blue light from the 4D object washed over him as he drew closer to the great opening, mortarchain rifle in hand.

"Great heights!" Hagan repeated. "Great! Heights! Great! Heights!"

The vols joined in the chant: "Great! Heights! Great! Heights!"

His limbs shaking, Hagan climbed up onto the giant window's lower sill, which hung about five feet from the floor, and continued to backstep his way across the width of the opening, which cut through a hundred feet of earth to the mountain's exterior. Scores of vols hopped up onto the stone still with him until the white-haired old man found himself standing on the outer edge of the great window, a three-hundred-foot drop beneath him, a mass of vols blocking his way out, the entire scene bathed in glimmering blue light. The slope of the mountain afforded him a view of its peak, and in his peripheral vision, Hagan sensed that the 4D object had changed shape. If he wasn't mistaken, the boot-soles of giant blue *feet* were hanging in the sky over Torsten's mountain.

"Walter. Torsten. Is dead. Walter. Torsten. Is dead."
"Great! Heights! Great! Heights!"
"Walter. Torsten. Is dead. Walter. Torsten. Is dead."
"Behold!" Hagan cried.

He turned around and looked out. A hive of street-blocks stretched out before him, while the remnant's mouth-ceiling hung hundreds of feet above. Boris Hagan raised the mortarchain rifle.

I hope this thing's got range.

He fired. The triplet of spires spat forth a triplet of electro-crackling chains that flew into the air and tinged the mountainside with a snaky shadow of purple light. The longer Hagan held the trigger, the longer the chain extended. Because the chains themselves were essentially electromorth constructs, Hagan was betting that they would continue ad infinitum until something blocked their path.

Luckily for him, he was *almost* wrong.

Hagan's chest tightened as the chains gave out hundreds of feet overhead. They hung in the air like three giant red stalks growing from the mountainside—and then they implanted. Swaying in the sky inches away from Hemming's ceiling, the mortarchains suddenly lanced into the rough stucco surface and took hold. The chains drew taut and nearly jerked the rifle out of Hagan's quavering hands. The vols cheered. Hagan spoke over his shoulder.

"*Flight* is necessary to bring any Odd back from the grave!"

The old man closed his eyes. A mad drumbeat sounded from within his chest, his heart rate having climbed near two hundred beats per minute. His last meal seemed like it had never happened. One of his ankles spontaneously rolled, forcing him to prop his hand against the side of the windowsill, but he managed to stay upright. He inhaled for a full fifteen seconds and envied the redhead's Narsyan training.

And he ran up the mountain.

Keeping a firm grip on the rifle, Hagan ran to the edge of the great windowsill and jumped out onto the mountainside itself, his feet churning though rocks, grass, and loose earth. Back on Tucker Beelzebub's barge-brick, the old man had found his second wind when he slipped into a hatch and waited on a ladder just below the deck. Clinging to that ladder in the dark, he felt a crazy burst of energy well up inside him—and it wasn't adrenaline. He had spent his supply of that handy secretion before they arrived in Penticton. No, Hagan's second wind sprang from sheer necessity, and as he sprinted up the side of Walter Torsten's mountain, he sensed that his second wind was almost over.

But he kept running.

Exhaustion transformed the affair into a meta-experience that carried Hagan back to his days of Zenning out with Zak Chamberlain, except in this case, he didn't have to concentrate in order to watch himself from the outside; the split between mind and body was automatic. The idea of sprinting up a mountainside in his current state struck the old man as darkly comic, an impossibility that continued to unfold as he ran higher and higher up the mountainside, his world saturated with the blue glare of the 4D hyperobject, which he could now see had transformed into a trio of 3D *people* who stood in a gigantic glowing tableau over the montainpeak as the wail continued:

"Walter. Torsten. Is dead. Walter. Torsten. Is dead."

Hagan's path up the mountainside tracked an arc away from the central great window. He course-corrected around one of the other great windows until he stood a good hundred feet higher, the mortar-chain rifle still in hand, its chains still implanted in the ceiling.

That's when the vols got it.

Their chant broke off midstream: "Great! Heights! Great! H—" A shouted garble of obscenity, blame, and *whatthefucks* interrupted the joyous chant as they realized that Hagan's promise might not have been entirely truthful. They streamed out of the great window, dozens of them crawling up the mountainside toward him. Hagan ignored them and scanned the city for a possible landing point, all while the wail continued and the citizens of Hemming spilled out into the streets.

Glass shattered and tinkled across the town as furniture started to fly. A riot was a-brewing.

Hagan didn't know how much control he might have over his swing, but he couldn't think about that. After all, a giant blue Eldridge was looking down at him.

"Eeeeg!" Hagan squeaked when he finally saw that the 4D hyperobject had transformed into a giant, three-dimensional portrait of himself, Quillig, and Eldridge. The three blue giants stood in mute shock over the mountainpeak—Quillig stood with his boltgun at the ready, while Eldridge and Hagan both *winced* at something, their eyes shrunk to slits, their hands rising to cover their faces. Over their heads stood gigantic blue letters that read THE CULPRITS.

The flash. Of course. When Torsten died, some kind of 3D smartscope must've snapped a picture of his murderer. Although why the hell did it scope him and Eldridge, when Quillig was the one who killed him? And had Torsten equipped his whole damn remnant with these smartscopes? What if he got killed somewhere *else*? *How fucking insane was this guy?*

"Kill the fucker until he's dead! Stab him in the butt!"

"Whoa," Hagan said as the shouts of vols brought him out of his confused reverie. A dozen vols had climbed up the mountainside, led by the chief lieutenant, who scrambled up the slope on his hands and knees, his fingertips tearing away patches of grass as he kicked his legs to propel himself. Hagan tapped hidden stores of fortitude to run forward and *jump.*

Hagan's boot caught the chief lieutenant in the face as he flew away from the mountainside. The lieutenant sailed backward through the air and landed on his cohorts, who tumbled down the mountain in a heap, all of them scrambling for a grip to stop their fall. As they fell, Hagan hugged the rifle and *soared.* He had leapt from a height of three hundred feet and now tracked a pendulous arc out over the city. The streets of Hemming rushed up below as his impromptu chain-swing found its nadir before carrying him skyward again, his plan to find a landing place quickly forgotten. City blocks smeared by, while dregs by the thousand gawked up at him and continued to wail in lamentation over their beloved Odd's death.

Finally, his velocity slowed. Hagan looked down and saw nothing but jam-packed streets a hundred feet below. As his momentum started to slowly carry him backward, he twisted around and looked for a place to land. He spotted a possible target. A few dozen yards back on his reverse course, an E-shaped building rose from a largely bare city block. Like the rest of the remnant, jagged brick walls surrounded the structure, but as Hagan hadn't hit the walls on his way over, he discounted the possibility of hitting them on the way back.

The citizens of Hemming changed that.

"There he is!"

Down at street level, thousands of pointing fingertips followed the arc of his swing as he passed overhead. A few of dregs were armed and started firing shots at his passing form. Some of the more cunning dregs shot at the ceiling where his mortarchains were implanted. A few of those shots dislodged two of the chains, which whip-cracked down to the street in a shriek of red lightning and struck down dregs by the score. Hagan lost altitude in a sudden drop that stopped his heart for an awful instant. It thumped back to life, and he tucked his knees against his chest to avoid hitting that jagged brick wall. He sailed over the E building and released the mortarchain rifle just as its third chain untethered and spilled to the street. He back-slammed onto the roof and rapped his head against its stone blocks. The rifle landed next to him and emitted a mechanical *yowl* as it automatically started the long process of retracting its chains. Hagan heard *oofs* and *ouches* from dregs at street level who got smacked by the chains as they slithered across the remnant and back onto the roof of the E building, where the old man felt his back seize up.

"Shit," he whispered. *Not now.*

Hot filaments of pain crackled along the sides of his spine. Hagan wasn't a sawbones, but he figured the injury was muscular, not skeletal. After all, he could still move his legs. Unfortunately, though, he couldn't move his *body*. Even *the thought* of sitting up caused his back to scream.

That's when an old friend came to visit.

That moron Zak Chamberlain spoke up from his past; Chamberlain, who, despite being a total spazzoid troxaholic, once walked himself across Dedrick to Doc Enki's office with a broken leg, the kook having somehow transmuted his shock into a Zenned-out bliss.

"Be a dude, Hages. Breathe into the pain," Chamberlain said, crouching over Hagan on the roof of the E building. Zak's leg was still shattered, his broken shinbone poking through the leg of his pants like an unwanted erection.

Hagan forced himself to relax every muscle in his body.

The wail continued. "Walter. Torsten. Is dead. Walter. Torsten. Is dead."

Hagan breathed deep. He never understood what the hell it meant to breathe *into* anything, but he tried to imagine his muscles inflating with air. Slowly, he rolled onto his side. A few muscle-spasms bubbled along his back, but no pain. He rolled onto his stomach, still breathing deep. No pain, so he pressed his palms into the ground and pushed himself up. He felt some pain then, but not enough to stop him. His legs came up under his chest, and he stood upright. A spasm rocked his back, but he started walking in slow, tight circles around the roof. Eventually, he paused before the mortarchain rifle and slowly bent over, both to retrieve the weapon and to stretch out his back muscles.

"Breathe *into* the pain, Hages," Zak said, a ten-foot top hat teetering on his head.

Hagan rasped as he grabbed his ankles and listened to the chaos on the streets below.

"Where'd he land?!"

"Get him!"

"*Kill him!*"

"Get him *and* kill him!"

And still the remnant-wide lament over the death of Torsten continued. Hagan snatched the rifle and made for a trapdoor laid into the roof. It concealed a set of stairs, which carried him past the E building's third floor packed with clothes and foodstuffs. He ignored the impulse to steal something to eat and plunged down to the second floor, which held nothing but art supplies—paint, pencils, paper, and *actual canvases*. Hagan was so taken with the sight of the supplies that he plowed right into a dreg blocking the staircase. The dreg must've been prepared for it, because he felt like a wall. Hagan fell on his butt, his face smeared with paint. The dreg, clearly the owner of the art supply store, rose over him and nodded at the mortarchain rifle he had clutched in his arm.

"Where'd you get that, friend?"

He grinned at Hagan with half a mouth and one eye. A bionic eye glowed yellow at him from one socket, while plastic webbing had replaced one of his cheeks. Thick rope-rivers of scar tissue coiled around his neck like his head had been severed and reattached. He grinned again.

"I said, where did—"

Suddenly they were face-to-face. Despite the dull agony in his back and his general being-an-old-man-ness, Hagan found the strength to ram the butt of the mortarchain rifle into the dreg's gut before he could finish his fifth word. He bent over soundlessly and sprayed Hagan with saliva mist. The riflebutt collided with his face next, and the dreg reeled backward down the stairs. Boris Hagan jumped—well, *eased his way*— to his feet, paused for breath, and stepped over the dreg on his way down the stairs.

The wail continued. "*Walter. Torsten. Is dead. Walter. Torsten. Is dead.*"

The stairs landed on the bottom floor (cooking implements) and spilled out onto a grassy hillock. Hagan stopped at the foot of the stairs. The three blue electromorph figures continued to slowly rotate over Torsten's mountain, while dregs by the thousands sprinted in every direction along Hemming's streets. All of the remnant's many footbridges were also jammed with dregs, who jabbed their fingers in unison at the culpable blue giants. A few score dregs seemed to be pursuing *him* specifically. They pointed at rooftops and screamed for the "head of the old man," but no one noticed the old man standing at the threshold of the E building.

Hagan checked the rifle's ammo readout. Only via the darkest rumortrysts had Hagan heard how mortarchain tech worked. Apparently the rifles were similar to the 4D hyperobject that hung over Torsten's mountain stronghold—they generated electromorph objects in the form of the chains, but they needed periodic recharges, and those could only be done at a secret bounty-merc base, wherever (and whatever) those were.

In any event, a small digital matrix-panel on the rifle displayed a red 01. His eyes rose to the image of the three blue giants that hovered over the mountain.

It would probably reveal my position, but . . .

From the foot of the grassy hillock, he took aim at the three blue giants. His finger coiled around the trigger—but someone shouted, "*Stop!*"

It was the one-eyed dreg, standing at the foot of the E building's stairs and clutching his stomach. Hagan's riflebutt had smashed his bionic eye, which sat is his socket, split in twain and bleeding bright green fluid. The dreg held up his palm, beckoning.

"Don't do it. Please!"

Hagan frowned. It occurred to him to ask *why* he shouldn't shoot, but an internal *fuck it* ended the debate. He pulled the trigger and fired his final mortarchain round toward the mountain. Three electric red snakes whiplashed across the remnant, the rifle humming as it fed out link after endless link. The triplet of hooks implanted into Quillig's gigantic blue-plaid face, which exploded like a splash of electronic blue water. A torrent of blue raced up the length of the chains and exerted a pull on the rifle itself. Hagan released the weapon, which rocketed across the remnant and smashed into Quillig's face. Hagan fell on his butt and shielded his eyes as the blue giants (and the accusing letters) shivered apart, their remains cascading down the mountainside like a crackling, luminescent waterfall.

When the blue waves had passed, the old man saw that the giants had vanished. In their place appeared more blue letters that read REBOOTING. Something else happened, too. The wail of Hemming stopped. *All* sound stopped. Silence filled the remnant. Over at the E building, Hagan saw that the one-eyed dreg had collapsed. Moments later, the word REBOOTING vanished, and blue cursive letters wrote out the message, WALTER TORSTEN: MAN OF THE YEAR, EVERY YEAR.

Hagan looked back at the unconscious, facedown dreg and started to slowly approach him. Had the flash from the exploding giants knocked him out? Was he stunned? Despite his fixation on the unconscious dreg, Hagan actually spotted the volley of mortarchains coming his way.

They lashed out from an alleyway like a triplet of red lightning-bolts. Hagan dove forward. Two of the chains sailed over him, but one lanced into his thigh and instantly yanked him backward. The old man left fingertracks in the grassy hillock as he ground his teeth and screamed in protest, but it didn't matter—one chain was enough. He whipped back and forth along the street as it reeled him in, and when it did, he looked up into the shiny, plastic-coated face of the bounty-merc called Kieron, who had a scorched black hole where her speechmouth used to be.

As crimson mortarchain-charge spun around him like a dozen electron shells, Hagan propped himself on his elbows.

"Congrats, jellywoman. You just blew my fucking mind. *You?*"

Kieron bent over and handed him a note written on old-fashioned paper.

I hereby claim you as my bounty, sir. And as our plight now stands, I'm your only hope to escape this remnant alive.

QUILLIG AND ELDRIDGE

HE HAD LESS THAN a day to get to Port Stafford, and despite that reality, something else nagged at him. Quillig turned and screamed at the redhead.

"Hurry it the hell *up!*"

Quillig ran around a giant stone circle that floated in the earth while Eldridge dawdled a few yards behind him. After they'd left the mountain's great hall, a series of stone hallways—all of them lined with various photographs, paintings, and etchings of Hemming's favorite Odd—led them deeper into the earth until they reached a massive cylindrical chamber. Roughly two hundred meters in diameter, the chamber sank into darkness below and stretched toward a pinprick of light above. The stone circle, which had no guardrails, hovered in the chamber, suspended by micromags. The wail of Hemming whispered through the half-mile of rock that lay between them and the remnant proper.

"Walter. Torsten. Is dead. Walter. Torsten. Is dead."

The bounty-merc's ass still stung from the singeing it had received from the piece-of-shit jetpack he had bought from a sniveling dreg in the far corners of Hemming. Regardless of the jetpack's value, Quillig had spent the remainder of his jenta on two *more* items that clattered together in his pocket.

A twin insurance policy.

His prized quarry, the Red Rook, Eldridge of Dedrick, shuffled along at a half-jog behind him, his head downcast. He had been like that ever since they left the great hall, and as they ran, Quillig bounced around him like an overeager child—a very pissed-off, overeager child—and berated him for his lollygagging.

I should've used my last round on him.

The bounty-merc was thinking of his mortarchains, of course, but once again, the redhead had surprised him. By his count, Quillig had captured more than two thousand bounties over the years, and he had never seen any of them grab live chains out of the air. If Eldridge didn't want to be implanted, then so be it. Still, he wondered exactly *why* Eldridge resisted implantation.

But the clock. He had less than twenty-four hours to deliver the redhead, and Stafford was almost a day's journey west.

Four dark passageways sank into the walls, the doors placed at the cardinal points of the stone circle. Quillig paused next to one of the passageways. To reach it, he'd have to perform a tiny jump across the divide and over a seemingly endless drop. On the wall next to the passageway sat a square control panel that flashed with red and green lights. He considered going back to retrieve the double-sidecar motorcycle he had left on the far reaches of Penticton, but he didn't like their chances of making it across Hemming unchallenged, unattached, or unkilled. So it was up or bust, but they had to find a way *up* out of these mountains. He looked back and watched Eldridge slouch his way around the circle until he stopped next to him.

"Where to, boss?"

"Look at me," Quillig said.

The redhead stared at the floor.

"Look me in the fucking face." Still no response. Quillig grabbed the redhead's jaw and pulled his head up, but still his eyes continued to droop. Quillig's hand dropped to Eldridge's neck. He squeezed. *"Look at me."*

Eldridge looked up, his eyelids red.

"You wanna come with me, you'll have to pick up the fucking *pace*. Any minute, Torsten's goons are gonna bust in here." The redhead looked at him with the eyes of a corpse, his gaze void of spirit. The bounty-merc began to choke Eldridge in earnest, squeezing his neck until his face flushed and he could feel the little shit's pulse throb against his palm. Quillig screamed, *"Say something, mactamerde! Aren't you gonna try and escape?! When's that old cunt gonna come and spring you?! Where are your friends?! Do something! Do something! Do—"*

The redhead's hand shot out over Quillig's shoulder and punched one of the flashing green buttons on the control panel. Trumpets blared. Quillig released the redhead and reached for his boltgun, but no attack came. Instead, a twenty-foot portrait of Walter Torsten floated up from below and hovered in the air. The late Odd stood with a foot propped on the upthrust rear end of a kneeling trixie. He squinted at the horizon, his chin tilted toward the sky, a sword in his hand, all while an orange sunset (or sunrise?) glowed behind him. Fireworks squealed up from below and exploded all around the portrait. Electromorph letters spelled out, BALLS TO THE WALL.

"What the fuck?" Quillig said.

"Sorry," Eldridge said, his voice husky from being strangled. "Wrong one."

He punched one of the red buttons, and they slammed into the floor. Or rather, the floor slammed into *them.* Propelled by an explosion of micromag energy, the stone circle soared up through the cylindrical chamber. As they flew skyward, Quillig hugged the floor, while the redhead lay on his back, his empty eyes watching nothing. High above, the pinprick of light became a circle that increased in size and luminance as they sped past level after level in the mountain.

The temperature increased, too.

Quillig continued to search the redhead's face for any expression, but he came up cold. Finally, the stone circle reached the top of the cylindrical chamber and let them out on top of a mountain that stood out in the blazing heat of the desert. Eldridge stood first.

"Better get off this thing. It goes back down after a minute."

The bounty-merc jumped up and off the stone circle. Moments later, it descended back into the mountain, which stood just outside Hemming as part of a small range of mountains that included Walter Torsten's stronghold. Torsten's mountain rose up before them, but was cut in half by the walls of Hemming remnant. It looked like someone had dropped a giant ball of wet plaster onto the region and smoothed it out over the mountains and surrounding foothills. Beyond Hemming lay more desert, and far to the west awaited the oceans and Port Stafford. Quillig shielded his aperture and looked at the sky, then at the redhead, who was already streaming with sweat. By contrast, Quillig *couldn't* sweat. He could feel his temples throb as his body began to overheat.

"Let's go. We need to find shelter and transport. The nearest confine is a hundred miles from here. I think."

"I've got transpo," Eldridge said.

Quillig glanced about. "Where?"

"We'll need to sneak back into Hemming."

"But—"

"Don't worry. It's near the entrance. I know where."

"Same way you knew how to work that thing?" He hooked his thumb at the cylindrical chamber.

"Something like that. Come on."

Eldridge jogged down the mountain, which descended on a gentle, rocky slope. Quillig followed. Halfway down, he grabbed the redhead's elbow.

"Eldridge, why are you doing this? Why are you coming with me?"

The redhead swallowed. He spoke, toneless: "I can remember her face. I can remember her death. But I can't remember anything else. It's gone. She's gone. My daughter's gone."

―∽―

BORIS HAGAN

BORIS HAGAN'S DARK REFLECTION looked out at him from a yellowing mirror that bore black streaks of grime and dozens of cracks. Under the mirror, a ceramic sink protruded from the wall. Two spigots sat on either side of the sink, a straight razor waiting between them. The red nimbus of mortarchain electricity still crackled around Hagan's body, but he knew that the jellywoman would have to disengage the chains to let him do what he had to do: shave.

In order to alter the old man's appearance so they could escape

Hemming unmolested, he and the jellywoman had retreated into one of the few places in Hemming that had four walls. Needless to say, an Odd presided over the tiny room. The Odd wore a short-sleeved, white button-down and black slacks that stopped a full three inches above his ankles and revealed white socks and black shoes. A gold chinpiece clung to his mandible and glinted in the lamplight that shone from a single top corner of the small room.

From the outside, the room appeared to be missing two of its walls just like any other building in Hemming. When the Odd spotted Hagan, he recognized his face from Torsten's giant electromorph "culprits" poster—and leaned out from what appeared to be nothing.

"Hot new tech, my friends," he said. "You need to be invisible. Ned will make it so. On the house."

Hagan's huge swing had taken him halfway across the remnant. After capturing him, Kieron had led them from building to building, always staying out of sight, even though that didn't seem to be necessary—after escaping Torsten's vols, the Odd was the first person they encountered.

The *only* person.

This particular Odd, called Ned, preyed on what Hagan would call off-the-bussers, or dregs who just got into town. His invisohabitat hovered within striking distance of one of the remnant's main entrances—a gate blocked by a porous gray wall that kept out the elements—and when newcomers rolled into Hemming, he'd spring on them and make odds over how long it would take them to make their first billion jenta. It only cost a fraction of that sum to make the odds, and any dreg who was cocksure enough to make the wager would invariably predict a meteoric rise to the top, their confidence buoyed by the excitement of being in a new remnant and unaware that they would invariably fail. And that meant Ned always won.

Almost always.

"So why are you letting us in here for free?" Hagan asked, sitting before the mirror, his muscles aflame from the mortarchains. Kieron hovered behind.

"Ned'll tell ya. Here's the squeeze: only one of my bettors has ever collected. Guess who?"

Hagan didn't have to guess. "Torsten?"

Ned's golden jaw wagged in approval. "Ned gets schooled. That's *my* story when I don't check *their* stories. How was Ned supposed to know he was an Odd fresh from Glaucio?"

"You couldn't have. But now you've got a chance to make your name?"

"It's a brand-new squeeze. Full of hope. Ned'll make it so. But now you gots to shave so you can make the *escape magnifico,* no?" he said, modifier trailing.

"That's right," Hagan said before he twisted around, his body emitting red flicks of lightning. "And I need to shave. So you need to lose these."

He indicated the mortarchains. Kieron shook her head and produced her black poly-stylus. Hagan frowned as the jellywoman drew a black box in thin air. The box hovered over her head like an otherworldly hat. Kieron drew two diagonal lines that linked the corners of the box, which instantly filled with whitespace. Using her plastic-coated fingertips, the jellywoman pulled the white box down so that its plane passed through Hagan's head. The old man yipped in response, but no harm came to him. When the jellywoman was done, Hagan was wearing the white box like a collar—it seemed to slice through his neck as it hovered a few inches above his clavicle—but his head no longer crackled with red mortarchain electricity; his head was charge-free.

Shit, Hagan thought.

The jellywoman then opened the mirror to reveal a small set of shelves that included various ad-hoc toiletries—a toothbrush, nothing more than a bit of wood capped with black bristles; handmade soap that resembled chunks of multicolored marble. An old-style shaving bowl sat on the bottom shelf. Kieron wet the small brush and swirled up a good lather that she spread across Hagan's face, stopping to use her fingers to work it into his hair. Kieron plucked the straight razor off the sink and offered it to the old man, but when Hagan held up a quaking hand, Kieron stayed him and lowered the blade toward the old man's neck, intent on performing the shave herself. Hagan grabbed the jellywoman's wrist. Ned inhaled. Yellow light glinted off the razor. The white-haired old man looked into Kieron's black oculars.

"You were after Eldridge before. Why do you want me now?"

Kieron dipped her fingertip into the lather and wrote a single character on the mirror: a capital J with two bars across the top—the symbol of the jenta. Hagan frowned.

"I know Hanna put a bounty on me, but it was piddlyshit. Why go to the trouble? Just let me go."

Kieron shook her head and drew more jentas on the mirror.

"I don't understand."

Ned spoke up: "Hanna, as in the Lilya, upped your bounty. If'n you *are* Boris Hagan, friend of the Red Rook?"

Why deny it? "Yeah, that's me." Muttering to himself: "Why the hell would she increase the bounty?" A thought occurred to him almost too grim to acknowledge. It involved a room built entirely from purple glass and a close-quarters encounter that forced the old man to tell a fib: Boris Hagan knew that Jacob Tutweiler wasn't the sixty-first president of the United States.

But a certain Odd was so enamored of him that she gave him unwinnable stakes months earlier when the old man came to beg for Pell Yannick's freedom. She invited him up to her personal pleasure chamber (the room of purple glass) and asked him one question—Who was the sixty-first president of the United States?—and she gave him these odds:

If Hagan was correct, she would take him as her love slave, while Pell would remain captive as Lord Macta.

If Hagan was incorrect, she would send him to the Chain of Tears, but she would release Pell.

Fucking Odds and their odds.

Hagan suspected that she'd go back on her word, but all the same, he thought he'd have a better chance to escape the Chain than to escape Hanna's pleasure chamber and her army of pinkeyes. When he told her the wrong answer, her disappointment manifested itself in a storm of pink plasma that filled the purple glass room. She called on Quillig as soon as the storm cleared, and despite her rage, her cranial essence melted into gleaming wisps of pink when she watched the bounty-merc blast Hagan with mortarchains. Pistons firing, she knelt beside him and cradled his cheek in her cold, metallic hands.

"A final overture, my Boris. Stay and love me."

Hagan lay on the floor of her pleasure chamber, three mortarchains implanted in his back, Quillig standing over him. Rings of red lightning flared around his prone form.

"If I do, will you release Pell?"

The pink wisps in her cranium crashed to the bottom of her brainpan and sizzled. She rose before him, steam spraying from every joint.

"*That's. Not. His. Name. Chain him!*"

The straight razor hovered before Hagan's eyes, his elongated reflection staring back at him. Once again, he sat in Ned the Odd's secret room on the outskirts of Hemming. He couldn't be 100 percent sure why Hanna had increased her bounty on him, but he had an idea—and it had to do with his buns.

"The bounty's only good if I'm alive. You know that, right?"

Kieron nodded. Hagan inhaled and leaned back. The jellywoman set the razor on his neck and cut. She took off the old man's hair first, the locks putting up no resistance as they fell in clumps to the floor. Kieron rinsed off the razor after she had shaved the top of his head. Hagan's remaining hair hung over his ears. Combined with the bounty-merc's electromorph collar-box, Hagan thought he looked a little like that William Shakespeare guy (with darker skin, of course), but then Kieron shaved off the rest of his hair and destroyed the illusion.

While Kieron worked, Ned leaned out of the hidden room to check the street. All was clear while the jellywoman shaved away Hagan's beard and revealed a jawline several inches shorter than the old man remembered. He touched his cheek and grinned with one corner of his mouth.

"Haven't seen that mug in a while."

And he hadn't. By his reckoning, he had last shaved a few days before he met the redhead, all those years ago. He hadn't taken any photos of himself back then, so his brain had to reconstruct what he *actually* looked like. Kieron set down the razor and tapped the mirror to get Ned's attention.

Leaning back into the room, the Odd said, "What do it?"

Kieron wrote on the mirror: *Clothes.*

"Right here," Ned said, crossing to the room's rear corner, where a steel closet stood. It opened with a *clang* and revealed a new outfit—that looked exactly like his own.

"Nice duds," Hagan said, then hissed as Kieron used her black stylus to tap the corner of the X-poly. The white box vanished, allowing the red mortarchain charge to engulf his head once more. He snapped, "This would be easier if you took off these chains. Every bounty-merc in a hundred-mile radius is gonna be looking for me. Don't you think you'd have a better chance to deliver me to Hanna alive if I was in a *complete* disguise?"

But the jellywoman was already jerking him out of his chair. She pointed at the clothes. Kieron used the straight razor to slice through the back of his new shirt, which Hagan pulled on. Ned sewed the holes shut. Once Hagan had changed, the jellywoman nodded her thanks at Ned, who offered these parting words:

"One tip, buddy-o's: *The water. Do not drink.*"

Hagan frowned at the strange advice, then forgot about it when Kieron yanked him into the street, which was silent. On top of that strangeness, Torsten's mountain no longer bore the deceased Odd's "man of the year" message.

The hyperobject had returned, but it wasn't blue. It was purple.

And it was growing.

ELDRIDGE AND QUILLIG

THE REDHEAD HAD ALREADY forgotten when he forgot his daughter.

after he and the plaid-faced bounty-merc, Quillig, emerged from a mountaintop just outside Hemming's walls, they scrabbled their way down that same mountain under the perpetual downblast of sunfire. Eldridge figured it for 160 degrees. Every drop of sweat that fell from his body hissed and steamed off the rocks, which constantly slid from underfoot.

Intellectually, Eldridge knew *what* was missing. He knew that he had raised Zora Tola himself after parting ways with his wife—he stopped himself. She wasn't his wife, but she was most certainly Zora's *mother*.

Nadia. Nadia Tola.

Boris Hagan used to ask him about Zora's conception, his tone ginger and gentle.

"How old were you when you knocked up Nadia, El?"

"Fifteen," came the redhead's answer.

"And how old was she?"

"I don't know. Older."

"How much older?"

"I don't know."

"How do you feel about that?" Hagan asked, like he always did, probing beyond the surface in search of what mattered.

As he often did, the redhead blushed. And fidgeted. And fumed. He'd start to say something, only to stop and course correct around his urgent silence, his mouth producing a succession of grunts and *ummms* as his face contorted its way through expressions that ran the gamut from rage to a verging-on-tears grimace.

"I don't fucking *know*, Boris. She's special to me is all. Special."

Indeed, the redhead had just turned fifteen when he met Nadia. He had left the order only a year and a half before, and out of habit, he had kept up his training. As it happened, his training led him to meet the dark-haired beauty who would pass on her six and a half feet of height to their daughter, the future Dedrick constable.

Narsyans didn't recognize days. Most of the lower-level initiates didn't even know what they were, instead viewing time in a series of grand celestial events—eclipses, solstices, equinoxes. By contrast, the chieftains educated themselves about the customs of all macta (non-order members), but a typical Narsyan had no knowledge of the concepts of yesterday, today, and tomorrow. Eldridge had never been a typical Narsyan, but even after he got drummed out of the order, he would go for days without sleeping, instead passing the time by running megamarathons through the frozen desert night. (The redhead had never been able to fully meet the challenge of running during the day.) One night, he wanted to hang out with Crius Kaleb, but his old friend was too busy stalking a bug in the far corner of town. With a free night ahead of him, the redhead sprinted up the ramp from under-Dedrick and ran due south, following the bright southern star that glittered over the horizon, which Marko Marinus had pointed out to him years earlier.

Before he betrayed him.

Marko's betrayal before the council (that wasn't a council) of chieftains still enraged the young redhead enough to fuel his system with liters of adrenaline over the course of a megamarathon. Eldridge always figured that Narsyans, even *macta* ones, had as much adrenaline in their systems as blood, which contributed to their amplified strength. The redhead had called on his amplified strength (and speed) that night when he cut a wide path around a pack of dreens that were making the long journey up to the Old Mine. His course change coincided with an incursion of clouds that covered the moon and the southern star. He figured he could find his way south again, but it wasn't until his chest started to burn from the exertion of sprinting an additional thirty miles that he paused and acknowledged that he had lost his way. By that point, clouds covered the sky. Surrounded by his body's steam, the redhead stood in place and slowly rotated in a circle so he could soft-focus-scan the terrain for any landmarks he might recognize. He saw none—only a blank expanse.

That was when the sky started falling.

Eldridge saw the first bit of sky flutter down, and even though his Narsyan-honed reflexes helped him jump out of the way, he wasn't fast enough to dodge all of the snowflakes that drifted earthward. He chuckled at his folly. Training in the upper reaches of the Oasis Mountains, he had seen drift after endless drift of snow—most of which he had been forced to run over or dig through—but the novelty of seeing snow in the *desert* awakened a bright spirit of invention in him. He caught a snowflake on his fingertip and tasted it; a single frozen pinprick on the tip of his tongue. He cupped his hands and tried to fill them with snowflakes, but they all melted too fast, leaving only a small puddle of water in his palms. For a moment, he simply listened. Freezing air sighed across the desert and carried the snowflakes along a windwave that glided parallel to the earth, only interrupted by the occasional eddy that whipped the flakes in tight circles on their trip to the ground.

The redhead didn't notice that the snow had started falling harder. When he looked up from his cupped hands, he saw snow had gathered over his bootclad feet and heaped upon his shoulders and head. He peered into the swirling wall of white but could only see about twenty feet.

"Well, shit."

Only then did he realize that his entire body—arms, legs, fingers and all—was quaking. Even his internal organs felt like they were jittering back and forth inside his trunk. He hugged himself and concentrated on rubbing his biceps and vibrating his torso as hard as possible. It was a Narsyan technique to fend off the cold, but the redhead sensed that he was too late; his reverie had carried him past an internal threshold that he'd never see again unless he found some fire.

Think. Think. What did Marko say about situations like this?

Trapped in a desert snowstorm, the redhead's memory failed him. Forgotten ideas called out to him from a distance, but he couldn't make out their words. *Something to do with challenges.* The fifteen-year-old redhead felt his eyes start to dryfreeze in his skull as his eyelids drew back and his mouth curled in a grimace of panic. If could remember how to cry, he would have, but instead, he stood there in the snow, hyperventilating.

Until a skyfire saved him.

Actually, it was the *snow* that saved him because it added contrast to the landscape and brought a nearby butte into view. It stood like a dark table a few miles in front of him, and somehow, it appeared to have a fire burning on its *side,* up in the sky. How had he missed it? The redhead dismissed his confusion and started running on legs that had grown leaden in the cold. Snow had started to stick, forcing him to wade through foot-high drifts every few yards, his feet having vanished into the blocks of numbness that encased him to his knees.

Unconsciousness contracted the time it took to reach the butte. One moment he was running, the next he was dreaming of a better world where the weather made sense, and the next he was about to slam into a rocky face that rose before him. Quaking, he looked up and saw an array of spherical and hemispherical pods that hung from the rockface on steel rods that protruded from the butte, which looked like down at him like a giant, mouthless leviathan with a dozen blazing eyes, as all of the pods glowed with fires that burned from within. Eldridge looked for a place to climb up, but there was no ladder—only natural handholds.

Great.

The redhead bent at the knees and jumped to the lowest-hanging handhold. He caught it with two hands that intellectually he knew existed, but which had both been encased in the same numb-blocks that currently housed his legs. Proceeding on concentration and instinct, Eldridge commanded his frozen limbs to carry him up the side of the butte, handhold by handhold, foothold by foothold. Another lapse into unconsciousness erased the time it took to climb to the strange vertical outpost. The redhead pulled himself up onto a small outcropping and knocked on the nearest glowing geodesic dome. Dark shapes stirred inside, their outlines shifting into focus as they crawled toward the dome's wall. A black hand crept to the edge of the dome and swept in a wide circle, unzipping a door along the way. Warmth and light spilled over the redhead, who closed his eyes and basked with such abandon that when he came to, her hair was brushing against his face. He was also dangling from the side of the rockface, having fallen when the heat hit him. Fortunately, the woman who had unzipped the dome was fast enough to catch him—and there he dangled, hand in hand with a woman he would later describe as the "most unbe-goddamn-lie-va-fucking-ble beautiful woman I've ever seen or will ever see, ever. Ever."

For a moment, her dark hair created a tunnel between her face and his, its black walls lit with intermittent threads of golden light. They could breathe each other's air, smell each other's breath. A harsh breeze kicked away the tunnel and admitted the onslaught of snow once again.

"You're not too bright, are you?" Nadia asked the redhead.

Teeth chattering, he shook his head, and then in a burst of youthful pique and infatuated joy, he kicked himself off the side of the butte and flipped into the dome. He landed on a hemispherical floor-platform covered with blankets and pillows made from unfamiliar fabrics that shone in the tent's inner light. The instant he landed inside the dome, his energy evaporated and left him curled in a fetal position. From the floor, he had a view of the dome's firehutch—a small cubical device that housed a sphere of flame. The redhead had seen such devices around the streets of over-Dedrick. A firehutch's chief ends were safety and mobility. Once ignited, the hutch enclosed the flame in a magnetic sphere, and if something were to shatter the device, it was designed to instantly extinguish the flame. But otherwise, the flame would last for days. It could even go underwater safely.

The dark-haired woman, whom he would come to know as Nadia, zipped up the dome and sat in a ring of darkness that rippled beyond the edge of the firehutch's light. Her next words sent a jolt through him.

"Get naked. Now."

"W-w-what?"

"Naked. Now. Or you die. Show me your fingers."

His limbs still encased in blocks of numbness, Eldridge pushed himself up to his knees. He felt like his torso was hovering. Somehow, his hands rose before him. He held up eight fingers and two thumbs, most of them tinged a deadly blue-black he remembered well from his many sojourns in the upper reaches of the Oasis Mountains. In those cases, though, it had been his friends, and not he, who had succumbed to frostbite.

"Oh, no," he said and immediately started fumbling with his clothes—a heavy corduroy button-down, burlap denim pants, and heavy boots.

"No coat?" she said, unbelieving. "No hat? No gloves? Here, let me." She knee-walked into the light and revealed a glimmering blue gown made from the same unfamiliar fabrics as the pillows and blankets. She set to warming him up, though not in the way that would eventually be successful that night. From the folds of her gown, the woman produced a flick-knife that she used to cut away his bootlaces. The blade traced two parallel lines up his pant legs next, followed by a button-popping trip up his shirt. Her knife slashed and sliced and snicked and snipped his clothes away, the firehutch spitting spectral spires across the walls.

Part of the redhead wanted to protest, but it was a small part, an underdeveloped part of his personality. Other parts of his psyche were more than ready to speak up for him—he used to mouth off to his Narsyan elders a dozen times a week—but when it came to matters of sexuality, his vocabulary was a wasteland of false and strange notions fed to him by his fellow Narsyans. He was no longer a virgin, but he had no idea what sex really was, much less love. His mind was primordial, unformed, malleable.

Nadia peeled away his clothes and revealed the rest of him—none of which was frostbite-blue, thank Crom. His muscles were aflame with blobs of golden mercury from the firehutch.

"Better if we had a warm bath, but this'll have to do," she said.

She thrust her flattened palm into the sphere of hutchlight, then made a fist and extracted a palmful of flame. By that point, the redhead was already fading into unconsciousness again, and for years, he dismissed the images chronicled in his memory as a dream, but as he would learn later—*much* later—the woman who would bear his child was capable of many such wondrous feats.

In her hand she held a ball of fire, which she spread across his naked body like a salve. As she worked, she cupped her hands over his form and contained the fire within, her body seemingly endowed with magnetic properties of its own. Flames danced between his skin and her palms when she passed over him. It only took a few moments for blood to rush back to his limbs and banish the blue-black from his fingers.

Nadia finished by cradling his face in her fiery hands. She worked on him until sweatdrops appeared on his brow, then stopped. With a flick of her wrists, the fire vanished. Sweat started to chill his face and induce shivering, so she dabbed him dry with a blanket that she cast aside. Once he was dry, she shrugged out of her gown and wrapped herself into a blanket with him. Her arms and legs coiled around him. She pressed his face into her neck and hugged one of his legs with both of hers. He felt her moisture pressed against the top of his thigh.

He got conscious again. Fast.

"What are you doing up here?" he asked.

"Be quiet and rest, love. Try to sleep. You'll need it for the journey ahead."

"Where are you going?"

"We're on our way west."

"I live north of here."

"Where?"

"Dedrick."

"That's due *south* of here."

"Oh."

"You're shivering again," she said and held him close enough to flatten his hard cock between their stomachs. "What's your name, love?"

"Billy. *Bill*. Eldridge. Why do you keep calling me 'love'?"

She giggled. It sounded like a busted organ.

"What's so funny?" El asked, not knowing that he had just originated her future endearment for him. A sudden sweat created viscosity between them. Eldridge thought it was his, but it was hers. She burned against his thigh. Eldridge exhaled so hard he felt his breath condense on her skin. Her legs untwined, and before he could protest, she'd taken him inside her.

His mind was primordial, unformed, malleable.

"What are you doing?" he asked.

The busted organ played a few halting notes, alternating major and minor keys. The dome's walls bristled with shadow-armies of knives and fire that marched in hectic formations all around him. He had a million questions about what was happening but no words with which to ask them.

When she was done, she held him close.

"Do you need something to eat?" she asked. "You must be so hungry."

"I'm not hungry."

"Thirsty?"

"No. I'm not . . . anything," he said, looking into her eyes, a pair of dark tunnels that beckoned him. He wasn't hungry for food but *her*. Eldridge learned a lot about Nadia that night—that she was many years older than he, that she and her group were traveling around the world, that she had been on her way to Port Stafford, which lay roughly west of Dedrick.

Had been on her way. Because after that night, she parted ways with her circumnavigators and moved to Dedrick with the redhead. Good thing, too, because 221 days layer, she gave birth to a premature (but healthy) baby girl.

Twenty-seven years later, Eldridge looked back on Zora Tola's actual day of birth and saw nothing but a fucking black hole. Somehow, he was missing her memories and nothing else. Had the engineers behind mortarchain tech found a way to selectively remove such precious memories? Was Boris Hagan missing his own set of cherished times, but not yet aware of the loss?

Back in the present, an eroded sheet of rock-dirt slid out from under his feet. Eldridge clawed at the mountainside for a handhold, found one, and hissed through his teeth as the exertion squeezed even more precious moisture out of his body. Quillig bounded down the mountain and rapped him on the temple with his boltgun.

"*Get up.* You need to get us back in there."

The bounty-merc pointed down, where one of the gates into Hemming awaited. From that distance, it looked like nothing more than a giant rectangular gray window set into the side of a man-made mountain. Wide enough to admit the passage of three of Quillig's big rigs, the gate may have *looked* like glass, but it was actually a porous reverse-superfluid. Undisturbed, it congealed into a semisolid state, but when penetrated, it liquefied just enough to allow the comings and goings of dregs, their traffic marked by inward-spilling starbursts that usually dotted the gate's surface like a series of breathing anuses. But no such features marked the gate that day, and that gave the redhead pause. He hunched under the shade of a dead tree that extended from the mountainside like a twisted finger.

"Where is everybody?"

Quillig joined him under the tree, wheezing. "What do you mean?"

"Dregs are usually pouring in and out of here by the thousand."

"Does it matter?"

"It might. Torsten had everyone drinking his lemonade. When you killed him, he might've done something crazy."

Quillig turned his dark aperture on him.

"'Drinking his lemonade'?" A question.

Eldridge looked down. *Something Boris Hagan would say.* "Just something I heard. It means he had 'em all fooled."

"Do you mean, 'drinking his *Kool-Aid*'?"

Eldridge looked over. "What's Kool-Aid?"

"It's a beverage designed to delight children. I had it growing up."

The redhead gave him a look. "Where'd you grow up?"

"The fuck do you care? Just get us in there."

Eldridge stared at the bounty-merc for a moment longer, then sprang down the mountain in a series of flying strides that set off a series of small rockslides in his wake. Quillig chased after, cursing all the way. At the foot of the mountain, the redhead hid behind a boulder and waved Quillig over. The redhead pointed at the lower corner of the gate.

"In case there's a welcoming party, we don't want to announce ourselves. Stay low and move fast, because you won't be able to breathe, and if we get stuck, we're screwed."

They ran over to the near side of the gate, dropped to their hands and knees, and crawled into the gray wall, which slurped them inside. The redhead knew they had about fifty meters to cross, all without breathing, and all while struggling through the gray goop, which was still littered with the occasional skeleton, bone, or half-decomposed corpse. Most dregs knew to maintain a steady pace through the gates of Hemming, but some arrived at the remnant so exhausted that their slogging pace wasn't enough to keep the gate fluid around them. Torsten's vols did their best to keep the gates clean. It was possible to open your eyes while inside the gate, although most opted to keep them shut rather than contend with the unusual sensation of having your eyes frozen in amber. On his previous visits to Hemming, Eldridge had closed his eyes, but not this day. He wanted to be ready for whatever awaited them inside the gate. As they progressed through the gate, the wail of Hemming grew louder and louder.

"Walter. Torsten. Is dead. Walter. Torsten. Is dead."

Eldridge emerged from the gate and jumped to his feet, shaking off the bits of gate-goop that had condensed onto his clothes. Two main thoroughfares connected in a V at the gate. The redhead glanced down both roads, which were lined with hectic jumbles of brick and stone, wood and plaster. Dregs scrambled down the V-streets toward the far corner of town, where the mountain stood. Eldridge stood on a separate major street that ran along the remnant's perimeter. A white plaque bolted into the wall bore the street's name: EDGECUT. The redhead looked both ways down Edgecut for any signs of trouble. A few dregs piled out of their homes, headed for the mountain, but no one had seen them. He plunged his hands into the gate and yanked Quillig out by the shoulders. They collapsed onto the stone tile street. The beige-stucco slope of Hemming's man-made roof rose above them, its surface tinged with blue. Red lightning flashed across the sky, accompanied by a roar from the citizenry. Eldridge tried to see what was happening, but a pair of tall buildings blocked his view. The redhead plucked some gate-drops off of Quillig's clothes and pulled him to his feet.

"That way," the redhead said, pointing at a faded wood sign that read VEHICLE IMPOUND. They jogged toward it. A few empty blocks rolled by before the mountain came into view and revealed their gigantic blue avatars—Quillig, Eldridge, and Hagan—all of them rotating under the words, THE CULPRITS. The sight brought Quillig to a standstill.

"That ratfuck."

Eldridge grabbed his arm. "Keep a move on, B-M."

The wail of Hemming chased them along the street: *"Walter. Torsten. Is dead. Walter. Torsten. Is dead."* Eldridge darted down an alley and brought the impound into view. He and Quillig leaned out from the end of the alleyway. Across the street, a wooden guardshack stood empty next to a wall of cyclone fencing. Rings of barbed wire ran along the top of the fence. A few scattered dregs, still chanting the wail of Hemming, sprinted by, their eyes bulging in mania. Eldridge let the dregs run a few more blocks toward the mountain, then jerked his head at the impound.

"Let's go."

Quillig in tow, he dashed across the street in time to see another flash of red lighting, only it wasn't lightning but *mortarchains* that slashed through Hemming's airspace until they smashed into the three guilty blue giants over Torsten's mountain and sparked an electronic explosion that doused the city streets with pixilated water. Eldridge shielded his eyes, and when he lowered his hands, he saw a new message had replaced the three blue giants: WALTER TORSTEN: MAN OF THE YEAR, EVERY YEAR.

Dark sensations teased the redhead from parts distant. Had he lost *other* memories? He scanned his past and found nothing amiss, and what's more, the dregs had finally shut up. The wail of Hemming had ended. The streets were empty, too. The sudden silence posed a series of questions to the redhead: *What was your daughter's favorite food? Or favorite color? Or favorite toy?*

Eldridge kicked open the gate to the impound, snapping an

inch-thick chain in the process. He stomped into the block-wide parking lot, which was packed with a panoply of conveyances—trucks, cars, small skycraft. The redhead even recognized a few ultralite aircraft and one rickety ornithopter. And then it came into view in a shimmer of chrome.

His motorcycle.

Torsten hadn't lied. His vols had showered his ride with an affection that bordered on creepy. A new matte-finish paint job adorned all of the bike's tactile surfaces, while loving hands had scrubbed the chrome until it shone like silver glass. Tucked in between the exhaust pipes were his sun-goggles. He pulled them on. Old memories, most of them happy, babbled like a brook in his mind, including his first memory of the bike.

Under the shadow of Jeb Goldmist's tower—which at the time was only half its eventual height—Nadia flexed her bicep with one arm and used her other to present the bike to him as a present for his birthday.

"But I don't know my birthday," he said.

"I don't care," she said, the dark tunnels of her eyes beckoning him.

In his mind's eye, Nadia continued to show off her bicep muscle, and as Eldridge mounted the bike in the Hemming impound, he puzzled over why Nadia would do that. Quillig climbed on behind him.

"You know the way to Port Stafford, Eldridge?"

Port Stafford. That's where Nadia had been heading before he sidetracked her life. Before they conceived a child. Bathed in the silence of Hemming remnant, Eldridge grew still. Nadia hadn't been flexing her muscle. She had been holding their baby.

But the memory of Zora was gone, surgically removed. Forever.

He looked out on Hemming and suddenly understood why it had grown so quiet.

Quillig jabbed him in the kidney.

"Eldridge. *Port Stafford.* Can you get there from here?"

"Yeah. I assume that's where the man is?"

"If you mean the one from across the oceans, then yes."

"Got it. Yeah, I know the way."

"Then hit it. I don't want these dregs to catch us."

"They won't," Eldridge said as he activated the hydrocell. "They can't."

KIERON AND BORIS HAGAN

As soon as they left Ned's, Hagan aimed himself at the exit gate—a porous plastic membrane that covered an arched tunnel out of the remnant—but Kieron reeled him back in.

"What?" Hagan said. "That's the way out."

The jellywoman shook her head and wrote a note:

We need transpo.

A few blocks away, a sign rose up over the surrounding walls that read VEHICLE IMPOUND. Hagan waved his finger at the distressed, faded white letters.

"Look! Lots of transpo there. Let's just boost something."

Kieron shook her head. A note: *Mud tunnel.* Unless dregs had stolen it, Quillig's double-sidecar motorbike awaited them in one of the chambers that led back to Penticton, which was where he was headed anyway.

Hagan's eyes jumped from the note to the *other* far corner of town. The walls of Hemming outlined a rough rectangle. Two corners of that rectangle stood clear across town from their current position. One corner held Torsten's mountain. The other held the entrance to the mud tunnel.

"We'll never make it," Hagan said.

Kieron shrugged and pulled Hagan along through the streets, which remained empty and silent as they made their way across the remnant. There was no one to see them; no one to see the newly hairless Boris Hagan, dressed like Ned the Odd, all in monochromatic shirtsleeves and slacks. Even this far away, the purple light of the hyperobject shone off of Hagan's bald head and cast its glimmering light across everything. The old man grumbled at Kieron.

"You should let me go. You'll never win playing with the Odds."

Kieron ignored him, but damn if that *purple* light didn't turn *blue* and start flooding everything. The light reached the streets of the remnant until Kieron's plastic covering suddenly vanished, and she once again found herself home among her people some several months ago.

In the middle of the war to end all wars under the waves.

She walked along the floor of the oceans, a water-sky of pitch black hanging overhead, her tank of respiro-paste bolted to her chest. Intermittent bursts of light illuminated the path she walked—*intermittent* because her allies were running low on ammunition.

An underwater explosion struck the jellywoman as sacrilegious, the ancient faiths of her people having proliferated since the start of the war, their old myths bolstered by a need for meaning among the endless bloodshed.

No one was sure who had instigated the war, but Kieron had promised her people that they would be the ones to end it.

Walking along the ocean floor, the jellywoman saw that Boris Hagan was now equipped with a tank of respiro-paste. Good. Kieron's leaders wanted all prisoners of war taken alive.

But what was remarkable about Boris Hagan was his ability to talk underwater. All of Kieron's people communicated in sign language when submerged.

"Hanna'll never pay you the bounty. She's fucknuts. She just wanted *me*, and she'll do whatever it takes."

She ignored her prisoner, who was simultaneously Boris Hagan *and* a commander from Admiral Govannon's naval high guard. They crested a rise in the ocean floor and brought the battlefield into view. Once again, the unholy appearance of undersea explosions peppered the scene. Bright spheres surged in and out of existence, their interiors packed with millions of fireball-bubbles.

Kieron, general-prime of her people's military, watched as an explosion vaporized a tower that rose from the center of a circle of inward-leaning columns, all of which had generated hallways of superwater around the tower for years. Although her people revered ancient structures of brick and stone, they had little need for them since the advent of the hyper-dense fluid. All the same, the tower and its accompanying circle of leaning columns had housed the citadel where the jellywoman had sworn an oath to defend her people. And now it was no more.

Ageless structures older than the world fell under the blasts along with hundreds of foot soldiers, their deaths punctuated by chest-tanks that detached from their bodies and floated toward the surface, leaking clouds of black respiro-paste along the way.

But there was something else. Something far worse.

The dead were *blooming*.

As they rose through the water, their chests burst open, dislodging their respiro-paste devices and revealing seething pink-red blossoms of villi, the very inner workings of their lungs, infected until they swelled to ten, *twenty* times their natural size, giving them the appearance of zoanthids that oozed blood in expanding crimson clouds.

By the Many Almighties, he did it, Kieron thought. *Govannon used the Narsyan poison.*

That had been months earlier. Maybe.

Back then, Kieron had released her prisoner and swam for the ocean's surface, but now as she led Boris Hagan through the streets of Hemming, she had no place to flee, no strange new land to call her home. She only had the hope, the potentially foolhardy hope that the Odd Lilya Hanna would pay her in the form of *jenta* for her bounty and *clout* for her reputation. Among the extraterrestrials, no one knew that Kieron had innovated the dorsal-flank maneuver during the Battle of Laurentia. No one knew that she had slain more than a thousand marauders over the course of her storied career. No one knew that she and her many lovers (and their many lovers) had convened the natural-philosophical symposium that had brought about the invention of superwater. No one knew.

All that made it from the oceans to the surface world were spook stories. Superstition. "Rumortrysts," the extraterrestrials called them, except that when they regurgitated the rumortrysts about Kieron's people, they spoke them as fact.

Only the Narsyans knew better. But they hadn't been heard from in months.

Purple.

The jellywoman returned to Hemming and looked at the peak of Torsten's mountain, where the hyperobject continued to glow purple. What the hell did *that* mean? She led her prisoner up a set of stairs to where a rope footbridge spanned several silent city blocks. The footbridge passed between two walls of a red brick tower. Windows on either side afforded views of the remnant, so Kieron paused and peered at the purple hyperobject. Hagan walked beyond the boundary of the tower, but the jellywoman yanked him back and tapped his shoulder.

"What?"

Kieron pointed at her ear, then out at the remnant. Hagan listened.

"It's quiet. It's *really* quiet."

The bounty-merc scribbled a note: *What does that mean?*

"How should I know? Nothing good."

The bounty-merc pointed at the hyperobject and her question again. Hagan looked at the purple four-dimensional shadow and shook his head.

"No idea. But listen: You should let me go. Right now."

Kieron shook her head and started to walk past him, then stopped. She turned back to Hagan and wrote a note:

Why?

"Lots of reasons. You heard what I said about Hanna. She won't pay you. Some Odds pay their bounties. She's not one of 'em. But who cares? You should let me go because you're fucking up my life."

The jellywoman stared at him.

Hagan went on, "You're not going to understand any of this. My friends need help. All of them. One of the Odds snatched my best friend and destroyed our hometown, so a bunch of us went out to make it right. Turned out we didn't know what we were doing, and we all got waylaid here and there. Two of us turned into monsters up in Towertown. One of us is a freak back in Penticton. I actually managed to spring my best friend from the Chain, but now your buddy, Mr. Plaid, is taking him to someone really bad. Me? All I wanna do is sit on the rooftop at Nix's and have a beer with my best friend under catwalk city. And I know for a truth that I'm not asking for too much. But you and yours keep fucking it up. So make it right, and make it right now. Turn me loose."

Kieron wasn't familiar with Nix's or catwalk city, but the old man's words completed a circuit somewhere inside her. She thought back to times spent freediving into pitch-dark trenches that plunged into the earth. As she and her old friends dove deeper and deeper, they challenged each other to see who could venture the deepest. Kieron always won. For a moment on that footbridge in Hemming, Kieron felt less like she was standing *next to* Boris Hagan and more like she was standing *with* him.

And then it passed. The jellywoman shook her head and pointed at the mud tunnel. The mud tunnel lay about a mile straight ahead. Hagan stared into her black oculars for a good ten seconds, his eyes shifting about. Finally, he turned and continued the march down the footbridge.

Then he jumped.

As soon as they passed beyond the boundary of the two-walled tower, the old man propped a foot on the rope guardrail and launched himself off the bridge. Mortarchains spilled off the side. In an instant, Kieron had wrapped the chains around his forearm, her plastic coating absorbing the charge, but it didn't matter. The chains reached their limit and snapped taut, pulling Kieron toward the edge of the bridge. She hit the rope guardrail, which bowed outward under her weight. Leaning off the side of the bridge, she saw Hagan dangling at the end of the chains about twenty feet below, a few feet above street level. The old man was kicking his legs in a futile effort to generate some momentum. Hagan quickly changed tactics, choosing instead to *climb up the chains*, his body surrounded by blinding bolts of red lightning. Kieron commanded her mortarchains to start retracting, but it was too late: Hagan had reached the top. Panting, he drew nose-to-nose with the jellywoman, then let go. This time, the old man got his desired result: when he fell, the chains ripped out of his back. He slammed into the ground as the chains slurped back into the jellywoman's wrist-mounted module. Kieron gawked at Hagan, who lay still on the ground.

But not for long.

Arms stirred, followed by legs. Elbows quivering, the old man pushed himself up to his knees, then levered himself to his feet and ripped off Ned's shirt, revealing three smoking black holes in his back. Steam rose off his sweat-slick form. He pivoted away from the mud tunnel and the hyperobject and started to run at a limb-heavy lurch, his plodding footfalls echoing across the empty remnant.

Kieron raised her wristmount and fired. It squeaked in response, out of mortarchain rounds. She considered ducking into Scar confine to recharge, but that would take at least an hour. New course of action: she leaped off the bridge and activated her footthrusts. The soles of her feet glowed, their energy holding her a few feet above the stone tile street as Hagan hobbled away. She leaned forward, activated her handthrusts for stabilization, and hit the gas. Kieron surged ahead, barely noticing that the purple hyperobject had doubled in size, and barely noticing the light that flashed from behind—from the mud tunnel.

Pink light.

The first bolt struck Hagan in the back. He staggered forward a few steps before collapsing to the ground. Kieron wheeled around to see that the entire far side of Hemming remnant was filled with pink plasma that danced and licked across every surface. The jellywoman flew toward the mud tunnel, but she didn't have to fly very close to it, because at less than a mile away, she could see that the tunnel had transformed into a giant mouth vomiting pink light. It spewed hot pink plasma-blasts in every direction and heralded the arrival of a new army. From the mouth of the tunnel they marched, backs bowed, knuckles dragging and eyes pink. The pinkeyes spilled from the mouth like giant hands had just tipped Hemming on its side and dumped thousands of runaway ballbearings into it; they filled every crevice, every corner, every nook. The mountain was already swarming with them like a horde of gnats attacking a rotten carcass.

But of course, they were only the advance guard for the main event.

Her purple mezz had made the journey through the mud tunnels, hovering all the way and holding aloft the mighty Odd, who looked like a smear of watercolor atop the mezz, her hyped-up mechanorg movements too fast for the jellywoman's eyes to process. Her eyes spewed pink lightning across the remnant as she emerged from the mud tunnel and soared into the air, and even though she moved so fast, Kieron could see that her arms were spread like she was—what was the word?

Benediction.

The term bubbled up from her past, when she used to visit the currentkeeps and observe the ebbs and flows of the world. Not many in the military followed the old ways and paid homage to the ebbs and flows, but Kieron did. Or she used to. Her old life felt a distant dream on the day that Lilya Hanna staked her claim to Hemming remnant and doubled her influence in the east at the greatest of costs. Looking back, the rumortrysts would call this day "The Almighty Fuck You."

The Odd hovered down the street, her army of pinkeyes scurrying underneath. Kieron stood in shock for a few moments before her brain reminded her that she had a bounty to deliver. As the pinkeyes (and Hanna) drew near, the jellywoman whirled around and sprinted down the street to where Hagan was just starting to struggle to his knees. After delivering a kick to his ass that sent the old man sprawling, Kieron cupped Hagan's armpits, hoisted him to his feet, and dropped him on the ground before the Odd.

Hanna's glowing pink eyes landed on Hagan. Her purple mezz descended to street level, and she stepped off of it, still moving at superspeed. She addressed the jellywoman.

"Ztlkt."

Kieron shook her head and wrote a note.

I don't understand.

Hanna moved so fast that from Kieron's perspective, a new message magically appeared on her pulpaper pad, written in exacting cursive script.

Where is his lovely beard?

Kieron stared at the question, then shrugged.

A new message appeared: *I love his beardy-poo. A Boris Hagan isn't a Boris Hagan unless he has his beardy-poo.*

The bounty-merc tried to write out a new question, but her stone stylus vanished. A new message appeared.

This man is mine, whoever he is. You may leave Hemming now. I forgive you for failing to bring me my Boris Hagan.

A platoon of pinkeyes came charging from all around. They spanned generations—a gray-haired woman, a hale young man, a squalling child—and they worked as a team to hurl the unconscious Boris Hagan onto Hanna's purple mezz. In a flash she was back on the purple disk and rising back into the sky.

The jellywoman watched the Odd fly away toward the mountain. Even if she had been able to talk, she wouldn't have. Thoughts of the oceans washed over her, causing her to list leftward from the sudden wave of homesickness. After regaining her footing, the jellywoman trudged across the remnant, moving vaguely in the direction of the exit gates, but along the way she noticed a stone stairwell that led to the top of a grassy hill twenty feet high, covered with white flowers. She climbed the stairs and sat down. The mad ravings of pinkeyes sounded all across the remnant, but where were all of the dregs of Hemming? Where were all the thousands of citizens who had packed the streets to cheer for the mud races and extol the awesomeness of Walter Torsten?

Kieron wondered about that, among other things.

She wondered how the hyperobject had returned. She wondered why its color had changed. She wondered why it was growing. She wondered how she had landed herself alone in this strange world, jentaless and bountyless.

Bountyless.

The jellywoman hefted herself to her feet, her mind casting back to the remote chamber of Penticton where Lady Ragnarok had betrayed Quillig. It occurred to Kieron that Quillig didn't have a bounty, either. If the plaid-faced man delivered Eldridge to this mysterious creditor, the man across the oceans, he wouldn't receive any payment. Only his life.

But what if someone *else* delivered the redhead? Maybe he'd be more generous.

Kieron bounded off the hill, headed first for the sectan confine of Scar to recharge her mortarchain module, then bound for the Hemming impound.

—⚏—

BORIS HAGAN AND PELL YANNICK

ROUGH HANDS HELD BORIS Hagan aloft. His toenails scraped along stone tiles, his legs useless and limp. His world: a black void filled with chattering voices. They jeered at him as he floated by, borne by those rough hands.

Soon, light joined his world—strobes and flashes. Eyelids fluttering.

A hard, flat plane rapped his shins. The pain jolted his eyes wide and flooded his senses with more input than his brain could tolerate. His first sight: the world reeling, spinning. His second sight: an enormous, heroic and *upside-down* painting of Walter Torsten holding a sword and using a poor trixie's ass as a footrest. Hagan looked up and realized he was looking *down* into a bottomless black pit. He closed his eyes and heard fireworks explode all around him.

A voice, unfamiliar: "Shut that off and get him up to her."

Darkness. Time.

More sensations. The charred-paper smell of spent fireworks. A heaviness in his head from all the blood. *Must still be upside down.* He sat cross-legged on something hard and flat. Glass—glass that was now moving. His inner ear registered the distant *thrum* of micromags. The *thrum* surrounded him, its intensity depending on his trajectory. He felt himself moving through all three spatial axes. Still he kept his eyes shut. A sudden decrease in the density of sound around him suggested that he had passed from a small hallway into a larger chamber, but then he felt himself pass through another narrow passage and into a headwind of fresh air. *Outside.* When he emerged, the world fell out from underneath him as he rushed upward and almost left his consciousness below. Even with his eyes closed, the world seemed to darknen, but he forced himself to stay awake. Inorganic heat warmed his face, while pleasant, organic smells—flowers, grass, earth—filled his nose.

He stopped.

A voice, familiar: "Kghlrzt."

He opened his eyes to a jiggling pair of Lilya Hannas, a visual anomaly he rectified by rubbing his eyes. When he looked up again, Odd Lilya Hanna stood before him wearing a new dress—this one red paisley with a tussle large enough to house a small family of dregs. Lace-lined openings on her sleeves and cleavage revealed her brass inner-workings, which jitterbugged in tune with her consonant-clumps.

"Klvlknrep. Nqnvoomp."

The rest of the scene coalesced around Boris Hagan. He sat on one of Hanna's floating glass mezzes (this one green), floating upside down high above Walter Torsten's mountain. About thirty feet below churned the 4D hyperobject, still purple and twice its original size. Hemming stretched out above/below him—its streets, hills, and mini-mountains aglow with the scrambling activity of Hanna's pinkeye brigades. They swept across the remnant, filling in its every corner.

And Hanna kept jabbering.

"Jvlenrd. Klbwrnlbkn. Vioqniobn."

"Hang on, hang on."

The old man's eyes rolled back to whites. The Zenning had commenced. Down below, the pinkeyes slowed to a stop until the remnant looked like it was filled with thousands of pink campfire-twins. Even the hyperobject's rotation slowed, though not to a halt. When Hagan had successfully paused the world, he was able to watch the terrain of the hyper-object transform from one state to another in endless, mind-blowing detail. Mathematical mountains rose from vector-valleys that ran with algorithmic rivers, all of which melted into whirling rings of fractal-coils adorned with golden-ratio ellipses and millions of self-similar treegrowths that iterated away into elegant nothingness.

"Sweet damn, but. But. But I missed those buns."

Lilya Hanna twined her mechanorg fingers under her bosom, which heaved with delight. Pink cloud-fluffs drifted through her cranium. Hagan tried to stand, but his rear end weighed a thousand pounds. He fell back onto the mezz. A scrape of metal signaled the widening of Hanna's eyes in sympathy.

"Oh, cutie-cutie. Here..."

The Odd kick-stepped backward and whipped her fingertips at the mezz. All she needed to do was shout "alakazam," Hagan thought. Nonetheless, he felt his butt decrease in weight. He floated to his feet and hovered above/below the mezz, but Hanna alakazammed the mezz once more and righted the gravity. Hagan's feet thumped to the mezz. Hanna approached him on a wave of interlocking gears and servos, her movements a simulacrum of "walking" as approximated by an ancient clockwork ambulation contraption. She spread her arms, hug imminent. Hagan recoiled.

"I guess I'm not wondering *if* so much as *how* you're going to kill me."

Hanna's pistons slowed. Wisps of steam escaped her joints as she settled into place and showed him her brass teeth.

"Sweet Boris. No. You're in no. Danger, that is. *You did it.*"

"I did?"

The cloud-fluffs in Hanna's cranium suck-shrank into a pinprick of pink that flashed joy-joy off her brass inner-workings, all of which sprang to twinkling life. Her joints extended and added six inches to her height. Brass teeth shining, she glided over and swept him into an impromptu ballroom dance. She led.

"Boris, Boris, Boris! You've ridden me of the odious Odd whose name I won't deign, deign, deign to utter."

Hagan danced on his tippy-toes, his arms stretched to their limit above him.

"Torsten?" he grunted.

"You deigned! You deigned! You must never again deign to utter it. Or it will hurt my feelings." Thousands of ball bearings seethed under her face until its expression resembled a pout.

"O-*Kaaaaay!*" Hagan said as she swung his feet off the edge of the mezz and tossed him back on the glass ground. More facial seething brought about another smile. She removed her brass teeth and plugged in a *larger* pair of brass choppers that doubled the size of her smile. She used her spare teeth to puppet her own words.

"And an Odd is always as good as her word," Hanna and her teeth said.

"Not one part of that sentence was true."

That sound again: playing cards and bicycle spokes. Hanna's laughter.

"I'm going to inject you with silicone until you can sit. On your own balls. I'll put you on a permanent drip of vitamin-B and zinc. B and Zinc. You'll never not be erect, never not be in the remnant of New Mid-Cummington. I'll bathe in it, bask in it, lubricate my servos with it. Your cerebral cortex will wither away and leave. Leave you a limp-hard mass of ecstasy. I'll do this until you die, and. And. And then I'll reanimate your corpse and do it again and again until the heat-death of the universe."

Hagan revised his internal list of the Craziest Fucking Shit he had ever heard with a new number one. Gaping at her, he said, "Would it change your mind to hear that I'm not the one who killed Tor—I mean, Mr. Oddpants? Deign Utter? W.T.? I didn't kill him."

"I sent you to Hemming. You won the Mud Races. He is dead. That's all that matters. But first, as I said: an Odd is always as good as her word. Behold!"

It hung between two pinkeyes like a clothesline laden with soaking garments, bowed in the middle from its fantastic weight. Hanna's pinkeyes floated on footmounted micromags that looked like cast-iron frying pan shoes. Hagan's state of Zen slowed the proceedings to a maddening crawl as the scene unfolded in upside-down vision. He grimaced with heart-true empathy at the sight of the gigantic tub of shit being hoisted in the air. The pinkeyes wrestled with the creature's endless rolls of fat like they were manically rebuilding a melting mountain of wax; one fold would spill out of their hands, and they would swipe their hands in constant upward loops to maintain a grip they could never keep. When they drew within a few feet of the mezz, its micromags slurped the creature's girth up onto its surface. The pinkeyes released the creature, which slammed onto the mezz with a sickening *plorp*. It was still naked, its genitals flattened across one of its lard-continents and twitching helplessly in the air. Chunks of dried diarrhea crumbled off of its ass as it rolled around in an effort to bring its head out from underneath itself. From the old man's perspective, the creature struggled for ten minutes to right itself, and when it couldn't, he jumped up and buried his hands in its clammy flesh. It emitted gas so foul that Hagan gagged, but he held his breath and pulled its head to the top of the quivering mass, whereupon its maw stretched wide and moaned. In Hagan's Zenned state, the moan sounded like a distant foghorn that would never stop. He covered his ears.

The Odd curtsied.

"As promised. *Lord Macta.*"

Hagan had already recognized the lightning-shaped scar on the creature's leg. He dropped to his knees and sighed.

"Thanks."

Lilya Hanna chugga-chugged across the mezz and bent at the waist to give him a view of her clockwork cleavage. She continued to puppet herself with her spare pair of brass teeth.

"You're a Boris. And. You're *my* Boris. Forevermore. Your first year will be spent in a constant state of prostate-stimmy-stim-stim. Catch up with Lord Macta. And then we. We. We can . . . *begin.*"

Her giggle sounded like a thousand squeaky hinges. She drew up her skirt, dainty pinkies extended, and hovered off the mezz, where she flipped upright (upside down, from Hagan's perspective) and floated down to Torsten's mountain, surrounded by a platoon of micromagged pinkeyes. Pell continued his foghorn moan. Hagan set his palms on his thighs and soft-focused. The Zenning ended and brought Pell's moan to a sudden, barking stop as the world snapped back to its normal speed. Hagan searched for Pell's eyes amidst the piles of blubber around his face.

"Pell, I—"

"Cut."

Webbed with saliva and crusty with dried smegma, Pell's maw had spoken.

Hagan leaned in. "Say again?"

"Cut. Me."

"What? Why?"

"Just." He wheezed for breath. "Cut."

Hagan checked his pockets, but he hadn't carried a pocketknife in years. An idea: he removed his glasses and snapped off the end of one of the earholds, leaving behind a sharp point of plastic that he regarded with caution.

"Are you sure?"

"Do." Wheeze, wheeze. "It."

In his blurred worldview, Pell resembled an enormous hazy oval, while the 4D hyperobject morphed from one shape to another—sphere, cube, cone. Hagan laid the sharp plastic point against Pell's flesh, which swallowed it. He pressed, but the point got lost in a fold.

"Dammit. Hang on."

The hyperobject continued to cycle through shapes, leaving the realm of basic polyhedra and moving on to figures with more and more vertices. Despite his bad eyesight, Hagan's peripheral vision registered the emergence of a dodecahedron over the peak of Torsten's mountain. Pell fidgeted underneath him.

"Stomach."

Hagan nodded. The flesh was drawn much tighter across the region that had once been his stomach. The old man found Pell's navel and pressed the sharp plastic point into the unyielding plane of flesh above it, unsure of the result. The hyperobject, still purple, continued to cycle through shapes, and although he couldn't be certain, he sensed the emergence of octagonal prisms, stellated dodecahedra, and myriad great cubicuboctahedra. He wondered why his brain had socked away so much knowledge about higher geometric shapes, but he figured the factoids were holdovers from his youthful days of working as a tutor for a succession of privileged Odd youth.

"This isn't working, Pell. What am I supposed to be doing?"

"Cut."

Hagan wedged the sharp point in place and pressed down on it with his thumb, all while the hyperobject entered into a new phase of expression. It had left behind the world of polyhedra in favor of amorphous blobs and clouds that bubbled over the peak of Torsten's mountain. Boris Hagan pressed until his thumb turned white, and then two events happened simultaneously.

First, the sharp plastic point penetrated Pell's hide and spawned an elaborate grid network of tears that flash-ripped around his ruined body's circumference with a jagged *pow.* Hagan expected blood and gore to spew from the tears, but none did; instead, clear fluid gushed out, lined with the occasional phlegmmy vein of viscera. Hagan kicked away from the onrush of liquid, which rained down on Torsten's mountain below. The old man fumbled his broken glasses back onto his face and afforded himself a view of the other event:

The hyperobject made up its mind.

After cycling through countless different shapes, it finally settled into the strobing form of a sine wave, which then slowed and connected its loose ends into a figure eight. The figure-eight then started to spin on its lengthwise axis, slowly transforming itself into a three-dimensional hourglass.

That's when it burst into flame.

Still upside down, Hagan shielded his eyes and stared into the flame while a quickly dwindling Pell Yannick dumped his fluidic insides all over Hemming below. Purple flames flared from the hyperobject bright enough to catch the attention of Lilya Hanna, who soared out of the mountain with a crew of pinkeyes in tow. She darted around the hyperobject screaming speedspeech nonsense that Hagan couldn't decipher in his non-Zenned state. Meanwhile, Pell stood.

He stood.

The unspoken high chieftain of the Order of the Narsyan stood up on the floating mezz, upside down to the world, the remains of his deformed self hanging from his neck like a vast, deflated parachute.

The fluid drained from his face last, sluicing down his sunken chest and leaving behind cheekbones that jutted from his face like a pair of elbows. He hunched down and gathered up the parachute-remains in a pair of squeaking, folding bunches that filled the crooks of his elbows, and then in one great upward heave, he hurled them down and away from the mezz's micromags. Once skyborne, gravity quickly took hold of the flesh-parachute and yanked it down toward the mountain, all while the hyperobject continued to burn brighter and brighter and hotter and hotter. Pell's flesh-suit tore away from his true body with the sickeningly quiet sound of human skin ripping apart. Hagan barely heard it, but it gave him the sensation of someone shearing off his own scalp. He clutched his head in response but forced himself to look up and watch the hyperobject as the two orb-ends of its hourglass shape bent toward each other. When the two orb-ends met, Pell's flesh-suit fell away. Naked and soaking, he hung in the air for a stomach-turning moment—caught between earth's gravity and the faux-gravity of the micromags—before he collapsed back to the mezz, his whole body wracked with spasms. Above the mountainpeak, the hyperobject sprouted four nubs that Hagan quickly recognized as arms and legs. The emergence of the limb-nubs heralded a time-lapse trip through the gestation of a flaming purple hyperchild in an airborne uterus, all of it to the tune of Hanna's mad screams as she fluttered around like a helpless hummingbird. Three quarters of the way through the child's development, its gender was apparent: the skies of Hemming were giving birth to a gigantic baby girl who surged through the ages, her skin aglow with gleaming, iterating fractal sets as she grew older and older and larger and larger, her purple light shining brighter and brighter until the entire remnant was flooded with it. And still the hyperwoman grew.

But she never grew any *hair*, Hagan noted, and indeed, the hyperwoman was as bald as the old man.

That's when he knew. That's when he knew that he had nothing to fear, and Hanna had everything to fear. That's when he knew that somehow, word of his (and his friends') predicament must have found its way to the wandering tribe of human-machine hybrids, the psychoskags, because when the hyperwoman was fully mature, she rotated in the air to face Lilya Hanna, who froze in place. Bathed in purple flame, the hyperwoman stood two hundred feet tall, her feet hovering mere meters above the rooftops of Hemming, her boulder-sized fists balled at her sides, her pupil-less purple eyes glaring hate at the tiny Odd. When the hyperwoman spoke, her thundercracking voice shattered every window in town.

"Unhand my friends, Odd."

Shanta Feruccio was in the motherfucking *house*.

—⚊∭⚊—

QUILLIG AND ELDRIDGE

THERE WAS NO SECTAN confine in Hemming. Or was there? Quillig's ears popped as they climbed another thousand feet in elevation, the terrain having shifted from the rocky plateau that surrounded Hemming to an expanse of blank-faced desert before melting back into an arid red wasteland littered with rocks and dead, black weeds. As always, sunrays seared the daytime world, but the little shit's motorbike came equipped with a clever cooling system—eight pipes that delivered freezing air. Eldridge's leather jacket still bore eight screw-ons for the pipes. He attached four to himself and gave the other four to Quillig, who stuffed them into a vinyl bodysuit he had liberated from one of Hemming's many empty households before they left. The bounty-merc's skinless face still baked in the sun, but the cooling pipes kept his body temp within parameters.

A dozen miles back, he had considered telling the redhead to return to Hemming. During his stint in Glaucio with the up-and-coming Walter Torsten, Quillig had encountered rumortrysts telling of a sectan confine that resided far off the grid, somewhere in the eastern deserts. As the largest remnant in the east, Hemming had always been a prime candidate for its location, but he had never found it. Besides, the rumortrysts told even stranger stories about the secret confine, which was called either "Scar" or "Herod," he had learned over the years. Supposedly, it had entrances scattered all across the eastern continent. Whatever *that* meant.

They rode over a rock, which bumped under the bike's tires and almost sent Quillig toppling off the back. He held onto the redhead's midsection tighter as he steered the bike onto a path that emerged from the landscape and climbed upward, closer and closer to the sun. Quillig had traveled from one end of the continent to the other, and this particular region—due northwest of Hemming—he knew well, because he always used to avoid it when he drove his big rig.

"Eldridge, are you going where I think you're going?"

"How long do you have to deliver me to Port Stafford?"

Quillig thought. "I don't even know. Probably twelve hours by this point."

"Can you think of a faster way to get from Hemming to parts west?"

"No."

"Then shut up and let me drive."

The bounty-merc fought off the urge to strangle the redhead, the twenty-third such urge he had felt since taking him captive. As they rode higher and higher, Quillig narrowed his sight-aperture on the back of Eldridge's head. Fingertip-sized bumps of bald scalp peeked out from his close-cropped hair, each bump swimming in a network of hair-swirls that circled around his many cowlicks like they were draining into his head. Quillig felt the scarred remains of his own scalp and found similar bumps—the result of his anti-dreen treatments. His deep-desert sawbones had to attach dozens of electrodes to his skin as a part of the process, including several on his head.

Had the redhead ever been a dreen? Not possible.

"What are these bumps on your head?" Quillig asked.

"Scars."

"From what?"

"Dunno. Doc Enki said I might've got 'em before I was born."

A rocky bluff rose to their right. Eldridge drove around it and steered them onto a steeper incline that wound around boulders and rocks and crevices, the sun always beating down upon them from on high. The bike's hydrocell was incapable of making noise, but the inner workings of its engine groaned with the effort—and Quillig knew that the steepest part of their voyage was still to come.

Yet his thoughts returned to the bumps on Eldridge's head.

"How could you have been scarred *before* your birth?"

"No idea. Why do you want to know?"

The bounty-merc had no answer, but he kept asking questions as the path climbed higher and higher.

"Where were you born?"

"I don't know. On this continent, I guess."

"When were you born?"

"I don't know. I'm in my early forties, I think."

"Did you know your parents?"

"Nope. They left me in a garbage bag in front of the Narsyan stronghold up in the Oasis Mountains."

"Why didn't you ever try to find them?"

"Didn't seem worth the effort."

"What about kids? Didn't you have some kids?"

Eldridge jerked the bike to the side of the path at the same moment they emerged at the top of the incline. The path terminated into the edge of a rock shelf that dropped twenty feet down onto the longest and widest downward slope on the continent. More than fifty miles wide, the slope was a featureless stone surface that extended for two thousand miles on a constant downward slope westward. Hills rose in the distance on either side, while the end of the slope vanished into a heat mirage that rippled in the distance.

The enormous slope had a few names, depending on the dreg's remnant of origin. Dregs from Eldridge's neck of the woods in the west called it Killermount, while dregs from out east simply called it the Great Plane. Quillig had always avoided it because his big rig couldn't handle the plane going up *or* down. Now he was in danger of *stumbling* into the Great Plane because Eldridge had stopped his bike and yanked him off of it by the collar of his vinyl bodysuit. Cooling pipes whipped in every direction, spraying cold gray mist. The bike fell to the ground just as Quillig *hit* the ground, his sweat-free body already cooking inside his bodysuit. Eldridge stood over him, still clutching his collar.

"You goddamn well *know* I had a daughter."

"What? Who?"

The punch almost knocked him unconscious. Black starbursts danced in his vision, while invisible mufflers clamped over his ears. Eldridge reared back with his fist, but the bounty-merc held up a red-scarred hand.

"Stop. Wait. I'm sorry."

The redhead dropped him to the ground. Quillig crawled over to the bike and grabbed two of the cooling pipes. He stuffed one down his suit while he aimed the other directly at his face. Eldridge, his armpits already dark with sweat, stood with his back to Quillig.

"It was the constable, you sorry fuck," Eldridge said.

Quillig cooled his face and thought back. The constable? What the hell was a constable? He thought back to his time in Dedrick, and when he made the connection, he found himself walking down one of his mental hallways again, only this time, he had no decision to make, and the hall had to end. He simply walked past door after door, his feet splashing through multicolored fluids that seeped out from under them. Wood creaked with the strain of each door holding back a torrent of fluid, yet he felt no fear. Far from it. Instead, he took off his shoes and sprinted forward, feet splashing through the rainbow soup that flooded the hallway and started to mix together into a compound that burned his feet. His feet had already been boiled to the bone, and the reflection that looked up at him from the floor was lined with vertical clawmarks. Instinctively, he checked his fingernails and found them filled with newly scraped skin; skin from his face, which he touched and set aflame. His hiss of pain quickly escalated into a scream in that dark hallway, knee-deep in fluid that was no longer multicolored. No, the rainbow waters had mixed together into a black muck that suddenly had no bottom. His bone-boiled feet, still screaming with fire-pain, sank into nothingness.

A nothingness that he welcomed. On the crest of Killermount, Quillig smiled his cold smile and asked a question to which he already knew the answer.

"Zora Tola was the constable?"

No answer. Eldridge stood, his head hung. In Quillig's mind, the hallway had filled to the roof with black muck, but then from the depths of it, a drain opened and started to suck, suck, suck the muck down deep into its gullet. The drainsuck was Quillig's imaginary mouth, of course, and when the black muck had drained away, all that was left was a floorless hallway of floating doors and a Quillig-thing gleamslick and soulsick with black ooze.

On the crest of Killermount, Quillig kept smiling.

"Jeb Goldmist killed her, didn't he?"

Eldridge didn't move or answer.

Quillig continued, "He shot her so many times that her face fell apart. He shot her so many times that her brains spilled into her mouth."

The redhead turned around, his face blank, and moved to pick up the motorbike. Quillig's hand locked around his wrist. The bounty-merc knew that if the redhead wanted to, he could easily break his grip, but he didn't. Want to, that is. Quillig plucked out the staples he had gunned into his face one by one and released a corner of the plaid fabric, which he then pulled, popping the remaining stitches that held it to his face. If the unveiling of Quillig's true face stirred any emotions in the redhead, he kept them hidden. Even before he went dreen, Quillig seldom saw his reflection, and after he was cured, he had never, ever seen his reflection.

Until that day.

He had to narrow his sight-aperture to account for the sunlight that blazed off the motorbike's chrome, but once the device adjusted, he looked at himself for the first time in years. Red and black scar tissue covered his face, which had no lips and only the withered remains of a nose. It looked like someone had taken rotten ground meat and sculpted it into the visage of a burn victim. His sight-cartridge jutted from his eye sockets like it always did. He unplugged it. Blind, he turned his face on the redhead.

"Where are your friends, Eldridge?"

No answer. Quillig realized that the redhead could easily slay him, but somehow, he didn't think he would. The bounty-merc spoke again.

"I was a tary-fairy, sometimes called a hypofidget. A mirror-fearer. Did you know that? A spineless little hypofidget who didn't think he was pretty enough for his mommy and daddy, even though they gave me everything, and even though for the first sixteen years of my life, I didn't even know that the world was so fucked up. I thought it was beautiful and green *everywhere*. Turned out it's only green where *he wants* it to be."

Eldridge finally spoke. "The man across the oceans."

"That's right."

"You grew up on the eastern continent?"

"That I did."

"How'd you get over here?"

"I don't know. I went dreen over there, and the next thing I knew, I was in the middle of the fucking desert on this side of the world. I used to wish that I had never come back. Been *brought* back. I *used* to wish that."

"*Used* to?"

"Used to. Until just now. Until I found out that I was present for the death of your beloved child."

Quillig's sight-aperture vanished from his hand. He figured Eldridge was chucking it down Killermount, but then his vision returned as the redhead jammed the device back into his sockets.

"Get up. Let's go."

Quillig sniggered.

"Tell me one thing, redhead. How did you know I wasn't going to take you back to the Chain?"

"You brought backup. I figured you must be in deep shit. I didn't think the man across the oceans would get involved, but it told me that the stakes were bigger than a simple Chain bounty."

Quillig's dry chuckles sounded like coughs. "Bigger than you know. He even put a bounty on my head. I guess he didn't want me to lose focus."

The redhead grinned at that. "No. That was me."

Quillig tilted his head. "You?"

"When?"

"You should ask *which time?* I put out a few."

"A few? To who? I've been to every sectan confine on the continent, and I never saw my name on the board."

"You've got competitors."

"Competitors?"

"Your network of bounty-mercs isn't the only one. There are other networks, with their own zektar confines or whatever. I put bounties on you with three different networks."

The bounty-merc laughed outright, his lungs calling on deep reserves of moisture to make him sound normal, if only for a moment. When the laughter passed, his tone hardened like a heart petrifying in an instant.

"I'm so impressed, Eldridge. All this trouble, and you *still* want to win that deathday wager."

Eldridge stared at him, then mounted his bike and reattached his cooling pipes. Quillig looked at the patch of plaid fabric, then tossed it away. He climbed on behind the redhead and stuffed his cooling pipes back into his suit. The redhead wrenched the accelerator and launched the bike off the cliff. They remained airborne for a good ten seconds before the bike slammed down onto the slope of Killermount and started the two-thousand-mile trip to the bottom.

—⟪⟫—

BORIS HAGAN, PELL YANNICK, SHANTA FERUCCIO, AND THE PSYCHOSKAGS

LILYA HANNA SHRIEKED. It sounded across the remnant, rising above the roar of Feruccio's purple inferno as the Odd pressed her palms into the sides of her metallic face, which stretched in horror of the sight that dominated the airspace before her.

From his upside-down seat on the mezz, Boris Hagan smiled, both at Hanna's terror and in anticipation of the havoc that the world's most beautiful woman was about to wreak on Hemming.

And then she was gone.

Feruccio the gigantic hyperwoman vanished in a flash, her departure marked by a few extinguishing wisps of violet flame and the sudden increase in volume of Hanna's screams as the remnant fell silent—*and dark*. Although the sun still seeped through the stucco roof above, every interior light in the remnant winked out at the same time as the hyperwoman. Relief washed over the Odd and rendered limp her mechanical limbs. The appearance of the hyperwoman had transformed Hanna's cranial-cloud into an angry cyclone, while her disappearance dispersed it in favor of a pink morning glow. Hanna wheeled around to face Hagan, her jaw pistoning into a blur around the skipping squeal of her speed-cackles. She barked consonant-clumps at him.

"*Slnqbr! Zklbqnnr! Tvmleqlkr!*"

Hagan didn't need to be Zenned out to know that she was gloating in triumph over his and Lord Macta's abandonment. As Hanna and her pinkeyes advanced on them, the old man crawled over to Pell, where the formerly magnificent Narsyan chieftain had been reduced to a twitching mass of finger-thin muscles stretched across bones. Sweat covered his naked body, which continued to buck with spasms. Hagan held him and watched Hanna, who didn't notice Hemming's newest arrivals.

The psychoskags.

From a distance, Hagan recognized them by the box-shape of their heads and the absence of pink from their eyes, although to be fair, most of them didn't have *any* eyes to speak of. Most of them had replaced their heads with computer monitors, while those who hadn't had still *encased* their heads in the old metal boxes. Some of them scaled Torsten's mountain, their feet and hands equipped with metal climbing claws that extended their reach by two feet per limb. Still others scaled the walls of Hemming itself, although they didn't "scale" the walls so much as *run directly up them*, each stride launching them twenty vertical feet while digging out a chunk of stucco that rained on the streets below. Three of the skags on the wall drew even with the green mezz and launched into the following maneuver:

Two of them ran up the wall and stopped about thirty feet above the mezz, while the third one continued sprinting upward until it reached the top, whereupon it grabbed hold of the ceiling and scrambled out until it was midway between the wall and the mezz. It then detached and hooked one of its climbing-claws into the ceiling and looped a length of black cable through it. With the cable attached to its waist, the skag ziplined down until it was looking Hagan in the eye. The old man wondered why the skag didn't just land *on top of* the mezz, but the skag's next move allayed his concerns. One at a time, the two skags on the wall both detached and skydove toward their third comrade, their climbing claws extended and ready to grab hold of each other. When the first skydiving skag arrived, the ziplined skag hooked claws with it and hurled it toward the mezz, where it landed next to Hagan, upside down. This one still had its head, so Boris Hagan prepared his ears for a barrage of *bargs* and *boofs*.

Instead, he got: "My name is Magna. Would you and your friend be so kind as to stand up so that we may decamp from this location?"

The skag still shouted everything in the same gravely voice as the rest of his people, but Feruccio must've upgraded them since they last met. Not only was his voice different, but every square inch of exposed skag flesh was covered with diodes, raytubes, wires, circuit-boards, datareads, flashing lights, microchips, and buttons.

The second skydiving skag apparently wanted to have songs sung about its glorious demise, because it got hurled directly at Lilya Hanna and her platoon of flying pinkeyes. Hanna's protesting screech ended in a gigantic *oof* when the skag executed a perfect midair slam-hug attack and dragged her earthward with its weight. Hanna disengaged herself and slung the skag down toward the mountain—but the falling skag would have no songs sung in its honor, as the rest of its crew—about a dozen in all—converged underneath and broke its fall.

Simultaneously, Magna the psychoskag galumphed over and helped a shaking Pell Yannick to his feet, but the Narsyan immediately collapsed to the mezz, prompting Magna to scoop Pell into the linking, scabby stacks that composed his bionic arms.

"Climb onto my back!" Magna said.

Hagan did. Magna detached one of his climbing-claws and ran to the edge of the mezz, which was ringed with humming black rectangular solids—micromags. Magna popped open a small panel on the side of one of the micromags and revealed several buttons and switches, including a slide-switch labeled with two familiar symbols: plus and minus. Magna slid it from plus to minus. Instantly, one end of the mezz tilted earthward as it lost the repelling strength of one of the micromags, but in exchange, Magna was now able to magnetically attach a climbing claw to the micromag. It held the metal claw in place stronger than any tether. The skag looped some cable through the claw, tied it around his waist, and jumped—straight *up* from Hagan's perspective, but straight *down* from everyone else's. Hagan's inner ears clicked when they escaped the pull of the mezz. With Hagan on his back and Pell cradled in one arm, Magna flipped around the cable so they were now facing (and falling) rightside up. The skag let them freefall for a moment before he clamped hold of the rope and brought them to a jerking halt a few feet above the mountain. Hagan jumped off his back and was immediately beset by a dozen other skags.

And Lilya Hanna.

The Odd and her retinue descended from above surrounded by a halo of pink generated by her cranium and all of their many eyes. Her mouth snapped permanently open and howled consonant-blasts—orders, presumably—at her pinkeyes.

"*Fvonernb!*"

The pinkeye brigade, twenty in all, split into four groups of five and formed a skyborne perimeter around them, slowly drawing the circle tighter and tighter around Hagan, Pell, Magna, and the other twelve psychoskags, who all broke into spraddle-legged battle stances and blood-roared at the pinkeyes, who *struck*. Two of them left a V-shaped trail of pink as they slashed down and snatched a skag, whom they carried into the air and dropped to his doom. Magna recognized the threat, screamed, "*Let's get to the Machine!*" and turned to Hagan.

"Follow us to the foot of the mountain. I've got Pell. Don't get left behind."

"Got it," Hagan said with a confidence he didn't have. Despite the artificial gravity on the mezz, he had still spent the last hour with a blood-swollen head. The flip-spin down the cable from the mezz had upset his already muddled mind, while his depleted energy reserves had rubberized his joints. He staggered down the mountainside behind the retreating skags, three of whom perished from the pinkeyes' snatch-and-drop attack. As rocks and dirt slid out from under his scampering feet, Hagan realized that his second wind was long since over, and he wondered whether a third was on the way, and if so, from where it might arrive.

He soon found out the answers to both questions: *Yes,* and *from above.*

"*Borisborisborisborisboris!*"

Her shadow covered his path down the mountain. He hit the brakes just as Lilya Hanna swooped in front of him, her speedspeech uniform enough to be intelligible even to the non-Zenned. She must've been repeating his name a thousand times a minute.

"*Borisborisborisborisborisborisborisboris!*"

Hagan's legs almost left his torso behind. His feet sprinted out from underneath him, causing him to lean backward as he ran straight through Hanna's waiting embrace, his sudden burst of speed carrying him to the front of the phalanx of psychoskags and setting off a mini-avalanche of rocks that chased them all down the mountainside, which terminated into a wall that stood about ten feet off a street called Edgecut that encircled the remnant. Hagan leaped off the wall and almost got flattened by the Clean Machine.

He knew it was called the Clean Machine because the words had been white-stenciled onto the side of the hulking black truck, which stood twenty feet high and spanned the width of Edgecut Street. Giant mechanical forklift arms hung off its sides like vestigal wings, while a quartet of powerful headlamps set its path ablaze with blue-white light. Armor covered the truck from bow to stern, while a dozen deep-tread tires rumbled on the stone tile street underneath. Steel ladders climbed up its rear sides. Barely legible under the name of the truck were the paint-chip remains of another word: SANITATION. The rear of the Machine opened like a giant mouth, and Shanta Feruccio herself leaned out, holding onto the ladder.

"*Let's go!*" she shouted to her skags, who hustled into the rear of the Machine. Hagan got there last, but Feruccio was still waiting for him, smiling and offering a hand. Her beauty—the common ancestor of rumortryst bloodlines large and small, highbrow and low—still dazzled its way through her current attire: battle fatigues composed of a brown canvas cargo vest, cargo pants, and thick boots. Unlike the redhead's report about his last encounter with the world's most beautiful woman, her long white hair had had been shorn away.

But there was something else.

When Hagan took Feruccio's hand, he almost fell into the street because of the heat. *Her* heat. Holding her hand felt like grabbing onto a red-hot iron. Hagan winced as she pulled herself back into the Clean Machine with him in tow. Once inside, she released him and pounded a red button that simultaneously shut the rear door and brought the Machine's interior to life. Computer stations lined the walls and were immediately manned by skags whose forearms made X's across their chests as they uncoiled hardlink cables that they plugged into the walls. Some of the stations lacked monitors; those were manned by skags with monitor-heads, which they removed and plugged into the walls.

On her way to the front of the vehicle, Feruccio pointed at Hagan and said, "Nice to meet you, finally. Sorry about your hand. I'll explain later." She then shouted at the skag behind the wheel, *"We're ready! Hit it!"*

The Machine lurched forward, its hydrocells silently pumping power into the engines, which growled to life as they picked up speed. Its interior grew brighter and brighter with flatpanel map readouts of the surrounding region; lightjets that sprayed the walls with streams of alphanumerics; ceiling- and wall-mounted datareads that assembled into a video display of their outside view. (Hanna and her pinkeyes were in close pursuit, natch.) Floating in the center of the Machine was an electromorph rendering of the interior streets of Hemming itself. Feruccio spun around and walked straight through the electromorph map, which liquefied around her. The millions of luminescent polygons, vectors, and bucketfills of color that composed the map *melted* into her body like the surface tension of a pool of water bonding with a raindrop. Standing in the center of the map, Feruccio scanned it for their location, which was marked by a flashing green sphere at the edge of town. Hanna and her brigade were also represented on the map as a flock of flying red cubes. Feruccio pointed at the green sphere, then at the far side of town, where the exit gate stood. She then swiped the red cubes into her fist and squeezed. The skags spoke as one, their response instant:

"Two percent. Seventy-six percent."

They didn't need to say "one hundred percent," because the driver jerked the wheel to the right and sent the Clean Machine hurtling down a diagonal alleyway that ran through a series of covered bridges wedged between brick buildings. At the same instant that the Machine changed course, a dotted blue line flashburst onto the electromorph map, while the red cubes (the enemy tangos) swarmed around the map in a seemingly random pattern—but then the skags' vocal progress bar started again:

"Forty percent."

One hundred percent. Feruccio pointed at the map with four arms. *She had four arms.* They had sprouted out of her body like reeds. Now she had sixteen arms. Sixty-four. She was pointing at *everything* when her body dispersed into the map in a splash of bits and bytes. The map displayed an interlocking array of arrows, vectors, and intersections—all of which converged on one of the remnant's two exit gates—but:

"*Sixty p—*"

Now everything pointed toward the *other* exit gate, and the driver course-corrected again, this time roaring over a grassy hill that Hagan saw was covered with corpses. They were moving too fast for a close examination, but as far as Hagan could tell, the corpses looked undamaged; no blood, no gunshots, no trauma. As they sped through alleyway after alleyway, the old man saw more and more dead bodies strewn throughout the remnant, although by his count, he didn't see nearly enough dregs to populate the rest of the remnant.

Something bumped into his arms—from both sides—and he realized that the interior of the Machine was quickly filling with more and more technology as the psychoskags disassembled themselves and filled the vehicle's interior space. Arms and legs detached from torsos and shivered apart into servos, diodes, circuit boards, and circuit breakers that sprang to life and skittered around the rapidly shrinking interior space of the truck, plugging themselves in and unfolding across every available surface, one on top of the other. Tech covered everything, including the seemingly crucial rearview datareads, which folded back into the walls and vanished. Hagan checked Pell and found him supine across a burgeoning platform of technology that bubbled up underneath him and bore him upward, stomach first. Hagan was about to call out for the mysteriously absent Feruccio when a five-foot electromorph rendering of her head filled the truck.

"Hey!" she said, smiling. "Have you guys gone insane yet? No? OK, good."

She started to fade, but Hagan yelled, "Wait! We're getting kinda smushed back here!"

Feruccio scanned the space and barked an order: "Leave some room for the organics, ya boobs!"

Technology abated with a grumble as her giant head vanished. Pell sank back to the truck's original floorplates while thousands of modules of circuitry gathered into seething mountains of tech that coalesced into Feruccio's psychoskag platoon, once again arrayed along the walls on a series of workstations. The rearview datareads reappeared, along with the map of Hemming, which blinked back into view on a wake of shimmering pixel-ripples.

Once he felt sure that Feruccio's technology wasn't going to crush them, Hagan's attention alternated between the rearview display and the map, which zoomed in to track their position relative to the dotted blue line and the red cubes: Hanna and her pinkeye squadron, who continued to menace the airspace immediately to aft. Her mechanical mandible maintained its hyperjabbering repetition of Hagan's first name, while her pinkeyes fired rosy laser-bursts from their skulls. One pink bolt incinerated the stone tile street under one of the truck's wheels, forcing the driver to jerk the wheel to the right and diverge from the blue-dotted line's course. In response, the skags once again cried out:

"Seventy-seven per—"

The dotted blue line vanished and a new one appeared to direct them along a new course out of the remnant. They rumbled up a cobblestone pathway that cut through the top of a mini-mountain in the center of town like an inlaid reverse-Mohawk of pavement. To Hagan's disgust, they rumble-crunched over more corpses that lined the streets.

"Don't run over them!"

Filaments of lightsmoke plumed from the map and formed into the shape of a genderless humanoid form capped with the bald head of Shanta Feruccio.

"They're all dead. It doesn't matter."

"But they're people! We can't—"

"Half the people in this city were electromorph ego-figments, and the other half were brain-drained husks."

"What? Then why are they dead?"

Feruccio's internal processors chewed some numbers, then spat out a response:

"His hyperobject dispersed nanotroids into the water supply that infected the cerebral cortex of every *living* dreg in town. Apparently they were set to self-destruct upon his demise."

"But—"

Another radical course change cut off Hagan's words and caused Feruccio to wink out of sight. The Clean Machine clattered onto a wooden footbridge, then blasted off the side, carrying with it a collection of severed ropes and shattered wood beams. Landing, the Machine smashed a crater in the stone tile pavement, while more pink lasers *zammed* into the ground all around and immediately behind. A few of Hanna's attacks connected with the Machine and knocked divots into the steel roof. In response, some of Feruccio's skags detached smaller portions of themselves—fingers, ears, and toes—which sprouted spidery mechanical limbs and crawled up to the ceiling to make repairs.

And the gate approached.

They made a ninety-degree turn onto a diagonal street that pointed directly at the gate. Feruccio's voice sounded from all around.

"*Do not stop. No matter what.*"

The driver grunted an affirmation and accelerated at the same time that a pair of pinkeyes latched onto the Machine, their positions revealed though the datareads.

Feruccio's voice: "Take care of that shit."

"*Yessir!*" shouted Magna, who jumped up from his station and ran through the map toward the rear, where the aft doors (still covered with dataread video) yawned open and revealed the rapidly receding streets of Hemming while admitting an inrush of wind that kicked around the few wisps of hair that still clung to the withered remains of his scalp. A triangular module fastened to his chest blinked and hummed with lights and tech. As the gate approached, Magna grabbed hold of the exterior ladder and swung out onto the roof of the vehicle. Hagan watched the action unfold on the datareads, which even at the odd angle—the doors that bore the datareads were standing open, after all—still gave him a good view to witness Magna's dismemberment of the pinkeyes. Hagan winced as more brainwashed innocents perished, their limbs pressed into duty as improvised explosive devices. Magna detached shell-casing-sized charges from his triangular chest module and attached them to the gory elbows of fallen pinkeyes, and holding the severed limbs by their hands and feet, he slung them at Hanna. They exploded in starblooms of flaming black-red viscera, showering Hanna's mechanical eyes with blood and guts. Magna continued to hang off the rear of the Machine, hurling limb-bombs at pinkeyes, killing some and dismembering others for more bombs.

And the gate was there.

Feruccio's voice: "*Magna!*"

The skag dove back into the Machine as the rear-jawdoors chomped shut and they collided with the thick, gray membrane—*then stopped.* Everything inside the machine, Hagan, Pell, skags and all, slammed forward as the gate reduced the truck's momentum by 99 percent. But they were still moving.

Feruccio's voice: "That Odd bitch—*reduce speed!*"

Hagan didn't know how they could reduce their speed any more, but the driver must've done something right, because they truck actually started to *accelerate* through the membrane, which grayed out the datareads. Still, Hagan could see the dark ghosts of pinkeyes as they swam through the gate, still in pursuit and still firing pink laserblasts from their eye sockets; pink blasts that crept through the membrane like supercooled hot pink mercury flowing through an unfamiliar network of crevices. Some of the blasts struck home but fizzled against the Machine, their power blunted by the membrane. Around them, the gray started to grow lighter and lighter until they suddenly shot forward, free of the gate, free of Hemming remnant.

They emerged into a valley, a mountain rising immediately ahead. The driver turned right and headed (what Hagan presumed was) north. He was checking the datareads for any signs of pursuit when the map vanished and Feruccio reappeared, this time dressed in her cargo vest and pants. An electromorph chair materialized underneath her. She sat and addressed Hagan.

"Relax. Mechanorgs like her don't do well in the open desert."

Hagan exhaled and leaned his head against the wall.

"How'd you hear about us?"

"One of our contacts in Penticton sent us a hardline saying you and El were in trouble."

"Right." He shook his head and muttered, "El."

"I guess you two got separated."

"Something like that."

Another voice asked, "Where . . . is he?"

It was Pell. Elbows shaking, he pushed himself upright and sat back against the wall, his hollow chest heaving.

Hagan sat forward and asked, "How are you feeling?"

"Like someone inflated me with mucus, and I had to break out of it. Or as we Narsyans say, *'Like shit.'* Where is Eldridge?"

"He left with Quillig."

"What?" Feruccio said.

"Quillig, the bounty-merc Quillig?" Pell asked.

"That's the only Quillig I know, Pell."

"Why?"

"I don't know," Hagan said. "But if I had to guess . . . I think I watched that man's heart break right in front of me. I don't know why, but it did."

Pell expelled a series of rapid-fire wheeze-squeaks. Laughter. "Well, we'll simply have to find him and reassemble his heart so I can fucking kill him. Where'd he go?"

"I don't know, but not to the Chain."

Feruccio held up a hand. "Wait." She sat in silence among the clatter of keyboards for a moment, then said, "He was sighted ascending Killermount."

"Sighted? How?"

"I can explain later. He must be heading west."

"Forgive me for repeating myself," Pell said, "but: Why?"

Feruccio held up her hand again. More silence. More processing. She said, "Boris, is Eldridge still in thrall to someone?"

Hagan nodded. "Yeah, there's some big whatsamadoodle on the eastern continent who's got him in hock. He doesn't know who."

"The man across the oceans?" Feruccio guessed.

"That's all he knows, yeah."

"Who is this, this man across the oceans?" Pell asked.

"No one knows," Feruccio said. "How the redhead got in his bad graces must be quite a tryst. But now we know why he and Quillig have ascended Killermount."

"We do?"

"They're on their way to Port Stafford."

"Why there?"

"We got word that a vessel departed from the eastern continent bound for Stafford. Reportedly, *he* is on board."

Hagan held up his palms. "How can you know that?"

"I'll explain—"

"*Later.* Got it. Shanta, why are you doing this?"

"Eldridge made my life true again by killing Goldmist. And if we're going to accomplish what we need to accomplish, I need to pay him back. This is a start."

"What are you trying to accomplish?"

"I'll explain on the way up Killermount."

ELDRIDGE AND QUILLIG

The T-shirt read, THE PROMETERIUM. Eldridge knew the shirt was under his leather jacket, but he tried not to think about it. Why had he kept the damn thing? He had only visited the place once—but once was enough.

Killermount streamed underneath them, a flat, white plane on a slope that ran halfway across the country. As they raced down its surface, hills rose up on either side fifty miles distant. From space, it would look like a giant plank wedged into the earth, but of course Hagan had explained that after Deadblast, there was nothing left in space to look down and see.

Or was there?

Eldridge couldn't explain it, but something at the Prometerium made him think otherwise. Two years earlier—before his collision with Jeb Goldmist, before the deathday wager, before he got into so much debt, before he even knew he was sick—Eldridge rode his bike west away from Dedrick, he knew not where. As he raced down Killermount amidst a downblaze of sunfire, the redhead thought back to the evening he rode away from Dedrick into a strangely temperate purple dusk.

He had no idea why he left Dedrick that night.

But when he realized that his memory of that night had been split in twain by a certain yawning void, he had an idea: Tola. For some reason, he left town because of her. But why? Had they fought? Had she started to suspect that she was his daughter? Whatever the reason, he had left Dedrick that night headed west, and his path led to the port remnant of Stafford, home of the Prometerium.

KIERON

Standing under the white eye of the sun, the jellywoman realized she had lost the trail. She stood at the foot of a fantastic rise in the desert's elevation, surrounded by black weeds and red rocks. Her new conveyance, recently liberated from the Hemming impound, hovered nearby, its hydrocell engines humming in idle. She searched for tire treads left by Quillig's motorcycle. At least Kieron *surmised* that the bounty-merc was riding a motorcycle. Hours earlier, when the jellywoman decided to claim the redhead for herself, she had ducked into the confine of Scar to recharge her mortarchain module, but she only had time to charge it up to three shots. After that, she had ran through the strangely deserted streets of Hemming to the remnant's vehicle impound, where she found an inch-thick chain dangling from the cyclone-fencing gates. Something had snapped the chains in twain. Kieron entered the impound, wrist-cannons at the ready in case a certain chain-snapping someone was still skulking in the impound. She found it empty.

Almost empty. Every few feet, she spotted a patch of dusty ground, and a few of those patches bore fresh bootprints. When she examined the prints, she saw two distinct treads. Had Quillig broken in here with Eldridge in tow to steal a vehicle? It made sense. Hanna and her pinkeye horde were still mostly confined to the opposite side of town, close to the entrance to the mud tunnel, where Quillig's double-sidecar would still be waiting. Kieron returned to the impound's front gate and searched the dust for signs of tire treads, hoping for a clue that would reveal the nature of Quillig's conveyance. She found it in the form of a single tiremark that could have been left by a bicycle, but the treads were too broad. In addition, there was a larger problem—there were still dozens of other tire treads that cut through the dust from various parts of the impound. Big, small, thick, thin. How could she assume that the motorcycle treads belonged to Quillig?

It was a gamble, but then everything was among the extraterrestrials.

Now for her own vehicle. She searched the impound for an appropriately fast ride, and right when she was about to climb into an ancient internal combuster called a Plymouth, she saw her destiny.

It looked like an oceanic wavesled. When Kieron was a child, she and her kind would ride transoceanic currents on two-person sleds that they made themselves. Little more than a sheet of scrap metal to sit on, what made it a wavesled was the aft cone. Kieron innovated the cone design among her friends, and she did it by taking another sheet of metal and coiling it into a hollow cone that they mounted to the rear of the sled with the cone's point facing backward. When placed into an oceanic current, the cone acted as a buffer pad that propelled the sled forward. She and her friends rode the sleds two at a time, both of them on their stomachs, one on the other's back—and everyone expelling endless bubbles of mirth as they rode.

The vehicle in the Hemming impound was designed for terrestrial travel, but it had a similar design. About ten feet from bow to stern, the one-person sled bore a rocket booster on its rear. (To Kieron's relief, it was hydrocell-powered.) Similar to the sleds of her youth, Kieron would pilot it lying on her stomach. As she stood over the wavesled—not its formal name, she knew, but the one it would bear—her shadow grew taller. Across the remnant, the hyperobject grew larger, while from the interior of Torsten's mountain, a floating green platform emerged, surrounded by pinkeyes. Sitting upside down on the *bottom* of the platform was Boris Hagan. Moments later, Lilya Hanna emerged and flipped upside down to address the old man.

Kieron turned her attention to getting the wavesled operational. It didn't even need a key. A simple push of a button brought the sled to life, and a cursory check of its vital systems confirmed its good status. It even had basic environmental controls, although Kieron's plastic coating obviated such functions. She climbed on and coasted out of the impound against the backdrop of a rapidly expanding hyperobject. She eased her way through the streets of Hemming. Even though this side of town was largely deserted, she still encountered a few patrolling pinkeyes. Once she reached the membrane gate, she eased her way through.

And almost had a head-on collision.

When the jellywoman emerged from the gate, giant steel teeth filled her worldview in the form of the grille of a massive black truck rumbling into the remnant. Kieron steered the sled into the earth and ducked as the truck rode overhead, its wheels passing within inches of the sled. The truck slowed to a crawl when it hit the membrane. Kieron used the opportunity to glide out from underneath. As she rode away, she checked her rearview and watched the truck vanish into the gate. Overhead, Hemming and its vast, sloping stucco walls glowed purple from within. The hyperobject must have been growing out of control, because the whole remnant looked like an enormous mass of glowing putty glommed among the mountains of the eastern desert.

Kieron turned her attention to tracking Quillig and scanned the desert earth. The truck's passing had disturbed some of the bounty-merc's treads, but after a tense few minutes, Kieron rediscovered the trails and was soon gliding across the desert at 120 knots—or "miles per hour," whatever the ETs called it—following Quillig's tire treads and thanking a grim aquatic deity for her luck that the weather maintained a boring uniform standard of oppressive heat and low winds. Normally when tracking a target, she might proceed slowly, taking care to preserve the trail behind her in case she had to backtrack. Not so with this quarry. The jellywoman's sand-wake obliterated any trace of the redhead's motorbike treads as she raced along.

Until she lost the trail at the foot of this mountain.

She continued to scan the terrain at the foot of the mountain but saw nothing. She went on seeing nothing until she widened the scope of search to include the way she'd come. Stretching across the desert, she saw the dim outline of the curving sand-groove left by her sled, along with something else: a dark, watery smear on the horizon. Of course, it only *looked* watery because of heat distortion, and having spent a lifetime living among the waves, Kieron's eyes decoded the sight and told her that a familiar black truck was approaching, flanked by billowing upwaves of sand. *It's coming fast.*

Hide. The jellywoman spun around in search of a hiding place and saw a small cave that sank into the side of the mountain a few dozen yards up its slope. She dove onto her still-idling sled and speed-glided into the cave, where she waited at the mouth, watching. Yes, it was the same black truck that almost killed her at the Hemming gate, only now she could see it had a name: CLEAN MACHINE. Were they tracking the jellywoman?

No. They weren't tracking *her*, Kieron realized in a sudden surge of insight and memory. They were tracking *Eldridge*. Quillig's words from days earlier came to her:

He will always have help. He'll get help from strange quarters and at the very last motherfucking moment you expect it.

Kieron watched the Clean Machine roar up the side of the mountain. Once the truck had climbed sufficiently far up the incline, she glided out from her hiding place and followed it up.

BORIS HAGAN, ET AL

"YOU HAVE A *WHAT*-ELLITE?" Hagan yelled.

The old man felt sure that the Clean Machine would pitch backward as it climbed the increasingly steep slope up to the crest of Killermount, but the mighty truck's treads dug deep into the red earth and pulled its mass uphill, chewing through errant rocks and roots as its speed topped out around 70 mph, straight uphill. Inside, psychoskag technology, miffed at being forced to assume such a lowly form as a chair, morphed around the backsides of the two organics, keeping them upright with gyroscope-powered precision, all while the skags themselves continued to clack away at their keyboards, always processing, processing.

Hagan shouted over the din, "Run that by me again."

"We have a satellite," Feruccio said, still sitting before them and wearing her cargo fatigues. Hagan touched his forehead and responded with incredulity.

"In *orbit*?"

"There's no other place for a satellite to be."

"A satellite?" Pell asked. "Like our moon?"

"No," Hagan said. "Back before Deadblast, we used to have all these . . . well, machines and gizmos circling around the planet."

The Narsyan gave him a look.

"In space."

"In . . . space. I see."

Bam! They slammed over a huge rock and caught air, always moving upward. The walls produced handholds for Hagan and Pell. As their chairs morphed into a new configuration underneath, Hagan continued:

"But—they were all destroyed. During Deadblast, they think. At least that's what I read on the Arpa."

"Yeah," Feruccio said. "The Arpa. Thank you again for introducing us."

"Well, not like it's a person, but you're welcome."

"Isn't it?" Feruccio asked as her cargo fatigues melted away, leaving behind her genderless avatar.

"Oh, boy," Hagan said.

Pell held up a shaking hand. "Dare I ask about this mysterious Arpa?"

Feruccio fielded that one. "It's an ancient computer network. Most of it's been lost or otherwise corrupted. There's also a disproportionate amount of hardline smut that survived. I think I would've been queen of the Arpa before Deadblast."

"Anyway," Hagan said. "How'd y'all get a satellite?"

"The Arpa," she said. "During our exploration of its depths, we discovered an old control panel for a satellite that has a remarkable capacity for sight. We believe it to be the only one left."

"That's how you found out about Eldridge and the, uh, the oceans guy?"

Feruccio's face vanished. All that remained was a featureless blob of blue energy. A voice emanated from it that bore scant traces of Feruccio's rosy tones.

"Yes. The satellite revealed their locations to us. But it only passes overhead once every twenty-four hours. We gathered a lot of intel on its last pass."

Hagan and Pell shared a bewildered glance at the sight of the energy being before them. The truck caromed off a treestump and jolted Feruccio's face back onto the glowing blue form.

Hagan asked, "Shanta . . . what *are* you?"

"I am me. But with the exception of my brain, my corporeal form is no more. It's actually quite an effort to assume a form—or a personality—that organics can understand. We felt like our sudden appearance would frighten you less if I resembled some kind of military commander. With cleavage. Normally, the rear of this vehicle would be filled with technology, and my essence would simply be another program inside it. We can make use of quaint relics like maps and progress bars, but we prefer not to."

"Got it," Hagan said.

"So, was that really *you* back in Hemming?" Pell asked. "In the sky?"

Feruccio's blue mouth pixel-morphed into a smile. "Am I displaying an expression of happiness?"

"Um," Hagan said. "If you mean a 'smile,' then yes."

"Good. Yes, that was me. We sapped every ounce of energy from Hemming's power station to generate that diversion—a difficult feat after the hyperobject shorted out."

Something rustled inside of Boris Hagan. Previous words that made no sense at the time: *His hyperobject dispersed nanotroids into the water.* A question took shape and rolled out of his mouth without his assent: *"How . . . did the hyperobject short out?"*

Feruccio's face vanished, followed by her blue form, followed by her chair, all of which electro-splashed into nothingness. Her voice bleated from a ceiling-mounted speaker:

"It shorted out. That is enough."

After an instant's thought, Hagan's hands went to clutch his own hair, but only slid across his bare scalp like he was swiping away a layer of sweat.

"But . . . *I'm* the one who shorted it out. When I blasted it."

Feruccio reconfigured before them, once again dressed in cargo fatigues. Her voice came in clipped fragments.

"This was an extraction. We knew there was gonna be a body count."

"I killed them all, didn't I?"

"He killed them, Boris. The Odd. You're not the one who planted bombs inside their heads. You couldn't have known. When you blasted

the hyperobject, you shorted them out, yes. But you also gave us the opening we needed to insert me into his system."

The old man held his head. "How many people live in Hemming?"

Upward momentum halted for an instant as they reached the crest of the incline and flattened out. Hagan and Pell shifted forward slightly as their seats reconstituted themselves. The Narsyan, barely a wisp of a man, slipped to the floor. Hagan helped him to his feet. They looked out the front windshield and saw the endless, sloping plane of Killermount racing downward to a distant horizon. Feruccio's electro-hot hand touched Hagan's shoulder. She answered his question.

"*Enough* people, Boris. This is how the Odds work. It's not your fault. Now, let's go save Eldridge."

"I don't know how we can," Hagan said.

"Let me talk to him."

Pell had spoken.

"What are you going to say?" the old man asked.

"Whatever needs to be said."

"Very well," Feruccio said. "We shall ride out in front of them and let you out."

"I'll lend a shoulder," Hagan offered.

The Narsyan chieftain shook his head and rose to his feet, hunching over inside the truck's cramped confines.

"I. Can. *Stand*."

—⚇—

ELDRIDGE AND QUILLIG

DESPITE WHAT THE REDHEAD had heard, Killermount wasn't entirely featureless. Various structures jutted out of the flat slope and provided the occasional obstacle to dodge as he brought the bike to its top speed and let downward momentum do the rest. The rumortrysts held that fantastic winds blew through the great valley that enclosed Killermount, and those trysts were indeed true. Eldridge had heard about some travelers who dared to ride *up* Killermount who would find themselves locked in place by a hundred-mile-per-hour headwind and have to turn back. On the day he abandoned Boris Hagan in Hemming, the redhead took bleak pleasure at the powerful channel of wind that filled his sails as he rode westward.

He winced. *Filled his sails.*

It was something Boris would've said.

With Quillig the bounty-merc riding behind and clutching his midsection hard enough to expel a chunk of food stuck in his windpipe, Eldridge slalomed around an ancient house lodged into the flat plane. A thin haze of dust hung inches above the plane of Killermount and flowed around the house, with its yellow clapboard walls, green shutters, and plywood-blocked windows. Its foundation faced the sky, like the house was trying to dig its way to safety.

I wish I could join you, Eldridge told the house, wondering if Boris Hagan would be safe.

Or Pell.

Or Stewart.

Or Crius.

Or Oksie.

His hands tightened on the handlebars for a moment, ready to turn the bike around—but a moment of black hatred banished the impulse from his mind. He tried to imagine the scene when his friends agreed to team up and rescue him from the Chain. According to Hagan, Dedrick had already been overrun by dreens. Crius had been abducted and made the new dreenking. Oksana had vanished. So that meant Boris, Pell, and Stewart all must've met somewhere to discuss their plan to rescue Oksana from her new dreen stronghold in Towertown. Where had they met? Probably the jail, which must've been deserted after Tola's death.

Tola's death. It was the only memory the Odds had let him keep.

He imagined Boris Hagan sitting behind her desk, playing with her quill and laughing about old times. He imagined Stewart telling bawdy jokes that Pell didn't get. He imagined them deciding to put their own lives at risk for a guy who couldn't even keep himself out of trouble.

Who couldn't even keep his daughter safe.

On Killermount, Eldridge jumped his bike off the roof of an old chrome camping vehicle, its chrome long since burnished to gray by the constant dust. Quillig yelped. They hung in the air for a long while, the horizon swimming in the distance while streams of dust flowed by underneath. Competing voices in the redhead's mind vied for his sympathy. One vocal contingent pointed to the image of his friends teaming up to rescue him and tried to cast it in a positive light, while a single voice sat in a spotlight and merely repeated a litany of gibberish and indicated an image of Dedrick overrun by dreens. Boris Hagan's words sounded from somewhere within.

Home? Where the hell is that?

The old fuck really looked tired after the Mud Races, didn't he? If the poor son of a *macta* didn't have it in him to mount a transcontinental rescue attempt, then why the hell even *try*? So *what* if Crius was the dreenking and the Narsyans had vanished and Pell was a monster and Stew was a fire warden and his Oksie was a dreen? *Who the fuck even cared after Deadblast?* Who cared that Eldridge couldn't remember how Zora Tola's eyelids got burned so bad—only that he knew it was his fault? His friends only wanted to go home and rest. Hagan in his shitty little apartment full of motionshow posters and an Arpa hookup; Pell up with those Narsyan assholes; Crius and Stew inside of that marble mausoleum they called a casino. They didn't need Eldridge back. They didn't *want* him back. They just needed the redhead's help to go home.

To hell with them.

And me.

The bike touched down. Its wheels swerved out from underneath them for one head-spinning moment, but Eldridge steered them back on course: straight down, and straight toward Port Stafford, where the redhead *thought* that this entire tragic chapter of his life began. That's what he *thought* as he remembered the night two years ago when he reached the terminus of the Aester Road and turned north, riding along the sheer cliff that marked the western boundary of the continent. A road followed the jagged edge of the coastal cliff and led straight to Port Stafford, where the Prometerium—and a very simple game—awaited him.

Despite the miasma of self-loathing that englazed his mind, Eldridge chuckled. Everyone thought that he had made dozens, scores, *hundreds* of odds to have buried himself in so much debt, but the truth was: Eldridge had only made odds four times in his life.

Once was when he made deathday odds with Crius Kaleb. Once was with Yasim, Odd of Dedrick; Eldridge had needed jenta to replace the cooling system on his bike, and he had only made those odds because he had acquired intel from the corpse of Qi Li that guaranteed his victory. The two times he competed in Xiang tournaments didn't count because you simply won jenta for *fighting* in those tournaments.

The other time was two years earlier. In Port Stafford. On a lark.

At the Prometerium.

The redhead had arrived in Stafford around three in the morning, but unlike some remnants that followed the old circadian rhythms of day and night, the port remnant was always awake. Its climate-controlled streets were packed with dregs that crisscrossed its wide boulevards with drinks in hand, dodging around passing forklifts that hovered from one warehouse to the next, bearing cargo bound for parts distant up the coast. Warehouses alternated with saloons and inns throughout Stafford, which was linked to its subterranean portion by one of three roadways that descended into the earth from the middle of the main boulevard. To the west, the ocean churned away, its green waves rendered black at night. Barges sailed alongside the cliff, passing underneath giant steel arms that lifted freight boxes from their decks. That night two years ago, Eldridge took one of the downramps to under-Stafford, whose black streets stank of newly poured pavement. While riding through its neon-glimmery, climate-controlled streets, he realized why he had chosen Port Stafford when he blew out of Dedrick, hoping to clear his mind.

Stafford had no Odd.

Well, it had no *resident* Odd. The rumortrysts held that someone from across the oceans held sway over Stafford, and if that certain someone were powerful enough to control a remnant from that far afield, then they were axiomatically an Odd. Various small-time Odds scurried around the wet-slick streets of under-Stafford, some of them hiding behind arching buttresses that held up the street overhead, while others sat in some of the dozens of portholes that looked through the red-brick walls at the ocean. That night two years ago, Eldridge ignored them all and simply wove his bike through the glut of chattering dregs that crowded the streets and parked by the nearest place that looked like it served food.

The Prometerium.

Like most of the establishments in Stafford, neon letters spelled out its name in a glowing swoop over the door, which stood on a curving corner at the crux of a triple intersection where three streets created a giant analog of an old glyph that Eldridge remembered from his mathematicalogical studies as a Narsyan youth: $\neq$

The redhead strode into the Prometerium, a man free of debt, free of responsibilities. When he walked inside, an attendant handed him a pair of micromag implants for his boots that let him walk up to the bar, which coiled through the building and around all three spatial axes like a loose length of ribbon. Eldridge climbed a micromag-friendly footpath up to an open stool. He sat down, his body parallel to the surface of the earth, and ordered a plate of slop that he shoveled into his gullet. He also ordered several drinks that he drained in an eager effort to inebriate himself. A mirror hung behind the bar and gave view to more neon letters; these letters, however, gleamed from *within* the Prometerium, advertising a simple game of chance. The name of the game caught his attention and sparked a receptor inside him that had heretofore lain dormant.

The game was called, WHAT HAPPENED AT DEADBLAST?

—⚋—

KIERON

Only the Emilian Drop had caused the jellywoman's stomach to perform the kind of backflips that it did as she flew down the massive, featureless, sloping plane that greeted her at the top of the mountain near Hemming remnant. As a child, she and her friends had ventured a few leagues from their native habitat to the drop, which slanted into the depths of the earth much like the terrifying mountain she currently descended at more than ten knots, taking care to leave sufficient distance between her wavesled and the Clean Machine, lest she risk detection. Onrushing dust maintained a steady, beating rhythm against her face as she rocketed down the mount, listing laterally around the rare stone or the occasional strange structure that protruded from the otherwise featureless surface.

Meanwhile, the Clean Machine continued to roar down the mount, far ahead. Kieron marveled at the enormous truck's ability to adjust to any physical situation. Rocket thrusters bloomed out of its rear like fiery flowers; when the truck flipped into a barrel roll after nicking a rock, more thrusters spewed fire to stabilize the truck. Its surface liquefied, morphing into thousands of tiny, interlocking modules that allowed the truck to reposition its tires. The jellywoman felt a brief flutter of panic when the truck vanished ahead into the heat mirage, but she increased speed and brought the truck back into view.

Unfortunately, she still saw no sign of Eldridge or Quillig, and the Clean Machine was starting to move at speeds faster than she could match on her wavesled.

The jellywoman hit the gas and felt G-forces reverberate through her plastic coating and press against her face. She reflected that if she were uncovered, her face would be stretched in a permanent grimace, her teeth clenched and exposed to the sand-blast of dust that she realized was eating away at her plastic covering as she rode down the mount faster and faster. Tiny brown pockmarks filled up her visual sphere in rapid-fire succession, like she was watching a virus multiply out of control under a microscope. She wiped dust-sand off her plastic face and tried to shield her eyes, but her efforts were for naught. When she had scraped away enough sand to allow herself to see again, she saw that the Clean Machine was gone.

But Eldridge was in sight.

Kieron veered starboard and rode a half mile away directly north, keeping the redhead and Quillig in view. They were indeed riding a motorbike, but curiously, it appeared that Eldridge had been driving. Even curiouser, it seemed that Quillig hadn't blasted Eldridge with mortarchains; the redhead had come on his own accord. Kieron also noted that Quillig had removed his plaid face covering for some reason.

The jellywoman positioned her fingers above the wavesled's accelerator, ready to bolt, but it appeared they hadn't spotted her.

Kieron then saw the Clean Machine a few yards ahead down the mountain, surrounded by a cloud of kicked-up dust, its tires still leaving long skid-tracks on the mount as it drew to a halt. The truck's rear-mounted rockets reverse-bloomed, leaving only flat, black rear doors, which yawned open and revealed an interior, dark but for a few multicolored flashing lights. A man Kieron didn't recognize crawled out of the back. The jellywoman didn't have mops where she came from, but she had seen the cleaning implements above the water. The infirm man who crawled out of the Clean Machine had limbs as thin as mop-handles. He wore only a patch of threadbare fabric wrapped around his loins. He lurched forward, walking up the mount toward Quillig and Eldridge on a pair of rattling knees.

They exchanged words. The howling winds along the mount drowned out their words, but Kieron heard the infirm man yell, "Eldridge!" The infirm man's words must have failed to move the redhead, because he disengaged his brakes and started to ride past the Clean Machine. But the infirm man must've had a final appeal, because he yelled one last thing at the redhead, who brought his bike to a halt.

They spoke a moment more—and then *Quillig* leaped into action.

The barefaced bounty-merc wrapped his arm around the redhead's neck and dragged him off the bike, which fell to the ground and slid a few feet down the mount. Quillig pulled something from his pocket; actually, it was *two* things.

His voice floated on the wind, *"Get back! Get back!"*

Quillig chucked one of the items—a palm-sized, rectangular black item—while holding the other item aloft. The first item clattered to the ground in front of the infirm man, who staggered back and fell to the ground. Quillig waved the second item (a small, pink rectangle) in the air, still shouting at them to get back. But then the infirm man crawled over to the first item, picked it up, and shouted something. In response, the redhead rammed his elbow into Quillig's stomach and dove forward.

Kieron would only have a vague recollection of what followed.

As near as she could remember, the skies turned purple, and the side of the mountain imploded. A bolt of unimaginable force, like a fist from the heavens, punched into the mount and left a hundred-foot crater in the slanted slope. The jellywoman couldn't tell which was louder—the thundercrack from above, or the shattering of the mountainside. As the cloud of dusty debris dissipated, Kieron watched the redhead hoist the infirm man into his arms and jump into the quickly closing rear of the Clean Machine, which had an unexpected passenger. Kieron's head jerked up in recognition when she saw Boris Hagan—incredibly free from Lilya Hanna's clutches less than two hours later—looking out from inside the black truck. Once again, Quillig's words came to her.

He will always have help. He'll get help from strange quarters and at the very last motherfucking moment you expect it.

Apparently that help extended to the redhead's friends as well.

The truck closed up around them and wheeled about. As it roared back up the mount, it extended a robotic arm and picked up the motorbike.

—⚙—

QUILLIG AND ELDRIDGE

A JETPACK AND TWO CELL phones. That's what the last of his jenta cost him back in Hemming.

After Quillig shot the jellywoman in the face, he found himself rushing through the cheering crowd at the end of the Mud Races, his hands scrabbling to reattach the patch of plaid fabric and hide his face from the endless eyes, eyes, *eyes* all around him—none of which paid him any mind, of course, but nevertheless, the bounty-merc (and recovering dreen) glared at every passerby with the dark aperture of his sight-cartridge, and even though every eye in town was trained on their beloved Walter Torsten and the two magnificent winners of the Mud Races, Quillig saw nothing but whites and pupils, *thousands* of them, all of them following his path through the roiling crowd in terrible twos, like he was walking down a haunted hallway with no end.

He dropped Mac's gun somewhere. He didn't remember.

But he had his stylus. Oh, did he have his stylus, and it was packed with the last of his jenta. He scurried through the streets of Hemming, his subconscious reminding him of the possibility of a *hidden* sectan confine somewhere within the remnant's boundaries, but Quillig ignored the thoughts and simply searched for an armory.

It hung suspended between two buildings on a foundation of

cables and ropes. The bounty-merc had to climb a flight of stone stairs and crawl out across a rope bridge to reach the armory, which was little more than a single wooden platform packed with armaments, all of which were hung by their bullet-guards from poles that dotted the platform. The proprietor was a squat dreg whose mandible had been surgically replaced with a failed attempt at an organic facsimile. Fist-sized clumps of scar tissue joined the hairless, white-pale mandible-mistake to his head. When he spoke, muscles flexed and jumped through the scar tissue like fingers trapped under his skin. The proprietor happily sold him the rickety jetpack, which looked less like a jetpack and more like a fucking food processor with shoulder straps and rocket mounts. Quillig bought it anyway and was on his way out when the dreg's mandible started flapping around the shapes of words he understood: *Edict. Cell phone. Deadblast. Want, want, want?*

Quillig didn't know why he bought the damn things. He had planned to simply drag the redhead's ass to Port Stafford via mortar-chains, but an old voice from behind one of the many doors that hid in his mind-hallway whispered that he might need a backup plan. When Eldridge declined mortarchain implantation in such dramatic fashion, Quillig thanked that old voice for the suggestion. The redhead was nothing if not unpredictable, and the bounty-merc was glad to have the cell phones just in case the little cocksucker decided to change his mind.

Riding down Killermount, Quillig actually let himself believe that Eldridge would follow through with his promise to let the bounty-merc deliver him to the man across the oceans. For a while.

But when a goddamn fucking *black dumptruck* blasted by and cut them off, Quillig's hands—heretofore clamped around Eldridge's midsection in terror—dipped into his pocket and palmed the two cell phones. Pursuant to the Cell phone Edict of Deadblast, everyone knew that cellular technology was *macta*, and in the wake of the last Dedrick Xiang tournament, the rumortrysts had received (and dispersed) word of how Eldridge used cell phones to slay his old friend, Marko Marinus. Those same trysts had also carried with them the information that the proprietor-dreg grumbled when he handed over the phones.

"Only two. One to call. One to go *boom.*"

Eldridge brought his bike to stop a few yards above the drumptruck, which skidded to a halt. Rockets had been mounted to it, but those same rockets disassembled themselves into thousands of tiny modules and melted back into the rear of the truck, which then opened like a pair of giant jaws. A few multicolored lights blinked within the dark interior. A single man struggled out of the truck, his body having been reduced to a jumble of quavering flesh and bone. Eldridge exhaled a long breath when he saw the man. Quillig didn't recognize him, but he had a pretty good idea who it was.

"One of your friends?" the bounty-merc asked.

Eldridge ignored the question and waited while his friend stumbled up the slope toward them, his knees threatening to buckle with each step. Finally, he stopped.

"Eldridge! It's Pell."

"I know who you are," Eldridge said. "What're you doing here?"

"I'm not alone. I'm here with Boris and Shanta Feruccio and the psychoskags."

Eldridge shifted in his seat but said nothing.

Pell took a few deep breaths, then said, "Did you know that when Boris Hagan and Stewart Kaleb first asked for my help, I refused them?"

"Can't say I'm surprised."

"Do you want to know what changed my mind?"

"Nope."

"I had ascended the mountain peak to work on the new conventuary, and when I returned to Burbage, I found it deserted. They waited until I was gone, and then they left me."

Wind howled around the redhead's response. "That's because Burbage was a systematic *abuse* factory, and you were the head of it. You're a fucking asshole, Pell."

Pell. Pell *Yannick*. Burbage. Quillig recognized the names from Narsyan lore, but how could this be Pell Yannick, unspoken high chieftain of the Order of the Narsyan? The rumortrysts held that Yannick could run a hundred miles at a dead sprint. This man could barely hold his own weight upright.

As if in response, the man who called himself Pell Yannick forearm-wiped sweat from his brow and leaned over to catch his breath. When he stood up, he said, "I don't dispute the charge. That's why I'm here to apologize. I should have said yes when Boris and Stewart first asked my help. I'm sorry that it took the loss of my home to force my change of heart."

"Pell—"

"We're not done yet. Oksana and Stewart remain trapped within the Fallen Tower, and Crius Kaleb is still the parasitic king to the dreen-queen of Dedrick. Eldridge, I don't know what's happened to you, but I call upon you to reconsider your course of action. We need your help. They need to be rescued, and they need to be cured."

Quillig's hand tightened around the cell phones. He waited for the redhead to change his mind and decide to go help his dumbshit friends. But for the second time in the last twenty-four hours, the redhead surprised him.

"You'll have to cure 'em yourself," he said as he disengaged the brake and started to ride down the mount.

Pell shouted, *"I can't cure them!"*

The bike jerked to a squeaky halt right next to Pell.

Oh, shit, Quillig thought.

"What do you mean you can't cure them?" Eldridge asked.

"You saw what Hanna did to me," Pell said. "My body is ruined. My *blood* is ruined. I can cure no one."

"What does that mean?"

The Narsyan coughed on dust and said, "It means *you* will have to brave the Maiden."

The redhead's shoulders slumped, and for a moment, Quillig thought he was going to ignore Pell's words, but then his head rose, and he tightened both hands around the handlebars. He muttered one word:

"Naughty."

"What?" Pell asked.

"Nothing," Eldridge answered, then spoke over his shoulder. "I'm sorry, Quillig. I can let you off back at—"

The bounty-merc dragged the redhead off the bike before he could take another breath. He pulled both cell phones out of his pocket and tossed one of them on the ground between them, screaming, *"Get back! Get back!"*

The former Narsyan must have recognized the device, because

he reeled backward and fell in a cloud of dust. Creatures stirred from within the dumptruck, but Pell held up his hand.

"He's got a cell phone! Don't move!"

And no one did. Fuckers. Quillig brandished his cell phone, a pink gizmo that bore the strange word BARBIE in idiotic, girly cursive script. He continued to scream, *"We're leaving!"* He lowered his voice and hissed, "Redhead, you are getting back on that bike, and we're riding west."

But like always, the son of a macta's friends surprised him. Pell scrambled through the dirt and picked up the second cell phone.

"El! *Move!*"

The redhead must've *really* changed his mind, because he rammed his elbow into the bounty-merc's midsection and jumped away from the purple blast of energy that slammed down from above and rendered Quillig blind and deaf one instant, unconscious the next.

Darkness and silence reigned.

His next sensations included the pitter-patter of dust-chunks that rained from above. His sight aperture expanded to take in all available light. He realized he was lying on his back. He tried to roll over and found himself tumbling into a crater that had been blown into the side of Killermount. The fall detached his sight cartridge. He fell to the steaming, smoking bottom of the crater and cooked in the sun.

Footsteps. Soft ones, plodding down the inside of the crater.

Once again, someone plugged his sight-cartridge back into his sockets, but this time, he didn't see the redhead. Instead, he saw the jellywoman, only she wasn't covered with quite as much jelly anymore. The top half of her head lay exposed, the plastic covering having been scored away. Black oculars remained lodged in her eye sockets, while her nose was still hidden underneath her plastic covering.

The jellywoman handed him a note.

He took it, but before he could read it, the jellywoman pressed one of her wrist-cannons into Quillig's forehead. Kieron tapped the note with her other hand. Quillig read.

I've decided to let you live. Eldridge shall be my gift to the man across the oceans. I advise you stay out of my affairs.

She lowered her wrist-cannon, turned, and climbed up the crater.

"Hey, jellywoman!" Quillig yelled.

Kieron stopped halfway up the crater and turned.

"You saw that, right? A dumptruck full of assholes comes all this way to save him. And that poor bastard on the ground? Half dead, could barely walk? You saw it, right? He dialed the fucking number himself. Could've been blown to bits. But he did it anyway. To save him."

The jellywoman continued climbing while Quillig kept yelling.

"You'll never beat that! Never! Never! Never!"

ELDRIDGE, ET AL

"I can't cure them!"

Pell's words froze the redhead's blood. He squeezed the brakes, his subconscious mind already a few steps ahead of his conscious mind. His subconscious had a question: *Would Quillig be a threat if I changed my mind?* But his conscious mind was still blundering its way through the choice that the withered Narsyan chieftain presented him, and as his subconscious took note of the tightening of the bounty-merc's arm around his midsection, his conscious mind spoke:

"What do you mean you can't cure them?"

His former Narsyan nemesis, whom he had seen transformed into a blubberous monster in the bowels of Penticton, stood before him, trembling in the 160-degree heat. At the same time, the redhead's subconscious mind delivered a missive to his forebrain: *Quillig's not armed. You can safely change your mind.* But Pell's words distracted him.

"You saw what Hanna did to me," Pell said. "My body is ruined. My *blood* is ruined. I can cure no one."

But why—

Eldridge ignored the rustlings in the back of his mind.

"What does that mean?"

The redhead knew the answer before he even asked the question. He had suspected it for years, and in the wake of Pell's ruination at the hands of Lilya Hanna, he knew that his future had one more stopover in his past. Dust whiplashed across their faces, borne by an especially violent upcurrent from the west. Pell coughed, then spoke.

"It means *you* will have to brave the Maiden."

Why is Quillig only holding you with one *arm?*

It was a good question, but the redhead ignored it, feeling his shoulders slouch under a sudden weight. He only heard the wheeze and whine of the winds across Killermount as he looked deep, deep, deep into the grinning chasm that his daughter's absence left in his mind. Time telescoped, and for the first time, he actually imagined what would happen if he followed through with his promise to Quillig. In his mind's eye, he watched as Quillig turned him over to the man across the oceans, who in turn would enslave him or torture him or kill him.

And that would be it. And Quillig was right. He'd be a few months late, but he could finally collect on his deathday wager.

Why is Quillig only holding you with one *arm?*

The prospect that his death might leave his friends hip-deep in trouble presented a conundrum, and for a dilating instant, the redhead considered leaving his friends behind. After all, they were only *in* trouble to begin with because he had gone to Hemming to play the hyperlotto. That's when Walter Torsten snatched him, which set off the destructive sequence of events—the dreenqueen's invasion, Oksana's disappearance, his friends' failed rescue attempt—that eventually led him to Killermount. He couldn't make it all right, he *couldn't,* but if he were gone, then he would take all his troubles with him.

They'd be safe.

Why is Quillig only holding you with one *arm?*

But then the redhead remembered why he had ridden out of Dedrick that night two years ago. He remembered why he had needed to clear his mind, and he remembered what led him to Port Stafford, specifically.

Nadia was dead.

Tremors ripped through his mind. The grinning chasm into which his memories of Constable Tola had vanished emitted a thunderous groan and hacked up that information; information he had almost lost. He had actually forgotten that she was dead, but dead she was, and someone in Stafford had managed to send a moto-express carrier to

Dedrick to inform him that he could claim her belongings in the port remnant.

At the Prometerium.

Deep inside his thoughts, the redhead saw the humor of it. Her death had led him to Port Stafford, which led him to the Prometerium, which led him to play the game: WHAT HAPPENED AT DEADBLAST? The Odds would've called it a threshold-trox; an easy game to rope in a dreg who might not otherwise be accustomed to the dopamine-burst delivered by a successful bit of oddsmaking. When Eldridge spotted the game that night in the Prometerium, three dregs were already waiting in line to play. The redhead downed a few shots of bourbon, finished his meal, and escher-strolled around the bar's corkscrewy perimeter until he reached the booth manned by a small-time Odd he knew, Zak Chamberlain. A ten-foot top hat teetered atop Chamberlain's bushy unibrow, which waggled in tune with his crowd-barking lantern jawline.

"Solve the mystery of our times! Answer the greatest question of them all—*What happened at Deadblast?* Counter-odds extraordinaire, my dregs! Step up and *stand* up for knowledge of the unknown!"

Eldridge stood on the micromag-friendly path and waited his turn. The three dregs all made their guesses. One speculated that a nuclear holocaust brought about the planet's demise. Wrong. Another suggested that a celestial collision was the culprit. Also wrong. Of course, the whole game was a joke, given that *nobody* knew what happened. Dregs who guessed incorrectly—which was everybody—actually *won* a few jenta for their troubles, hence the game's reputation as a threshold-trox. Even the smallest taste of winning could hook a dreg for all time.

The third dreg swayed up to the booth and caught himself from falling with his palms. A tumbler full of booze splashed onto his hand as he made eye contact with Boris Hagan's old friend. Naturally, the third dreg had red hair and was several drinks into his evening of mourning for the beloved woman who had never been his wife but whom he should have made his wife.

"Thanks for sending the message, Zak."

Despite the concern on his face, Chamberlain continued to wag his unibrow and mug for the crowd.

"You're welcome, El. Condolences. Care to try your luck?"

Eldridge peered at the dataread that displayed an overhead view of the eastern continent. He frowned.

"How'd you get that overhead shot?"

Chamberlain glanced over his shoulder. "Oh, it's just an effex." He raised his voice for the dregs waiting to play. "So, good sir! *What happened at Deadblast?!*"

As he sat on Killermount weighing the potentialities of the future, Eldridge thought back to that night two years earlier and felt his memory skipping through the past like a slimstone across a pond; a pond polluted with flaming slicks of oil. He remembered his first night with Nadia—the way she felt, the way she touched him, the way she controlled him—and he remembered opening the smartpaper message from the moto-express carrier that told him she had been slaughtered at the hands of undersea marauders while braving a voyage to the eastern continent.

He thought of her giggle; the way it oscillated between major and minor key, like she couldn't decide whether to laugh *with* him or *at* him. He thought of Boris's ever-present question about her:

How much older was she?

Had she always been laughing *at* him, never *with*?

Sitting at Zak Chamberlain's booth that night, Eldridge drained his drink and spouted forth the craziest idea he could possibly conceive for what caused the Deadblast cataclysm, and in response, Chamberlain pressed a brass horn to his lips and tooted a doleful note.

"Sorry, sir! Wrong again!"

He scribbled out a modest payment of jenta that the redhead scooped up. Chamberlain leaned over to whisper in his ear.

"I tossed in a little extra. Meet me out back in an hour."

An hour later, Eldridge was puking behind the Prometerium when Chamberlain found him. The redhead palm-leaned against the wall like a constable was patting him down and ducked his head between his arms to achieve an optimum barfing position. Chamberlain kept a respectful distance in the dark alley and waited for him to finish. When he did, the Odd stepped forward and held out a small canvas bag.

Eldridge took it and spoke with drunk-numb lips. "How'dja get it?"

"Y'know how it goes, El. One dreg passed it on to another dreg. Her name was in there. *Your* name was in there. So it goes, and so it came to me. Bor's an old bean, and I know you two are onesies, so I felt the obligation. It's no big."

Eldridge hesitated a moment, holding the bag by its handles. Then he spread his hands and pulled it open.

It was filled with light.

An up-shining cone of white slashed up from the alley. Inside the bag sat the very same hutchlight that Nadia had once used to warm his body in the middle of a desert snowstorm.

"How . . . ?"

"Like I said, there was a note," Chamberlain said. "She asked me to light it before I handed it over. Here you go."

The Odd handed him a folded-up piece of old-fashioned paper. A brief note at the top laid out the request to ignite the hutchlight, while below it sat her final message to the redhead:

I don't blame you for what happened to our little girl. I regret that you couldn't make space for me in your life to raise her. Maybe if I had been around, she might not have suffered the fate she did.

They're coming for me. I don't have long.

In place of my light, I give you the first light we shared.

I trust you'll always love me, my Billy-Bill.

Nadia

"Nadia," Eldridge muttered on Killermount, his decision made.

Pell frowned. "What?"

"Nothing," the redhead said before he craned his neck. "I'm sorry, Quillig. I can let you off back at—"

In the moments that followed, his subconscious mind wagged its finger at him, telling him a thousand *I told you so's*. With his free arm, the bounty-merc dragged the redhead off his motorbike, which slid down the mount a few feet while Quillig waved something over his head. As it turned out, he was waving *two* somethings.

Cell phones.

Shit, Eldridge thought while Quillig shrieked.

"Get back! Get back!"

The bounty-merc chucked one of the phones into the dirt, where it acted like a repulsor to the weakened Pell Yannick. The Narsyan fell to the ground in a heap of swollen joints and shaking limbs. Movement from inside the black truck caught Pell's attention, because he held up his hand.

"He's got a cell phone! Don't move!"

Quillig continued to drag the redhead away from the phone. His next words steamed against the redhead's ear, somehow hotter than the sunblaze of Killermount.

"Redhead, you are getting back on that bike, and we're riding west."

As usually happened in moments like this, when an insane bounty-mercenary held a lethal device to his head and a truckful of cyborgified robot-monsters stood nearby and an old nemesis lay in the dirt, his body having wasted away to its constituent parts—a typical day in the post-Deadblast world—*time extended.* As the moments stretched out before him, Eldridge realized that even though he had *thought* about Nadia's final note many times over the years, he had never actually *read its words.*

Blame. Regret. Suffer. Fate.

Light.

If pressed, the redhead wouldn't be able to explain why he had changed his mind and decided to once again take up the cause to rescue his friends, but as he looked into the eyes of Pell Yannick that day atop Killermount, he figured it was because something had finally dislodged Nadia's words from his mind. They fell away, leaving only the image of the other woman in his life—Oksana the trixie, still trapped in Towertown—and he just couldn't bear to think of her being anywhere but in his fucking *arms.*

Quillig didn't see it, but Eldridge and Pell *smiled* at each other.

"El! *Move!*"

The redhead rammed his elbow into the bounty-merc's stomach before Pell even lunged for the phone on the ground, and just like the day Marko Marinus died, Eldridge felt the heavens rend themselves apart in anticipation of the call. The Narsyan pressed the *send* button just as Eldridge performed a running dive down Killermount. A column of pure purple energy blasted into the mount, its impact sending the black truck rolling down the slope, but the psychoskags' tech was nimble enough to reposition its tires and stop its slide, although Eldridge soon found himself sliding headfirst down the endless plane.

He spun around, flipped over, and dug his bootheels into the dirt to stop his descent. When he looked back up the mountainslope, he saw a rainstorm of debris falling across a newly blown crater that dipped into the earth. He leaped to his feet and sprinted up the mountain. Incredibly, Pell was lying on the ground near the crater. He must've pressed send, chucked the phone, and crawled out of the way—all on an empty fuel tank. Not bad. The redhead scooped the frail Narsyan chieftain into his arms and turned to the truck, which still stood with its rear doors open. A face appeared in the doorway that was familiar, yet different.

"Get in!"

It was a bald, clean-shaven Boris Hagan, who grinned in spite of the carnage and the sight of an injured Pell Yannick in the redhead's arms. Eldridge jumped into the Clean Machine as its rear doors clamped shut. He laid Pell on the floor, then looked up.

"Where's Shanta?"

An electromorph avatar of Shanta Feruccio crackled into view behind him. Still kneeling, the redhead spun around and kick-crawled back against the wall.

"Holy Crom!"

"Hello, Eldridge!" Shanta's avatar yelled, before she aimed her ire at the psychoskag driver. *"About-face! Move! And grab the motorcycle, too!"*

She vanished as the truck wheeled around and started the long ascent back up Killermount. Presumably, robotic arms extended from its exterior and snagged his motorbike. Eldridge saw a lot of familiar psychoskag faces, some of them having been detached from their host bodies and plugged into the wall. Even Magna was there, grinning down at him with black teeth.

"I thought you were dead," Eldridge said, and instead of a *bargle*, he got:

"No. I live. It is agreeable to see you."

Pell coughed and opened his eyes. Flat on his back, he took the redhead's hand.

"Thank you for changing your mind. You fuckwit."

"Good to see you too, Pell," Eldridge said with a chuckle, then hung his head. A hand touched his shoulder. He looked up at Hagan, who smiled down at him. Eldridge noticed his attire—no shirt and black pants.

"What are you wearing?"

"Oh, this dumbshit friend of mine decided he wanted to give himself up for bounty and leave us all to die, so I figured I ought to dress up for the occasion."

"Ah. I probably would've worn a tie for that."

"As soon as I regain the strength to dead-press a thousand pounds," Pell said, "I'm going to crush both of your larynxes."

Eldridge and Hagan smiled.

"You think I jest. I do not. Larnyxes. Crushed. *Soon*. Oh, my head . . ."

His words trailed off into the silence that filled the truck. No one said anything until they reached the top of Killermount and started the descent back toward Hemming. Eldridge spoke first.

"Thanks for coming back for me."

A moment passed, and then: "You're welcome."

Pell had spoken. He pushed himself up to his elbows and regarded the redhead with his gaunt face. Eldridge looked him in the eye.

"I'm so sorry this happened to you, Pell."

The Narsyan shook his head. "It is nothing. Another Great Challenge for me to conquer."

Eldridge nodded, then addressed the truck's interior. "Shanta?"

Feruccio's avatar rematerialized, this time divested of her military trappings. A genderless, blue energy form floated before him.

"Yes?" she said.

"I don't know how far west you can take us, but we need to get back to Dedrick. Well, to Burbage, really. Up in the Oasis Mountains."

Pell preempted Feruccio's response. "That won't be necessary."

"Why not? The Typhoid Maiden's in Burbage."

"When Yamuna absconded with the rest of the Narsyans, she took the Maiden with her. But there is another. In Penticton."

"Penticton?" Eldridge asked. "Why?"

"In the elder days, Lilya Hanna ascended to our highest ranks."

Hagan spoke up. "Right. We knew she used to be a Narsyan."

"But she has a Maiden?" Eldridge asked.

"Indeed she does," Pell said. "She never actually performed the

Circle Walk, but neither did she successfully brave the Maiden. In the intervening years, she constructed her own. When she took me captive in Penticton, she showed it to me."

"Well, that's good news," Eldridge said.

"I presume you need to brave the Maiden to become a full Narsyan chieftain, Eldridge," Feruccio said.

The redhead blinked owlishly, then nodded. "Right. I always forget you used to be a Narsyan yourself."

Pell looked up. "When?"

"Many ages ago. Before the Order moved from the eastern to the western continent."

"You were present for the Inculta Wars, Shanta?" Pell asked.

"I was present for Deadblast. I lived *before* that great cataclysm, although I have no memory of either time."

"And now you're a living computer program," Hagan said.

"Not exactly," Feruccio answered. "As I said, my brain still functions. This electromorphic avatar is being generated by this." Her avatar reached into itself and extracted a small blue orb. Her electromorph-self flickered away a few percentage points of opacity when she pulled it out, but she remained visible enough to show them the device, which sprouted six spidery couplings that formed a tiny blue cone. At the point of the cone, a starburst of blue-white energy shone.

"This device allows me to move about and interact with organics and other non-virtual physicalities. It has a range of about a hundred miles."

"A hundred miles from *what?*" Hagan asked.

"From my brain."

"Um. So where's your brain?"

Feruccio nodded at Magna, who stood and opened a panel on his chest. A glass cylinder housed a human brain inside his chest.

"My lady?" Magna said. "I don't like to keep this exposed for so long."

"Quite right." She nodded her thanks. He returned to his station.

Hagan frowned. "Isn't that a little—I dunno—*dangerous* to stick your brain inside of someone else? What happens if you go out of that hundred-mile range?"

"I would die."

Magna spoke up. "We *think*."

Impatience crept into Feruccio's tone. "Yes, yes yes—there are . . . *hypotheses* that my 'essence,' so to speak, might be permanently transferred or 'downloaded,' in organic parlance, into a virtual sphere."

"It's *possible*," Magna snapped. "My lady just won't admit it."

Something registered on the redhead's internal sensors.

"Uh . . . do you two have something to tell us?"

Feruccio's reinserted the electromorph device and increased her luminance by a few hundred candles. "Yes. We are mates."

And even though Eldridge was spoken for and neither of the other organic men in the truck had any intentions to court the electronic essence of the world's most beautiful woman, they all sighed: "Oh."

"That's great!" Eldridge said, casting aside his irrational disappointment.

Pell shook his head in wonderment. "You have some fascinating friends, redhead. But there's a problem."

"Crom. What?"

"I have no memory of the location of Hanna's Maiden."

"Great," Hagan said. "That remnant's nothing but sprawl. We'll never find it."

"Plus I've got the big you-know-who on my tail."

Feruccio spoke next, her words sparking surprise from all around.

"I may be of further assistance." She addressed Eldridge: "I am in your debt, and I will aid you until that debt is satisfied."

"*You're* in *my* debt?" Eldridge asked. "How does that work?"

Hagan elbowed him in the shoulder. "You killed Goldmist, goof."

"Oh. Right. Well, that guy needed killing, Shanta. No need to—ow!"

Hagan's thumb and forefinger pinched the soft tissue between his deltoid and pectoral. He whispered, "Shh. We could use the help."

Feruccio's avatar smiled. "This truck is equipped with sensing apparatus powerful enough to hear your mitochondria metabolize sugars. We've been monitoring your vital signs since the moment you joined us. So there is no need for subterfuge. I plan to satisfy my debt with the redhead, and it would seem that part of my repayment will take place within the many rooms of Penticton remnant."

"Thank you," Eldridge said. "But how do you even know *where* the Maiden is?"

"I don't. But I just so happen to know the map man of Penticton."

TOWERTOWN
&
PORT STAFFORD

KIERON

THE JELLYWOMAN'S JELLY WAS failing.

She knew it. When she had originally met with the mysterious deep-desert physician who had encased her in the protective covering, the sawbones had warned her that an excess of trauma might cause the plastoid compound to lose integrity. Apparently a trip down the sandblasting slope of an endless, mountainous plane was enough to make that happen.

But she had to keep the Clean Machine in sight.

She had been following the vehicle at a discreet distance for hours. First they had descended the far side of the strange mountain, and then they had turned west, moving away from Hemming. Kieron suspected that they must be returning to the remnant of Penticton. Days earlier, Quillig mentioned that one of the redhead's friends was being held captive there. Her earlier conversation with Boris Hagan confirmed it.

One of us is a freak back in Penticton, the old man said.

So off to Penticton it was. Kieron thanked her aquatic deities for the calm winds along the desert plains between Hemming and Penticton, but it didn't matter. As she coasted along the ground, her plastic covering started to peel away from her body sheet by sheet, leaving her with a progressively thinner layer of protection. By her reckoning, she lost a centimeter of plastic every hour. That in itself wasn't a disaster—after all, her coating encased several key pieces of equipment and weaponry.

But her *lungs*.

Kieron hadn't actually *respirated* since the encasement. The same plastoid compound that coated her also filled her lungs, and swarming throughout the plastic were nanotroids that did all her respirating for her. What would happen when her layers of failing plastic reached that deep inside her?

For now, the jellywoman ignored that question and focused on the black speck that rolled across the desert in front of her: the Clean Machine.

ELDRIDGE, ET AL

"Well, if it isn't the world's most beautiful woman."

The map man of Penticton, a guy called Conrade, stood next to an open porthole that sank into the earth about twenty miles from Penticton proper and at least twenty-five miles from the standpipe where Eldridge and Boris Hagan had originally driven down into the remnant. The Clean Machine had carried them across the desert in less than a day's time. The skags had provided Boris and Pell with some new duds that they had seemingly generated from nothing; Hagan wore a gray zip-up jumper, while Pell opted for a canvas jacket and pants similar to Feruccio's. The Narsyan filled every pocket on his outfit with whatever heavy items he could find—bits of metal or other tech. All told, his clothes weighed about fifty pounds alone. After the rapid trip between the remnants, the Clean Machine stopped at a seemingly random point. But it wasn't random to Shanta Feruccio, who evidently had a past with Conrade—a past that twisted the map man's prosthetic face into an expression that sat in a netherzone between aroused and annoyed.

Here was the scene: Conrade stood next to the porthole, accompanied by a lackey whose jiggling muscles looked like they had been inflated with water. Idling across the way was the Clean Machine, which had parked with its rear facing the porthole, still bearing the redhead's motorbike on its side. Standing outside were the military-garbed avatar of Feruccio, Eldridge, Hagan, and Pell Yannick, who was doing push-ups in the dust, his elbows trembling under the weight of his clothes. As the sun dive-bombed behind the horizon and incipient nightfreeze settled over the land, Conrade drained a tumbler of bourbon that he had carried all the way up from the deepest reaches of Penticton. Just to look cool, apparently.

Eldridge snorted. Conrade turned his black-within-black eyes on him.

"What's the gas, Red Rook? The rumortrysts say I'm about to do you a favor. Best you stow the lip for another time. This one—" (he indicated Feruccio's avatar) "—*lost* her Penticton privileges a long time ago."

Tattoos rode rippling musclewaves along Conrade's arms when he pointed at Feruccio, who waved away his ire and stepped across the divide, her electromorph feet hovering centimeters above the ground.

"I come bearing gifts, Conrade. More precisely, a *gift*."

Feruccio's martial trappings melted away, leaving behind a radiant blue superversion of herself. She looked like she had been carved out of a flawless vein of sapphire that glowed from within. The map man shuffled to the left, unsettled but trying to save face by masking his side step as a tough-guy shift of weight between feet. He raised his drink, saw the tumbler was empty, then smashed it on the ground.

And Feruccio kept coming closer.

"Come here, Conrade."

Conrade's mouth spurted white clouds of breath-fog faster than an old steam engine. He took a step forward and looked up into her face.

"What do you have for me?" he whispered.

Feruccio cupped her hands around the remains of his cheeks. He gasped. She guided his face closer to hers. When their lips were inches apart, she drew back and held up a shiny black cylinder. Conrade's eyes took a moment to refocus around the item, but as soon as they did, he snatched it out of Feruccio's hand and dropped to his knees.

"Light! *Light!*"

Muscles swaying, his lackey stomped over and shone a flashlight on the object. Conrade turned it over and over in his hands, then reached into his pockets and produced a small black card equipped with a male out-port. He plugged the card-sized hydrocell into the black cylinder—and the hyperobject returned.

"Sweet damn all," Conrade said, shaking his head. The longer he kept it activated, the larger the hyperobject grew and cycled through one iterating shape after another. An incredulous smile spread across the map man's faces, organic first, prosthetic second. He looked up at her and asked, "How the hell do I *have* this?"

The sapphire angel of Shanta Feruccio smiled. "We liberated it from Hemming earlier today. Poor Lilya Hanna." She glanced over her shoulder at Hagan. "She went to all that trouble to conquer her rival remnant, only to find it full of dead bodies and missing the key piece of tech she would need to expand her oddsmaking empire." Feruccio addressed Conrade: "So my initial statement was correct: I bring you *gifts*. I present you with the hypergenerator, which in turn will give you the means to become a full-fledged Odd. Might I suggest that you conquer Penticton during Hanna's absence?"

Conrade stood and deactivated the hypergenerator. "Now *that's* what I'd call an almighty fuck-you. What do you want?"

Feruccio turned to the redhead. "Eldridge? Pell?"

Pell stood up, refusing an offer of help from the redhead. They walked over. Pell spoke first. "Hanna has a special room somewhere. In this room is a glass chamber."

"The thing's built to hit you with a bajillion different bugs—viruses, bacteria," Eldridge added. "It's an old Narsyan test."

Conrade made a face. "I had heard the Narsyans were banannakers. Are you serious?"

Pell nodded. "Yes. She showed it to me."

"One minute," the map man said, withdrawing to talk with his lackey. After a moment's intense discussion, he returned. "Buds, I know every millimeter of this remnant, but Hanna has some deep-darks I've never sounded. I might be able to point you in the right direction, but—"

Pell broke in, "It would be made of purple glass. The whole room was purple glass."

Another voice said, "Holy shit."

Hagan had spoken. The old man crossed over. "I know what room that is. That's her . . . well, her *love room*."

Pell propped his hands on his hips, aghast. "She would *dare* juxtapose the greatest of the Great Narsyan Challenges with mere *lovemaking?* Even the youngest, greenest initiate knows that would be an outrage!"

They all stared at him. Pell cleared his throat, then looked at the ground. Hagan elbowed-prodded the redhead.

"Right!" Eldridge blurted. "An outrage. Totally."

"*Thank* you!" Pell said.

Hagan addressed Conrade: "Does that information help?"

"Does it ever," Conrade said, already smiling. "We sounded her fucknest just a fortnight ago. Follow me."

—◊—

KIERON

KIERON'S SOCKET-MOUNTED OCULARS ZOOMED in on the porthole as Eldridge and his comrades disappeared into it. It sealed shut with a *hiss*. She hadn't been able to hear much of their exchange, but it was of no consequence. The Clean Machine hulked close by, no doubt keeping watch on the opening. She looked to her left, where she had drawn an X-ray-enabled X-poly over the ground that gave her a view of a brick-lined hallway about ten feet below her current position.

The jellywoman activated a hot-cutter from within her plastic covering. It jutted out of an opening on her wrist and dislodged two whole layers of plastic that rained off her arm in sheets and pooled on the ground like translucent jelly. Icy night air stung her exposed forearm and froze her sweat to her bare brow.

But all the same, she started digging.

—◊—

ELDRIDGE, ET AL

ELDRIDGE SMELLED PAVEMENT.

Lilya Hanna's love room, as Hagan so named it, lay almost directly above the Venn Room, which placed it at almost the exact geographical center of Penticton's three-space. Conrade led them to the love room, but everywhere they went, the redhead smelled pavement.

He tried to ignore it when Conrade led them through a network of hallways made from brick, slate, stone, and wood. He tried to ignore it as they progressed deeper into the earth and passed dozens of windows that peered through dozens of nearby rooms, all of them choked with the stench of newly laid pavement. It got worse when the map man led them through a set of double doors that opened onto a miniature underground train. A platform barely large enough for all of them stood on a small track that coiled away through a tunnel. Eldridge felt sure he could see black smoke billowing ahead, but they never reached it. By the time they dismounted the mini-subway, they were only a few minutes away from the love room—and its Typhoid Maiden—and the redhead's breaths were catching in his chest. Conrade led them down a cylindrical steel hallway that melted into purple glass. Up ahead, the purple glass continued into the room itself, although foggy imperfections in the walls and doors blurred the interior of the room into ghostly shadows.

Both Eldridge and Hagan hesitated before the love room. Pell, limping around under the weight of his clothes, turned to them.

"Are you men feeling well?"

Eldridge chuckled. "Funny *you* asking *us* that, Pell."

"El, your breathing's pretty ragged," Hagan said. "Everything OK?"

Hagan's appearance—gaunt cheeks, red-ringed eyes, shaky joints—rekindled the rage he felt on Killermount, a rage *self-directed*. The absence of hair on Hagan's face only made the old man look older to the redhead.

"Hey," Eldridge said, forcing a smile. "Hages is the one who oughta be going all yellabelly here, not me." He retched and dropped to his knees. Hagan knelt beside him.

"El! What's wrong?"

Pell knelt next, his entire body one big wobbling mess. His back bowed under the weight of his clothes. The sight of his friend's sorry state felt like an incendiary agent inside the redhead's mind. He had heard tales of powerful magnets that could hold antimatter in a perfect vacuum, but when released, the antimatter would collide with regular matter and annihilate itself in a burst of gamma rays.

His friends were antimatter.

But then he looked into the shimmering eyes of Shanta Feruccio, whose appearance had settled somewhere between "genderless sapphire angel" and "pin-up general badass" as her luminescent blue form wore its battle fatigues. She gave him an encouraging smile. For a moment, he could practically imagine her with long black hair and trixie overalls—although he'd never insult Oksie by comparing her to the dowdy likes of Shanta Feruccio.

The redhead waved them off and struggled to his feet.

"Just being a drama king. Let me at 'em."

Conrade slowly opened the door into the love room. His lackey whimpered and cowered outside. They entered and found it deserted. *Almost* deserted. The room was diamond-shaped, and they entered at one of its far corners. Directly opposite them stood the petrified remains of a human man whose limbs had been tension-stretched to twice their natural length. He faced them from the far corner, his arms and legs extended against the walls like he was trying to keep himself from being sucked through an imaginary hole in the wall. A rictus of climax-torment elongated his face, which was crumbling away along with the rest of his long-since-dried-out flesh. Other such remains littered the room like disintegrating statues—some male, some female, Hanna's appetites unbound by gender.

Or species.

The freeze-dried corpses of dozens of animals were scattered across the purple glass furniture like cremains spread across a forgotten room. Eldridge grimaced and felt his gorge rise, both at the sight of the dead bodies, and at what awaited him: the Typhoid Maiden. Like the Maiden of Burbage, it was a vertical glass cylinder that spanned the space between ceiling and floor, accessible by a single sliding door. Unlike the Maiden of Burbage, its glass was purple, and a pile of decomposing corpses was heaped around its bottom like an ash sculpture of a mass grave. A half-dozen dead bodies cradled each other in death.

"Oh, my god," Hagan said.

Eldridge turned. "What?"

"She made them all do it. After she . . . stimmy-stim-stimmed them within an inch of their lives. She made them do it. The Maiden."

The redhead scanned the room, starting and finishing at the Maiden. When his eyes fell on the glass tube again, its interior was filled with black smoke. He blinked, and it was empty.

"Looks that way. I'd ask *why*, but this is the same Odd who turned Pell into a giant booger. No offense."

"None taken," Pell said.

Conrade leaned against the Maiden and rapped on it with his knuckles.

"Can we raise curtain on this? I don't know when she's due back."

Eldridge took a breath. "Yeah. Open it up."

The map man jumped away from it. "*I'm* not opening this fucking thing. You said it's full of diseases."

The redhead crossed the room, stepping over corpses along the way.

"No problem," he said, touching Conrade's shoulder to dismiss him. The map man stepped away and left the redhead to the Maiden. Hagan sat down, while Pell had removed his weighted pants and draped them over his shoulders so he could do squats. Eldridge used his foot to nudge away some of the corpses, but they disintegrated on contact and collapsed into a pile of dust around the door to the Maiden.

"Dammit."

Eldridge spent the next few minutes kick-shoving their remains out of the way, staining his pants black with ash and coughing as he worked to clear a path to the door. When he finally did, he experienced an awful moment of fear that he might not be able to remember how to open the damn thing, but a memory-trip back to Burbage reminded him—you *didn't* open it. Marko Marinus spoke in his head:

It opens when you're ready.

Eldridge rolled his eyes.

Pell spoke in mid-squat. "It'll open when you're ready, El."

"I know. What the hell is that supposed to—"

Vumm-vumm-ummm. The door slid up with a menacing groan. Corpse-ash went flying as Eldridge and Conrade both duck-and-covered away from the opening. Conrade remained in place with his arms over his head, while Eldridge straightened and strode into the Maiden, where he did an about-face and strode right back out. Then back in. And out. He repeated this pattern three times before muttering, "Fuck it," and going inside. "Somebody close this fucking thing before I change my mind!"

Still doing squats, Pell said, "It'll close when you're ready—"

Eldridge spun around. "*God-damn you Narsyans and your stupid mimbo-jimbo!*"

"Mumbo-jumbo?"

"Shut up, Hages! I mean, this shit is important! Why not just put a *switch* or a *lever* or a *button* on the damn thing?!" As he ranted, his vision turned purple with rage. He rambled on for a moment more—"The problem with Naryans is fourfold: One, you're ugly. Two you're stupid. Three you're ugly, and four is *fucking—every—thing*"—before he realized that the door had slid shut.

"Oh, shit," he said, the screamed, *"Let me out! Lemme out! Oooout! I'm not kidding!"* He held his head. "No! No. I'm completely kidding. *You assholes.*" Something drew his gaze upward, and he lurched backward at the sight above him. *"Fuck."* He fell and got lodged inside the Maiden's cylinder.

Lilya Hanna was looking at him.

Or rather, her *head*. The top of the Maiden was ringed with a circular vent that he knew was about to spew all manner of contagion, but in the center of the circle hung the Odd's severed head. Eldridge had heard rumortrysts tell tales of how Hanna kept her own brain preserved somewhere within Penticton, and here it was. She had preserved her organic visage with skill, and were it not for the seven layers of psychedelic makeup that turned her face into a paisley-kaleidoscope of eye shadow and lipstick, she might have looked comely. Thankfully, someone had closed her eyes.

Eldridge wasn't sure if he could've continued if her eyes had been open.

That's when two things happened: He noticed her scar, and the Challenge began.

Black clouds concealed her face, but not before he saw that Hanna was still a Narsyan. Her vertical forehead scar, the product of many a headbutted Narsyan greeting, remained untouched. If she had been drummed out of the order, then one of the chieftains would have dug a circular divot of flesh out of her forehead, marring the perfect line and condemning her to life with an imperfect shape on her head—a circle—for according to deep Narsyan myth, the only perfect shape was the ellipse.

"Because it has a solar-center," went the Narsyan adage, acknowledging the role played by the fabled golden ratio in the creation of the hallowed shape.

Those memories faded into the pitch-stench of darkness that

enveloped the redhead inside the Typhoid Maiden of Penticton. Eldridge closed his eyes and relaxed, his mind accessing two different stores of memory—one on command, one in spite of his efforts to forget it.

But the smell of pavement was simply too strong to forget.

Inside Hanna's Typhoid Maiden, the midnight cloud of contagion parted to reveal the Aester Road once more. The redhead winced at the memory. He knew where it was going, and he cursed mortarchain tech once more. Why couldn't the Odds have robbed him of *this* memory instead of his daughter? His silent complaints moved no one that day in Penticton, though, and as the first illness welled up within him, Eldridge watched himself drunkenly ride east away from Port Stafford, bound for Dedrick with the last of his deceased wife-but-not-wife's possessions. As the sun threatened to break over the horizon ahead, his motorbike weaved back and forth along the road, which was mostly deserted. The occasional passing dreg gave him a wide berth and shook their fist at the drunk asshole as they passed, but Eldridge rode on, wondering why Nadia's death failed to inspire any tears in him. He *felt* sad, but he didn't feel like crying. He just felt drunk.

Drunk. The first illness made him feel drunk. He dislodged himself from his prone-suspended position and dropped his feet to the glass ground as the Maiden's black smoke flooded his lungs and he called on the memory he actually *wanted* to remember. Although for years he had wanted to forget *any* image of Pell Yannick, recent times had changed his opinion of the Narsyan chieftain. The redhead thought back to his time in Burbage as a child and remembered a night high up among the mountainpeaks on a three-week hike with only him, Marko, and Pell, who had recently become a full Narsyan chieftain. They had paused on a three-foot-square outcropping to construct an igloo-habitat around themselves. They rested standing up, shoulder to shoulder. Marko looked at the new chieftain with wide eyes and an eager smile.

"How'd you do it, Pelagius?"

Even then, Eldridge wanted to roll his eyes at Marko's brown-nosing. No one called Pell by his full name. Pell, still covered in healing lesions from the ordeal, offered a magnanimous smile.

"The key is to take control of your internal forces. You are your own general, your own field marshal, your own supreme commander."

Knock, knock.

Eldridge returned to the present, where his skin bubbled with pox-sores, hives, and a hundred other lesions. Mucus filled every cavity above his neck and post-nasally dripped into his lungs, which were drowning with fluid. His vision had been reduced to a pair of bright slits among the darkness as his eyes swelled shut. His arms had fallen limp by his sides, and when he tried to lean forward to see who had knocked, he *fell* forward onto his face, which appeared as a flattened, swollen grotesque among the black smoke to everyone outside. Dimly, he registered that everyone drew back at the sight—everyone but Pell.

"Command your forces, Eldridge!" he screamed through the glass.

But he couldn't. Not when the pavement monster stared at him with its non-face. Standing in the Typhoid Maiden, he looked up and searched the black smoke for Hanna's face, but what emerged instead was a featureless black cylinder head that looked like it had been carved out of newly poured concrete. The Maiden faded away, and Eldridge again was forced to countenance an unwanted memory. The creature had risen from the Aester Road itself, morphing up out of the pavement like it was a superfluid, sheets of tar dripping from its arms like slime, its blank face staring at him with no eyes. Eldridge dismissed it as a drunken hallucination at first. But then it spoke, its voice childlike.

"Hello, sir."

Eldridge tried to stay upright, but he staggered off his bike. It fell to the earth as he fell to the ground, his breath still clouding around him in the chill of breaking dawn. The pavement monster rose over a quickly brightening horizon.

"You owe *him* a lot of jenta," it said.

"What? Him? Who?"

The creature sounded like it was five years old. "The man across the oceans."

"Who the hell is *that*? And how does he know *me*?"

"He doesn't. But I monitor his games. And you lost one of them. Therefore, ergo, you owe him a lot of jenta."

Drunk, the redhead tried to remember what games he had played, but he had never made odds in his life. That he could remember.

"What game of his did I even *play?*"

"I believe it was called 'What Happened at Deadblast?'"

Eldridge laughed. "Wha-? Back in Stafford? I *lost* that game. Everyone does. *That's the idea.*"

The creature leaned over, pavement crumbling from its steaming joints. A red gash split across its non-face.

"I'm sorry to report that you did not lose, sir. *You guessed right.*"

—⚋—

KIERON

THE TRAIL THROUGH THE remnant of many rooms had been fraught with obstacles, but the jellywoman had tracked her quarry around every turn, even going so far as to ride her hoversled along the miniature train track that led her to the purple, glass-blown heart of Penticton.

Of course, she had been leaving her own trail along the way.

A jagged line of congealed plastic followed the jellywoman wherever she went. Somewhere between the entrance-porthole and the glass heart, her plastic feet had unseamed and fallen away, leaving her vinyl-clad feet exposed. (She wore a singlet underneath the plastic coating that covered her feet but not her arms or head.) Still she pressed on until they reached the mysterious purple room—the glass heart. Kieron hovered farther back in the passageway, listening. She couldn't make out everything they said, but she caught one snippet:

"Funny *you* asking *us* that, Pell."

The redhead had addressed the emaciated man, who Kieron recognized as the same person who successfully appealed to the redhead on the strange mountain.

So that's the freak from Penticton, Kieron thought, wondering how he had been freed just as she wondered what business Eldridge and the rest of his crew had with Conrade. She had watched the ghost-woman, whose name was *Chantal,* she thought, trade Conrade something for his help, but she hadn't seen what it was.

After they entered the purple glass room, the jellywoman scanned the passage for a way around. She found a small tunnel that, while it appeared to lead *above* the glass heart, was still made of glass, and therefore would open her up to detection.

Black ink, like a squid attack.

Up ahead, Kieron looked into the glass heart and saw the redhead step inside a cylinder of glass with black ink. Everyone stood around the cylinder, watching. The jellywoman decided it would be distraction enough. She climbed into the glass tunnel and followed it, crawling her way out *over* the glass heart, which was joined to her tunnel via hundreds of tiny glass tubes. As she made her way, her knees and elbows shed a few more layers of plastic until her shoulders were exposed. By the time she found herself kneeling over her target and separated by a few dozen layers of purple glass, only her pelvic region and chest were still encased in plastic. A trio of transparent plastoid pseudopods reached into her mouth and nostrils and extended into her lungs, where the respirating nanotroids did their work—for now.

Kieron waited and watched the redhead writhe in the black ink.

ELDIRDGE, ET AL

"Command your forces, Eldridge!"

Despite his weakness, the Narsyan chieftain had stood his ground before the Maiden when the lesion-riddled face of the redhead smacked against the glass, his skin spurting abscess from a thousand sores. He slid down the glass, leaving a trail of pus and blood. Everyone but Pell backed away from the Maiden at the sight, including Feruccio, who was once again clad in her military garb. Conrade didn't have to back up because he was stationed by the door, keeping watch and chain-smoking his way through a pocketful of black cigarillos.

Boris Hagan, who had staggered back at the sight, stepped forward. "He can't do this."

"He *can*," Pell said.

"How many of you wackos *die* during this test, Pell?"

"Most."

The redhead's face fell back into the black smoke only to be replaced by the rapid drumbeat of his forearms, knees, and feet as he convulsed inside the Maiden and pounded on the glass. His screams echoed from within.

"So if someone fails, they just stop moving," Hagan said.

Pell nodded.

"How do you know when someone passes?"

"Well..."

Bootsoles smacked into the side of the Maiden and remained stuck there, two beige ovals among the black smoke. Eldridge wailed.

"What?" Hagan said. "When will we know?"

"We won't know until he stops moving. And dies. At least once," Pell said. "That is part of the Challenge. The initiate not only masters control of their immune system, but they also figure out a way to revive themselves."

Hagan shook his head. *"Fuck. This.* I'm getting him out of there. How do I shut this thing off?!"

Shanta Feruccio floated over. "May I answer this one, Yannick?"

Pell nodded. Feruccio started to address him, but Hagan interrupted.

"Don't tell me it'll open when he's ready!"

"I won't," she said. "There is a way to open it, but the shutdown subroutine takes approximately three hours. If we were to open it before the system had time to properly scrub the interior for contagions, we would wipe out all of Penticton at a stroke, and possibly risk more widespread infection."

"What if he's successful? Will we have to wait that long to take him out?"

"No," Pell said. "If he's successful, there won't be anything left in there more dangerous than a common cold."

—∞—

KIERON

THE MAN CALLED PELL, the freak from Penticton, had said something about common colds, but the jellywoman couldn't quite hear it. Kieron watched and listened from above the glass heart. She had an idea. She started to crawl again, only to find herself bonded in place with congealed plastic. She unstuck her elbows and knees from the glass with audible *pops*. She froze and watched the room below. They continued to jabber amongst themselves, having failed to detect her.

The jellywoman crawled, feeling her final layers of plastic drizzle onto the glass tunnel as she moved closer and closer to the glass tube of ink; the device that the redhead's friends had called the Typhoid Maiden. The jellywoman couldn't fathom what was driving her to risk being seen. She tried to imagine what she would look like from the perspective of the people in the room—Hagan, Pell, Conrade, and the electronic woman, whose name she hadn't been able to make out yet, although her face aroused old memories that had yet to coalesce. In any case, if they were to look up and peer into the countless glass hallways that ran above the Maiden, they might see a spectral dark form hovering above them.

But Kieron felt sure that their gaze wouldn't stray above the Maiden.

The jellywoman made her way out above the Maiden, and even though the primary chamber enclosing the redhead stood below a few layers of glass, that chamber was topped by a squat black cylinder that (presumably) held all of the device's inner workings, including its store of diseases. That portion of the overall device extended up through the layers of glass up to the jellywoman's level—and now she knelt right above it, her mind aglow with a new idea.

It occurred to her to disable the device and kill everyone in the room, including the redhead, but Quillig had already said that the man across the oceans wanted Eldridge alive. But Kieron had another idea *related* to her first one. She plunged her fingertips into the layer of failing plastic that covered her chest and produced a small metallic device shaped like a polyhedral trapezoid. Among her people, it was called a *safepod*.

She held the device between her thumb and forefinger and pinched it. In response, one of its flat planes dematerialized and revealed a hollow interior. Kieron laid it down, then turned her attention to the Maiden. She popped the top off of the black cylinder and revealed its inner workings. Three separate tanks, each labeled with a different series of strange glyphs, fed into the same dispersal unit. If Kieron had to guess, he'd say that the three compounds were inert when separated, but would combine to generate the black smoke that currently filled the Maiden.

Kieron picked up the safepod—which was still open—and laid it on top of the dispersal unit. A moment later, its color shifted from metallic silver to a deep green. She placed her fingers on it, thought a prayer to one of her undersea demigods, and then lifted it. It had successfully sealed shut, and Kieron knew that the device would hold the contagion in suspended animation until she chose to deliver it.

She crawled back to her original position. She had no desire to kill every dreg in Penticton, but as a soldier for her people's military, she had already killed so many, and as general-prime of her people's forces, she had brought about the deaths of thousands more. *Tens* of thousands. What mattered the deaths of one more city, if it meant she could proclaim her status as the mightiest bounty-merc in the land and win favor with one as powerful as this mysterious man across the oceans?

A man whom the jellywoman would later topple, of course.

She would be Kieron the Conqueror, and her reign would begin with this room full of dregs, who would die from the diseases she held in her safepod. Thinking back to Quillig's grudging praise for the redhead, the jellywoman felt sure that the redhead would survive the test of the Maiden, but he would emerge to find his friends dead. Her plan had two potential weak points: the ghost-woman and her own failing plastic system. She wasn't sure what to make of the glowing ghost-woman, but she would contend with her later; and as for her own safety, she knew that her nanotroid respirators were equipped to filter out a thousand different pollutants and ailments. She would survive—as long as her lungs were filled with plastic, of course.

And then Kieron the Conqueror would capture the Red Rook.

Hundreds of tiny glass tubes ran between his glass tunnel and the room below. The jellywoman placed the safepod onto one of the openings and pinched it.

—ɯ—

ELDRIDGE AND THE TYPHOID MAIDEN

THE PAVEMENT MONSTER HAD him.

The redhead was lodged in the Maiden with his boots pressed against the glass, his mouth a fountain of pus that sprayed from his lungs as he screamed. His entire body—head to toe, arms and legs—swelled up until he could feel himself filling the glass cylinder with his soon-to-be corpse. His memories had faded into living nightmares. The head of Lilya Hanna had sprung to life moments before to cackle at him, while the pavement monster that had beset him outside Port Stafford hovered behind her, silent. The redhead's body fell still. He watched his vision fade to darkness.

But then someone slapped him in the face.

Only they hadn't. They *couldn't*. He was alone inside the Maiden. Wasn't he? Eldridge felt boils burst around the circumference of his neck as he turned to see who had slapped on the glass.

It was Feruccio. She was screaming something, but his ears had sealed shut. (He had sensed the power of her slap, but he hadn't actually *heard* it.) Boris Hagan, Pell Yannick, and Conrade had all collapsed to the ground, where they thrashed back and forth, clutching their throats. Feruccio kept screaming at him, and although he couldn't read lips, her words were so emphatic as to be unmistakable.

There's a leak. The Maiden has leaked into the room. You have to help them.

―⁂―

QUILLIG AND THE
MAN ACROSS THE OCEANS

THE PAVEMENT MONSTER FOUND him.

After the jellywoman had left him to die, Quillig crawled out of the cell phone crater and started stumbling down Killermount while bathed in the constant blast of sunheat. He skim-walked down the slope, buoyed by the westerly wind. Night fell at some point, and with it came a cold that soothed the bounty-merc's ruined flesh.

But the night brought something else: the deadline.

Quillig smiled when his internal clock registered the passage of the thirty-six-hour ultimatum delivered by the creature in his sawbone's shack. He assumed that the man across the oceans had the means to find him, and he did. Waiting for him along the slope of Killermount was the pavement creature. The bounty-merc had settled into a state of exhaustion in which it was actually *easier* for him to keep moving. As soon as he stopped, he crumpled.

That's when he saw that the pavement creature wasn't alone. The man stood next to his monstrosity wearing a simple blue tunic, his black hair braided into cornrows. Lying in a fetal position, Quillig spoke.

"Not what I expected."

"I seldom am," said the man across the oceans.

"So what now?"

"You're to be taken into captivity, of course. And I will have to fetch the redhead myself."

"Why him? Why's he so important?"

The man across the oceans smirked. "Because he knows what happened at Deadblast."

Quillig's aperture *whirred* open. "You're lying."

"I assure you I am not."

"No. I'm sure he *does* know what happened. But that's not why he's so important."

BORIS HAGAN, ET AL

It smelled like cinnamon, Boris Hagan thought. Yasim used to keep a store of the precious spice in the back of his joint for special occasions, and Hagan never forgot its sharp-sweet smell.

So when the smell of cinnamon wafted down from the ceiling of Lilya Hanna's purple-glass love room, he didn't think anything of it.

Until they all started dying.

The diseases dropped him in an instant. One moment he was watching the redhead inside the Maiden, the next he smelled cinnamon, the next he was on the ground, his lungs full of liquid. He crawled for the door, but Conrade was already pounding it to no avail.

"Sealed . . . shut," the map man said. "Feruccio. Get. Help."

So Hanna hadn't been *totally* insane if she had equipped this room to quarantine itself in case of a failure with the Maiden. But the Maiden *hadn't* failed. Hagan felt suddenly sure of that. The damn thing was filled with *black smoke*, for Crom's sake, and if there were a leak, wouldn't they be able to see it spewing from the sides of the Maiden itself? Abscess flooded into Hagan's eyelids and sealed his eyes shut, but the last thing he saw—besides Feruccio screaming into the Maiden—was a faint, black cloud emanating not from the Maiden but from one of hundreds of small, circular openings in the ceiling above.

Had they been followed?

His vision faded as his eyes sealed as tightly shut as the room. Something dripped from his ears. He wondered if it was blood. A smash, like someone broke through the glass doors. But the smash didn't come from without; it came from *within*. Footsteps, stumbling ones. The footsteps turned into *knee*-steps as someone stumbled to the ground over him, his voice a distant, frantic whisper.

"Holy Crom do I suck, suck, suck, *suck!*"

The old man recognized the voice, but given his last vision, it didn't make sense to hear it. *Pain* was his next sensation; a sharp pain that sliced through the agony of his multiple infections and centered on his arm—the inside of his elbow, specifically—and almost instantly, light blinded him. He blinked, and when his vision had fully returned, he sat up to find the avatar of Shanta Feruccio kneeling over him, pressing a piece of fabric into the crook of his elbow. She bent his arm around the fabric, a bit of T-shirt that read THE PROMETERIUM.

"Hold this in place while the cut heals."

Across the room, black smoke poured out of a huge, shattered hole in the Typhoid Maiden, while Eldridge knelt over Pell Yannick, who had collapsed to the ground as well, his skin covered in boils and lesions. The redhead was topless, having doffed his leather jacket and T-shirt, which Feruccio was tearing into pieces. Eldridge squeezed his own wrist, which pumped blood all over the floor. Using his fingernails, the redhead pricked open Pell's blood vessel and fed his own blood into it. Feruccio crossed the room.

"Be careful, Eldridge. We can't have you bleed out."

"*Fuck* me. They need this. I don't."

Another voice: "Yo."

It was Conrade, who had slid to his chest with his head lodged at a grotesque ninety-degree angle against the door. Eldridge jumped up, while Feruccio ripped the T-shirt. While Eldridge performed the same rescue operation on the map man, Hagan touched his face. Boils continued to seethe under his skin, and a few lesions remained as open sores across his body, but his head was clearing. His first attempt at speaking ended in a rasp that caught Feruccio's attention. She raced over.

"Lie down, Boris. You're going to be fine, but you need to rest a moment."

"El . . . Eldridge?" he asked.

Eldridge knelt over by the door behind Hagan. His voice floated over.

"Hages, hang on."

The redhead stepped over and knelt by Hagan. Feruccio handed him the remains of his shirt, which he used to bind his wrist. Hagan smiled.

"You did it."

"Yeah."

"You're a Narsyan chieftain."

Eldridge took a breath and shook his head. "Well, I don't know about that. But . . . my blood is righteous. And I've got some good news. I know how we're going to save Oksana and Stewart."

—m—

KIERON

KIERON THE CONQUEROR WATCHED her prey fall to the ground and convulse from the contagion she had just delivered. The ghost-woman watched in horror as her comrades fell one by one. Conrade was the first (and only) one of them to try the door, only to find it sealed shut.

But his next words, although he wheezed them with a pair of diseased lungs, sounded like a shout in the jellywoman's ears.

"Feruccio. Get. Help."

The jellywoman flinched at the words. She jumped. She bucked. She leaned down and peered through the layers of glass. She retracted her oculars to get a better look at the blue ghost-woman, whose name wasn't *Chantal* but *Shanta*.

Shanta Feruccio. The myth that repeated itself.

As general-prime of her people's forces, Kieron had been sworn to protect her waters and bring about the rightful destruction of their nemeses. The jellywoman had since foresworn her duty when she saw the destruction wrought by those wars, but something else disillusioned her: the original cause of the war.

It sounded too insane to believe, but according to the singer of her state, the war had started when a pack of extraterrestrials had brought the world's most beautiful woman into their midst. They were carrying her across the oceans and so needed the blessing of the Phocas to secure safe passage from the eastern to the western continent.

But the woman's beauty had stirred the passions of the Phocas neighboring state, a splinter colony known as the Musroks, and when they tried to kidnap her, war broke out. The idea that a full-scale conflict had broken out over someone's beauty outraged the jellywoman almost as much as did the wanton destruction of her homeland, which was why she would have to return to her home with the means to end the war and restore order for all time.

Didn't she?

The myth that repeated itself spoke again: "There's a leak. The Maiden has leaked into the room. You have to help them."

Her elders had told her that an ancient extraterrestrial war had broken out over a woman, although they didn't know when or where it took place, only that it predated Deadblast. And there she was. In the room below. Somehow, the redhead's friends included this legend from her people's past. Perhaps Kieron the Conqueror could claim *her* as a trophy for her people, too. She would return to her underwater state with unstoppable extraterrestrial weaponry and the myth that repeated itself. And all would bow down before her. The thought took her breath away. She had been basking in her own imagined future triumph when she realized that her breath had *indeed* been taken away.

Down below, the Typhoid Maiden exploded.

Kieron grabbed her neck as a newly smashed hole in the Maiden disgorged a horizontal column of black smoke. Eldridge emerged from the smoke, already ripping off his jacket. Up above, the jellywoman's plastic coating finally failed, and she realized that she was breathing molten plastic. *Trying* to. Her nanotroid respirators had drowned in the liquefying plastic instantly, leaving Kieron with nothing to do but grab the pseudopods that protruded from her nostrils and mouth—*and pull.*

Black smoke from the Maiden seeped up through the layers of glass into Kieron's tunnel and flooded it. She had two choices: leave the plastic inside her lungs and die, or pull it out and die. She decided to pull, all while remembering how she had escaped her homeland by spreading her trip to the surface over almost a month, allowing her body to decompress every few hundred meters.

The jellywoman pulled.

As she abandoned her homeland, conflicting feelings and thoughts besieged her. Was she leaving her people to die at the hands of the Musroks, or was she expressing a true and proper discontent with the state of her undersea nation?

Kieron imagined the inside of her lungs and saw two pear-shaped pods of plastic that remained. She realized that if she tried to pull them out at the same time, they'd get lodged in her windpipe. They probably would anyway, but extracting them one at a time would be her only chance. She leaned over, feeling the need to retch, but her stomach was still filled with plastic, too. She released one of the plastic pseudopods and clenched both fists around the one leading to her left lung. She pulled, and when enough of it was out, she wrapped it around her foot and used the strength of her leg to bring it up the rest of the way. The blob got stuck at the back of her throat for one awful instant, but then her foot kicked forward, and an audible *pop* marked the exit of the first lung-blob of plastic, which slung out of her face and smacked against the far wall, trailing a dissolving line of plastic. More plastoid compound dribbled out of her mouth, but she still couldn't breathe. She kept pulling as the scene below unfolded.

After the redhead emerged from the billowing black smoke, he pulled off his shirt. Topless, he tried to bite the inside of his elbow. When his mouth wouldn't reach, he bit directly into his wrist, drew blood, and knelt before Boris Hagan. He plucked open a blood vessel on Hagan's arm and transferred some of his own blood to him. The redhead repeated the process with Pell and Conrade, and as the jellywoman pulled the other lung-blob out of her head, she watched everyone in the room start to heal themselves right before her eyes. Once again, she heard Quillig's words.

This little macta's got more respawns than a neckbeard, but more important: He's got friends. He will always have help. He'll get help from strange quarters and at the very last motherfucking moment you expect it.

Immediately following Quillig's words, she heard *her* speak again.

"Be careful, Eldridge," the myth that repeated itself said. "We can't have you bleed out."

"*Fuck* me," Eldridge said. "They need this. I don't."

Conrade mumbled something, and the redhead ran across the room to save him, as well. Up above, Kieron started to retch up the liquid plastic that filled her stomach and digestive track. The clear gel spilled out of her mouth as the last bits of plastic that clung to her body finally fell away, leaving her surrounded by all of the technology she had packed into her plastic armor when she arrived among the extraterrestrials, ready to make a new life for herself—a life that never quite materialized. The myth that repeated itself spoke again, this time addressing the old man, Hagan.

"Lie down, Boris. You're going to be fine, but you need to rest a moment."

Hagan said something inaudible. Eldridge looked up from where he was.

"Hages, hang on."

He stepped over and knelt by Hagan. The myth that repeated itself handed him the torn remains of his shirt, which he used as a tourniquet around his arm. He and Hagan exchanged a few sentences that Kieron couldn't hear, but then the redhead spoke up.

"Well, I don't know about that. But . . . my blood is good. And I've got some good news. I know how we're going to save Oksana and Stewart."

"How?" Hagan asked.

Eldridge addressed the myth: "Shanta, you and the skags have already done so much, and I hate to ask any more, but . . ."

"Ask it," Shanta said.

"Well, okay. Can we borrow some of those electrobarf doodads of yours?"

"Electromorph," she corrected. "And of course. But for what purpose?"

Eldridge and Hagan looked at each other.

The redhead said, "I don't even know where to start. Two of our friends are trapped in this really tall building—Hages, what'd you call it?"

"A skyscraper."

"Anyway, it's really hot, and we need to get into the hottest room. We can't do it as humans, but I think we could do it if we were like you. I mean, that's assuming you don't have to scoop out our brains to make it work."

"No, there are other ways," Shanta said. "And yes, we would be honored to provide you with the devices."

"El?" Boris said. "That still won't work."

"Why not?"

"We need to cure Oksana and Stewart with the blood of a Narsyan chieftain."

"Right."

"How are going to cure them without your body?"

Pell spoke up. "Hagan is right. The restorative effects of the blood fade after approximately sixty seconds."

After a pause, the redhead said, "We're going to bring my body in there. We'll carry it with us."

"*What?*" Hagan said. "That doesn't make any sense. I don't even know how these electromorph thingamajigs work, but we'll have to tote your carcass all the way in there? That's crazy! You'll never make it!"

"Your avatars will have heightened strength," Shanta said. "You would be able to easily bear the redhead's weight."

"Shut the fuck up, Feruccio!" Hagan said. "You don't have a say in this." He addressed Eldridge: "El, we'll go in there and *extract* them! You don't need to do this."

"*Extract* them, Boris? With Stewart turned into a fire-whatzit and Oksana turned into a White Queen? Do you really think we'd be able to wrestle *her* all the way out of the Fallen Tower the way she is now?"

"Your Oksana is a White Queen?" Shanta asked.

"Yeah. Hagan tells me she got hooked on Doc Enki's serum."

The myth that repeated itself floated back away from the redhead. "I am sorry."

"Me too," Eldridge said. "But this is the only way, Boris. We just have to keep my body alive until we reach the central room in the Tower, and then we'll find a way to get my blood into both of them."

"And then we will have to race out of the Tower before the heat kills them," Pell added. "We'll still have to contend with Oksana in her hulking form as she heals. It won't be an instantaneous recovery as it was for us just now."

Hagan yelled, "Everyone shut up! There's another way to do this that doesn't involve a macta-fucking *body count!*"

"What is it?" Eldridge asked.

They sat in silence and absorbed the truth of the redhead's words. Overhead, Kieron heaved up the last of the plastoid compound, her mind swimming with memories—her homeland, her families, her friends, Quillig, Lady Ragnarok, Kieron the Conqueror—and as she vomited up the last of the covering, she realized two things: One, she saw that she was breathing in the black smoke that had floated up from the Maiden; Two, she realized that she was pounding on the glass hard enough to cause shattering white starbursts. As she pounded, she heard someone she hadn't heard since she'd first arrived on land.

She heard *herself.*

"*There is another way! Look! Look! Look up here!*"

QUILLIG AND THE
MAN ACROSS THE OCEANS

Incredibly, Quillig wasn't dead.

The man across the oceans had bid farewell to the pavement creature, which lumbered off into the night. Dozens of the man's guard-troops materialized from the darkness to take hold of Quillig. He had expected to be executed without delay, but instead, they loaded him onto a gigantic white hover-fortress shaped like a giant letter C that spanned a thousand feet from side to side. When it hovered, it led with its two points like a crescent moon flying across the desert.

They removed his sight-cartridge and stuffed him into a holding slit half a foot too narrow to hold him. He felt like he had been crammed between two boulders. The man stood outside his holding slit.

"Where did the redhead go?"

Quillig spoke, the scarred remains of his lips smashed against the metal interior of his tiny cell: "It's funny. I'd love to tell you where. But I actually don't know. Penticton, maybe."

The man didn't move.

"Are you going to torture me?"

"No, I believe you. I have other sources on this continent. I'll find out."

"You mind if I ask you something?"

"Go ahead."

"If the redhead is so important—which he is—why didn't you come across the oceans to begin with? Why leave his capture to me?"

The man thought. "I didn't know he was important until I found out who he was. Now, I believe you have something of mine, Mr. Quillig?"

"Right," he said. "I'd hand it to you, but you seem to have taken away my third dimension."

"That's fine," the man across the oceans said as he reached into Quillig's pocket and pulled out the tiny castle.

—⚍—

KIERON

ELDRIDGE LOOKED UP AND saw a complete stranger wearing a singlet pounding the glass a few levels above them. They all forced open the door to the love room and helped the woman down from the glass tunnels. In addition to her singlet, she was soaked with some kind of viscous, shiny gunk, and she had retractable black oculars lodged in her sockets, which was a good move, because she looked like she had been swimming in lube. She had pale skin and a dusting of brown hair. When they helped her out of the tunnel, the redhead noted the stranger stood taller than everyone else and had enormous lat muscles and long limbs. She also brandished a small, metallic object in his face.

"Quick! Before I die, let me explain how to use it!" the stranger said, shoving the object into the redhead's hand.

"Wait, wait—" Eldridge said.

"I don't have long! I breathed the smoke from the—what did you call it? The Maiden. *I inhaled it.* You need to carry your blood in a *suspended* state, correct? This device can do that!"

"You were *listening* to us?" Hagan asked. "Who are you?"

"Please listen! If you pinch the device, you can store some of your blood in perfect suspended animation until you need to administer it to your friend. Wait! You have *two* friends trapped! Damn my memory!"

Tears had started to stream from the stranger's eyes as her hands moved in a blur across her body before she realized she had forgotten something.

"Oh! I'm no longer wearing it. It's all right. I have several safepods—these devices—you can use." She paused for breath, her tale apparently complete. "I'm so, so sorry. For everything. I did not see. I did not know."

"Sorry for *what?"* Eldridge asked. "Who are you?"

"The jelly—Kieron. My name is Kieron."

Boris peered into her eyes. "I *do* know you. You're one of the bounty-mercs that's been chasing us."

"I am."

"You grabbed me in Hemming," Hagan said. "Turned me over to Lilya Hanna."

"Quite so."

Feruccio had been hovering alongside Conrade, behind Eldridge and Hagan. She stepped forward. "I recognize you."

"And I you," Kieron said.

"Your heart has grown trifold," Feruccio said. "What changed your spirit?"

Hagan rolled his eyes. "Why did everyone start talking in verse?"

Kieron ignored him and said, "It . . . is a long story. And I'd like to spend my last moments in repose, if you don't mind."

Eldridge grinned. "You keep talking like you're gonna die. Are you sick?"

"I—I inhaled the smoke. From the Maiden. Am I not going to die, as you were?"

Eldridge's head tilted up as a few pieces fell into place.

"Oh."

Hagan realized it, too. "Wow. The Maiden *didn't* spring a leak."

Kieron shrank back a step. "I beg your forgiveness. And I ask you accept my help. I do not ask for the Red Rook's wondrous healing powers. I will accept my death as a general-prime."

"As a general-*what?*" Eldridge asked.

"A general-prime. I am general-prime of my people. I hail from under the oceans."

"Oh. Well . . . Ms. General-Prime . . . you're not going to die. At least, not right now."

"I'm not?"

"No. The smoke's harmless. I had to do that to—oh, who cares. It's a bunch of Narsyan horseshit."

"El, do you even know what a horse is?" Hagan asked.

"No sir, I do not." He addressed Kieron: "Hey. You said you have a few of those things?"

Eldridge indicated the safepod. Kieron nodded and climbed back into the tunnel. When she returned, she handed over six of the devices.

"Accept them with my compliments. And I bear one more crucial piece of intelligence: you are being pursued by—"

"The man across the oceans," Eldridge finished for her. "I know. Story of my life. Thanks. And hey—thanks for . . . well, for coming around."

Conrade spoke up: "We need to *vacate*. Hanna could be back any time."

Hagan added, "Or the big guy. Mister Oceans."

"Wait! Lemme get my coat!" Eldridge said. "Shanta! How far can you and the skag-brigade take us?"

"As far as Ikraam, which will put you close to Towertown."

"When we're done, maybe we can finally get back to Dedrick and set it right," Hagan said.

Pulling on his coat, Eldridge said, "I dunno, Hages. That might be a lost clause."

"Lost *cause?*"

"Shut up."

"Eldridge, I'd like to go home one of these days."

"Okay."

"Isn't Dedrick your home, too?"

"Not really." He addressed Kieron: "Thanks again."

Kieron nodded and watched them leave.

—⁂—

KIERON

As they hustled down the hallway, Kieron listened to their conversation.

"El, if Dedrick's not home for you, what is?" Hagan asked.

"Oh, wherever you assholes are."

"Oy," Hagan said. "Even by post-Deadblast standards, that's fucking sad."

Already running, Kieron shouted, *"Wait for me!"*

—⁂—

ELDRIDGE, ET AL

Their next moves came quickly. After collecting Kieron's equipment, which was plentiful and valuable, they said goodbye to Conrade and got the hell back topside, where the Clean Machine was waiting. Everybody—Eldridge, Hagan, Pell, and Kieron—climbed in. Before they left, Conrade was kind enough to provide the former jellywoman with new attire: a Kevlar-reinforced sweatshirt, cargo pants, and boots.

The truck took off and hauled ass across the desert on a northeasterly course, which would take them across the Chain of Tears under the traffic bridges.

They rode through the rest of the night and another day, during which Feruccio briefed them on the electromorph tech while wearing her full military-virtual regalia. First, she reminded them of the basic tech, holding up the tiny, spheroid emitter, which was capped with a cone built from spidery electronic legs.

She detached the cone. "Here's how it works. You put this in your ear. Can I get a volunteer?"

No one raised their hands. Then they *all* raised their hands.

"All right. Pell."

She handed him the cone. He inserted it into his ear and leaned back.

"What now*EEEEEEEEEEEEEEEUUUUUUH.*"

His face flick-froze into a slant-jawed grimace and buzzed forth an electronic wail that settled into silence. Feruccio pinched the other half of his emitter between her thumb and forefinger. It flared to life and generated an electromorph version of Pell Yannick resembling Feruccio's own genderless blue avatar. Pell looked down and touched himself.

"It would appear that in this state, I lack the senses of touch, taste, and smell."

"That's right," Feruccio said. "That's one of the trade-offs."

"We're going to need better disguises, Shanta," Eldridge said.

"He's right. We'll need to make odds with the Creep to even get *into* the Tower, and if he suspects a ruse, we'll be kind of screwed. And dead."

"Becalm yourselves," Feruccio said. "Pell, if you concentrate, you will be able to assume almost any form you like."

The Narsyan nodded. "Very well." After a moment, clothes appeared on his avatar, while its blue luminescence dimmed until he looked like a normal person. He turned and lifted one of the larger psychoskags by the shoulders. Smiling, he set it down. "Your claim about the enhanced strength was correct."

"How strong will we be?" Eldridge asked.

"You will have access to roughly ten times your normal strength."

"Damn, El. You'll be able to lift Quillig's big rig," Hagan said.

"But," Feruccio said, holding up a finger. "The more you access this enhanced strength, the more you will tire out your host body. There are limits. Any other questions? Eldridge?"

"Nah. I'm still trying to figure out how to becalm myself."

Feruccio smiled and moved on. "The outpost of Ikraam is roughly six miles away from Towertown. There is an inn there. We'll need privacy so your host bodies can slumber while you infiltrate the Tower."

"It's gonna be tight," Hagan said. "If the man across the oceans picks up our scent, we're screwed."

Eldridge nodded and shrugged. "Not much choice."

Kieron raised her hand.

"I have a question. What happens if our emitters get damaged? They can withstand the heat inside the Tower, correct?"

"Yes. They're built to survive radical changes in temperature and pressure. But they're not indestructible, and if they're destroyed *while you're within the hundred-mile radius,* you will suffer no damage. You'll simply awake back at Ikraam."

"But if for some reason we go farther than a hundred miles?"

"That won't happen. As I said, Ikraam is only six miles—"

"I know. But if we do, we're . . ."

"Kind of dead," Feruccio said.

They rode in silence until one of the psychoskags spoke.

"We've arrived at Ikraam, sir."

—⚍—

BORIS HAGAN, ET AL

Boris Hagan's third wind had ended.

They arrived at the outpost a few hours before sundown and

just as the sun's sky position provided a perfect view of Ikraam, which wasn't so much an outpost as a *home*. The Clean Machine rode through a dry riverbed until they reached a canyon.

Hagan chattered away to distract himself from the sinkhole of exhaustion that had opened up inside him. "Before Deadblast, there used to be a gigantic waterfall here. Hundreds of rivers all flowed into this canyon."

All that remained of the ancient waterfall was the riverbed, which ran off the side of the canyon. Right at the cusp where the earth made a ninety-degree turn straight down, wooden support struts extended out into the sky and held aloft a four-story house. But the platform held more than just the house; it was wide enough to sustain actual foliage—trees, shrubbery, vines, and ivy—all of which held the house in an embrace of green. The house itself had been constructed from the same faded, distressed wood as the platform holding it up. Wood beams carved up the front of Ikraam house, and within those carvings, the smooth plaster panels of the house had been painted a deep, rich red; like dried blood or the skin of a perfectly ripe apple. By the front door hung a painting of a young girl. Weathervanes and dozens of windmills dotted the roof, while an awning-covered deck ran around the outside of the house. At either end of the circular deck, two wooden bridges curved across the divide to the land. The Clean Machine parked by one of the bridges. Everyone got out, Hagan last, as he hoped his quaking limbs and cold sweat would go unnoticed by the others. They all squinted into the sun, except for Kieron, who had slid her black oculars back into place as soon as they left Penticton.

"I've never quite gotten used to all the light up here among you extraterrestrials," she said, drawing funny looks from everyone, including Pell and Feruccio.

Amidst a blaze of sunlight, they approached one of the bridges and admired the silhouette of Ikraam before they stepped into its shadow and heard the *click* of several different handheld weapons. Eldridge recognized the *thrum* of other ordnance, too. Ikraam outpost came alive at their approach and opened several dark eyes—mortar cannons that appeared from flipping platforms in the roof and looked down at them. A woman appeared at one of the fourth-floor windows, bearing a shotgun.

"You the supply train?!" she yelled.

Eldridge called back, "No! We're here to stay at the inn!"

The woman waved her shotgun. "Y'all don't look like no supply train I ever seen."

"*We're not a—*" Eldridge cut himself off and addressed Feruccio. "How much jenta do you guys have?"

"Enough to spare."

"Thanks." Eldridge addressed the woman: "We have jenta! We need to pay for lodgings!"

"Don't want yer jenta. Why y'all look so fuckin' weird? That one looks like a daggum fish."

She seemed to indicate Kieron, who shrugged. Eldridge rolled his eyes.

"Shanta, I can't believe I have to ask for more, but do you guys have any food?"

"Not unless she consumes plasma energy."

Eldridge turned and called up, "By any chance, do you consume plasma—"

"*Fuck off!*" yelled the woman and vanished.

"Okie-dokie," Eldridge said. "Are there any other outposts nearby?"

Feruccio nodded. "There's one located roughly midway between here and Towertown, but it lacks privacy. I wouldn't feel safe leaving you there unconscious."

"Fair enough," Eldridge said.

"We could hole up in a cave," Pell suggested.

"Bad idea," Eldridge said. "I don't want my head getting chomped by a suprafeline while we're in the Tower."

Hagan had taken a tentative step forward. He examined the painting of the young girl by the front door and noticed something very interesting: dates. Specifically, *two* dates: birth . . . and death. He turned to Eldridge.

"I've got it. Shanta, let me into the truck and hand me one of the emitters."

Moments later, the young girl in the painting stepped out from the Clean Machine and walked up to Ikraam house. She wore a dark green gingham dress that offset her bright blue hair.

"Mama?"

The woman reappeared in the window, gaped at the sight, and vanished.

Eldridge covered his face. "Great. We're screwed unless this poor old lady's kid sounded exactly like you, Hages."

Hagan whispered, "Just wait." He called again, "Mama?"

The front door opened, and the woman emerged, still bearing her shotgun. In his electromorph form, Hagan's vision was tinged blue, and the absence of the major senses made it difficult to tell where he was walking. He found himself checking each footstep to make sure he wasn't about to walk into a hole. He turned his attention to the old woman, who scuttled across the bridge and stopped a few feet away from Hagan.

"Cycil?" she asked.

The old woman's eyelids drooped so low they resembled a pair of parantheses tipped on their sides across her face, which looked like a hanging ream of old burlap pinned up in several places to mark where her facial features had once been. One pin marked the remains of a dimple, while two others held the burlap secure to the corners of her eyes. A kerchief covered her head, while a combination pantsuit-gown covered her sphere of a body. Hagan surmised she had cut up an old skirt and fashioned makeshift pantlegs out of it. She squinted at Hagan's disguise-avatar.

"Cycil? I watched them dreens tear out your insides. Oh, I tried to get there in time, but my heart done gave out."

"*Crom*," Eldridge whispered. Pell had walked back to the truck to check on something. Kieron watched on, confused as always.

The old woman took Hagan's electromorph hand and placed it on her chest. "But Cycil, *feel*. The sawbones done fixed me up with one of them new contraption pumps. And if'n any of them dad-blamed *goblins* come lookin' fer organic vittles again, yer mama Tru Serene'll be ready." She took Hagan's hand and turned to the rest. "Why din't y'all tell me you found my Cycil? I'm Trudy."

Hagan glared at Eldridge, who said, "We . . . forgot."

"Speak up, son. I din't quite make that out."

"*Nothing*," Eldridge said, raising his voice. "*So we can stay at the inn?*"

"Long as I get to spend time with my Cycil," Trudy said. "Come on inside."

―⚇―

ELDRIDGE, ET AL

IKRAAM HOUSE FELT WARM, even in the blaze of daytime or the frost of nighttime. Trudy lived alone and had some kind of powerful environmental controls that kept even the outside decks at a comfortable temperature while also dimming the brightness of the sun. She took them around the house's exterior deck first and showed off the view from the *back* of the house, which looked off the side of the dry waterfall into the sweeping canyon below. Feruccio had yet to depart.

Trudy was still holding Hagan's hand.

"Right this a-ways," the old woman said.

Pell took the redhead by the elbow and pulled him away from the old woman. Eldridge, Pell, Kieron, and Feruccio remained on the rear deck while Hagan and Trudy went back inside.

"Eldridge, we need to speak."

Feruccio added, "Yes, we do."

"I know, I know," Eldridge said. "It sucks what we're doing to this nice old lady. We need the place to crash."

"That's not it," Pell said. "I checked on Boris's body."

"And?"

Pell nodded at Feruccio. She spoke. "His heart rate has climbed to three hundred beats per minute, and his blood pressure is only seventy over fifty."

"I don't understand anything you just said."

"El, he's *dying*," Pell said. "The concentration needed to maintain an electromorph being is extremely taxing."

"No," Feruccio said. "That's not the case here."

"What do you mean?" Eldridge asked.

"He would be dying anyway," she said. "Asking him to maintain an electromorph is only hastening the process. And, Eldridge?"

"What?"

"My people and I need to leave."

The redhead propped his hands on his hips. "Oh, fucking *fantastic*. As soon as one of my guys is about to croak, you and the skags wanna pull up and bolt."

Pell touched the redhead's forearm. "Eldridge. Calm down."

"I'm becalmed!" he said before he stopped and rubbed his forehead. "I'm fine. Sorry, you're right, Shanta. You've done so much already. We'll get him out of your . . . um, mobile-fortress thing. And . . . well, Hages'll have to wait here while we go into the Tower."

"He's not going to agree to that," Pell said.

"I can't ask him to take that kind of risk."

"You're asking it of me," Pell said.

"I don't follow."

The Narsyan offered a grim smile. "My body is just as ruined as Hagan's. I only have the advantage of a few years' youth and the echoes of a Narsyan upbringing to gird me."

Eldridge was already shaking his head. "No. No, no! Fuck it! I'll go in there alone!" He addressed Kieron: "You can stay behind, too. You don't even *know* these people."

"If it please you," Kieron said. "It is my intention to one day count you among my friends and allies, and to do that, I wish to offer my services on this mission. I am a soldier. It is the only way I know."

The redhead's chest swelled in admiration as he smiled. "Dude, are you reading from a script or something?"

Kieron tilted her head. "Pardon?"

"Nothing," Eldridge said, turning to Pell. "Listen, I can't ask that of you or Hagan. I won't."

Another voice: "Won't ask what?"

They turned to see Boris Hagan coming around the side of the deck. He walked like he was ten-drinks drunk and trying to look sober—every step precisely chosen. He came up to them and pointed up at the house.

"Poor woman's pooped. I put her to bed. There's lots of space for us. Come on, I want to get to Towertown by nightfall."

"Boris—"

Hagan advanced on him. "El, this isn't *your* rescue mission. It's *mine*. It's mine and Stewart's and Pell's. *We* set out to save you and

Oksana, not you. You just went and got your dumb ass scooped up by an Odd. You're the one who needed saving—*twice*. If I die in the Tower, then I die in the Tower. But I'm going to finish this, and a dumbfuck like you isn't gonna stop me."

Eldridge's eyes darted in thought. When he looked up, Boris cut him off:

"And you don't have to thank us. They're our friends, too." He noticed Kieron. "Well, almost."

Kieron nodded. The redhead smiled. He nodded and whispered his next words.

"OK. Then let's go to bed."

―⟶―

THE MAP MAN OF PENTICTON

THE MAP MAN OF Penticton sat in his office, sipping on a glass of bourbon and fiddling with the hypergenerator. His lackey stood guard by the door.

"How many thick-n-thinners you think we got in Penticton? Enough to take down Hanna?"

His lackey said nothing.

"I mean, army or not, I can start making odds with this sucker right away. Any time. Big-time odds. Odds of destiny."

His lackey frowned, glancing upward.

"Maybe I'll book a trip across the oceans. Set up shop where it's green. Wouldn't that be a mind-blower? Tickle my toes in the greengrass."

His lackey turned into strawberry jam. Not that Conrade had ever *eaten* or *seen* strawberry jam in person, but he had heard about it, and when the shockwave from above ripped through his office, his lackey's swollen body must not have been sturdy enough to withstand it, because it emulsified his body in a blinking instant. The map man's desk shattered, too, as did the tumbler of bourbon. The map man's prosthetic face fell off, leaving behind nothing but a dark hole capped with two beady black oculars. He stood up, clutching his prosthetic face, but before he could bolt, his ceiling turned black. The stain started small and spread to engulf all above before it bubbled downward. The black bubble drooped to his floor and stuck there as more and more black gunk rained from above and assembled itself into a creature with a concrete cylinder for a head. From above floated someone whose face Conrade didn't recognize, but who was holding an object the map man *sure as shit* recognized.

Holding his tiny castle, the man across the oceans floated over the rubble of the map man's office and stopped.

"Hello, Mr. Conrade. Quillig tells me you might know the whereabouts of a certain redhead."

ELDRIDGE, ET AL

THE ELECTROMORPH AVATARS OF Eldridge, Boris Hagan, Pell Yannick, and Kieron rode in an old internal-combuster car (a "station wagon," Hagan called it) Trudy had been kind enough to loan to them.

"If by 'loan,' you mean we boosted it from her garage while she was conked out," Eldridge said from behind the wheel.

"We needed the ride," Hagan said. "We need to *look* like we're real people or the Creep won't make odds with us. We couldn't all pile onto your bike, El. Well, we *could*, but it would look suspicious."

Back at Ikraam house, they had said their goodbyes to Feruccio, who left them one more gift—a small speaker.

"Play this sound quietly near the old woman, and she will remain asleep."

After they had climbed into their beds and activated their electromorph avatars, they had been ready to run out the door when Hagan stopped Eldridge.

"Forgetting something?"

Eldridge almost knocked over a water cooler in Trudy's kitchen when he realized what he had neglected to do. Moments later, he was tying off his own arm to draw some of his own blood.

"This is weeeeeee-irrrrrd," Eldridge said while Kieron's avatar assisted him. They transferred some of the redhead's blood into all six of the safepods, which Eldridge divided among them.

"This way, no one person has 'em all," he said. "I'll keep two. Pell, you take two. Kieron, two for you."

Hagan protested. "I should carry at least one."

"Okay. Kieron, give him one of yours."

Kieron obliged, not noticing the way Hagan glared at the redhead. Later, on the car trip to Towertown, Eldridge grumped about Hagan's involvement.

"I still think you'd have been useful back there, Hages. You could have stayed in disguise and kept the old lady occupied. That way our bodies would have some defense in case someone came by."

"All her defenses are automated, El. One more old woman with a misfiring shotgun wouldn't make any difference."

They rode on, covering the six miles between Ikraam and Towertown with speed. As the white-hot disk of the sun began its descent toward the horizon to the west, they rode north across a desert that rolled over one hilly range after another. Besides one small outpost, the terrain was blank.

By nightfall, they saw a haze of golden light glimmering from within over the horizon ahead. They crested a rocky hill and stopped as the remnant of Towertown—and the Fallen Tower itself—came into view.

Towertown *looked* at them. That was the redhead's first impression, and he presumed it was Kieron's too, as this was her first visit. Eldridge had encountered rumortrysts about this remnant, and in this case, they sang true: A stone head rose out of the earth. If the head were attached to a statue of proportional size, it would stand three hundred feet high, Eldridge estimated, although he didn't want to imagine the possibility that a massive stone giant was hiding under the earth, and his mind reeled at the notion that *something* in the past had buried such an enormous statue up to its lower lip. The giant head appeared to be covered in fireflies, which it also yawned across the desert basin stretching out before it. Of course, they weren't fireflies but the *fires* of the remnant's many residents, all of whom eschewed electricity. Unlike most remnants, Towertown had no generator. They received news of oddsmaking and oddsmanship from parts distant exclusively via moto-carrier, rumortryst, and hearsay.

The Creep and his mighty fire wardens would have it no other way.

This was because they lived in the shadow of the remnant's oddsmaking source and all-central shrine: the Fallen Tower and its accompanying river of lava. The molten red river originated from the base of a rocky hill rising to the south of the remnant; the same hill that Eldridge, et al, currently sat atop. The river spilled out of the hill and cut a snaky path through the remnant, effectively dividing it in half. Three major bridges arched over the river, which flowed due north and under the Tower.

Viewed from above, the remnant would look like a misshapen exclamation point, with the Fallen Tower as its vertical line, while the stone head (the exclamation point's point) sat off-center, just to the east of the Tower's base. The remnant's other houses, huts, and hutches were all spread out directly to the south of the tower. To the north of the Tower rose an enormous mountain range centered about an active volcano that spat forth lava in a constant loop of leaping, fiery gouts.

From their vantage point, they looked at the bottom of the skyscraper's foundation, as it had fallen northward, directly over the river of lava. Hundreds more fires burned across the face of the foundation—all of them controlled fires manned by dark figures who scurried back and forth along metal walkways built into the foundation. Despite the dramatic change in brightness, the three men and one woman were immediately able to see that the walkways built onto the Tower's foundation had been built in an elaborate pattern. (Unlike their organic eyes, their vision as electromorphs required no time to adjust to changes in brightness or darkness.)

"Let's go," Eldridge said as he put the car in gear and drove down the hill. A rocky access road came into view, and he followed it down into the village that spread out below the Tower's foundation. A strange sense of claustrophobia settled over the redhead as he realized the stone face blocked escape to the east, while the Tower blocked escape to the north. To the west and south rose more rocky hills that were *passable,* but by no means easy to climb. If they wound up running for their lives, of course.

Soot-covered dregs glared at them with the whites of their eyes as they drove past. Black ash seemed to cover everything in town, and Eldridge felt relief that he wouldn't have to *breathe* any of it while they were there. His connection to his organic body felt like a barely remembered dream. If he concentrated, he could feel himself breathing back in the beds they had arranged for themselves back at Ikraam, but that divided his focus. He brought himself back to Towertown.

The road melted from rocks to black dirt when they reached the perimeter of town. They arrived on the west side of the river and immediately looked for a safe place to park. Eldridge finally spotted something resembling an inn, and they stopped.

"OK," Eldridge said. "Lame faces."

"*Game* faces, El. Jiminy Christmas—how'd you goof *that* one up? We still *have* games after Deadblast, man."

"All right, all right. Just concentrate on your disguises."

Because he still feared a bounty might be on his head, Eldridge had assumed the likeness of a much darker-skinned man, with black hair and brown eyes. Thanks to the old woman's private stash of weaponry, he was able to arm himself with a pair of shotguns he had sawed off and outfitted with sharp kitchen knives from Trudy's kitchen as makeshift bayonets.

"I'm not going to be able to carry live rounds too deep into the Tower, so we'll have to rely on hand-to-hand," the redhead had said.

Having already been to Towertown, Boris Hagan *knew* he'd be recognized, so he transformed himself into a hale teenage boy with white hair and red eyes. He had raided Trudy's armory for a 9mm pistol and an aluminum baseball bat.

Pell had also been to Towertown, and he went so far as to take on the form of a powerfully built woman with close-cropped blond hair. He took no weapons.

"I shall rely on my amplified strength to combat the horrors inside the Tower."

Only Kieron retained her actual appearance, confident that no one among the extraterrestrials would recognize her. She had armed herself with the weaponry left over from her plastic armor. They bound her wrist-cannons to her virtual forearms, and she even brought her mortarchain rifle at Hagan's behest.

"That came in handy for me back in Hemming," Hagan said.

Armed and disguised, they marched across the remnant of Towertown, passing by hundreds of dregs who bartered food and water, all while making the occasional odds. The structures were hewn from stone, brick, and mortar—anything that wasn't flammable. Soot and sweat covered everyone. Eldridge shook his head.

"How can anyone *live* here?"

"Hey, at least no one's gonna plant a bomb in their heads."

"What?"

"Nothing."

They crossed one of the footbridges and looked out at the river of lava.

"I wonder if we could swim in it?" Kieron said.

"I wouldn't try it," Hagan said. "Remember, our emitters aren't indestructible."

Eldridge gave Hagan a look, but they walked on, twisting through more streets as the stars came out overhead. The stone head grew larger as they approached, its pupilless eyes staring down at them. As they got closer, they could see that ancient hands had built the stone face from dozens of larger blocks, which had then been carved down to resemble a face. Hundreds of fires dotted the surface of the head, some of the fires burning on stone perches, while others burned from *within* the head, which they could see had been hollowed out. The mouth and nostrils of the stone head gave view to an elaborate network of passages inside.

But the main event was stationed on the exterior surface of the head; on its *face,* to be exact. Between the village and the head was a strip of bare land, all of it covered with ash, soot, and black-glass lava stones of all sizes. They arrived at the foot of the head and looked up at its face, which was covered with the keepers of Towertown: the fire wardens.

Hagan had been right—they looked like they had lava for blood. Glowing veins covered their bodies from head to toe and burned brightest around their hearts and lungs. But more than having lava for blood, the dregs of Towertown could recognize a fire warden by their face, because all wardens looked like horrific burn victims *who were delighted about being burn victims.* Most fire wardens couldn't talk because their faces had melted so horribly. Their lower lips had melted into their chests, which were covered with hexagonal- and diamond-shaped scales of scar tissue and skin grafts. Some fire wardens had no necks, their heads having melted into their shoulders, while others glare-grinned at the world, their eyelids and lips having been scorched away. Despite their appearance, fire wardens retained some semblance of modesty, covering their nether regions with pants or other loincloths. Having braved the dreeny depths of the Old Mine, Eldridge didn't blanch at the sight of one. Neither did Hagan or Pell, having seen it before.

But Kieron hesitated. Eldridge turned.

"You all right?"

"I am most certainly not. But thank you for asking, sir."

The redhead nodded, then addressed Hagan: "We're here. Where's this Creep?"

"He's already here."

One of the fire wardens perched on the brow of the stone face spotted them and raised up a deep wail to the heavens. The rest of the fire wardens followed suit, including all of the wardens inside the stone head. After a minute's chanting, they fell silent. Hagan prodded Eldridge.

"Go ahead, El."

"What do you mean, 'go ahead'?"

"I can't talk, or they might recognize my voice. The Creep is here. Address him."

Eldridge looked up at the stone head, then called out, "We . . . uh, want to make odds with the Creep!"

As one, the fire wardens responded: *"Make your odds."*

The redhead did a double take, then turned to Hagan and Pell. "OK, what odds did you guys make last time?"

"Say, 'deep-tower' odds."

Eldridge shouted, "Deep-tower odds!"

"How deep?"

Off Hagan's prompt, Eldridge said, "To the heat-heart!"

The Creep—and by association, all of the fire wardens—laughed.

"Only the fiercest, the most savage of my wardens has penetrated the heat-heart. You've lost your jenta before you even laid it down."

Hagan whispered, "That's fine. Tell 'em we don't have any."

Eldridge said, "We don't have any—" he broke off and addressed Hagan: *"Are you out of your fucking mind?"*

Hagan shushed him. The Creep spoke:

"Then you make life-odds?"

Eldridge glared at Hagan. "Forget it."

"El, *think* about it. It means if we don't win, they'll kill us."

After a moment's thought, the redhead nodded. "Got it. Sorry." He addressed the Creep: "We make life odds."

"Very well. Two of my wardens will escort you to the Tower gates."

The fire wardens raised up their deep wail once more as the Creep apparently made his exit. Hagan turned to them. "Get it?"

Eldridge nodded. "Even if we 'die,' we'll just wake up back at the ranch."

"Right."

Rapid footfalls heralded the arrival of a pair of fire wardens. Up close, Eldridge saw they had other qualities: Fire-spheres glimmer-burned around their fists. One of the wardens, who was taller, had wrapped his legs in fire-resistant vinyl, while the other wore a simple set of leggings. Both were barefoot, their feet scaled over with burn-tissue. The shorter one looked like his entire mouth had melted across his chest, his black teeth spread over his torso. His unblinking eyes bulged out of his face.

Pell whispered, "Boris."

Hagan nodded. "Right."

"What?" Eldridge asked.

"These are the same two who escorted Stew into the Tower on our first trip. One of 'em doesn't talk. The other is Dredge."

The taller of the two wardens, Dredge, spoke.

"You guys know what you're doing?" he asked.

Eldridge grinned at his polite tone. "Yeah, we're good."

"No, listen," Dredge said. "The Tower's not for everybody. I *chose* this life. I know you're fuck-ugly, but it's nothing to feel bad about."

An imaginary question mark appeared over Eldridge's head. Dredge must've noticed the change in expression, because he wrapped his arm around his shorter partner. Their blood glowed twice as bright.

"Maybe one day you can look like Tox," Dredge said. "If you listen to the Tower close enough. Come with us."

The fire wardens, Dredge and Tox, took off at a full sprint, moving faster than expected for two men who could barely bend their knees. Eldridge and his crew fell in behind. Hagan ran up next to the redhead.

"Careful. Don't trip into the fire."

As they approached the Tower's foundation, ten steel staircases rose out of the earth and swooped up toward the bottom-center of the skyscraper's foundation. Dredge and Tox took the steps two at a time, while Eldridge—leading the way for his team—chose one of the center staircases and immediately tripped and wiped out, causing the whole structure to give a menacing wobble. The redhead gawked at the lava, which flowed by a few yards underneath. Hagan's young man avatar lifted Eldridge by the shoulders.

"See what I mean? C'mon."

Hagan stepped over him, followed by Pell and Kieron. Eldridge hopped up.

"Wait up, you assholes!"

He lowered his head and jogged up the stairs toward the face of the foundation, which evoked memories of catwalk city back in Dedrick, except that the steel walkways of the psychoskags' old home were always a hectic, crisscrossing mess that belied the computerized, ordered nature of skag central command. By contrast, the walkways covering the foundation of the Fallen Tower formed a web of concentric circles that sketched the likeness of a labyrinth filled with flames.

When Eldridge reached the top of the stairs, he saw the network of walkways had been built over the jagged, crumbled remains of the foundation itself. Ancient I-beams and thick metal rods protruded from the layer of cement that had once held the skyscraper secure to the ground.

Hagan hooked his thumb at the walkways and whispered, "Looks like a dirty-glass window."

Eldridge grinned. "Don't you mean *stained* glass?"

Hagan looked tremendously impressed. "Yeah, I guess I did."

Various wardens maintained fires across the foundation's many platforms—huge, bellowing bonfires large enough to conceal the wardens, who embraced the flames while drumming out ritualistic rhythms on the metal, all while singing call-and-reply hymns with each other in unfamiliar tongues.

"Luca! Giambat-frej!" some would call.

"Halvard-hal, presco! Rasim!" others would respond.

At the point where the ten staircases converged, a twenty-foot gate, most of it concealed by the stained glass network of platforms, rose up. The wardens had cut through the foundation itself to construct the gate, which they had shored up with *actual* glass; specifically, volcanic glass bricks of varying shades of red and black. Dredge and Tox stopped on either side of the gate.

"You wanna know something? I fucking *hate* the Creep," Dredge said.

No one responded. If Tox had the facial acuity to change expression, he didn't.

Dredge continued, "Odds let us maintain the beauty of this house of worship, but never forget that when you step through these gates to test your mettle against the heat and legions of dreens, *you will look into the face of god.* Your deaths would bring honor to us, but if you should succeed, do not emerge from the Tower cheering. Do not emerge smiling. Do not emerge celebrating. Emerge *chastened.* Emerge *humbled.* Emerge *anew.*"

No one said anything until Tox, his mouth permanently melted open, let loose with a guttural howl that called down the attention of the wardens above, who all turned their charred and scarred faces earthward and hurled fistfuls of flame at the group.

"All hail the all-fire!" Dredge screamed.

The three men and one woman ran through the gates just as a few score fireballs smashed into where they had been standing—Eldridge with his bayonet'ed shotguns strapped over his shoulders; Pell unarmed; Kieron with her wrist-cannons and mortarchain-module; Hagan with a 9mm stuck in his virtual pants, his hands full of an aluminum baseball bat. They passed underneath the stained glass platforms and ran into the gate, which stretched on for hundreds of feet through solid cement, the walls dotted with the occasional cut-off bit of steel piping. High above, the ceiling made a perfect arch of black glass. Ghostly bits of wire mesh seeped through the cement, while up ahead, the gate-tunnel terminated into a dark beyond that gleamed with golden heat.

Eldridge felt his breathing speed up. He chuckled at what the four of them must sound like back in their bedroom in Ikraam. They passed through the gate and immediately hit the brakes as they spilled out onto a stone platform that ended in a sheer drop down to the lava-river. The redhead recalibrated his senses for the journey through the Tower—

everything was on its side. The walls of the ancient skyscraper composed the outer floor and ceiling, while the skyscraper's original floors stood on their sides before them.

The gate cut through the *center* of the foundation, and were it not for the efforts of the elder fire wardens, they would be suspended in the air. Over the years, the fire wardens had built a basic path through the Tower, smashing their way through the original floors toward the top of the tower, which now lay submerged in the river of lava. The top of the Tower was its *heat-heart,* presumably.

All around the initial chamber, hulking electric generators sat on their sides, covered in more fire wardens, who chanted by bonfires. The path split in two and made an O through the old power room, the lava-river visible in the center of the O.

"Left or right?" Kieron asked.

"Left," Eldridge said, leading the way.

As they ran, they saw the fire wardens had constructed the path by any possible means. Parts of the path had been cemented to neighboring walls, while other parts of it had been suspended from steel cables hanging from the ceiling-wall overhead. Chunks of pathway crumbled from underneath their feet and pitched into the lava below.

Eldridge stopped up short. "Wait!"

They did, under the watch of a pair of wardens. Hagan walked up to the redhead.

"What's wrong?"

"I never apologized."

The old man rolled his eyes. *"Some other time."*

"No, now. I need to tell you why I turned myself over to Quillig."

"Eldridge, you need not trouble yourself," Pell said.

The redhead yelled, *"I lost my memories of Zora."*

They fell silent.

Kieron whispered, "Forgive me. I presume Zora is of some importance to you?"

"She's his daughter," Hagan snapped.

"Well, she was. The mortarchains took away all my memories. All I remember is her death."

Hagan laid a hand on his shoulder. "El, I'm so sorry."

"Me, too," Eldridge said before he pushed Boris Hagan into the lava.

—ɯ—

[AUDIO: A MASSIVE CRASH, MORTAR CRUMBLING, GLASS SHATTERING.]

[AUDIO: THE CLICK OF A DICTATRYST DEVICE DEACTIVATING.]

What the fuck was that?!

[AUDIO: A MALE VOICE: "What? Who are you? No. *No!"]*

"Oh, my god—he found us! The man across the oceans found us! Pell! Pell, brother, I'm coming for ya!"

—ɯ—

PELL AND KIERON SWIPED at the old man's falling avatar, but the redhead's push was too strong. Hagan plunged into the lava and vanished, along with his electromorph emitter. Kieron was babbling.

"What? What? I don't—"

But Pell was already grabbing the redhead by his virtual lapels.

"Goddammit, Eldridge! How *dare* you?!"

"He's going to be *fine*," Eldridge said. "He'll just wake up in bed."

"I *know* he's going to be fine!" Pell released him and leaned off the edge of the path to check the lava for any sign of Hagan's avatar. There was none. He turned and addressed the redhead: *"Damn you* for endangering this mission. He had one of the doses of blood. We needed all four of us to have a hope of reaching the heart. We—"

Eldridge said, *"He. Had done. Enough.* And besides, I made sure he only had one of the doses. We've still got five, which should be more than enough. We only need two."

Pell sneered. "Oh. Of *course* he only had one dose. You *tried* to prevent him from carrying *any* of them, but your plan didn't work to perfection, did it? You better hope we can reach them with enough of your blood."

"Great, I'll do that," Eldridge said. "Now, are we going to move forward or are we going to keep bellyaching?"

Pell glared at Eldridge, then felt the gaze of the fire wardens immediately behind him. They had stopped chanting to listen to the argument. Pell spun around and snapped, "What the fuck are *you* looking at?!"

They went back to chanting. Pell turned around and marched past the redhead, who offered Kieron a wry smile.

"Still wanna be friends with us?"

Kieron flattened her palms and raised them over her head to form a triangle with her long arms. "More than ever, sir."

"What was that?" Eldridge said, mimicking the pose.

The woman from the sea shrugged. "Something we did back home."

She jogged past the redhead, who followed her around the pathway through the rest of the generator room. A serrated mouth of shattered steel and concrete greeted them and yielded entrance to the remains of an ancient basement. The lower wall of the skyscraper had been completely burned away so that the *entire floor* of the ancient basement was lava. Despite the protection from the senses his avatar afforded him, the redhead still *imagined* the heat. The path led straight out over the lava and toward the far wall. Various old platforms and stairways hung from the walls and ceiling, all of them packed with fire wardens, who raised up a joyous howl at the entrance of the two men and one woman. The wardens beat out a vicious drumbeat as Pell led Kieron and Eldridge across the room. As they ran, the redhead pulled up next to Pell.

"So Stew did this alone?"

They dodged around hanging wires that held aloft the next section of path. A steel chain hung over a gap in the path. Pell stopped and tried to judge the distance of the jump.

"He felt he was the best equipped to brave the journey to the heat-heart."

Pell jumped and swung across the fiery pit. He teetered on the far side for a moment before he found his footing, then slung the chain back to Eldridge, who called across the divide.

"Even though he used to be a dreen?!"

The redhead swung across. Pell caught him.

"If you think we should have proceeded differently, Eldridge, I am open to correction and suggestion."

Eldridge whipped the chain across the pit to Kieron, who caught it and swung across in one smooth motion.

"I have a question," Kieron said.

"Shoot," Eldridge said.

"What is a dreen?"

Eldridge and Pell looked at each other.

"It's hard to explain," said the redhead. "Your buddy Quillig used to *be* one."

Pell said, "They are mutants of their own making. Quite fearsome."

"Do you have to shoot dreens in the head *and* heart?" Kieron asked.

"That's right," Eldridge said. "You've tangled with 'em before?"

"One," Kieron said. "When can we expect to face off with them here?"

Another voice: "What's the opposite of 'later'?"

They turned to see a sniggering, smirking fire warden female manning the door to the next chamber: an archway of flowery, intricately woven barbed wire filled with fire from the next room. Eldridge peered into the bright flames, then looked at the female warden, who was forced to stomp her feet in tune with her comrade's chant, because her arms had melted to her sides. Eldridge only *guessed* she was female based on the shape of her mouth, so misshapen was the rest of her—except for her full lips, which curled around a smile.

"Worship hard, gentlemen," she said with a cackle. "Only the faithful may pass the following tests. I'd start running now."

"Why?" Eldridge asked, although his ears already told him the answer. Mad shrieks called up nightmare-visions from his past as the lava below spat forth dreenthings covered in molten rock too horrible to be countenanced. One of them soared out of the lava below and slammed into Kieron, driving her back against the wall. A halo of red surged from between them, the blast hurling the lavadreen back into the river. The female warden continued her cackle as Eldridge waved his hand and shouted.

"Let's boooooook!"

They ran into the next room, which had a lot more floor than the previous one. The pathway cut a path across the entire lobby of the old skyscraper, while on the wall directly facing them—the *ceiling* of the old building—an enormous bonfire burned, tended to by dozens of fire wardens who stood astride the flames and hurled fireballs at the lavadreens attacking them.

The group sprinted across the lobby, pursued by an instream of lavadreens that stagger-swarmed into the lobby, dripping red-hot molten bits with every searing step. One of them ran ahead and cut off Eldridge, who drew his new scatterguns and spent two rounds—one for the head, one for the heart.

But it kept coming.

"*Guys?!*" Eldridge shouted. "This one didn't die!"

Echoes, echoes, echoes. Echoes sounded from all around as the fire wardens howled with ecstasy, and Eldridge realized what they were all sitting on: *a chandelier.* An ages-old steel frame for a chandelier protruded from the wall/ceiling ahead, and in the intervening years, the wardens had turned it into an infernal altar. Black-and-white tiles checkered the wall/ceiling behind the flaming chandelier, which was flanked by a pair of doorways leading deeper into the Tower.

And which were both thronging with lavadreens.

"*Breej-donwat! Hok-hok-hok!*" the wardens chanted. "*The Tower is the motherlord, the fathergod, the all, the all, the all-flame! Breej-donwat!*"

More fireballs came hurling down from above, some of them connecting with lavadreens, most of them aimed at the two men and one woman, who dodged back and forth before lowering their heads and running headlong into the lavadreens.

"Let's take these avatar-thingies out for a—*ooof!*" Eldridge said as he slammed into a lavadreen and drove it into the next chamber on a wake of churning legs and sheer, pissed-off certitude. Kieron followed behind, bearing two lavadreens over her head. She chucked one skyward and blasted it with her wrist-cannon, which illuminated the next chamber as a mezzanine giving view to the rest of their journey.

The Fallen Tower was an atrium.

A cross-section of the Tower lay exposed before them. Each floor had a balcony running around the curved exterior of the skyscraper. The fire wardens' makeshift pathway spanned the width of the following chamber for a few hundred meters before it narrowed into a twelve-foot-wide bridge snaking over the river of lava, which consumed everything below. Buttresses rose up from the lava and held the bridge-pathway aloft as it stretched into the deepest reaches of the Tower, always descending lower and lower until it reached the far end, which was submerged in lava.

Pell kicked a lavadreen in its swollen head, which popped and spewed forth flaming viscera. Another beset him from his blind side, but Kieron pulled him out of the way, causing two lavadreens to collide.

Planters filled with fire instead of greenery lined the mezzanine. Fire wardens hung from the wall/ceiling overhead and fast-pitched fireballs at them. Kieron jumped out of the way, then backed toward her comrades, firing one red wrist-blast after another, each one sending a lavadreen flying away, only to regain their footing and come running at them again. Eldridge blasted another, then checked a sidepurse he had strapped to his waist.

"Shit! I dunno how much longer these shells're gonna hold out!"

"Are you running out?" Kieron asked.

"No! Before it gets too hot in here and they go blammo! I can't tell how hot *anything* is!"

Boom, boom! Eldridge blasted two more lavadreens, one of which split into a darkfire splatter of lavarock and glowing molten lead. Another lavadreen, this one a hulking torso with blackglass eyes and flaming feet, charged them from across the mezzanine, the volleys of fireballs from the wardens above only adding to its rage. Kieron blasted it, but the massive lavadreen simply soaked up the energy.

"Stand back," Pell said.

"Pell!" Eldridge shouted. "You're not strong enough, even as an electer-mop-fucking whatever thing!"

But the great Narsyan chieftain strode up to the lavadreen and drove his palms into its midsection, delivering an avatar-amplified blow that shattered it from nave to chops and sent flaming chunks of lavadreen rock everywhere.

The fire wardens cheered. What a show.

Pell turned around. "Let's move!"

He motioned toward the treacherous stone bridge leading deeper into the Tower. Eldridge nodded, and they all three sprinted out onto the bridge as the chants of the fire wardens grew louder and louder from all around. Eldridge wondered how far Stewart had made it before he—how would Boris put it? *Went native?*

And he wondered if Oksana would be awaiting him at the end of this bridge, and if she was, what would she look like?

The redhead dismissed those thoughts and wondered what the Crom he was doing running across a tiny bridge over a river of lava that ran through a tipped-over skyscraper. He also wondered why, when the agent of the man across the oceans had confronted him, he didn't just kill himself?

"*How* the fuck much do I owe him?!" Eldridge had shouted in a tiny black steel room back at Port Stafford two years before. The pavement monster had dragged him back to the seaside remnant to inform him of the terms of his debt. The creature had melted back into the street when they reached the boundary of the town, where a man covered in horizontally flowing lines of red smartcharacters met him. Several heavily armed dregs accompanied the smart man, who all led the insta-sober Eldridge into the tiny room and told him how much he owed.

The smart man used his stylus-enhanced index finger to write out the figure on the table between them. Eldridge grabbed his hand.

"*Stop* writing zeroes already!"

"That is how much you owe him, sir."

Eldridge covered his face. "That's not even a *number!* How am I supposed to come up with that kind of jenta?!"

"Oh, this actually isn't the *final*-final figure." He started writing zeroes again.

"Wait, wait—what if I told you I don't remember what I said?"

The smart man looked up.

"I don't!" Eldridge said. "I was so wasted, I could've said *anything!*"

And he didn't. The redhead's memory of the night before was a strobing patchwork montage of corny jokes, body shots, and maudlin moments shared with total strangers. The smart man smeared away the figure on the table.

"That is what you owe. You have thirty months to pay in full to the man across the oceans."

"Or I'm dead?"

The smart man rolled his eyes. "Well, *yes.*"

Eldridge stood. "Fuck it and you. I ain't paying. I'll just kill myself."

The smart man's sigh rattled into a yawn. "Do I need to say we will find any of your family, friends, and loved ones and slaughter them as well?"

The redhead's chest deflated. "Daggummit."

The smart man walked around the table and opened the door. "You're free to leave. Remember: thirty months."

Eldridge started to leave, then stopped. "Wait—you're not going to kill Zak, are you? It's not his fault!"

"Oh no. I wouldn't worry about Mr. Chamberlain."

The smart man left and walked down a wood-paneled hallway. Eldridge tried to follow, but a steel wall slammed down and blocked his path.

"What the hell is *that* supposed to mean?!"

Years later in the Fallen Tower, Eldridge thought back to how he had tried to warn Chamberlain about an attack from his bosses, only to find that the WHAT HAPPENED AT DEADBLAST booth had disappeared and the Odd was nowhere to be found. The coming realization hit Eldridge so hard he almost didn't notice a huge chunk of rock fall from above and shatter the bridge in front of him. He was about to run straight into the lava before Pell pulled him back.

"Eldridge! Stop!"

"Holy Crom. That's it. That's *it*," Eldridge said, his eyes bulging.

Kieron came jogging up behind them. "What's wrong?"

"I know who it is," Eldridge said. "I know who *he* is."

"He? Who?" Pell asked.

"The man across the oceans. It's Zak Chamberlain."

―⚏―

QUILLIG AND THE MAN ACROSS THE OCEANS

THE MAN ACROSS THE oceans stood on the bridge of his hovercraft and watched the desert landscape roll by. Visiting the western continent always depressed him. He yearned for the lush green of his adopted homeland, the eastern continent.

But that was one errand and one return trip across the oceans away.

From his slim cell, Quillig asked, "When you find the redhead, what do you plan to do with him?"

The man across the oceans considered the question, then chuckled. "I have so many ideas."

Quillig sensed the loss of light.

"Where are we?" he asked.

"Oh, we've entered the remnant of Hemming. I'm taking a little shortcut."

—⁂—

ELDRIDGE, ET AL

THE SHATTERED CHUNKS OF the bridge fell into the lava river below. The group huddled on the edge of the bridge while fireballs rained down from above. A phalanx of lavadreens advanced up the bridge, all of them swarming around the bridge's circumference with their preternaturally prehensile claws and talons.

"There has to be another way," Kieron said.

"There is *no* other way," Pell said. "We should throw ourselves into the lava and regroup back at Ikraam."

"No!" Eldridge said. *"How* are we gonna get to Oksana and Stew?"

"We can muster forces and invade the Tower from the north. Access them directly."

"Pell, are you kidding? 'Muster forces'? *What forces?* We're no one. It's just us, and we can't raise an . . . an . . . and I think I've got a boner."

"*What?*"

"No! I've fucking *got it!* Where's the elevator?!"

"Eldridge, what does that *mean?!*" Pell said.

"An *elevator!* Tall old buildings had 'em. They carried dregs from floor to floor." He looked around. "Shit. It must've gotten smashed."

"Did you really expect it to *work? In here?*"

"No, no! But we could've used it to—"

"Is that it?" Kieron asked.

The woman from the sea pointed directly up at the outer wall of the old skyscraper. About a hundred feet overhead, what looked like a train track ran along the interior wall of the building.

"That's great—*shit!* Where's the car?!"

"The what?"

"The car! The elevator car!" Eldridge impaled a lavadreen and slung it off the bridge, where it fell into the lava. He looked deep into the tower. "It must be on the top floor. *Shit.* What if it got melted?" The redhead's eyes lighted on something. He whooped with glee. "I see it! I see it! Look!"

He pointed, and incredibly, there was indeed a glass car hooked into the track far ahead into the Tower. Eldridge stepped over to Kieron and pointed at her mortarchain module.

"How many more shots you got?"

Kieron checked. "Three."

"What's the range?"

"Virtually unlimited. What is the plan, sir?"

As the lavadreen brigade closed in on them, Eldridge did some math in his head.

"That should be enough. But everybody listen! These are my orders: *Do not, under any circumstances, fuck up.*"

Pell rolled his eyes. "Okay."

"May I?" Eldridge asked. Kieron handed over the module. Eldridge said, "Everybody grab onto me!"

They did, and Eldridge fired a round of licorice-lashing, electro-crackling, crimson-flashing mortarchains into the ceiling/wall overhead. The chains found purchase. Eldridge tugged on the chains to make sure, then started fumbling with the module.

"Retract! Retract?! How do I—"

Kieron pressed a button, and just as the tidal-rush of lavadreens reached them, they zoomed into the air, the module slurping its chains back into itself and hoisting them toward the elevator track, which they reached in a few mad instants. They hit the ceiling/wall next to one of the Tower's many sideways balconies a few yards away from the elevator track. All three climbed into one of the balconies, which circled the outer wall of the skyscraper.

"This way!" Eldridge yelled.

The balconies were filled with fire wardens, who hurled more fireballs at them even as they cheered their progress through the Tower. Deep chants rolled through the Tower like thunder, the wardens' rhythmic synchronicity total and subliminal. One of the fire wardens scurried across the outer wall toward them, his head bent back at an impossible angle because the back of his scalp had melted to his back. He spoke through a gaping hole in his neck.

"*Freelon-dreej-tot! Scaldlove awaits!*"

He fell from the wall and spun down into the lava. The plummeting warden's motion drew the redhead's gaze downward, where he saw the Tower's outer walls darkening as lavadreens by the thousands started to swarm the balconies. And then he finally got it.

"Our emitters. Dreens love synth-tech. That's why they want us so bad."

"No time to fret about that now—the elevator awaits," Pell said.

They scrambled along the balcony out to the elevator track, where Eldridge handed the mortarchain module back to Kieron.

"You're tallest. You'll have to do it."

Kieron understood. The elevator track cut a fairly narrow path through the balconies—narrow enough for a tall woman like Kieron to lie across the gap and aim at the elevator. She took aim at the car, which waited, scores of stories away. Eldridge looked down and saw the wave of lavadreens consuming more and more of the wall, while the fire wardens retreated.

"Hurry up, jellyw—"

Before he could finish, Kieron kicked Eldridge in the face and fired. As the redhead fell backward, the mortarchains lashed a straight line along the outer wall and implanted in the base of the elevator-car.

"Got it," Kieron said.

"Retract!" Eldridge yelled. "And I'm really sorry I almost called you jellywoman!"

Kieron pressed the *retract* button. The mortarchains snapped taut . . . but nothing happened. They sat there, listening to the oncoming wail of a lavadreen horde and the deep gurgling groans and moans of the lava-river below, all while the mortarchains vibrated and a reverberating buzz. *Then it happened.* Something dislodged with a distant *clank*, and the elevator car came screaming toward them as the chains retracted into Kieron's module. Kieron crawled back onto the balcony, still holding the module.

"Uh, how do we stop it?"

"Elbow grease," Eldridge said. "Come on!" He leaped across the gap to the other side of the balcony, dodging the whiplashing chains, and then leaned out with his hands extended. "I'll need help! Kieron, you sit back and *keep a tight motherfucking grip on that module!*"

She did, while Pell leaned out from his side of the balcony. Cables, dormant for untold centuries, rushed along the wall above them, followed by the onrushing car, which reached them an instant later—*smash!* It crunch-halted into the outstretched palms of Eldridge and Pell, the two Narsyan chieftains. Pell wheezed from the exertion, his amplified strength no match for the redhead's, whose physical form hadn't been ruined the way Pell's had.

On his hands and knees, Pell swayed, but Kieron caught him before he fell off the balcony. Eldridge extended his hand. Pell took it. They clasped thumbs, as if arm-wrestling, and squeezed each other's virtual forms—one of which faded away. Pell Yannick's female disguise morphed into his true form before their eyes.

"You still with us?" Eldridge asked.

"I am with you," Pell said.

"All right, then let's get this mother moving."

The elevator car had once been enclosed with glass. Steel rings coiled out from the back of the car. They had once acted as the frame for the elevator's glass walls, but no more. Eldridge climbed out onto the rings and extended his hand for Kieron, who reached out just as the shotgun shells in the redhead's side-purse exploded. The explosion didn't harm him, of course, but they were powerful enough to interrupt the signal from Kieron's emitter, which fell *out* of her chest. As her emitter fell and her avatar dimmed, Kieron instinctively grabbed for it and fell.

"No! *No!*" Eldridge screamed.

When Kieron realized it was over, she simply relaxed, rolled over, and fell into the lava, smiling. She vanished. Eldridge hung his head for a moment before Pell smacked it. When the redhead looked up, he saw Pell had caught the mortarchain module before it fell. Pell glared at him.

"Kieron is *unhurt*, Eldridge. We almost lost the module. Do. Not. Lose. Sight."

"All right, all right," Eldridge said. "I'll take the shot."

"Very well. And do not dawdle."

Eldridge noticed that the wave of lavadreens had reached the top of the outer wall and now advanced toward them. Pell detached the chains from the base of the elevator. They slurped back into the module, which Pell handed over. The redhead took aim at the far wall—the ceiling—of the skyscraper. Pell chuckled.

"Have you given any thought to how we're going to get out of here once we cure them?" he asked.

"None," Eldridge said, then fired. Once more, the mortarchains flashed along the length of the skyscraper as the module spat out link after link after link after—*thunk*. Contact. Eldridge tugged on the module. "We got it. Climb on."

Pell did. Eldridge took one last look below and saw the wave of lavadreens advancing closer and closer as the shrieking creatures crawled along the outside of the building, leaping from balcony to balcony, all of them dripping with molten blood and flaming dopamine.

"Let's finish this," Pell said.

Eldridge nodded and pressed the *retract* button. The module screeched, and in the next instant, the interior balconies of the Fallen Tower were racing by as the mortarchain module hauled them and the shaking elevator-car along the wall. Eldridge and Pell grabbed onto each other's hands and held on with all of their avatar-amplified strength as their imaginations projected the sensation of incredible momentum directly into their brains. Floor after floor smeared by, the Tower's circumference narrowing, all while the downward-sloping angle of the outer wall carried them ever closer to the river of lava below.

And then they slowed. Some kind of ancient braking system—crumbling rubber pads set into the track above—stopped the car. Eldridge reflected that those same brake pads were what held the car in place when they first tried to retrieve it. They had reached the far end—the *top*—of the Fallen Tower.

He looked down and saw nothing but lava. And dreens. And lavadreens.

Islands of solid rock floated through the lava, all of them crowded with dreens, while their fiery counterparts, the lavadreens, swam through the lava itself. Not a fire warden in sight.

"Pell, let's—"

They hung in the air. Eldridge didn't even hear the *snap* that marked the severing of the the elevator car's cable. One instant he was crouching on one of the car's steel rings, the next they were both dangling from the car, which clung to the wall by a few fraying strands of steel cable. Pell lost his grip and went flying by the redhead, who snatched his hand and held him aloft.

"Let go, you fool! I'll bring us both down!"

"No!" Eldridge said. "Hand me the blood!"

Pell reached with his free hand for a pouch on his side that contained his two safepods, and then his expression quantum-leaped to another place. A shockwave of static ripped through his avatar. His eyes lost focus, and he peered at something close by. His next words sounded muffled, like he was speaking from the bottom of a well.

"What? Who are you? No. *No!*"

"Pell!"

Life vanished from the avatar of Pelagius "Pell" Yannick, whose limp virtual hand slipped from the redhead's grasp as he tumbled away. Halfway down, his avatar shimmered out of existence, leaving only his emitter, which fell into the lava and vanished in a white flare. His two safepods fell with him. Eldridge watched him fall, filled with terror, and waited for his own life to end.

But it didn't.

And yet he still dangled from the elevator over a river of lava. He couldn't think about Pell, or what had happened to him back at Ikraam. Had they been *found*? Had Quillig tracked them down somehow? What about Kieron? Or Boris?

Mind-divide the challenges.

The words of Marko Marinus calmed him and set his mind to the task at hand. He looked down and watched the lavadreens swim through the lava. Too deep. There's no way he could keep his emitter intact if he jumped into the lava, so he looked to the islands of rock floating below. Could he jump it? He wasn't sure–*snap!* It tore through his ears, the next snap did, and entirely on instinct, he found himself scrambling up the side of the elevator and leaping for the track above, but it was *too high* above, and yet someone was there, waiting on the elevator track, hanging from the elevator track, extending his hand, but it was impossible, impossible.

Eldridge heaved himself off of the falling elevator and grabbed Boris Hagan's hand. As the elevator fell into the lava, Eldridge cried out.

"*Bull. Shit.* No, Bor—this isn't you. You found another emitter. Shanta. Shanta gave you another fucking one. You're lying. This isn't really you."

Hagan, his skin bubbling with heat blisters, his face one bright shade of red, his body and clothes soaked through with sweat, clung to the elevator track, teeth bared, every muscle bulging, every vein on his body throbbing with his final efforts.

"El, listen. He's got your body."

Eldridge spoke through his virtually clenched teeth. "Quillig?"

"Not Quillig. You know who. *Him.* The man across the oceans. He came all the way here. Kieron was gone. I couldn't save Pell. The man and his goons snatched your body and took off. You don't have much time. Save Oksie. Save Stew. Get back to Ikraam."

"Boris—"

A harsh sigh racked Hagan's body. "Grab onto something! Don't waste this chance!"

Eldridge swung his hand around and grabbed onto the elevator track, his grip sure and solid. He pulled himself up and hung from the track next to Hagan, whose entire body shook with effort.

"Hages, I'll carry you out of here, okay?"

"No time. You need to save them."

"Boris, no, please—"

Hagan's brow made a sorrowful arch over his eyes. "You're an asshole, El. I love you. And you just might try to carry me outta here, but I'm going to let myself fall in a second to make sure you don't. I'm dead anyway. *I love you.* I'm so sorry I never did enough to help you when the darkness came. And I'm so sorry I never did enough about Nadia."

"Boris—"

"That woman did one helluva number on you, my brother. I'm

sorry, so sorry for what she did to you. What she *took* from you. I know you can never get it back, but I hope you can find some peace knowing she's gone. She can't take anything else from you. She can't hurt you any more, brother. Now listen: You've got two doses of blood left. Go save Stew. *Save your girl. And get back to Ikraam. You're out—of—time."*

With that, Boris Hagan let go of the track and fell.

Eldridge didn't watch.

—⚋—

[AUDIO: THE CLICK AND WHIRR OF A DICTATRYST DEVICE COMING ONLINE.]
[AUDIO: RAPID FOOTFALLS.]
[NOTE: SUBJECT IS BREATHING HARD.]

Pardon my huffing and puffing here, everyone. It's been a long time since I did any kind of running, much less a full-tilt run across the desert.

I still can't believe it was only a little while ago—Eldridge pushing me into the fire, me waking up back at Ikraam House, the man across the oceans finding us.

Me losing Pell.

I'm so sorry I couldn't save ya, brother. I tried.

I didn't hear her wake up, but Kieron had already am-scrayed by the time the house got smashed in. the man across the oceans came busting in. Hope you're all right, sister. Here's hopin' the man across the oceans won't find ya.

I don't know how I'll make it into the Tower in my own real body, but I've got to try—because this is it. This really is the last of my great labors.

Someone has to warn Eldridge.

. . .

Before I say goodbye, I've got a few things to say:

Y'know, all this time, I've been addressing alla you folks listening from the shores of a better world—all of you Shore-Riders. God's honest truth, I've been envious of you, wherever and whenever you are. You live in a world of comfort and safety, while I'm running across open desert to certain death.

But y'know what? I wouldn't trade my life for anything.

Even with all the folks I've let down.

Even with a brother dying of depression.

Even with the man across the oceans hot on my trail.

Sometimes I wish I lived in your world, but the only problem is . . . your world ain't got my friends.

Oksana.

Stewart.

Zora.

Pell.

Hell, I'll go ahead and jump Kieron into our clan.

And Eldridge. My brother. I'm sorry I never helped you conquer the darkness inside you. I tried. I tried so many times to reach out to you, to say hi, to . . . just ask you how you were doing. I know you did the best you could, and I know I didn't do enough. I didn't do enough when the darkness fell. I didn't do enough when you pulled away.

And I didn't do enough when Nadia came around.

Sweet blue Jesus. Nadia.

And for all the rest, I love you too.

Oksana, Stewart, Zora, Pell, Kieron, Eldridge.

To every Shore-Rider within the sound of my voice, know this: These people are the only good thing I ever did.

They're my friends.

They're my family.

I've let a lot of folks down over the course of my life, and I'm so sorry to each and every one of ya. I spent most of my early years drinkin' myself to death, the last few trying to become an Odd.

But amidst all my bullshit, I managed to do one good thing, and that's build a family; a real, honest-to-Crom family.

[AUDIO: ECHOES, VOICES; THE SUBJECT HAS MOVED INDOORS.]

For those of you still reading, don't worry. There's an outpost between Ikraam and Towertown. I'm gonna duck into it and send word to Feruccio and the psychoskags about this dictatryst device. They'll read the logs on this gizmoid and pan the stream of whispers that runs among the remnants for the rest of the tale.

But for now, this is Boris Hagan, Chronicler of Dedrick, signing off. With love.

—ɯ—

ELDRIDGE

Once the old man was gone, Eldridge looked down again at the lava and watched as one of the rock islands floated closer. When it was close enough, he propped his virtual feet against the wall and propelled himself downward, executing a midair flip that landed him on his feet on the edge of the island, where he swayed for a moment before he found his solar-center and bulled his way through the mass of dreens awaiting him. After clearing the first island of all things dreenish, he leaped to the next, his sudden appearance on the island freaking out some of the dreens, but only for a second. The *next* second, they were swarming at him as his senses took in the larger scene and he planned his next move.

But there were no signs of Oksana or Stewart. Not yet.

Eldridge spent a solid ten minutes wrestling a shrieking gaggle of dreens into the lava, and then moved on to the next rock island. Eldridge sprang from one to another, wondering what the *hell* had happened to Pell back at Ikraam. And what had forced poor Boris to trek *all the way* back up here to warn him? And, well—to save his life, too.

And what about the jellywoman? Kieron?

He couldn't worry about that. *You're out of time,* Hagan had said, and he knew it was true. *Wait. Hagan.* Hagan's friend in Stafford. Zak. The man across the oceans. Of course. Eldridge knew the man across the oceans was a player in all this, his presence terrifying enough to force the fearsome Quillig to take on extra help. Had *he* found them?

He reached the northernmost island of rock and looked into the heat-heart of the Tower. A great, vaulted archway—all of it on its side, of course—rose out of the lava ahead. He thought back to the first look he got at the Fallen Tower. The upper floors of the Tower lay in the middle of an active volcano. He must have been standing in part of the volcano at that moment, and the upper spires of the Tower must have been extending before him, sticking up out of the lavabed.

But it was too far to jump.

He looked around for another platform, another *way* to get himself into the heat-heart, but he was trapped in the middle of a sea of lava. The prospect of abandoning Oksana and Stewart occurred to him in a dark rush of desperation, but the sight of a lavadreen walking up *out* of the lava ahead cleared his mind. A few yards away, one of the creatures marched up from the fiery pool and into the heat-heart. Eldridge gauged the distance and figured he could make the jump, but he'd have his emitter and the safepods stayed above the lava-level. He had stowed the safepods in pockets on his shoulders—one on each—but his emitter was roughly stationed at navel-level.

He probed his stomach with his fingertips, which then lanced into his virtual body. His avatar fritzed and crackled as he fished around inside his virtual guts, but in another bizarre sensory epiphany, he *felt* it—the emitter. Once he had it pinched between his thumb and forefinger, he pulled it up through his form inch by agonizing inch—this shit *hurt*—until he had it stationed in his head. His feet lost a few points of opacity, but fuck it. He backed up to get a running start, then jumped.

As he fell, he locked his knees and held his arms up over his head. The lava slammed up underneath him, but he felt bedrock and stopped cold with the lava at chest level. A pack of lavadreens spotted him and immediately charged. He still had his shotguns strapped to his back, and even though he had no rounds, he drew them both and ran at them, kitchen-knife bayonets at the ready. On some kooky intellectual level, it occurred to him to marvel at how he was *running through lava* but he felt nothing but the resistance the lava gave his numb legs. A lavadreen sprang up out of the lava next to him, but he swatted it across the face with one of his bayonets, which was already melting from the heat.

The redhead reached the edge of the lava and jumped out onto a thick arch of stone covered with intricate carvings. The arch curved forward, toward the old top of the skyscraper. But still no sign of Oksana or Stewart. Eldridge sprinted forward, ready for his life to blink out of him any moment, but still it didn't—and then the moon shined in his eyes.

Overhead, the outer wall of the Tower had been torn away, leaving a giant hole that gave view to the inner wall of the volcano. Behind the redhead, a wave of lava washed up the inside of the Tower, forcing him to run forward, dropping his melted scatterguns along the way. He touched his shoulders to make sure the safepods were secure. All good. He looked up and saw nothing but the night sky.

"Oksie?! Stewart?!"

A shadow appeared over the moon. *Two* shadows, one of them glowing. Eldridge looked up and saw the same hulking golem who had helped him storm another tower—Jeb Goldmist. In the center of the creatures glittered two dark eyes. Oksana's.

Next to her stood what could only be a fire warden, the mightiest of them all. Its skin glowed from within with pumping, superhot luminescent bloodfire. His old friend, Stewart Kaleb, looked down at him.

And then they jumped, followed by a swarm of dreens and only the most faithful of fire wardens. The two titans struck the ground before the redhead and rose up before him, the Oksana-dreen twice as large as Eldridge remembered. Her descent into dreendom must have brought with it an increase in size and power, as well. Stewart hovered next to her, his dark eyes gleaming, all while dreens and lavadreens infested the space behind him, swarming their way onto the interior of the Fallen Tower's topmost arch. They surrounded the redhead, who realized he was still wearing his avatar disguise. He looked up at Oksana.

"Oksie," he said, then closed his eyes and transformed himself back into his true form. The Oksana-dreen tilted her head, her eyes glinting. Eldridge held eye contact with her for as long as he dared, then turned to Stewart. "Stew. You're a fire warden. I've made it to the heat-heart. Can you see that?"

Whatever Stewart had become—this otherworldly amalgam of dreen and fire warden—its senses were apparently too dulled, because it merely exhaled a chestful of smoke and thudded its way closer to Eldridge, who drew back, feeling the wave of dreens behind him. He looked again to Oksana the trixie.

"*Oksie. Little girl. It's me. El. Eldridge. Buttwad.*"

Oksana and Stewart stomped closer. And the redhead shrugged.

"Well, shit."

He vaulted skyward, attacking Oksana first. He jumped and grabbed onto her face, holding on tight against the momentum of her instant reaction: a lightning-fast rearing back. She whipped back and forth, but the redhead clung to her face with his legs while he pulled out one of the safepods, laid it against her eye, *and pinched.* As the Oksana-dreen squeal-howled in protest, Eldridge sprang off her face at Stewart, who saw his first attack and parried, although for a gigantic fire warden-dreen creature, a "parry" was more like an "open-palm smack across the room." Eldridge smashed a divot into the far wall and dropped the other safepod. *Shit, shit, shit, shit!* He jumped to his hands and knees and scrambled for it as Stewart roared and came stomping after him. A bit of lava licked out from the nearby river and landed on the roof near the safepod, which was sliding down the archway toward it. Eldridge lurched to his feet and dove for it, but it skittered just out of his reach.

Until a foot slammed down and blocked its path.

He looked up into the eyes of the Oksana-dreen, only it wasn't the Oksana-dreen anymore. Not entirely. It couldn't talk, but it stood in place while Eldridge snatched up the safepod. Once the redhead had it, the Oksana-dreen wheeled around and cracked Stewart across the face. He staggered back. The Oksana-dreen shrank before his eyes. *Hurry, hurry.* He jumped up and ran toward Stewart while Oksana used her rapidly diminishing dreen-power to fend off an attack from the dreenhost advancing from below. Eldridge jumped and caught onto Stewart's scaly lower lip. He performed a one-armed pullup.

"Sorry about this!"

He pinched the safepod and rammed it into Stewart's eye, bursting it in the process. Stewart reeled backward, his arms pinwheeling as he yowled in torment. Then a voice sounded.

"El?"

Eldridge turned to see Oksana smiling at him. Half her size when he'd first arrived at the top of the Tower, she nevertheless was still three times the size of an average dreg and ten times as strong.

"Oksie! You need to get us out of here!"

Fear shook her quickly healing face. "Where *am* I?!"

"Uh! Long story! In a volcano! And a building! *Just grab me and Stew and jump us the fuck outta here! Now, girl!*"

Oksana's expression steeled, and she swept the redhead into her massive, calloused arm. Stewart shrank before them as he writhed on the ground. Oksana picked him up and heaved him over her shoulder.

"*Quick!*" Eldridge shouted. "*While you still can!*"

She jumped. They flew. She shrank. They fell.

—⚉—

THE FIRE WARDENS

THE STAINED GLASS PLATFORM of the Fallen Tower shook with the mad chants of the fire wardens. They sang and sang through the night, stoking their flames and beating out an endless rhythm on the steel.

And then the three New Wardens appeared above them all.

They bore no scars, no burns, no injuries from their journey through the tower. Two men and one woman. One of the men they had seen before—a black man who had arrived with three others who didn't make it out of the Tower. He arrived with the other two—a woman and a man who pressed his hand against an empty, bloody eye socket—both of whom stood with him atop the foundation of the Fallen Tower, all three of them having walked the full distance back from the heat-heart.

Or so the rumortrysts would later sing.

Dredge and Tox looked up in wonderment from their stations by the gate. They watched in awe as the three people clambered down the stained glass platforms, sometimes falling over each other, until they dropped to the ground before Dredge and Tox and ran past, the mysterious black man rattling off this speech as he moved:

"We give our thanks to the Fallen Tower. And to you, the fire wardens. Thank you for letting me venture into its hallowed halls."

They started down the stairs, still moving at full speed, only to be stopped by Dredge's shouted words:

"You forgot your winnings!"

All three people halted and conferred for a quick moment before the black man ran back up the stairs.

"Sure—whatever you think's fair."

Tox crossed to Dredge and handed him a jenta-stylus and a jenta-catch. Dredge deposited the winnings into it. As the huge stream of jenta smartcharacters streamed into the catch, Dredge spoke: "You honor us. My siblings in flame saw you soar along the ceiling toward the heat-heart on an avenue of crimson. Songs shall be sung in your honor."

He handed him the jenta-catch, and instantly the three New Wardens were on their way again, but then the black man halted halfway down the stairs and jogged back up, brandishing the jenta-catch over his head.

"This is too much. *Way* too much."

"Do not dishonor the heat-heart by refusing our homage."

The black man made a fist around the jenta-catch and pumped it in thanks. He left with his two mysterious companions.

ELDRIDGE, OKSANA, AND STEWART

AFTER STOPPING IN TOWN to clothe Oksana and Stewart, they all climbed into the station wagon as the redhead dropped his virtual disguise.

"El!" Oksana said. "What! The *hell*. Happened?!"

"I don't even know where to start. Pell's dead. Boris is dead. Fucking *everyone's* dead, and we need to get back to Ikraam."

He floored it and kicked up sooty gravel everywhere.

From the back seat, a grimacing Stewart spoke. "El-dawg, how'd I lose an eye? And why are you a hologram?"

"How *else* was I supposed to get in there and rescue you two?! Sorry about your eye, Stew. I had to shove a dose of Narsyan blood into your face."

"Oh. Thanks?"

"And I'm a Narsyan chieftain now, not that anyone gives a shit."

"How much jenta did you win?" Oksana asked.

Eldridge chuckled. "Enough to pay back the man across the oceans."

"Who's that?" she asked as they motored over the hill out of town and going south toward Ikraam.

"I'll tell you on the way—*shit!*"

They almost had a head-on collision with a woman on a motorcycle. Specifically, it was a lanky woman with black oculars sitting astride the redhead's motorbike.

"Eldridge!" Kieron shouted.

The redhead stopped the car and leaned out the window. "K! Are you all right?"

Kieron jumped off the bike and leaned into the window.

"Hagan was gone. I woke up moments before he struck. They killed Pell. But, Eldridge, *they've taken your—*"

"Yeah, I know!"

—⁂—

ELDRIDGE, ET AL

O NE HUNDRED MILES, ELDRIDGE thought. That's how far ahead of them that motherfucker Zak Chamberlain would have to get before the connection between his brain and his avatar would give out, and he'd vanish into nothingness. He kept the station wagon floored and aimed it at Ikraam.

"Shanta said they were going to Port Stafford. Shit. *Shit.* We're almost out of gas. What was he riding, Kieron? Was it fast? I need to keep it range, or I'm gonna die."

Kieron said, "I heard them say they were headed for *Hemming*, not Stafford. They said they were going to take a shortcut, and I think I know what they mean."

"What? What're you talking about?"

"There's a secret passage—a portal—from Hemming to Stafford. But Eldridge?"

"*What?!*" yelled the redhead as he course-corrected toward Hemming.

"Why not just return to your body? You could fight your way out their clutches, couldn't you?"

The redhead slammed the brakes. "You're right."

"What da *hell* are you guys talking about?!" Oksana asked.

Eldridge jumped out of the car into the freezing night and yanked his emitter out of his body. Oksana yipped, while Stewart looked on in bafflement. Eldridge handed the emitter to Kieron.

"Listen, *deactivate* it and then *reactivate* it a minute later. I just want to get the lay of the land."

"Very well," Kieron said, then deactivated the emitter.

Eldridge vanished. Oksana screamed and jumped out of the car, where she took a swing at Kieron.

"Where'd he go?!" she screamed. "And who the fuck *are* you?!"

"I am a friend of the redhead's."

"*You* can't call him the redhead. You're a *stranger*. Only his friends get to call him that. And his sweeties."

Stewart climbed out. "This is a mactatrox, dude. Bring him back."

Kieron nodded and reactivated the emitter. Eldridge was already snatching it out of her hand when he reappeared, his entire virtual body's momentum carrying him toward the station wagon on the leading wind of his shouted pleas.

"*Get in! Get in! Get in!*"

They all piled into the station wagon. Eldridge tore out in the direction of Hemming. Sitting next to Stewart in the back, Kieron spoke.

"What happened? Where had they taken you?"

"Beats the shit out of me. I landed in a fucking *dreamland* when you switched that thing off. I think they've put me in a coma. We need to get to Stafford and catch Zak Chamberlain before he gets on a boat bound for the eastern continent."

THE BOUNTY-MERCENARIES
OF THE SECTAN CONFINE OF SCAR

Looking back, the dark rumortrysts of the bounty-mercs would report that one day in the secret sectan confine of Scar, the Red Rook, Eldridge of Dedrick, led a group of three other people—Stewart Kaleb, Oksana the trixie, and an unknown tall woman—screaming through the confine, bound for the portal into Port Stafford.

—⚎—

ELDRIDGE AND THE
MAN ACROSS THE OCEANS

Eldridge, Oksana, Stewart, and Kieron sprinted along the wet streets of Port Stafford in the dead of night as stars twinkled overhead and dregs by the thousands streamed from one establishment to another.

"Move, move!" screamed the avatar of Eldridge as they elbowed their way through the crowd to the cliff marking the coastline. Eldridge scanned the black waves for a telltale sign, which he spotted about a quarter mile up the coast.

A white barge, just setting off.

No other barge would dare be so ostentatious as to proclaim its presence with the color white. Eldridge and his three friends sprinted along the coastline, dodging around dregs right and left, pushing a few to the ground until they reached the mooring where the white barge had set off. Eldridge stopped by the coastside and watched the barge sail away with his body. As soon as it got a hundred miles away, he was dead.

And then he saw him. The man across the oceans. Zak Chamberlain. There he was, the son of a macta. Standing on the stern, watching the western continent float away.

"Zak! Zak! I've got your jenta! Stop!"

He waved the jenta-catch in the air, but the white barge was too far away for Chamberlain to see or hear Eldridge. The redhead stood in stony silence until another voice interrupted his thoughts:

"What jenta, El?"

Eldridge turned and looked straight into the face of Zak

Chamberlain, who stood on the coastside next to him, his top hat teetering on his head. The redhead staggered back a step.

"Wha—? What? But aren't you the man across the oceans?"

Chamberlain laughed. "Me? You kiddin'? No way. You just missed him. *That's* the man across the oceans." He pointed at the blue-clad figure on the white barge.

Eldridge looked into the distance. The density of his eyes shifted as he saw the person on the barge clearly for the first time.

"But . . . that's a *woman*."

Chamberlain laughed again. "Yeah, I know, right? Who'da thunk that the man across the oceans was actually a *dame*?"

Eldridge stepped up onto the coastside shelf and squinted into the distance, looking straight at the woman across the oceans. It took a moment to figure out who he was looking at, but when he did, every star in the sky went dark, while flames licked from the horizon like the oceans had suddenly caught fire.

He whispered one word. A name.

"Nadia?"

ACKNOWLEDGMENTS

Karl Mueller provided invaluable feedback on early outlines of this book as well as two separate drafts. But more important, he's been a tireless champion of my work for many years. Thank you for believing in me.

The team at Fanbase Press worked with me on an adaptation of this book's predecessor, *The Odds,* and I can't thank them enough. Over the course of three years, we explored the post-Deadblast world together. Our work deepened my knowledge of my own world in ways I couldn't have predicted. **Barbra Dillon** was our conscience and guide, while **Bryant Dillon** was a steadfast proponent of the original text. **Sam Rhodes** was good enough to let me steal one of his lines for this book. All three of them are artists of the highest order, and I'm honored to have worked with them.

Brett Jackson is one of the best writers and artists I know. He not only provided excellent feedback on a draft of this book, but he also typeset the cover. It's spectacular work, and I'm honored to have it grace the cover of my humble sci-fi romp.

Thanks also go out to the team at **Rare Bird Books** for their unending support, our interns **Meg Eden** and **Karen Shih,** and to **Andy Bartlett** and the team at **Brilliance Publishing** for producing such wonderful audiobooks based on *The Odds* and *The Remnants.* Thanks to all of you for believing in me.

But more than anyone, thanks go to my partner, wife, best friend and favorite person, **Lauren Rock.** I finished the first draft of this book right after we met (and while you were at the Burn), and now it's coming out when we're married. There's a cosmic rightness to that.

I love you, Lauren.

ABOUT THE AUTHOR

ROBERT J. PETERSON is a writer and web developer living in Los Angeles. A Tennessee native, he graduated from Northwestern University's Medill School of Journalism. He's written for newspapers and websites all over the country, including Welcome to Twin Peaks, the Marin Independent Journal, PerformInk, Space.com, the Telluride Daily Planet, and Geekscape.net. In 2004 he co-founded the pop-culture emporium CC2KOnline.com. He's appeared on the web talk shows Screen Junkies TV Fights, Collider Heroes, Comics on Comics, The Fanboy Scoop, Geekscape, and Fandom Planet.

He's the founder of California Coldblood Books and the author of two previous novels, the YA sci-fi thriller *Omegaball*, and *The Odds: Book One of the Deadblast Chronicles*.

His friends call him Bob.

CPSIA information can be obtained
at www.ICGtesting.com
Printed in the USA
LVHW030306011019
632757LV00002B/2